DEATH

Enjoy!

This edition first published 2021 by Fahrenheit Press.

ISBN: 978-1-914475-08-5

10 9 8 7 6 5 4 3 2 1

www.Fahrenheit-Press.com

F 4 E

Death At Dukes Halt

By

Derek Farrell

A Danny Bird Mystery

Fahrenheit Press

Also published by Fahrenheit Press

- *Death Of A Diva*
- *Death Of A Nobody*
- *Death Of A Devil*
- *Death Of An Angel*
- *Death Of A Sinner*

This one – like all of them – is for my dad, with all my Love.

For David, whose love keeps me going.

For everyone who came to Walnut Tree Barn and allowed me to steal their names.

And for Neil, who gently but firmly persuaded me to try it without a parachute.

And it's for you: Thanks for waiting.

"Nothing is perfect. There are lumps in it."

~ *James Stephens, The Crock of Gold (1912)*

She's running around the room in a panic as the people on the other side of the door hammer relentlessly.

The sideboard has been ransacked. Piles of napkins and tablecloths are scattered all over the floor. Most of the antique dining chairs are toppled on their sides, the seat cushions discarded haphazardly. The ornamental fireguard is lying on the same Persian carpet where, a few feet away, a man is sprawled on his front.

The back of his head has a deep dark hole in it, and glistening blood is spreading down over his collar and shoulder to pool around his head.

She's stopped now, and is standing over him, a small dark pistol in her hand.

Her eyes turn to me and she reaches out, the gun pointing directly at me for a moment before she stares at it as though for the first time ever and drops it.

"I can't find it," she says, panic mixed with despair clear in her voice. "I've looked everywhere, and I can't find it."

Sunlight, thin and golden, catches the blood still crawling slowly across the floor.

"Help me." She locks eyes with me. "You have to help me find it."

"Find what?" I ask as the pounding on the opposite side of the door increases.

"The book. His black book. Without it I'll never find her." She steps back, noticing for the first time that, in her panic to search the corpse, she has gotten his blood on her hands.

She looks at me, accusation clear in her eyes. "He must have hidden it. He must have realised that you'd come to find him and hidden it."

She stares at her blood-soaked hands, her whole body slumping as though every last drop of hope is draining away, and then wrenches her eyes away from the gore to look straight at me.

"Oh God, Danny. What have you done?"

And then, with an ear-splitting crack and a splintering of wood, the door bursts open.

WEDNESDAY

CHAPTER ONE

"Absolutely not." I stared at my best friend in horror.

Across the table from me, Lady Caroline Victoria Genevieve Jane de Montfort – Caz to her friends – looked at me as though my horror were absolutely incomprehensible.

"But why not?"

"Why?" I was resisting the urge to ask how many Martinis she had. "Are you serious?"

"Deadly," she said, sipping from her glass. "It was Georgie's dying wish. His living one too, come to think of it. And if his father wasn't such a complete bastard, he'd have been granted it years ago. Well, he mightn't have been able to do it in life, but I'm going to do it in death. And permanently."

"I'm not even sure it's legal," I protested, and she snorted.

"It's probably not," she said, "but it's a dying man's wish and are you - a person who works for a gangster renowned for jointing his enemies with a large machete – really going to talk to me about legality?"

"Well, first off, I don't work for him; I'm my own boss. He just happens to own the pub that I'm running. And second – and you know this perfectly well – Mr F. has never been convicted of any violent act. So, y'know, it could be nothing but scurrilous rumours that you're adding to by your insistence in referring back to unproven here say."

"He's known as Chopper Falzone," she stated baldly, swallowing her Martini, fishing out the olive and popping it into her mouth.

She had a point. And that was the first solid I'd seen her consume in months.

I tried another tack.

"How? I mean, the logistics."

"Leave logistics to me," she said, a smile that intimated she'd not only worked them out, but had had a trial run in Hyde Park, settling on her face.

"No, I mean the logistics of this place. I mean, I'm trying to organise that Cabaret Night- Elephant's got Talent."

"Despite the fact that this bar is not situated in The Elephant and Castle." Caz dipped into her handbag and extracted a shiny silver cocktail shaker. She wiggled it at me and I waved it away, my own glass still containing what I'd discovered on first sip was basically pure gin with a homeopathic quantity of vermouth.

"It's in the environs," I said. "And anyways, The Cabin Boy and Codpiece on Borough High Street's already got a 'Southwark's got talent' night on a Wednesday."

"Bastards!" Ali – my bar manager – strolled over on hearing the name of her nemesis. The Cabin Boy had been taken over by an ex- hedge fund manager, and Ali was convinced the pub was stealing her customers at an alarming rate. She spat her condemnation and began polishing the bar with a rag so filthy that she didn't polish so much as move the grease from the left to the right, the right to the left, up then down and then back up again in a bizarre housekeeping version of The Hokey Cokey.

"Well quite," I couldn't really argue with her hatred of the competition, but facts were facts: They were offering a Savoy-trained mixologist, leather banquettes and a Sunday roast that delivered recipes by Heston Blumenthal to a selection of the ex-hedge fund manager's mates.

The Marquess of Queensbury, meanwhile, served bottles of Czech lager that bore labels claiming the contents were brewed in – and managed to misspell – Czechoslovakia, despite the country in question not having existed for twenty-five years or more. Our clientele could binge on out-of-date pork scratchings whilst lounging on bar furniture that looked like it had been acquired some time before the great fire.

Said clientele, in fact – such as it was - consisted of regulars who'd been coming here since the trouble with Europe was Joan of Arc, unemployed drag queens who still thought Danny La Rue was recherché, and a selection of people who either came for the ambience or who, having heard about the ancient plumbing and rarely cleaned toilet facilities, came to test the efficacy of a new yellow fever vaccine.

"So, who've we got lined up for the first night?" I asked, and Ali stopped polishing, focused her eyes (and, I suspected, her mind) into the middle distance, and begun to recite the bill:

"We've got Benoit Balls. French. No," she held up a hand, "Belgian. Does something amazing with ping pong balls. Works up to tennis balls and the finale involves something jaw dropping with a rugby ball."

"It's almost like being at the Folies Bergere," Caz said drily.

Ali ignored her. "We've Lardy GaGa. Morbidly obese tribute act. Comes on wearing a dress made out of sliced ham. Sings the hits. Finishes the night wearing only her wafer-thin chicken knickers having eaten the costume as she sings. Brought the house down at The Rotary Club do last Christmas. Oi lads," she called to my nephews Ray and Dash, who were serving a shitfaced but oddly quiet hen party, "Who else we got on this talent thing?"

"We got Gary Klinkerhaus and Marco. A vent act," Dash said, taking his top off and exposing his defenestrated and oiled chest to a round of applause from the hen party, and – without pausing for breath – pocketing the tips that hit the bar in seconds, "and a folk singer called – what's her name?" He asked his brother "Callisthenic Arsehols?"

"It's Cullinan Arsene," Ray corrected, losing his t-shirt too, "and he's a man".

The Hens – all deaf and all signing their approval of his physique in ways that even I could understand – clinked glasses of 'Prosecco' that I suspected was made in a lockup in New Cross Gate, and leered at the boys who – used to being objectified – carried on reciting the bill for the upcoming talent night.

"We've got a rock band called Jihadi TukTuk. Well, we might have. They're still looking for a drummer. With his own drum kit."

"So, you see," I gestured at the trio behind the bar, "I couldn't possibly go away at such short notice.

"Balls," Caz snorted. "The boys can run a talent night. Sounds like they've basically booked the whole thing any way."

"You're not wrong there," Ali muttered, casting her most opprobrious glance my way.

"So," Caz said, and waited.

"Well, what about the logistics of getting there?" I persevered. "Of getting him there."

"Sorted," she replied instantly. "Paolo will let me have his car."

I blanched. "Two things: If I recall correctly you don't actually have, at this moment in time, a licence to drive, and also Paolo? Are you still seeing him?"

Caz blushed, fiddled with the stem of her glass, shrugged. "Well, let's put it this way: I'm seeing him, but he's not exactly seeing me."

"He's in a coma again, isn't he?"

I'd never asked how Caz had met the vastly wealthy Paolo and I wasn't entirely sure how he or his ancestors had actually acquired the fortune that he seemed happy to shower Caz with, but I did know that the man – a bon vivant whose weight tended to yo-yo from Nijinsky to Hindenburg (by which I did not mean the race horse or the count) – had acquired the habit, when he could no longer fit into his designer jeans, of having himself put into a coma in Zurich and fed a liquid diet til he had wasted away to the desired weight, then brought back around and sent straight out to Alain Ducasse at the Dorchester.

She shrugged. "Just a little one. He thought he looked a bit puffy around the eyes, so he had Doctor Kevorkian put him out for a week or two."

"Kevorkian?"

"Different one. I think." Caz frowned, sipped her drink. "I'll check."

"And how do we get George down there?" I asked. "I mean, we can hardly stick him on the roof rack?"

"A roof rack? Do you think Paolo would own – or that I would be seen dead in – anything with," she gulped back what appeared to be a sudden rise in gorge, "a roof rack?" She presented me with her most offended front while rooting around in her handbag and snorting a little cry of triumph as she located the olives and dragged a fresh one out to drop into her neat gin.

"So, are you in or not?"

I was still looking for a get-out. I do not normally like the aristocracy. I mean, I've met a few, and I'm sure they were perfectly pleasant people, but – especially en masse – they tend to make me feel that perhaps the Bolsheviks were on to something at Yekaterinburg.

"I mean, if you were such a close friend of George's," I pressed on, "why would the father even allow you over the threshold? Surely you're tarred with whatever brush he tarred his own son with."

"Ah but that's the point," Caz smiled gnomically. "I met Georgie long after he was ejected from Eden. By that stage he was Georgie, and he was the funniest, sweetest, smartest man I'd ever met."

"Really?" I attempted – and failed – to suppress my bristle.

"Before you, dear heart. But you would have loved him." She paused, inspected me with a raised eyebrow, and smiled. "Yes, you would have loved him, and he you.

"But I met George when his first gallery show was the hit of the season. I was GLAM's culture editor in New York, and he was the hot new British artist in town, and they assumed that we'd have something in common, so we were thrown together."

"Culture editor?" I marvelled at the idea of Caz deciding which deconstructivist poet would feature in the magazine that month or whether she'd go with a performance artist who inserted guavas where they were never meant to be inserted whilst reciting Baudelaire, then realised I was probably being a snob.

Caz ignored me. "And who'd have guessed," she said, her smile wavering, "that two aristos would have a bond. Years later Pamela - one of my oldest friends - tells me she's met this very charming farmer called Henry Warren.

"By farmer I'm assuming you don't mean he mucks out every morning at five."

She ignored me. "So, Pamela and Henry marry and it was ages after before I realised Henry was Georgie's estranged brother. It was the first time I was due to visit Dukes Halt. The father – Sir Philip Warren – has a huge fireworks party every year at Hallowe'en, apparently it was his late wife's birthday and became something of a tradition during her life, so he's kept it going ever since. So I mentioned where I was going to Georgie en passant, and he – so quietly, as if he were talking to himself – said something like 'Oh that's where I grew up.'"

She paused, sipped her martini, put the glass back on the table and adjusted it as though she were trying to stay anchored in the here and now while her mind drifted back. "'Well,' he said, 'I suppose technically I grew up at a series of boarding schools, but Dukes Halt is where my family lived.' I was a bit confused, to be honest, I mean I'd thought that the place had been in Henry's family forever, so I ended up saying 'Oh, where do they live now?' assuming his family had sold up and moved on.

"And he looks at me with surprise as though he'd understood simply everyone must know, and says 'Oh they still live there. You're going to visit them this weekend.'"

Caz looked at me as though awaiting a response, and so I said "Wow," though I was wondering where the story was going.

"And so I asked him if he'd be there that weekend and he laughed. 'No,' he said, 'I've written a few times and asked if I can come visit but you know how it is.'"

"Wait," now I was piqued. "He wrote? A letter? Asking for permission to go back to his family home?" I was remembering how, when my relationship of several years had ended one sunny morning, I had simply walked to a train station, boarded a train to Waterloo and a couple of hours later been ensconced in my childhood bedroom while my parents openly debated having my ex-boyfriend kneecapped.

"He was sent away, he said, two months before his sixteenth birthday."

"The fuck," I gasped, and Caz nodded, a look on her face that said, 'see what I mean now?' and sipped again from the cocktail.

"He wouldn't ever speak about it. Just said his mother died and his brother died, and terrible things happened that he would never be able to forgive himself for, and if the punishment was banishment from Dukes Halt he'd take it a million times over if it could reverse a sliver of the damage he'd done."

"Fuck," I said again. "What did he do?"

"No idea," Caz said. "A couple of times I tried getting the skinny out of Henry but he really clammed up. He was cast out over thirty years ago and nobody, it seems, has spoken of it again."

She swigged the cocktail, a larger mouthful this time.

"I'm not unfamiliar with, shall we say, the eccentricities of some of my social class, but I have to say even I found it all quite shocking. But Georgie laughed it all off as though it was some silly misunderstanding and he was embarrassed for bringing it all up.

"When he got sick I asked him once or twice whether he wanted to go back, and he'd get a bit misty-eyed then shake his hand. 'Not gonna happen,' he'd say 'I can never go back there.' And then he'd ask me what I thought of the new show at the Saatchi. It was only at the very end – when he knew that he was dying – that he told me he'd written asking his father to allow him to return one last time, and that the letters had been returned unopened."

"Jesus. Why didn't he just get into a taxi and go? I mean they'd hardly have slammed the door in his face, surely?"

Caz smiled sadly. "They might have. And the one thing that nice boys and girls who remember the lessons they learned at boarding school will do almost anything to avoid is the causing of a scene. I think Georgie was afraid that, if he turned up and his father slammed the door in his face, it would mean all hope was lost. Maybe sending letters meant that there was hope of a positive response, an invite to tea."

"Until it came back unopened," I said, and she nodded, sipped her Martini again.

"Quite."

"So, none of the family know that you were friends with George?"

"Well Henry does, because I asked him outright what they all had against his brother, and Georgie and I were papped at a few of his openings, so it's possible if Sir Phillip ever switched his subscription from Horse & Hounds to Vogue or Tatler he might have seen us, but whether they know or not, I have never been refused entry to Dukes Halt, so I suspect their issue is with George and George only."

"Only now George has died," I said, prompting her back to her story.

"And I promised him that I'd get him back. I hadn't achieved it in life, and so that's why I need your help."

"Okay, but I still don't understand how I can help or how, in fact, you're going to get him back there. Unless you're just going to knock on the door and tell his father that you've come round for tea, oh and you've brought his dead son's remains."

Caz stopped me. "I've – we've been invited by Henry and Pamela. It's October, Danny."

Realisation dawned. "George's mother's birthday."

Caz nodded. "It's too good a chance to miss. And besides, Pamela wants me to go and have a talk with Lottie."

"Okay, now I'm confused: Who's Lottie?"

"Well Pamela met Henry. They married, and had a daughter

– Carlotta, who everyone calls Lottie. And I'm Lottie's Godmother."

"You? Godmother?"

"I'm sensing some moralising, Daniel. And you know my thoughts on moralising; it gives you lines."

"Well, it's just I thought Godmothers were supposed to be all about religious and moral education, y'know?"

"Well, that's how little you know. In some sets, perhaps, but in my set it's all about having someone who can help introduce the child to the right sort of people when the time comes and get them the right unpaid internship to launch them in life and – if they play their cards right – get them the right husband."

"Caz, you're unemployed, spend half your life in this dump, and the man you're currently having a relationship with appears to be addicted to elective comas."

Caz sniffed dismissively. "Well, all that aside, here we are: I have a Goddaughter, and her name is Lottie. And Pamela wants my help, because the girl, apparently, has been acting up lately. She's just been expelled from a very prestigious boarding school for smuggling in an entirely banned mobile phone."

I gaped. "A mobile phone? Did you say boarding school or high security prison?"

"Whatever, this is the third expulsion in as many years. Apparently, she's become over-argumentative and obstreperous."

"Really? And she's your goddaughter?"

"What's that mean?"

"I'd say they chose well. But why can't her parents deal with whatever is making her act up?"

"Ah." She shifted uncomfortably. "Well, you see, the thing is, there is only really the one parent. Henry Warren. He's a lovely old thing really, but Henry is one of those people who was made for the nineteenth century and – unfortunately for him – launched in the latter twentieth."

"Wait. Where's Pamela in this?"

"Gone. They divorced about six years ago. It was a shock, to be honest, because they seemed so solid, but then poor Pamela's brother died, and, out of the blue, she announces she needs space, goes off to become games mistress at some posh school, and leaves Lottie with Henry. I mean the two of them seem to have remained great friends. She spends time at the house, he sees her when he's in town."

"And the obstreperous daughter?" I asked. "Where does she fit in?"

Caz sighed sadly. "Where indeed? The Warrens – and I count Pamela in that, though she's obviously only a Warren by marriage – are not exactly renowned for their parenting."

"No shit."

"I need to sort out whatever's happening with Lottie," Caz watched a bead of condensation run down her glass and ran her finger alongside it. "She needs to be back in school. I need to get her away from that place. I'm genuinely fond of Pamela and Henry, and Sir Phillip is just one of those types that are trapped in this sort of provincial Rep Edwardian paterfamilias role, though it seems never to have brought him a moment's joy. But there's something about the place – about Dukes Halt – that," she shrugged, the shrug a failed attempt to hide a small shudder, "something that frightens me, to be honest, Danny. I don't know what George's crime was and I don't really care anymore, but almost at the end - when he was on more morphine than the entire front row at a Babyshambles gig - he looked at me, and said that Dukes Halt was cursed. He said that the place had been poisoned forever but he'd destroyed the last slivers of goodness in it."

"And you want to bring his remains back there?"

"It's where he wanted to go. He also said that some of the happiest days of his life were spent there." She smudged the drop of condensation. "Maybe he hoped his return would exorcise the place."

"Brilliant," I said, knowing I was caving in and knowing – from the satisfied look on Caz's face – that she'd picked up on my acquiescence. "So, I'll pack my holy water and brush up on my Latin. You need to figure out how we're getting there."

CHAPTER TWO

My mother called to tell me she was going on holiday with my dad, which put the kibosh on Caz's suggestion we hire him to take us to Dukes Halt.

"Portugal," my mum said, excited and happy.

"Is it okay?" I asked, knowing as the question came out that she wouldn't be going away if it wasn't.

"It's okay," she said, something in her voice shifting on the last syllable. "*I'm* okay."

My mother, a year before, had been diagnosed with cancer. She'd told only my father. To this day, the only other person who knew of her diagnosis was me, and that was only because I was the sort of son who couldn't leave things lie.

But she'd had treatment. The prognosis was good. Her health was good. She was still recovering, but she was well enough to go away on holiday.

"Are you sure?" I asked, as Ray – wearing a Hawaiian shirt with a deep v-neck over a rather sheer sarong – entered the kitchen and gestured that I needed to come into the bar.

I waved him aside. Whatever it was, it could wait.

This was important.

"I'm sure."

"So how long you going away for?" I asked, wondering why – despite her assurances – I was still worried.

"Just a couple of weeks, but, oh, Danny, it'll be wonderful to dip my toes in the sea, get some sun on my face."

"Not too much sun," I said, "and wear a high factor sunscreen."

She chuckled. "You're a good boy Danny."

"A regular saint," I deadpanned back, as Ray leaned in and stage-whispered "There's someone to see you."

"You've visitors," my mum said, hearing his words. "So I'll let you go."

"You don't have to," I said shooting daggers at my nephew. "Whoever it is will wait."

"No, it's okay," my mum said, a smile in her voice. "I've told you my news now."

"When do you go?" I jumped in, concern suddenly flaring up once more.

"Saturday. Morning. Early," she answered.

"But that's the day after tomorrow," I said back and again she chuckled.

"No flies on you. Go see who wants you. I'll bring you back some sardines. And don't worry. Oh, and Danny: Love you."

"Love you too," I said, and the call ended.

I knew, of course, why my mother had called to tell me only a day or two before she went away: It was a done deal and I would have less time to worry about the decision. If she'd told me a month before, I'd have spent four weeks agonising over whether it was the right thing to do or not. This way, I had to let go of it.

So that's what I tried to do.

I almost succeeded.

"Right," I turned back to Ray but he'd already gone back to the bar, which - even from my seat at the kitchen table in The Marq – sounded busy.

Thursday night was free prawn cracker and half-price Lychee Gin cocktails night, and featured a regular weekly floorshow by the aptly named Ms Opium Waugh, so it tended to draw a good crowd.

As I entered the bar I could see that the sign-up sheets for Elephant's Got Talent were doing a roaring trade, and was pleased to think that the twins' idea looked like it might have legs after all; if even half those who were expressing an interest in performing came down on the night we'd be in line for the best Monday night bar takings in ages.

My visitor was standing in the middle of the bar, her back to me as she surveyed the throng, and even though I couldn't see her face I knew who she was.

As though sensing me, she turned around.

She was tall and blonde, her hair tucked behind her ears, and she was wearing dark blue jeans and a crisp white button-down shirt covered by a lightweight beige mac, and everything about her made her seem like the last person in the world who would be standing in my pub on Lychee Tuesday.

Which was how I knew who she had to be.

"You're Arianna," I said, and she smiled at me.

"Hello," she said, her voice smoky. "It's lovely to finally meet you. I wonder if it would be possible to speak in private?"

In case you haven't been keeping up: Once upon a time I spent several years living with a man called Robert, who was a city lawyer, a great success and a total shit. I discovered the latter fact when I came home one day and found him in bed with our window cleaner.

I'm no snob; I really don't mind that the man he was shagging behind my back was the window cleaner as opposed to, say, a senior partner at his law firm.

But I was particularly stung by the fact I'd been paying the window cleaner's bills out of my own pocket forever, so I'd effectively been paying for someone to come round and give my boyfriend a weekly seeing to while I was working my little legs off to pay for the cleaning.

So, I left Robert, ended up running The Marq (Don't ask how; this is already running too long for a quick catchup), and met Nick.

Who seemed nice.

So, Nick and I sort of drifted into a relationship, then Nick went on a secondment to Albania – something to do with a training exchange and an opportunity to network with other forces – and some months later I discovered that, whilst in Albania, he'd married. A woman. Named Arianna.

I know: I was as shocked as you are. More, probably.

I led Arianna behind the bar and back down the hallway into the kitchen.

I gestured at the seat opposite the one I'd just vacated, and she slung her mac over the back of it. "Can I get you something to drink? Tea? Coffee?"

"In a pub?" she asked, a slight curving of the lips, aligned with a gentle tilting of the head lending her a mildly sardonic air. "Don't you have a good vodka? I think, somehow a good vodka would be more apropos."

I paused, my hand still reaching for the kettle, and smiled uncertainly.

"In this pub," I answered, "we only have vodka that's never been further east than Canvey Island. But in this kitchen," I crossed to the fridge, opened it and extracted a bottle of Chopin. "Neat or over ice?" I asked, crossing to the cupboard and running my eyes over the glass options.

"If it's cold, then adding ice is unnecessary dilution," she said, her voice tone still seeming to have a smile as though at a private joke she had yet to share with me.

"Shots, then," I answered, reaching up for the top shelf and realising I couldn't quite reach it unaided.

"Here," she was suddenly beside me. "Let me help you." She reached over me and removed two shot glasses from the top shelf while I was wondering why I was playing nice when every fibre of my being was calling out 'Something funny's going on.'

Don't get me wrong: Any concerns I may have had about Arianna and Nick had long been resolved. But I've seen enough Turner Classic Movies to know that when The Other Woman turns up placidity is not a state one should adopt.

Arianna stepped back, smiled and, as I turned, still holding the chilled vodka, resumed her seat at the table, the glasses placed carefully in front of her.

I uncapped the bottle and poured a measure into each, then placed the bottle back on the table and sat down before lifting the glass and raising it in a silent toast to her.

She mirrored my toast and we slugged the shots.

"You did not put the cap back on the bottle," Arianna said, the smile back and this time reflected in her eyes. "In my world, that means an invitation to stay."

I poured two more shots.

"I don't really know what I'm toasting," I said. "This feels odd. I mean, you're Nick's-" I froze on the word, suddenly embarrassed by it, and her smile changed from being a hint of an upturn at the corners of her lips to a full beam, exposing perfect white teeth.

"Wife," she laughed, toasting me and slamming the vodka back again. "And you," she said, seeming not even to have swallowed the spirit, "are the man he loves. In another time, this would be some terrible arthouse movie, and we would all be miserable. And yet here we are."

I sipped my vodka and she raised an eyebrow in rebuke.

I swallowed the shot.

"Yes," I said, feeling my cheeks start to burn. "Here we are."

Arianna looked around the room. "This, then, is the famous Marquess of Queensbury Public House of which I have heard so much?"

"Well, it's a bit of it," I answered, noticing the smell of onions and garlic still hanging on the air from lunchtime, the spatters of grease all over the hob, and the trail of dark black splashes – a sauce, perhaps, or blood from some poorly handled meat – running across the floor tiles to the overflowing bin in the corner. "Perhaps we should have gone upstairs."

"This is perfect," she answered me, the private joke seemingly banished. "And before we go further, I am truly pleased to meet you Danny, and grateful for your time."

She noticed my discombobulation and reached a hand out, resting it gently on mine. "I meant what I said, you know: He really does love you."

"I know," I said, because I did. But in that moment I realised he'd never really said it. The words 'I Love You' hadn't reached my ears from his lips, despite his every action and his every look telling me he cared so much that he had tipped over into love.

"Do you love him?"

Now that was a question. And one which, to be honest, threw me a little. I did, and everyone seemed to assume I did. Even Caz, who'd been known to forensically dissect the emotional entanglements of complete strangers hadn't ever bothered to ask me what I felt for Nick.

My millisecond of hesitation caused a frown to flicker momentarily across her face before I watched her almost consciously replace it with that Buddah-like half-smile.

"I'm sorry," she said. "It's rude of me to ask. Your life – your relationship – is none of my business."

"No," I interjected, "you're fine. And yes, I do love Nick." I sighed. "It's just hard."

She tilted her head, the smile dimming, her focus turning entirely to my words.

I sighed again. "There was a man. I was very much in love with him. I thought he loved me."

"A story I'm familiar with," she said quietly.

I nodded. "He didn't. Or rather: he loved me, but not enough."

"And you're afraid of loving Nick," she said quietly. "Afraid of being hurt again."

I shrugged. She was hardly Sigmund Freud, but she was right. I loved him, and I wanted him to love me, and I knew he loved me, and yet…

And yet we both sort of danced around all of the absences, the obstacles, the uncertainties in our relationship, each of us seemingly accepting of the imperfections. And yet I worried that every accepted imperfection would read – to him – as a licence to appreciate me less, and that that licence would lead me inexorably back to the day I walked in on Robert and the window cleaner.

"He's a good man," Arianna said. "An honourable man. If he hurts you it will be because the only alternative will be worse than hurt."

I felt my chest tighten. What was Arianna doing here? What news had she brought me?

"When he found me – when he saved me – he did so from a sense of right and wrong, Danny. I was," she paused, reached for the bottle, a look asking my permission which I, in turn, gave with a slight nod.

She poured two more shots, downed hers while I was still lifting mine to my mouth and refilled her glass instantly.

"I was born in a part of what was, at the time, the Union of Soviet Socialist Republics. I had a mother and a father and a brother – his name, I think, was Stefan." She stopped, suddenly, her eyes taking on a faraway look, and nodded "His name was Stefan. I do not think this, I know it. And I had a sister. A twin sister. Named Klara."

Arianna smiled now, and a deep sigh came from her. I noticed her hand, laying on the table, was trembling, and she reached for the vodka, lifted it to her mouth and slammed it.

"And then the empire fell," she continued, putting the glass down. "And everything… imploded. We lived in a village that had been part of the USSR, then was part of Yugoslavia, then was in Bosnia.

"And then the war came."

I reached for the vodka. Stopped. I was already buzzing. This felt like something I needed to be sober for.

Arianna poured two more shots.

"I – we – saw our father murdered outside our house by," she smiled bitterly, "they called – and still call – themselves soldiers, but they were gangsters in uniform. My mother," she paused, the first time since her arrival that I'd seen her search for the appropriate word, "broke."

She nodded as though deciding that that was the only appropriate word.

"My brother – Stefan - was fifteen. Klara and I were 7. A man came. His name was Sergei Maximov.

"He told my mother he would take care of Klara and I. Get us to a place of safety while she and Stefan buried my father, sold what could be sold, and came to meet us in a month or two."

Arianna reached out and pulled the glass nearer to her,

toyed with it, staring down into the clear liquid. "I never saw my mother or my brother again."

She looked up, her eyes locking with mine. "This man – Sergei Maximov – was a predator. This word is used a lot these days, but I think, whenever I hear the word, not of an animal which hunts it's prey, but of one which, having caught its quarry, devours every last piece."

She paused again, lifted the glass and swallowed the vodka.

"When Nick met me in Tirana," she said, changing tack suddenly, "I was the property of a man. He called me his girlfriend, but we both knew what I was. He was a violent man, and a dangerous man, and – god forgive me – I stood by for many years while he did terrible things. But then he killed a man. Not much more than a boy, really.

"And I discovered that the boy he'd killed – for some minor infraction, some stupid bullshit – had a brother. A twin. And just like my mother, something in me broke. And I went to the police to tell them that I had tape recordings, copied documents, diaries, lists of politicians, businessmen, contacts. I had been this man's girlfriend, but I had also been the only person he thought he didn't need to worry about. And do you know why he didn't think he ever needed to worry about me?

"Because he thought I was nothing but a whore. Correction," she raised a finger, "nothing but an *old* whore. I had nowhere to run. I had nothing of value any more, and so – being valueless – I had nothing to fight for."

"Nick told me this," I said. "How the local police admitted, once it all kicked off, that they couldn't protect you. How they accepted you'd probably be dead in a year."

"A month," she corrected me. "And so – to get me away from that place, and because there was no other way to be sure – Nick married me. I'm alive because of him. My sister and I were trafficked. Sold. Rented. Passed on, and always under the control of Sergei Maximov."

She lifted the vodka now, and barely sipped it, her eyes closed, her hand no longer shaking, then placed shot glass back on the table.

"And this is why I am here today."

"I'm sorry," I said, quietly, feeling it needed to be said. "I'm so sorry for all you went through."

Now she looked at me with a blank look, the sardonic smile gone, the beatific grace evaporated.

"Why?" She asked. "You had nothing to do with what happened. From you, I do not need sorrow."

She smiled, the smile – this time - not reaching her eyes. "And *now* you're wondering what I *do* need. From you I need *assistance*."

I waited. Her smile widened, this time some of it reaching her eyes. "I can see why he likes you."

"I thought you said he loved me."

"He cares," Arianna answered. "The world is full of men who tell you they like you and – just before they cry – tell you they love you. But a man who cares? That's," she waved her hand, turning around to reach into the pockets of her mac, the movement causing her hair to slip forward so that her face was masked until she straightened up, ran her left hand through it, and placed her right hand on the table, removing it to leave a phone sitting on the scrubbed pine.

"I need your help," she said, businesslike. "I need you to do something for me, and I ask you to join me in keeping my request from the honourable man we both know. He's made you happy, Danny. Despite your fears, you know this to be a fact, as I know you have made him happy. And he – and you, by accepting this situation – have made me safer than I have felt since I was seven years of age.

"And what I am about to tell you, I do not want him to know."

I frowned. I needed to hear what Arianna had to say, but the idea of keeping secrets from Nick bothered me. In the end, my curiosity got the better of me; once I knew, I could decide how much of Arianna's secrets I'd keep.

I nodded.

"My sister Klara and I were twins. That made us especially valuable to Maximov. He," she paused, sipped again at the vodka, then "he whored Klara and I out. But he made sure he took more than money from many of the men who paid for us."

"Blackmail?" I asked, my voice sounding odd to me.

Arianna nodded. "He kept a notebook. Everything was on it, and it empowered him. He moved, as the world seemed to shift from war into peace, from selling girls and boys to selling the secrets and fears and desires of his customers.

"And that was when he sold my sister."

I'd been watching her all this time, seeing a woman who had been containing her feelings since childhood relate this tale of horror. She didn't flinch now.

"Klara was gentle. Easy. I was always the difficult one. Always, I would be the one who acted if there was a problem. By then we'd reached Grozny," she waved her hand again. "You don't need to pretend you have a clue where it is. It was a shithole before, a shithole during, and a shithole after a bombardment that reduced it to rubble. But it was the point at which Maximov decided he no longer needed to sell flesh above secrets.

"And so he sold me to a man who abused me for three years."

"I'm sorry," I said reflexively, realising as she refocused on me, that my apologies were unnecessary.

She shrugged, sipped the vodka once more. "He's dead. I hear he died painfully."

I looked at the phone.

Cleared my throat. "So how can I help you?" And wondered how I'd got from unease at this woman being in my kitchen to openly asking what I could do to assist her.

"I've found him," she said and I realised the vodka had kicked in. "Maximov."

I opened my mouth. No words came out.

Arianna touched the phone, tapped the screen a couple of times, turned the device around.

A man, somewhere between sixty and seventy, his silver-grey hair swept back exposing a widow's peak. A pronounced, hawk-like nose. High cheekbones, eyes sunk in shadows. He was talking on a mobile phone. She touched the screen, the angle changed, he was standing on the opposite side of an obviously high-end car, a shop window behind him.

"I had an interview with the Home Office. Afterwards I was walking aimlessly around the west end and found myself close to," she named a super high-end hotel, one of those that have been around seemingly since the dawn of time without ever needing to advertise. "I think the interview went well, and I felt like a small celebration, so I thought while I'm here, I'll have a coffee.' And I did.

"They had a cafe in the lobby. It was very expensive, but very chic. If I'd gone straight home after the interview I would have missed him. But I was sitting there with a cappuccino, trying to make the tiny biscuits they gave me last a little longer and I heard his voice."

Her eyes took on a faraway look, as though she were back in the hotel lobby.

"I froze," she said. "I thought I was going to have a heart attack, so fast was my heart pounding. And then I thought I'd imagined him. That he was just in my mind. Or that he was a different man; one who sounded like Maximov but who wasn't him.

"I turned. He was talking on the phone and he was just stepping into the revolving door, so I couldn't see him full face. But I knew. And so I threw some money on the table and I went after him. I wanted to run after him, to scream his name, to stop him, but I knew that anything that drew attention, that caused alarm would make him vanish.

"I have spent so many years looking for this man, and he has always been a week ahead. As though somehow he knew that I was close and he would simply vanish like smoke. But this time he was there. He was real. And so I walked out of the hotel as he stepped into his limousine and I took these pictures to prove he exists."

She stopped, tapped the screen once more and, the picture reappearing, looked at it with a discomforting intensity.

"So what are you going to do?" I asked, and she tore her eyes away.

"He was staying at the hotel. I'm sure of it. I need to know where he went to. I need to track him down."

"Well surely Nick can help," I said, and she looked up from the photo, a bemused look on her face. "Arianna, this man is a criminal. Nick is a policeman. You need to tell Nick."

She shook her head, anger flashing across her face. "Not Nick. Have you heard nothing I said? Danny, Maximov was a criminal when I knew him, and he still dined with diplomats, rich men, powerful people. He's untouchable. If I report him to the police and they visit him, what will happen? I tell you what will happen: Nothing. There will be no proof of any crimes. There will be phone calls from people to people. And he will vanish again."

"But how are you going to get justice?" I asked, puzzled still.

She smiled that faintly pitying smile again, as though she were humouring a small child.

"I don't care about justice, Danny. There is no justice anywhere in the world. A man like Maximov – even if he goes to prison – lives a better life than any of the widows and orphans he left behind. The world is made by and for men like Sergei Maximov, and I no longer care what happens to it or to him. All I want from him is my sister. She's still alive. I can feel it. A part of me is still out there somewhere. And I need to find her. You locate Maximov for me and I will make him tell me where she is."

The kitchen was warm, and the vodka coursing through my veins made it even warmer, but I still felt a chill run through me.

"That's all I need from you."

THURSDAY

CHAPTER THREE

"Come on you piece of shit," Ali snarled, flashing her lights at the car in front of her. "It's a motorway, not a kiddies' ride."

I blanched as the little car swung out, rocketed forward and swerved back into the left-hand lane before overtaking another car on the right, earning a chorus of horns by swerving back right, across two lanes and shooting forward.

Beside me on what felt like a parcel shelf Ellie, Caz's glossy black Staffie/Lab cross whined, looked at me with what can only be described as a plea for help, and let loose a fart of such noxious odour that I became certain I would not live to see Duke's Halt.

Caz reached forward and pressed a button, the window on her side sliding down a fraction of an inch.

"Jesus, Danny," Ali gasped, doing the same, "what you eating back there?"

"Me?" I opened my mouth to protest, and shut it as quickly. Speaking seemed to increase my opportunity to consume the toxic gases.

Ellie lifted her head, gave me a dolorous look and settled back down, her head on her paws which, in turn, were resting on one of Caz's antique Louis Vuitton trunks.

"It's awfully nice of Paolo to lend you his matchbox," I said – for not the first time - to Caz as Ali once more swerved left and shot forward, "shame he didn't have something a little more suitable for a crowd."

I fidgeted on the trunk I was half perched on and shifted my feet so they were placed more squarely on my own luggage, the better to retain my balance next time Ali swerved like a maniac.

To my left, sandwiched between me and the side of the car,

was a sealed Fortnum & Mason's cool bag which housed the remains of George Warren.

I'd been fairly sure that Caz – despite my agreeing to help her on her crazed mission – wouldn't be able to find a driver at such short notice, and so my agreeing had been done with a fairly strong sense that I'd never have to actually deliver on the promise to join her on this trip.

I don't think that makes me a bad friend, just one who thinks smuggling a dead man's ashes back into a house he seems to have been permanently banned from in life is an unnecessary aggravation to put oneself through.

But I'd reckoned without my best friend's famous persistence. And without Ali's desire to 'have a gander at a real country house'.

"She can't drive us," I'd protested when informed that Ali had offered to do the honours. "She's got a pub to run."

"She's standing right here," Ali had answered dryly, "and it's your pub. *And* the twins are perfectly capable of looking after it for a few days. My boy Carlton and his girlfriend Tara have offered to help out behind the bar, so they won't be short-handed. And, to be honest, I'd rather not be around for this bloody talent competition. It's shaping up to be like purgatory with novelty acts."

"All the more reason, surely, that you should be around. The twins are lovely but can they be trusted not to burn the place to the ground?"

"Mate, I'm due some holidays, and her ladyship has asked me to accompany you both to this posh gaff. So if you think you're going to stop me having a few days living the high life in a mansion you've got another thing coming."

The tone of menace had been explicit: deny Ali this and I would pay dearly.

"Has Caz told you why we're going?" I asked her.

"If you mean the ashes of this bloke what got kicked out of his own home," Ali answered, "then yeah; she's told me. I think it's disgusting that anyone would do that to their own child."

"And yet you'll still accept their hospitality," I noted dryly.

"Payback, mate. I'll accept their food and drink, lounge around their," she closed her eyes as though recalling the phrasing, "gracious drawing room and shelf-lined library which contains volumes as diverse as 'an original copy of Darwin's Origin Of The Species and a long-rumoured King James Bible.' You don't get shit like that at a Holiday Inn. Not even the Premier ones. And all the time I'll be sticking it to the man."

I was losing this battle, and the final nail was when I'd raised the request from a friend to track down someone for her.

"What friend?" Caz perked up. What someone?"

"Just a friend," I said, and Ali sniggered.

"Mate, every friend you've got is in this room."

"There's Nick," I said, realising as the words came from my mouth that I'd basically agreed with Ali. "And besides, there's nothing wrong with having a small group of friends."

"So Nick – Detective Sergeant Nick Fisher – wants you to hunt down this mysterious person for him?" Caz asked. "Rather than use the resources of the Met Police, which is almost literally what they're there for?"

"Not Nick," I said grudgingly. "Another friend."

"Oh-ho-ho," Ali hooted, "he's got them coming out the woodwork now. Which friend?"

"Just a friend you," I answered, beginning to feel outgunned, outmanoeuvred and out of my depth. "One you don't know. I said I'd keep things discreet."

Within minutes they'd got me to admit that my unnamed friend had seen someone in a hotel and needed them tracked down to return something that they'd dropped.

"Well surely this unnamed friend," Caz said, "could just explain that they have this person's belongings and leave them with reception?"

I was close to drowning. "No," I finally said, attempting to put some grit into the statement, "they really want to find the person themselves, but of course the hotel won't disclose guest details."

"Whatever," Caz – tired already of the discussion – waved a hand airily, "Hacking the reservations system of the hotel isn't a job for you, and you know it. And turning up at reception asking to be told the name of a guest at places like that one is guaranteed to have Nick and his ilk escorting you from the building in no time at all. So leave the details with the twins and let Ray do his thing while you escort me to Duke's Halt."

"But Ray has the talent show to organise. And the bar to run," I tried desperately, and both Ali and Caz gave me a look that told me they were tired of my shit and if I didn't start packing immediately they'd do it for me.

"This is all sorts of wrong," I said now as Ali honked the horn once more and the car swerved across lanes of the M1.

"This is justice," Caz answered, half-turning in her seat to look at me, and I couldn't help but be reminded of Arianna's line about there being no such thing.

"We don't even know what he did to get kicked out of the house," I answered. "He might have murdered someone. We might be bringing a murderer's ashes back to the place he committed his crime."

"You never met Georgie," Caz answered quietly, "or you'd not even joke about that. He was the gentlest of souls, and there's no way he did anything like that."

"Then why leave the place and stay away for over thirty years?"

"Families," Ali said gnomically, before loudly questioning the parentage of the driver in front of her and demanding to know if he knew the speed limit wasn't just aspirational.

I'd given Ray and Dash the background on Arianna's problem without naming the lady herself and asked them to do what they could to locate the name of the guest.

Arianna, when I'd called to confirm I had some associates looking into her request, had seemed a little disappointed.

"Not you personally?" She'd asked.

"It needs some special skills," I'd explained, "but the associates who are working on it are top notch, and I'm confident we'll have something for you soon."

The thing was, I *wasn't* sure that, if we did acquire the desired information, whether I wanted to share it with Arianna.

Something about how she'd said 'You locate Maximov for me and I will make him tell me where she is,' had unnerved me. I knew that the Home Office was watching Arianna and Nick like hawks watch chicks in an abandoned nest. Man goes to Albania, comes back with wife. The sort of people who specialised in identifying immigration scams and punishing those responsible had to have bells going off over that one, and even though Nick marrying Arianna had been the only way to get the woman away from almost certain death, he'd still basically entered a sham marriage and she was still, basically, seeking to acquire the right to live and work in the UK without providing full background details.

And anything that rocked the boat – any hint of illegality or even of scandal – would put them at risk. She'd be shipped back to her fate and he'd face an investigation and possible loss of his job as well as his liberty.

So while I appreciated Arianna's need to find Maximov and locate her sister I knew I'd need to think long and hard about how I managed the situation before just handing his whereabouts over to her.

But first, I had to have his whereabouts, and I hoped that the twins – Ray especially – were working on that.

Duke's Halt – according to the research I'd done – was one of the best examples of late Elizabethan architecture in private hands today.

There were references to a folly, to the famous library and a long gallery supposedly filled with treasures dating back to the Renaissance as well as a small collection of ancient antiquities and to the 'checkered history of the Warrens themselves', and none of this meant much to me to be honest.

"So Caz," I said, leaning forward and receiving, for my efforts, a lazy growl from Ellie, "have the Warrens been living at Duke's Halt ever since it was built? And who was the Duke in question?"

"Well the Duke is one of the Plantagenets who supposedly stopped at the house on the way to one of the battles during the war of the Roses. A war the Plantagenets eventually lost, which – since the place is named after the fact one of them used it as a sort of proto air bnb – would, one might assume, have put it and its inhabitants on some sort of blacklist. But the Warrens are either the most politically astute family or the luckiest aristocrats in the country.

"A few years later Henry Tudor granted them their own Duchy, which of course lead to suggestions they'd been playing both sides in the war, and a generation or so later they sided with the Catholic church during the Reformation. Hid priests. Once had a Bishop leading masses in their cow sheds. The Duke at that time nearly lost his head for it. Was in the Tower when Mary came to the throne and reversed all findings against him.

"Course Mary didn't last long and by the time she was gone and the winds had blown the other way again that duke was dead and his son was holding the title with complete deniability.

"Same thing happened with the Civil War. Total Royalists, but managed to play both sides against each other until Charles the first," she drew a line along her throat with her index finger and I was fairly sure that that was not how Charles was beheaded, but she was off again on the potted history.

"The Puritans were all for pulling the title, confiscating the land, only the Duke at the time had a sister who was married to one of Cromwell's right-hand men, so they got away with it again. Just. Until Cromwell popped his clogs and Charles the second came back to the throne, at which point they switched sides yet again, went spying for old Charlie and helped round up a load of Puritan sympathisers at court."

"Jesus," Ali muttered, suddenly deciding, as we moved off the motorway, to start using her indicators, "I thought we were doing well tracking my family tree back to the eighteen hundreds and finding some bloke what might have helped build the Commercial Road."

"Slow down," Caz softly instructed Ali. "The turning's coming up." I wondered if she had some sort of built-in Aristo GPS that could sense a country house from miles away.

The hedges on both sides soon gave way to trees, densely packed as though to create an impenetrable wall and then, in short order, a high, red-bricked and fairly impenetrable wall appeared, about six or seven feet high, the forest dark and dense behind it.

The car slowed and Ali – now we were on a road with not another soul in place - rediscovered her indicators, clicked them on, slowed and turned left off the road and through a pair of huge and ornate metallic gates.

The car's speed dropped now, and we wove our way up a slight but persistent hill, deep forest on either side, the road curving gently left then right until it slowly curved back to the left and, eventually, the forest dwindled away.

We turned gently left once more, and then, suddenly, across a wide, perfectly manicured lawn, we saw Dukes Halt.

The house sat on a hillock so that it was raised above everything. It was a long, solid-looking three-storied building with a high sloping red-tiled roof surrounded by an ornamental turret. Off centre, five tall slender chimneys jutted into the sky, and I could see another two of the same chimneys – one at either end of the building – coming from the rear of the roof.

The doorway was set in the middle of the building, which was constructed of a golden-yellow brick, and seemed to have grown organically from that main portal so that the eves on the left hand side of the property jutted out further than those on the right hand side, and the high, mullioned windows – their scale shrinking slightly on the first floor and shrinking again on the top floor – were leaded, the glass panes (even from this distance) looking thick and inconsistent, the top portions of some of the ground floor ones decorated with stained glass.

To the left, across the rolling green lawns, another hill – taller than the one Dukes Halt sat on – jutted upwards and on that one, silhouetted against the afternoon sky – was what looked like the ruins of some ancient church, the shattered wreckage in direct contrast to the serene-seeming, implacable solidity of the house in front of us.

In front of the house, in the middle of the lawn, a pair of huge circular flower beds flanked a massive ornamental fountain, the water stilled now, what looked like laughing nymphs and dryads frozen in gold grey stone as the wind whipped over them.

As we drove slowly forward, Dukes Halt, constructed as it was of that yellowish brick and elevated as it was above the surrounding landscape, was suddenly caught by the autumnal sun and – as though putting on a show for our benefit – it glowed, golden and red, seemingly illuminated from within.

"Christ," Ali exhaled. "I bet that's a bastard to heat."

CHAPTER FOUR

As the car pulled to a halt, the front door of Dukes Halt opened and a man stepped out followed by a woman dressed in a long black skirt and a white puff-sleeved blouse, her steely grey hair backcombed and coiffed in a way that suggested a tornado would have trouble shifting a follicle.

The woman stood impassively as the man jogged around the car to Caz's side and opened her door. Caz crawled out of the sports car and they embraced.

"Thanks for coming," he said, hugging her again. "And – in advance – I apologise for whatever happens this weekend."

They laughed until Ali, tired of waiting for someone to open her door kicked it open and half-fell out of the motor, catching herself at the last minute and hauling herself upright whilst issuing the sort of groans that one usually associated with medieval torture or modern pornography.

"Jesus, my pants are wedged in parts of me that haven't had wedging in decades," she muttered to nobody in particular while reaching behind her and yanking at her jeans.

I reached forward and grabbed at the catch on the back of the driver's seat, triggering it forward and allowing Ellie to leap from the car and run around to Caz, bark at her mistress then charge off into the middle of the rolling lawn where she squatted and did a perfectly lady-like wee.

I swear, as I grabbed the Fortnums cool bag and hauled my own stiff, sweaty body out of the back of the car, that I heard the woman who had been standing immobile actually crackle, then glanced upwards just in time to see Ali rise from a curtsey that I swear she'd been practicing it in front of a mirror.

I didn't have the heart to tell her that I was fairly sure she'd just abased herself to the housekeeper.

"Darling, you must meet my friends." Caz put her hand under the arm of the man – tall, late fifties, high cheekbones, deep-set eyes of a very dark blue that bordered on black, precision-clipped goatee and a tightly cropped head of salt-and-pepper hair.

"Daniel," Caz said, as the two strolled around the back of the car to where I stood stretching, "this is Henry Warren. Major Henry Warren," she said, presenting the man as though this were her house and both of us guests at a drinks party.

Close up, I could see that his dark colouring was a suntan and I wondered, briefly, where he'd acquired that in late October, but before I could wonder any more, he reached a hand out and shook mine enthusiastically.

"Wonderful to meet you," he said. "Wonderful. Caroline has told me so much about you," he smiled at Caz who smiled back and reached out to take the Fortnums bag.

"Really?" I asked, and he laughed.

"Really: No," he said, laughing again, "but I'm absolutely looking forward to finding out all about you this weekend."

"And this is Ali. Mrs Carter."

Caz gestured at Ali, who said 'Charmed, I'm sure," attempted another curtsey, lost her balance and ended up leaning against the side of the car as though holding it for support.

Henry Warren smiled, confusion clear in his eyes, and turned back to Caz.

"If you get your driver to park the car around the back by the stables, Mrs Chapman," he indicated the wraithlike figure who clearly shopped for all her fashion in the late 1890s "will show them to your rooms and she can bring the luggage in while I get you a drink. You must be arid after that journey."

"Driver?" Ali bristled, and seemed about to explain just what she thought of the suggestion that she was little more than help, when Caz, smiling beatifically, jumped in.

"Sadly Carter can't do bags. Scoliosis as a child, you know. Handles a jalopy like a champion, but the legs are just too bowed for any weight-bearing activity."

Ali, no longer sure what to be outraged at, favoured Caz with a glower so intense I suspected a nuclear blast was imminent.

"Danny here will take them, won't you sweetie," Caz patted me gently on the arm, and Ali sniggered, the word *mug* being clearly heard, even though her lips didn't seem to move.

I found myself bristling as much as Ali had while Caz and Henry Warren – still arm in arm – turned towards the door.

"The blue room, is it?" Caz enquired, and Chapman nodded. "Your," she eyed me suspiciously as though uncertain whether the fact I'd just been delegated as porter made what she was about to say suspect, "*friend* is in the green room."

"Perfect," Caz smiled at me, "we're next door to each other."

"Chapman will show you where to go," Henry Warren said airily. But before he could lead Caz inside, the front door swung open and an angry-looking woman stormed out of the house.

Her red hair was pulled tight in a ponytail, and everything about her clothes – from the oversized man's shirt to the jeans belted tightly at her waist and on down to the muddy Wellington boots – seemed too big for her frame.

"Impossible," she snarled, her furious face flushing red and her eyes, for a second, filling with tears.

Then, seeing the assembly on the doorstep, she blinked, clenched her jaw and her fists, inhaled deeply through her nose, and smiled brittly at Henry.

"Major Warren," she said, nodding and making to move past us.

"No joy, Beth?" Henry asked, and she paused.

"Joy?" The woman laughed bitterly. "If I was one of his bloody paintings or one of his stupid horses he'd find me a home. But I'm not. I'm just a woman and thus incapable of doing the bloody job I've been doing half my life. I've lived here since I got married. Gaia's lived here her whole life. And he's just told me I have a fortnight to pack and get out. He's got some temporary man coming from Cornwall."

Henry held a hand out to her and she shrank from it.

"I've got nowhere to go," she said quietly, then turned as though noticing Chapman for the first time, and shot a look of pure hatred at her.

"Look," Henry Warren released Caz, stepped forward and put a hand on the other woman's arm. "Don't do anything. Let me talk to him. We'll sort something out after the weekend. Please. It will be okay."

"Okay?" She shook her head. "Nothing's ever going to be okay again. But if you can do anything…"

She trailed off and he patted her arm. "We'll sort something," he repeated. "I promise."

She clenched her jaw again, as though biting back words she suspected would make her position worse, then nodded at him, muttered a "Thanks," and made her way past us all, making as though to head for the lawn before suddenly swerving away from it and walking – each step still seeming to telegraph her emotion – back down the driveway we'd just come up.

I watched her go as Henry and Caz went into the house.

Ali dragged all the luggage from the back of the car and unceremoniously dumped it on the drive. I glanced at the housekeeper, and for a moment I was sure that, just as I'd looked her way, she'd reassembled her face. It was impassive now, but for some reason I was certain that, just before I'd glanced her way, it had been home to a quiet but triumphant smirk.

"Right," Ali said, clambering back into the car, "where do I dump this thing then?"

The housekeeper, as though voice activated, turned her eyes on Ali. "Follow the drive around until you come to a fork. Take the right fork and go on a couple of hundred yards until you see a turn on the left. Take that turn and you'll come to the vehicle parking area. Please reverse park neatly so that your front end is pointing forward and ensure you leave sufficient room for other vehicles to do the same."

Ali opened her mouth, doubtless to make some comment about her front end, her thoughts on reverse parking, or her feelings about the suggestion she might be an inconsiderate parker, but got not a word out before the woman, still talking to her as though she were an Edwardian scullery maid and the housekeeper a reincarnated Queen Mary, added "when you've parked walk back to the house and enter by the staff door. Cook will show you where your quarters are."

And then, as Ali, the car door still open, gawked at her, Chapman swooped down, lifted two of the four suitcases from the drive and, nodding at me, said "If you will follow me, sir," before entering the house.

I snatched up the other two suitcases, glanced back at Ali, who looked genuinely bemused, and followed the straight-backed woman into the house as the Ferrari roared to life and, with a tsunami of marble chippings spitting from behind its back wheels, shot off towards the vehicle parking area.

Inside, the hallway – a vast space dominated by a huge staircase that Ali could probably have driven the car up if she'd been so inclined was chilly and echoing and filled with a selection of furniture so old I suspected it had been hand whittled from the Ark by one of Noah's sons once they'd all finally settled on mount Arrarat. In one corner under the turn in the stairs a rather impressive suit of armour, the scrap value of which, alone, would be worth more than almost everything I possessed – was dimly lit, the low autumnsal sun adding a flickering orange light as though the whole place were aflame.

The space smelled of wood smoke, tobacco, vanilla, something sweet and floral and, underlying it all, of money.

Money so old it had been around before currency was invented.

Chapman – who had to be well into her seventies, though she seemed as robust as the straight-backed chair to my left – was already halfway up the stairs en route, I supposed, to mine and Caz's rooms, so I followed her in silence.

Our rooms were beside each other, with a shared and connected bathroom which contained plumbing that she described as "not original but still rather traditional".

I couldn't help wondering if she really spoke as if she'd been beamed in from the nineteenth century or whether this was all an act to fit in with the space then decided, as she looked me up and down as though I'd crawled from under a rock, and suggested that I might like to freshen up "Before joining The Major and Lady Caroline for tea in the drawing room," that Chapman had never seen – and never would see – the inside of a Gala Bingo hall, and she left me to it, explaining that she had "Some correspondence to work on with Sir Phillip."

Chapman had suggested that the plumbing was 'Rather Traditional,' but I'd have gone more with 'The sort of shit Edgar Allen Poe would have done if writing had paled and instead he'd gone in for indoor water engineering.'

I used the loo, which appeared to be an original Crapper, and was large enough, if one felt so inclined, to baptise a small elephant in. The flush, I ascertained after some minutes, would be achieved by yanking on a long ornate chain which ended in a gilded orb the size of a Jaffa orange and I duly yanked on the chain.

Nothing happened.

I yanked again, and the orb came off in my hand.

I swore under my breath, and spotted that the last link in the chain had come undone, slotted the orb back into place and pressed the link shut with my thumb and forefinger then grasped the chain further up and pulled it more slowly this time.

And an almost perfect replica of Victoria Falls drained into the gargantuan bowl while somewhere in Sub Saharan Africa a village experienced a cataclysmic drought.

Next, I crossed to the sink – large enough this time to baptise the elephant baby's mother if she fancied converting – and turned on the tap.

And again – apart from a noise somewhere within the bowels of the house that suggested someone was rehearsing the bass part from Cole Porter's 'I've got you under my skin,'

– nothing happened.

I put my hands under the tap.

Still nothing.

I turned the tap off then back on, and still nothing, though the melodious bass part had now sped up and become more of a punk drum track.

I frowned, and reached for the tap again just as a torrent of scalding water shot forth with the force of an espresso machine, slammed into the porcelain and ricocheted straight off that and into my crotch, soaking my trousers and parboiling bits of me which I was fairly sure the owner's handbook recommended should never be parboiled.

I swore again, dabbed ineffectually at the soaking, contemplated changing trousers and decided, after everything that had happened, that I was not only past caring but, more importantly, desperately in need of a drink. And thus it was that I went downstairs to join Caz, Major Henry, and to meet his charming and delinquent daughter, while looking like I'd wet myself and hadn't noticed, incontinence and dementia seeming to fit perfectly into the weirdness of the whole place.

CHAPTER FIVE

I found them in the drawing room, Caz and Henry seated in two high wing-backed chairs upholstered in pale green silk, while across from them a teenaged girl lounged on a sofa upholstered with the same fabric and flicked listlessly through a magazine.

A low coffee table was placed between the sofa and the chairs and on it was a silver tea service.

The girl's hair was dark and glossy and cut in a Louise Brooks bob that fell down so that her face was partially obscured, only the chin – small and pointed – and a lower lip were visible.

"Ah," Caz smiled, gestured at the sofa opposite, "here he is. We were wondering what happened to you. Danny, this is my goddaughter Carlotta."

"Lottie," the teenager looked up from her magazine, did a double take (which she attempted to cover by glancing back down at Tatler) then glanced back up again as I squeezed on to the sofa next to her. "Have you wet yourself?" She asked, and I winced.

"Plumbing accident," I said, miming a torrent cascading and then ricocheting towards me, and realising too late that the mime looked more like I was drawing attention to my crotch than actually explaining what had happened. "The water came out of the tap quite forcefully."

"Ah yes," Henry smiled benignly, "our famous Traditional plumbing."

People seemed determined to use that phrasing, though I was fairly certain it didn't actually mean what they thought it did. Traditional plumbing was, surely, an unplumbed latrine in a shed out the back with a sponge on a stick in a bucket; what they had here, it seemed clear to me, was ineffective, wasteful and possibly dangerous plumbing, and I wondered how many guests had, in their time, been maimed by the "traditional" aspects of Duke's Halt.

The room we were in was long, with several more sets of sofa/chair combinations dotted around it. One side of the room was taken up by the leaded windows looking out on to the lawn while much of the opposite side of the room was taken up with a fireplace so huge that my parents' flat could happily have fit inside it and still left room for a garden shed.

In the fireplace a rather pitiful fire sputtered, and above it a portrait in oils of a woman, seated and staring with a somewhat melancholy air off to the right, her gaze focused on the middle distance as though she was looking towards the doorway I'd just come through, or hearing intriguing sounds from the hallway itself, was hanging.

The woman had honey-coloured hair styled in a chignon, part of which – because of the turn of her head – was just visible on the left side of her head. She was wearing a light summer dress of a pale ivory silk covered in what looked like oversized peonies, their colours bleeding into the silk like watercolour paints into blotting paper, and her hands were resting in her lap as though sitting here listening to – but being unable to get up and investigate the source of – a series of mysterious sounds from the hallway was the most relaxing thing in the world.

Perhaps, I mused briefly, she was listening to the sounds of Traditional Plumbing.

On the mantlepiece in front of her was a large Chinese ginger jar, the delicate white china covered in the same peonies on the dress, and I knew instinctively what was inside the ginger jar and who the woman in the portrait was.

"That's my grandma," the girl – Lottie – said, her eyes watching me closely now as I slid back on the sofa, my hands on either side of me to stop myself sliding off the bloody thing. "She died a long time ago. But she was a great beauty they say. What do you think?"

I jerked from my reverie, glancing back at the portrait, the ginger jar, the Fortnum bag resting by Caz's left foot, the duo opposite me, Henry's neutral gaze and Caz's faintly amused one, and back to Lottie, before saying: "Yes, she looks beautiful."

"What can I get you to drink, old man?" Henry suddenly came to his feet. "Chapman's put tea out but if you prefer something more robust I've a Lagavulin."

I suddenly felt as though I'd stepped out of reality and into some sort of theme park without fully understanding where the theme park ended and reality restarted, and in my confusion I heard myself say that tea would be fine, before realising that the teacups were the size of eggcups and I'd need about twelve of them to quench a thirst.

"Here," Caz leaned forward, "let me be mother."

She lifted the heavy silver tea pot and poured a cup for me, whilst asking Lottie if she wanted one.

The girl's response – "A tea or a whisky?" didn't even receive an acknowledgement and, as Caz handed me the cup and saucer with a whispered 'relax; it's all fine,' Lottie loudly announced, "I hate tea. Coffee too. Horrid stupid pointless stuff."

I glanced at the crystal tumbler in front of Caz and – remembering my friend's dislike of the drinks that fuelled the nation – wondered if this hatred was evidence of Caz's influence on the girl.

"Thanks for taking the bags up," Caz said, settling back into her chair. "I suppose I should go up in a minute and freshen up. Wonder where Ali's got to?"

I blushed. "That lady – Chapman? – said she should go round to the kitchen door and cook would sort her out," I mumbled.

"Oh dear," Caz frowned slightly, "Ali's not going to like that, is she? I'll go find her once I'm freshened up."

"Oh you met Mrs C, did you?" Lottie had continued, through my exchange with Caz, to watch me closely, her eyes – as dark as her father's – observing me from under her fringe.

"What did you think of her?"

I paused, unsure how to respond, but Lottie had already carried on.

"I don't think she's all there. I mean, it's the twenty-first century and yet she carries on like Mrs Danvers."

"Last night I went to Manderlay," I misquoted, only to have Lottie correct me.

"Dreamt I went to Manderlay," she said. "Again. Do you like the film?"

"Not sure I've seen it," I said, "but I've read the book."

At the mention of the word book she smiled. "I think it's a hoot. All that repression and melodrama. Mind you," she gestured around the room and went back to flicking through her magazine.

"Lottie, dear," Henry said, "why don't you show our guest around the place?"

"Cos I don't want to," she said without looking up, her tone embarrassed and a tiny bit angry.

I knew that feeling; the feeling of being a teenager and accidentally giving away too much of yourself so that people assumed you wanted to play nice and be part of their gang when really all you wanted to do was hold tight to the bit of you that wasn't theirs while you figured out how to be the you that you were becoming.

So far, I liked Lottie Warren. She wasn't the Caz clone I'd been expecting, but she had enough spirit to seem like a chip off the bouffanted block.

"Oh go on," Caz encouraged her. "Show him the Long Gallery before the light goes entirely."

The girl sighed, shoved the magazine behind a cushion, and stood. "God," she sighed theatrically, "all I ever get in this place is sent out of rooms. Well let's go."

This last was addressed to me, Caz and Henry having already gone back to talking about whatever it was they'd been discussing when I'd entered the room.

I paused, frowned at the two of them already gossiping about someone Henry admitted he hadn't heard from in years, felt a little like I'd been shut out, then shrugged and stood. What the hell: I might as well see some of the house while I could.

Lottie had already stomped out of the room and was halfway across the hall by the time I caught up with her.

"So," I said in what I hoped were encouraging tones, "the Long Gallery. What's that then?"

She didn't look at me, merely marched up the stairs in front of her. "Most people would call it a load of stupid paintings of dead white people. Gramps calls it his 'Collection.'"

We reached the first landing, walked down a corridor lined on both sides with closed doors and came to a secondary, but almost equally impressive stairway at the end, which Lottie again attacked as though she were Hillary on the last stretch of Everest.

At the top, she stood to one side and swept an arm as though presenting an amazing trick to me.

We seemed to be in another long and dusty corridor. I say seemed because this one was in almost total darkness, every single one of the windows shuttered fast against any outside light.

Lottie reached behind me, flicked a switch and a low glow began to fill the room, its intensity growing slowly until I could see that we were standing in an almost equivalent space to the drawing room downstairs, albeit that this one was two or three times longer, and I realised with a start that it seemed to run the whole length of the building.

Hence, I supposed, the name The Long Gallery.

The ceiling was plastered and stuccoed like something from Versailles and – despite the presence of a vast crystal chandelier suspended in the middle of the space – the lighting here came from a series of recessed halogen spotlights in the ceiling as well as a number of delicate light fixtures placed over some of the dozens upon dozens of paintings that lined the wall opposite the shuttered windows.

Lottie crossed to the first window and flung open the shutter, repeating the action all along the space so that the artificial but dim light was joined by the soft golden autumn sunlight, lending a somehow more peaceful feeling to the space.

"Right," she announced, joining me at the top of the stairwell. "No photography, no smoking, drinking, spitting and," she finished, shouting the last phrase, "no touchin' the artwork."

She grinned at my confusion. "Just kidding. You can lick the bloody things for all I care."

Right beside me, I could see, was an oil portrait, another of the woman from the living room. She was older in this one, the full face from downstairs a little gaunter, a slight hint of grey in the hair at the temples, her hands encased in artfully rendered silk opera gloves as she sat, again, looking off to the right, and I realised with a start that in the space behind her was what looked like Dukes Halt, the building seemingly afire.

Then I looked again and realised that what I'd taken for flames were fireworks painted all around the house.

"That's my grandma Lady Marion," Lottie said. "Again. She died, years before I was even born, though I suspect my grandfather had her murdered. I mean, all of this 'Marion's birthday' nonsense, the guests who never knew her, the bloody fireworks: Don't you think it stinks of guilt?"

"Maybe your grandfather just really loved her," I offered apropos of nothing else, and she sniggered.

"You haven't met him yet. He thinks love is a cryptic clue in the Times crossword. So here they all are," she gestured at the room ahead. "All my ancestors, and all the shit they managed to buy, beg steal or borrow from whoever previously owned it."

I began walking the room, and actually whistled at a couple of the pieces. There was a Caravaggio – not a very good one, but a Caravaggio nonetheless – a couple of Gainsboroughs, a smattering of pretty but unattributed ladies in jewels and finery, and a rather alarming handful of very outrageous looking gentlemen in doublet and hose that left little to the imagination.

Some of the smaller pictures, I noted, were hanging in spaces where larger paintings had previously been, the previous pictures having left ghosts of themselves in the faintly sun-bleached shapes surrounding the newer works.

Under several of the paintings were small glass cases, lit internally, and containing small pieces of what looked like pottery.

"Great grandfather picked up half the Middle East back in the day," Lottie explained as though the telling itself were enough to kill a girl of boredom, "and dad bought a few pieces when he was in Iraq a few years ago."

"Iraq?"

"Decorated war hero, don't you know. Killed a bunch of the locals and ended up with a selection of wall tiles from Ur for his trouble. That's them there," she indicated a small collection of glazed wall tiles laid on a blood-red velvet background in a small display case.

The colours were as iridescent as a peacock and so fresh they looked as though they'd been painted yesterday.

Beside the tiles, on the wall was a small shelf, and on it a vase filled with fresh white Dahlias. Beside the vase was a small toy fire engine, the red paint chipped and scratched.

And above the odd display were the only photographs in the room: One of a very young Lady Marion cradling a baby, one of a young boy – about four or five - wearing an antique sailor's suit and looking at the camera with the same look of alarm I think I'd have if someone dragged me up like a nineteenth century Romanov and took a picture for posterity – and another, in a simple black frame, of a tired looking Lady Marion and a man who – based on the familial resemblance – I assumed was Henry's father Sir Phillip, the same small boy in a variation of the Victorian cosplay from the previous shoot, and – so close to the edge of the frame that his left shoulder was cut out – a teenager I assumed was Henry himself.

I frowned at the photo. Something was wrong.

"That's Marion again," Lottie indicated her grandmother,

"and my uncle Edward."

Caz hadn't mentioned another brother. I was about to ask Lottie whether Uncle Edward would be joining us this weekend, or whether he too was barred from the property when she added, almost nonchalantly, "he died too. Three days after his mother. I think it was a terrible accident, but nobody here will ever talk about him, so maybe whoever bumped off Marion did for Edward too."

And suddenly I knew why the picture looked so odd: The framing was all wrong. There was too much dead space on the right-hand side of the picture, but this was not because of poor photographic composition.

This was because someone – before putting the picture in the frame – had taken a pair of scissors and cut a huge chunk of the left-hand side of the photo away, including a bit of young Major Henry's shoulder and – I realised, my unease growing – all trace of the other boy who had been in the photo.

Of George Warren.

"Tell me," Lottie suddenly demanded, her voice lighter as though she'd decided not to be bored any longer and was going to play a new game, "d'you like tits?"

I was taken aback, but styled it out. "Tits? Wrens? Ravens. I love all birds of the British Isles," I deadpanned.

She 'tsked', then pushed me roughly forwards. "Well tit-lover or not, you have a treat in store. We've tits and peen aplenty in the next lot."

She shoved me onwards to a selection of Italian Rennaisance works, huge overdone paintings that did, indeed, seem to belong in an exhibition entitled 'Clothing Optional.'

Even one called 'The war between the angels and Satan' by, according to the the tag, School of Giorgione managed to make the cataclysmic battle look like kicking out time at a South London swingers club.

"I can't wait til I'm old enough," Lottie said absent-mindedly, "to get away from here. I think I'll go to Italy and see if I can become an artist's model. Do they still have artists in Italy?"

I nodded. "They still have artists. But I'm not sure that they still have models."

Lottie considered this, then paused in front of a painting of a periwigged and beruffed female of a certain age - the age being the late 1600s and her years being, according to a glance at the smooth hands visible just above the gilded frame, far fewer than the hangdog expression and droopy jowls suggested; I wondered, for a moment, whether she might have approved of Paolo and his never-ending search for youth.

"I think she was an ancestor," Lottie said, staring up at her as if trying to recognise someone in the darkly lacquered paint, "but for all I know the previous generation might have bought her from a sale of pictures of miserable old bitches who look like they might belong here. Does that bother you?"

"What? The suggestion that your family might be faking their history?"

"No; my use of the word bitch. Some people are upset by it."

"I've heard worse."

"May I ask you a question?" she suddenly asked, barrelling on before I'd responded. "Are you what my grandfather's generation referred to as a sodomite?"

"Not as frequently as I'd like to be. May I ask you a question?"

She stared back, clearly unhappy that she'd failed to outrage me.

"Why are you so unhappy?"

"Unhappy?" She bristled, and I thought for a moment I'd lost her.

"What on earth makes you think I'm unhappy?"

"Well you just seem angry and unhappy," I said trying to make eye contact as she suddenly found the old girl in the frame incredibly interesting.

There was a moment's silence, then: "I hate it here," Lottie said. "This place is full of dead people and dust. My turn for a question: Have you ever seen a priest's hole?"

Now I was definitely lost for words. Lottie snatched my hand and, giggling, dragged me down the gallery and into a far more informal room containing an overstuffed sofa, a couple of huge armchairs and a coffee table. The ceiling was lower and the whole place felt like an average living room, albeit one with what looked like a genuine Ming Vase on a low table in the one corner that – had it been my living room – I'd have rested the telly on.

Lottie released me and walked across the room, shoving – with some struggle – one of the armchairs to one side, and doing the 'Ta-da' motion towards a corner of the room.

"Nice," I said, wondering what it was I was supposed to be finding nice.

The top half of the room was papered in a pale blue silk wallpaper that complemented both the upholstery and the vase, and the lower half of the walls were panelled in a dark wood that, now I looked, appeared to be very old.

As old as the vase, perhaps, or older.

Lottie reached forward, pressed something in the dado rail separating the two and, as I wondered whether the wood panelling was original to the house, a chunk of it – maybe two foot wide by three feet high – swung open revealing an empty darkness.

She looked at me and grinned.

"Gotcha," she said as a car horn sounded from somewhere.

"Ooh, new people." She reached forward and yanked the wood panelling back into place.

"Wait," I said. "What- "

"We didn't go over to the Reformation right away," she said, shooing me from the room. "Typical Warrens: They waited to see which way the wind would finally settle on blowing and while they did so my ancestors had the odd priest over to do whatever it is priests do. Mass? Dinner? Altar boys? Anyways, if the rozzers turned up, they needed somewhere to stash Father Michael or whatever, so they build a few of these things. Eventually the wind settled and one of my ancestors gave up a dozen priests and all their parishioners, who were promptly burned to death."

She was at the door now, clearly eager, despite her conscious adoption of an air of ennui, to get downstairs and see who the new arrivals were.

"They were terrible people, really, my ancestors. Disloyal, treacherous. They were spies and turncoats and thieves. This place is littered with booty from god knows where and secret tunnels and spy holes. And I'll let you in on a secret."

She stopped in the doorway, grinned impishly at me, and said: "We're as bad today as we were then. Nothing and nobody here are what they seem, really. Watch your back, my friend. Oh, and do a girl a favour, would you? Put that chair back in place, close the shutters, and switch off the lights when you're finished up here.

"I'm going to see what fresh meat's arrived. I like you. You're so much nicer than most of the dreck hereabouts. That lot, I'd murder in a heartbeat."

And so saying, she bolted for the stairs.

CHAPTER SIX

By the time I got back downstairs the new people were settling in. I crossed the hallway as another car pulled up outside and made my way into the drawing room, lit now by another chandelier and a battalion of lamps dotted around the place.

The two new arrivals – a pair of women – were sitting primly on the sofa that Lottie had previously been sprawled on.

"Well that's quite surprising," one of them was saying in a deep, American accented voice that I vaguely recognised. "I mean John was absolutely certain he'd be here before us. I guess our driver knew some short cuts."

She glanced my way and I immediately knew who she was.

Sara Simone had been one of the most successful movie stars of the nineties, making millions of dollars for her role as Carillion Virtue, the arse-kicking, gun-toting bounty hunter she'd played in three movies before the studio that owned the franchise had announced they were going to reboot with an origins story, and hired a younger (and cheaper) actress for the part.

She'd become better known these days for the lifestyle brand that sold chakra realigning shower gel, womb purifiying bath salts and a series of soft furnishings that bore the brand 'sacred feminine' and featured hand embroidered vulvas on each throw cushion (and which had been proven to have been sewn by Bangladeshi women who'd been separated from their children and forced into virtual slave labour), and I had to admit that whatever she was doing, she looked fabulous: Her skin was tight and yet dewy, a rose-coloured blush seeming to glow from her face.

She looked younger than Lottie, who was slumped, now, in

a chair across the room still ostensibly reading her magazine but ignoring the two women with a studied deliberateness that gave away how star struck she was.

It occurred to me once again that for all her bravado and attempts at world-weariness she was a girl stuck in a house full of – as she'd put it - dead people and dust, and whose exposure to the world was limited.

Henry noticed my arrival and stood.

"Ladies," he said, "let me introduce another of our guests this weekend. Mr Danny Bird, this is Miss Simone the Actress."

"And philanthropist," Sara said, extending a slim pale hand.

I shook her hand as Henry introduced the other woman. "And her mother Mrs Gerber."

"Francine," the other woman – her elongated 'a' testament to the fact she did not share a voice coach with her offspring.

Sara's focus shifted to a space beyond me and the beaming smile I'd seen photographed on countless red carpets was suddenly switched on. She stood, effortlessly moving me to one side, and stepped forward, her hands outstretched.

"Honeybun," she almost sang.

I turned. A young posh male straight out of central casting – all floppy hair, red chinos, weak chin and Merchant Ivory good looks, stepped forward.

"Darling," the Hugh Grant tribute act smiled, taking Sara's. "I'm so sorry sweetie," he leaned in to her, his voice dropping but not enough to prevent me hearing every word. "My boss is here this weekend, so I fear I'll have to do some work."

"Work?" Ms Simone pouted. "Oh honeybun. I thought this would be an us weekend."

I looked around for an escape, fearful that any more saccharin sweetness and I'd be in a diabetic coma.

"Warren, Old man!" A bulky middle-aged man stood in the doorway. If the floppy-haired youth currently plighting what was left of his troth to the Hollywood actress was the 'before' picture, the man standing in the doorway was the 'after' half of the equation.

He had the look of someone who'd once taken care of himself and been feted for his efforts, but who had since decided that brandy beat bench press every time. And yet he still carried himself with the assurance that comes only from a youth of beauty, a middle-age of self-delusion and a lifetime of privilege.

And there was something familiar about him.

He stepped into the room, clapping Henry Warren on the arm and making some vaguely off-colour comment about the drive to Dukes Halt. And when he spoke, it came to me.

I looked at Caz, who'd been abandoned by Henry, nodded at the Fortnum's bag still at her feet, the snoozing figure of Ellie in front of the fire, and suggested we get the hell out of the drawing room before I said something I'd regret.

Up in Caz's room I turned on her.

"What the hell is he doing here?"

"He? Who?" She placed the Fortnums bag carefully on the dressing table as Ellie snuffled around the room hunting for the source of the feint odour of dampness.

"Digby bloody Smith," I said through clenched teeth.

"Oh," a light came on behind Caz's eyes, "is that who he was?" She crossed to a large chest of drawers in the corner and opened the top two. "I thought he was familiar."

"Familiar? Caz, he voted against the equal age of consent, the repeal of Section 28, against equal marriage, and in favour of every bill that's been put before Parliament that would knock back rights for LGBTQ people. I've heard he left his mother's deathbed to vote down a Transgender Recognition Bill. The man's a fucking monster."

"Darling, I didn't know you were into politics." She opened her suitcase and began lifting clothing from it and placing it into the drawers.

"Politics?" I was struggling to keep my temper, "I'm not talking politics, Caz; I'm talking spending the weekend with a bloody Homophobe."

Caz patted the last of her smalls into place and turned to face me.

"Homophobe? Oh he's worse than that," she said. "The man's not just a homophobe; he's a," she searched for the word "complete and absolute misanthrope.

"His entire outlook is predicated on convincing everyone that people who aren't like them are simultaneously dangerous and worthless."

"And here I am," I said. "Worthless, in his eyes."

"And dangerous in mine," she said, lifting a vintage Janet Reger piece up for consideration.

"So what?" I asked, "I'm supposed to make nice? Smile across the canapes?"

Caz placed the lingerie back in its place, and turned to me, her moue and tilted head telegraphing unspeakable disappointment in me. "Make nice? God no. Where's the fun in that?"

I was angry. I felt destabilised in this environment. The last thing I needed was an argument with Caz.

"For clarity," she said, "I find Digby Smith to be one of the most loathsome creatures in the world. But I also know that it's important to know your enemy. And never – in any circumstance – to retreat. Calling Digby Smith a homophobe lets him off to easily. He's not a homophobe; he's a selfish, self-obsessed, spoiled manchild. And everything I've heard about him – along with everything I know about you – tells me that you need to stay here and help me make the fat bastard's life a misery for the weekend. Thoughts?"

And suddenly, just like that, I remembered why I loved Caz so much.

She'd been my best friend almost since the day we met, and she'd never given me a reason to doubt her. But most of our time together – as comfortable as she always appeared - was spend in my world, and reversing the roles had left me uncertain and a little paranoid.

She was right: There were Digby Smiths everywhere, and running from them wasn't the answer. Though I knew I had no chance of changing his mind, I would stay, and make him squirm every time I could.

"So what are you going to do with our friend?" I asked, nodding at the Fortnum's bag.

Caz had opened her second suitcase and a selection of frocks – already on hangers she'd brought with her, as though she'd literally scooped them off the rail in her Fulham flat and dropped them into the Vuitton – were now being stored in the wardrobe.

"Well here's as good a place as any," she said, putting the bag on the floor of the wardrobe and pushing it to the back so that the low hanging frocks hid it.

The sound of an engine, audible from outside, reaffirmed my fear that the rooms were not double glazed, and I wished I'd brought a pair of pyjamas with me.

"Oh good," Caz said, glancing out of the window, "it looks like Pamela's finally arrived.

I looked too. Outside, the sun had set to a thin red on the horizon. From this elevation we could just about see over the tops of the trees and, in the gathering gloom, I saw a large people carrier coming out of the dense forest and trundling towards the house.

My phone rang and I tugged it from my pocket, glancing at the screen.

"Ray," I said after hitting answer, "what's up."

"Just wanted to give you an update on your friend from the hotel."

I glanced at Caz, who was busying herself now transporting armfuls of cosmetics to the shared bathroom, and then turned my attention back to Ray, allowing my eyes to scan the trees, occasional flashes of headlights allowing me to follow the progress of the people carrier.

"Go ahead," I said.

"Well he was staying there. We ran the photo you gave us past a few of the chambermaids, and he'd been there for a few weeks, but none of them knew his name, and the suite was booked in a corporate name. Hang on," there was silence for a minute and then he came back on the line "Matheson Logistics. Ring any bells?"

Even though he couldn't see me, I still shook my head. "None," I said.

"No, none here either. Which is odd. You'd think a logistics company would have some presence: contracts signed, deals done, the odd press release, a web site. All we could find was a company registration in the Bahamas and a few other hotel bookings for short-term stays over the past couple of years."

"Do I want to know how you found the hotel bookings?"

"Not really," he answered.

The people carrier made its way slowly towards the house, and it crossed my mind to go looking for Ali before dinner.

"Anyway, long story short: he's gone," Dash said. "Checked out this morning. One of the porters called up, said the man in the Edward eight suite was packing up, so I sent Dash over to at least get a couple of decent shots of him.

"So then we ran the pics Ray got this morning – full face, nice and clear – through a couple of apps that aged him up and down and looked for images with similar faces in them, and we got something."

My ears perked up. "Tell me," I said.

"Danny, I don't know who he is, but this fella gets around. Someone's done a fairly decent job of scrubbing him from the internet but we got pictures of him in the background at a party on an Oligarch's yacht. Cannes last year. In the background at a mini riot in Crimea just before all the shit kicked off there a couple of years ago, and at a New Year's party in Mar a Lago about six years ago."

"So all the fun places."

Ray snorted. "Thing is, Dash got the pics and got the licence plate of the car he left in, but he couldn't follow him very far, and the plate turned out to be licenced to-"

"Matheson logistics," I filled in for him.

"Yeah," he said as the people carrier pulled up outside the house and a woman – Pamela Warren, I assumed – stepped from it, turning back to say something to someone still inside the vehicle.

"I'm thinking," Ray said, "we can ask around the West End,

see if we can at least find out where he went while he was here, who he saw, and maybe figure out what he was doing in London, but I'm sorry, Danny. Whoever Sergei Maximov is, and wherever he went, we've lost him for now. He's done another vanishing act."

And then the other person in the people carrier stepped out, and his head lifted.

And he stared right up at me.

And my blood ran cold.

CHAPTER SEVEN

What the hell is Sergei Maximov doing here?

I'd seen Arianna's photos, and they weren't great, but they were clear enough, and the face that had briefly stared up at me – the hawk-like nose, the swept-back hair and and the piercing dark eyes – was unmistakeable.

I'd instinctively jerked back from the window and fled to my own room, telling Caz I needed to unpack, when really what I needed was to escape.

My immediate thought was that he'd followed me – that somehow he'd discovered I was investigating him and had come to Dukes Halt to confront me - but of course that was paranoid nonsense. He couldn't have followed me. He was just here. As a guest.

His glance upwards – the laser-like stare – ran through my mind. It was almost as if he had sixth-sense; as if he'd known there was someone watching him. Which I suppose one develops after years of staying one step ahead of one's enemies. I knew I was being irrational now, investing him with almost hyper perception, and that he might simply have been checking out the house, looking up at the turreted rooftop.

As my heartrate came back to normal, I called Ray back and told him why I'd ended the call.

"Shit," he said. "What are you going to do?"

And I had to admit that, for once, I wasn't really sure. I mean one of my problems was solved: I no longer needed to find out where Maximov was, because he was here with me. But now I wanted to know what he was doing here.

I wondered, briefly, whether I should call Arianna, but decided against it. I'd told her I'd call if I had any news, and 'hey, I'm having dinner with him tonight' was probably not the news she wanted to hear. I'd figure out what was going on then decide, tomorrow, whether to call Arianna or not.

That decision made, I ended the call with Ray, unpacked and took a shower that – unsurprisingly – was accompanied by the soundtrack from an Am Dram production of the bombing of Dresden. My grumbling stomach reminded me I hadn't eaten for hours and that it would be dinner time soon, so I changed into my tuxedo as Caz showered and we both went down to dinner.

The first person we bumped into when we arrived in the drawing room for pre-dinner cocktails was Digby Smith.His eyes raked me over, a sardonic little smile on his lips, and he held a hand out.

"We haven't been properly introduced. I'm Smith. Digby Smith."

He virtually ignored Caz, who placed a hand in the small of my back as though to steer me away from him, but it was too late. Manners had gotten the better of me and I had instinctively put my own hand out to shake his.

His grip was tight, something in his eyes shifting as our hands touched, and Caz – sensing, perhaps, that she wasn't going to be able to shift me away from him - stopped, a smile like a mongoose might bestow on a cobra forming on her face.

"Digby," she said, the tone of her voice dropping a good twenty degrees.

"Lady Caroline," Digby smiled back, still not releasing my hand. "And you are?"

"Danny," I said as he shifted slightly, the grip tightening almost imperceptibly, the angle of his right elbow shrinking so that the gap between us shortened, like I was being pulled in to him. "Danny Bird. I'm a friend of Lady Caroline's," I added entirely unnecessarily, so flustered was I.

"A friend?" his right eyebrow rose in mock surprise. "Well isn't that nice. I didn't think you had many friends, Lady Caroline."

"I don't," Caz replied, her hand returning to the small of my back. "I'm very selective about them. *Very*. And speaking of which," she applied pressure, and I found myself being shoved away from Digby and steered towards the opposite side of the room, "I want to introduce Danny to a dear old school friend."

"Well It's lovely to meet you, Daniel," Digby smarmed after me, his eyes still looking solidly into mine as though he were attempting to guarantee my vote or to steal my soul. "I hope we'll have time to talk again later."

I was completely nonplussed, Caz's hand in the small of my back feeling more protective than anything.

"Don't look back," she muttered through a rictus grin. "Just imagine you're Lot's wife and don't look back."

Which – the implied reference to the Cities of the Plain and to Sodom perhaps triggering the thought – was when it hit me. Digby Smith, that famous homophobe, had just been flirting with me. The seemingly gentle mockery, the hand shake that went on slightly longer than it needed to, the eye contact and the attempt to push Caz away so he and I could be left alone together; all of that could be attributable to simply being a politician instinctively playing the 'you have all my attention' act they do so well, and admittedly it had been many years since I'd been hit on in that way, but I was fairly sure that what had just happened was something more than politics.

I had no chance to raise the issue with Caz, however, because I was momentarily stunned to silence and, before I could speak, we'd come to the couple by the fireplace, and Caz was depositing me before Pamela Warren and her date for the weekend.

Pamela was a tall brunette wearing a tight jade green dress, the front sprinkled with jet beading that sparkled softly in the light. Her auburn hair was piled on top of her head, the seemingly casual assemblage fixed with a large jet and jade pin.

She beamed at Caz, reaching her arms out to her in greeting, and – airkisses and compliments exchanged – I was then introduced and gifted with another air kiss on both cheeks.

"It's so lovely to meet you Danny," Pamela smiled at me. "Caroline's told me so much about you."

I glanced at the man next to Pamela, who was stood straight-backed, his eyes scanning the room in a way that suggested he had worked out every possible exit strategy from the joint and was now trying to decide which of the assembled guests would be the most useful human shield.

"And this," Pamela put a hand on his elbow, snapping his focus back to her, and he nodded to me, "is Sergei Maximov. Sergei, this is my dear friend Lady Caroline de Montfort."

Maximov stepped forward, accepted the hand that Caz had offered, lifted it to his lips and brushed them against the back of it.

"Enchanté, madame," he said, his voice low, his eyes never leaving hers.

Caz smiled, her eyes twinkled, and she murmured something about being charmed to make his acquaintance.

"I have heard so much about you," he added, releasing her hand, and Caz's smile dipped a couple of degrees.

"Well you have an advantage over me," she replied, indicating Pamela, "as this one has told me nothing about you at all. How'd you both meet?"

They glanced quickly at each other and, instead of answering, Pamela introduced me. Maximov held a hand out and I instinctively hesitated a millisecond, but this was not the time to announce what I believed him to be and, besides, I'd shaken Digby Smith's hand without hesitation.

"Is good to meet you formally, Mr Bird. We met very briefly before," he added, explaining to both Caz and Pamela, "at the window. When I arrived. You were, I think, an unofficial welcoming party."

So he had seen me looking down. I opened my mouth to say something, not wanting to appear to be a snoop, but not wanting him to think he'd caught me out in something, but before I could speak he'd added "do you prefer Daniel or Danny?" His curt firm handshake ended far faster than Smith's had.

"Danny's good," I smiled back, the act feeling tight and unnatural as my heart beat a little faster. Up close, this man just felt wrong. He had an air about him that – even if I hadn't known the story Arianna had told – would have destabilised me. The way he half-smiled at everything as though he knew a secret that the rest of us had yet to fathom.

"Have you met Doctor Stamford and his wife?" Pamela asked, gesturing over a couple who'd been hanging around looking as bemused as I'd felt.

The man was short and round, his egg-shaped and perfectly bald head, horn-rimmed glasses and owl-like stare made me wonder making him look like an academic Humpty Dumpty. His wife meanwhile, looked to be at least half his age, her statuesque athletic-looking figure encased in a pearl-blue satin sheath dress, a pair of sapphire and diamond earrings matching the simple diamond and sapphire necklace around her neck.

The couple introduced themselves as Richard and Karen. We shook hands, smiled politely and then, conversation having already dried up, stared at each other in uncomfortable silence.

"Well," Dr Richard said, "this is all so exciting."

I looked around the room. If this was Doctor Stamford's idea of exciting, he needed to get out more.

"Have you come far?" his wife - clearly a fan of the smalltalk styles of the House of Windsor - smiled at me.

"London," I said, dreading the small talk that I just knew was going to follow. "Southwark to be precise."

"Oh Southwark. Such an," her eyes glazed over momentarily "*interesting* part of London. Richard worked at Guy's for a time when we first came to London. I'd pop round sometimes. But there were so many homeless people in the area."

She shook her head sadly. "Sometimes you couldn't go twenty paces without another one sprawled on the sidewalk. So sad."

I was about to point out that the homeless crisis wasn't just present in Southwark, and that I doubted any of the people sprawled in her way were there through choice, when Pamela suddenly spoke up, breaking the spell and nodding over my shoulder. "Here comes my father-in-law."

I turned slightly. An elderly man somewhere north of eighty, his haughty Patrician stare raking over the assembled, was entering the room. He walked straight-backed and proud, but Henry's presence beside him, their closeness, suggested he could lean on his son's arm at a moment's notice, and that his strength might not be as vital as he wanted people to assume it was.

I watched as Henry led his father over to a long sideboard at one side of the room, murmured something and was rewarded with a withering look and a dismissive hand wave. Eve Chapman appeared, a silver salver in her hand and presented it to Sir Phillip, who lifted a glass from it and sipped an amber liquid before nodding approvingly.

Chapman smiled and turned to the door from where two teenage girls and a boy – all holding silver salvers with drinks on them – appeared and began circulating, offering pre-dinner cocktails to the guests.

"About time," Caz muttered, catching my eye. "The party doesn't start til Sir Phil arrives," she explained. "And by the looks of it, I think this is going to be a very interesting party."

CHAPTER EIGHT

Interesting was Caz being somewhat optimistic.

I would have called the party tense.

After a moment I was walked over to be introduced to my host for the weekend, who was half-leaning against the sideboard, a glass of whisky and soda in a hand that had a feint but noticeable tremble to it.

Sir Philip held the glass out to Henry, who took it from his father and placed it on the sideboard within reach.

"Sir Philip," Caz smiled, "lovely to see you again. Thank you for inviting me."

"I didn't," the old man – the family resemblance to Henry clear in the sharp cheekbones and the long sharp nose - responded bluntly. "Pamela said she wanted you here for the girl," he nodded across the room where Lottie, looking as though she'd rather be on trial for her life was sat on a sofa between the floppy haired youth, who Caz had told me was John Warren, a cousin of the family, and Francine Gerber, who appeared to be reciting the Gettysburg address without breathing. "And what Pamela wants…"

He tailed off, and Caz smiled her most gracious smile, though it failed to reach her eyes. "Well thank you for letting Pamela have what she wants," she replied, adding, before anything else could be said, "I'd like to introduce my friend Mr Bird."

A pair of watery but intelligent eyes turned on me. "The barman-cum-detective," he said, the tone of his voice making it hard to tell whether he found my mishmash of interests distasteful, comedic or actually quite interesting.

"More barman," I smiled, offering my hand, which was taken, shaken, and placed back in my care.

"You undersell yourself," he responded, reaching his right hand out towards Henry, who placed the whisky and soda back into it. "World's full of fools who undersell themselves. Think it's clever to make out they're really nothing much. Not clever. Stupid. If you're good at something, be good at it."

"Well Lady Caroline tends to make me sound far more effective than I am," I smiled, gesturing at her, and Sir Phillip frowned.

"Nothing to do with the woman. She's never even mentioned you."

I was puzzled. "Then how did you know about the," I searched for the right words, "the incidents I've helped the police out with?"

"Because I may be eighty-three years old young man, but I'm still capable of asking questions. And I like to know about the people who are coming in to my house. Even," he glanced towards the fireplace, his face tightening briefly, "those guests who are unplanned and unannounced."

"I've spoken to Chapman," Henry said in conciliatory tones, "and she's adjusted the table setting. It'll be fine."

"No thanks to you and Pamela," Sir Phillip replied tersely, his gaze roaming around the room. "What's that idiot Digby Smith doing now?"

I glanced over to where Digby was ensconced on a sofa with Sara Simone. The member of parliament was waving a handkerchief around and clearly doing an impersonation of someone to the great hilarity of the actress, who was wearing a pale green coloured silk dress, a pair of emerald and diamond earrings – each the size of a quail's egg – sparkling on her ears.

"Christ," Sir Phillip muttered. "John's got another bimbo. One wonders how two people so vacuous can actually exist in the same space."

Which was the point at which Caz placed her hand on my back again and suggested we'd circulate a little.

"I can't believe he actually Googled me," I said, glancing over to the sideboard where John was introducing Sir Phil to Sara and Francine. Sir Phillip's face had the look of someone who was unsure what it is that they were experiencing but was certain that they weren't enjoying it.

"I can," she muttered, and at that moment a distant gong sounded.

"Oh goody," Caz's eyes widened. "Dinner."

The Dining Room was off the Drawing Room. A long, polished table stretched the length of the room. To the left was a wall of French windows, the curtains undrawn showing a moonlit chunk of garden, blue and faintly menacing beyond the glass.

On the opposite side of the room another vast fireplace stood between two panelled doors. A meagre fire glowed in the grate, an ornamental fire screen – all filigree and curlicues – in front of it.

At the end of the room was a vast painting showing some sort of sea battle, huge battleships, their white sails billowing as their cannons spat fire and fury at each other in a sea which appeared almost alive.

Sir Phillip, still closely accompanied by Henry, made his way to the head of the table and sat, the sea battle behind him.

Each place setting had a small white card on which was inscribed the name of the person due to sit at that place. It felt, momentarily, that we'd reached Country House play acting now. I mean: who puts out cards that tell their guests where they're allowed to sit?

But then, from the very brief experience I'd had of Sir Phillip, it seemed clear he would.

The guests rambled around the table, finding places, bumping into each other and generally good-humouredly complying with the somewhat overbearing staginess of if all until eventually we were all seated, the antique wooden chairs made bearable by thick padded cushions that shifted disconcertingly as we moved around.

Working anti-clockwise from Sir Phillip at the head of the table, and arranged in a classic boy/girl arrangement, we had Lottie, then Maximov, Caz, John Warren, Karen Stamford, Henry Warren Sara Simone, Andrew Stamford, Digby Smith,

Francine Gerber, myself and Pamela Warren.

And looking around, it struck me that for a party to celebrate Lady Marion's life, there didn't seem – with the exception of her son and her husband – to be a single person there who'd known her in life.

And what's more, it hit me as the trio of (I guessed) local help started placing wide shallow bowls of soup in front of us, almost half the people at the table were total strangers even to the master of the house. Sir Phillip had clearly never met – and not expected this weekend – Sergei Maximov, and he'd never met me, Sara or Francine either, and yet here we all were at a jolly birthday party for a dead woman.

The soup was delicious.

Which was something, I supposed.

Pamela, on my right, was immediately collared by Sir Phillip who spoke in hushed tones, and with body language that suggested he was not complimenting her on her choice of frock, and so I turned to Francine, who'd already been snagged by Digby. Joining any conversation with the politician was the last thing I wanted to do, so I tucked into my soup, which was followed by a small but exquisite dover sole, simply fried in butter and dressed with a tapenade of capers.

I glanced across the table at Caz, who was deep in conversation with John Warren and Lottie, and at Sergei who, like me, was eating rather than conversing while beside him Sara and Henry chatted occasionally.

Sara, I noted, ate not a sliver of the meal put in front of her, and drank only water, smiling thanks when the food was delivered, thanks again when it was taken away, and thanks every time one of the staff refilled her water glass.

The Dover Sole was, in turn, followed by a trio of vol au vents, each one stuffed with a different filling, and a lemon and rosemary sorbet of which Sara deigned to sample a fingernail-sized bite.

The sorbet was removed, and in the gap between that course and the next, Maximov, as though deciding now was the time for some mischief, raised his voice.

"Sir Phillip," he said, and the volume of hubbub around the table dipped slightly.

Sir Phillip and Pamela parted, and our host turned a somewhat sour look on the Russian, who lifted his wineglass in a silent toast.

"May I thank you for having me to your beautiful house," he smiled, "for your beautiful food and for allowing me to settle my eyes on so many beautiful things."

Sir Phillip's sour expression softened somewhat, and he made some gruff comment about it being "quite all right," before turning as though to continue his conversation with Pamela.

But Sergei Maximov wasn't finished.

"Carlotta showed me the long gallery earlier."

I figured this tour had taken place while I was showering, and glanced at Lottie – who was studiously inspecting the tablecloth in front of her. I remembered her earlier jibe about being an unpaid tour guide. I wondered if she'd really spent the afternoon having to show guests around the house.

"Such beautiful portraits of so many ancestors."

Sir Phillip raised an eyebrow, but turned his expression back to Maximov, who took a huge gulp from his wineglass and smiled at his host.

"And that pretty little floral display under the family photos," Maximov carried on, looking around the table. "The boys in the photographs are Major Warren and John?"

The question seemed innocent, but something about the tone, about the way Maximov's eyes glittered, told me he already knew who the boys were and was simply playing with the table. Or at least with those around it who also knew who the other boy was.

"The other boy," Sir Phillip spoke clearly and coldly, "was my son Edward. He died in childhood."

"Ah," Maximov laid his glass down and held his hands out in apology. "My mistake. And my condolences." And then he carried on as though nothing had altered, though the look on Sir Phillip's face suggested he'd happily have turfed the man out of the house. "There also are so many beautiful ancient artifacts. So much history. And some of it yours."

Henry Warren cleared his throat.

"The sixteenth Earl," Pamela explained, "was a Classicist. His digs in Egypt and Syria were quite the thing in their time."

"In their time, yes," Maximov replied. "And yet to some they were – surely – little more than looting."

"My ancestor," Sir Phillip said icily, "was a preservationist."

"Quite," Maximov replied. "But surely to some people he must have appeared – what is the bird you English have – a cuckoo? No," he smiled wolfishly, "that's the one that lays its eggs in another bird's nest. What is the bird? Ah! A magpie. Taking what was bright and pretty. I mean, everywhere, there are thieves. Is that not right Mister Warren?"

He was prevented from saying more – and Sir Phillip from replying - by Sara, who had clearly decided she'd been out of the spotlight too long.

"That's so cute," the actress gushed. "My mom's a preservationist too."

"Jelly and Jams, mostly," Francine elaborated. "Though I've been messin' round with Chutney lately."

"Oh yes," her daughter raved, "you should try her Pomegranate and Pear. We're selling it on the website. Momma's recipe though of course she doesn't make every jar herself."

"Me in a kitchen in Boca Raton? Not likely."

"So Mrs Gerber, tell me," Digby piped up, in what seemed like a desperate attempt to move the conversation on from Maximov's insulting the Warren ancestors, "is there a Mr Gerber?"

Francine stiffened. "My husband," she said coldly, "is with Jesus." But before anyone could do more than frown and prepare their condolences for her loss, Sara expanded: "His name, momma, is Jesus," she said the name in the Spanish pronunciation, Hey-Soos, "and they live in Catalina, where Jesus is a Pilates instructor and my dad is very happy."

She smiled at me as though telegraphing "Got your

demographic sorted too, baby."

"Oh," Digby frowned as the roast beef arrived at the table, "how very American."

CHAPTER NINE

The remainder of the dinner was – well, as weird as the rest of the evening to that point had been.

Sara, rather than a plate of roast beef, was presented with another soup bowl containing some green sludge which she ate with a spoon. Digby – who had definitely had several wine top-ups – engaged in a debate with Francine Gerber around 'The Race Issue' in America, managing to leave the poor woman staring goggle-eyed at her plate until she took too large a chunk of Yorkshire pudding and started choking on it, at which point the MP attempted to do the Heimlich manoeuvre and was prevented from doing so only by Francine physically shoving him away from her.

Eventually – after an apple crumble and custard – the table was cleared and, as though on some inaudible signal, Pamela Warren stood and said "Ladies," will you join me in the Salon?"

I looked, in alarm, at Caz, who smiled and winked at me before putting her arm around Lottie and leading her, along with Karen Stamford Sara and Francine out of the dining room, so that I was left alone with Sir Phillip, Henry, John, Richard, Digby and Maximov.

"Wonderful dinner," Digby gushed at his host. "Great grub, old chap."

At the phrase 'old chap,' Sir Phillip bristled so hard that I swear I heard him crackle.

"Tell you what," Digby – either too drunk or too insensitive to note the disdain on the other man's face – barrelled on, "these foreigners know how to make a good bit of grub. What is she? Greek? Iteye?"

"I believe she's from somewhere in the Balkans," Sir Phillip responded with so much froideur that I felt ice form on my eyebrows. "Mr Bird," he turned to me, "I trust all was to your satisfaction."

"Me?" I felt myself blush, took a breath and smiled. "The dinner was wonderful, Sir Phillip. I really can't thank you enough for your kind invitation. And the house is beautiful."

I swear, if I'd been standing I would have finished the response with a curtsey, a mumbled reference to it all being too good for the likes of me and a suggestion I'd better be getting on with my coal scuttle cos them clinkers won't clean themselves.

But I wasn't, so I didn't.

Two of the boys who'd served dinner arrived, one of them wheeling a trolley containing dozens of bottles.

"Will you have a brandy, Mr Bird?" Sir Phillip asked, and I realised finally that he was addressing me as though I were the sole guest in the room, and explicitly ignoring both Maximov and Digby.

I took a glass of brandy – the bottle it came from bearing a label that looked hand-written, and a sip of the stuff told me that what I was drinking was a vintage Cognac, the spirit slipping over my tongue like honey.

I closed my eyes to savour the taste all the more, and when I opened them was horrified to discover that Digby had scooted up a chair and was sitting beside me.

"Smoke?" he leered, offering me what looked like a six-inch-long cigar.

I shook my head, explained that I didn't smoke, and he smiled, made some comment about how it's always nice to have some vices to look forward to when one's all grown up, and slipped the cigar from its casing, clipping the end with a cutter he'd produced from his pocket, and lighting the thing with what looked like a mini blowtorch.

"John," Sir Phillip immediately ordered, "open a window."

John Warren – who, for most of the evening so far had been almost invisible, walked around behind me and unlocked the French doors.

Across the table from me, Richard Stamford lit a cigarette, inhaled what looked like a couple of lungsful of smoke in one desperate drag, and stared morosely into his brandy glass.

Maximov, who had pulled a huge tablet-cum-mobile phone from his pocket as soon as the ladies had left the room and been tapping furiously at the screen as the brandys were being poured, suddenly grunted, chuckled, and put the phone back in his inside pocket.

"If you gentlemen will forgive me," he announced, the same amused curving of his lips that had been hanging around all through dinner announcing how humorous he found his use of the word 'gentlemen,' "I have some – ah – business to attend to." He bowed ostentatiously to the Warren men, nodded curtly to Stamford Digby and I, then left, closing the door silently behind him.

"God," Digby Smith leaned in to me conspiratorially and I got a waft of some woody scent, "I miss the days when one didn't have to actually dine with them."

"Them?" I leaned away slightly. He leaned in again.

"The Russkies. Back in the good old days people like Warren fought cold wars against them, they didn't have to have them at table."

I glanced quickly across at Henry, John and Sir Phillip gathered together by the vast canvas.

"Mind you," Digby continued, "it's been a bit of a rum crowd tonight. You did well to avoid that terrible American woman. And as for the effervescent chat from our bald friend over there," he nodded surreptitiously across at Richard, who had now removed his phone from his jacket and was either furiously tapping out an urgent email or playing the world's most energetic game of candy crush. "Lord knows what inspired old Warren to invite him down here. Man's a personality vacuum."

I'd had barely a minute of talking to Stamford, but he'd seemed a perfectly pleasant – if clearly introverted man, and I was loathe to side with the vile Digby in mocking him.

"He seems nice," I said, standing my ground. "Quiet, but

nice."

Digby, as though I'd been completely mute, barrelled on. "Started off as a medium, you know."

"Mr Stamford?"

"Stamford? God no. "No, he's a surgeon. Hearts, I think. Invented some methodology that cuts post-op infections by eighty per cent or something."

Digby squeezed my shoulder, his hand staying there a little too long for my liking, "The man's a life saver."

Digby wiggled his eyebrows and smirked, as though to suggest that he found the idea of being a 'Life saver' one big 'So What?'

He leant in closer and I could smell his expensive woody cologne. "Not saying he's not a good egg. Just that like all these worthy types, the fella's damn dull. Know what I mean?" He chuckled, leant back and dragged on the cigar again.

"The wife's more entertaining. But then she's in business. Some sort of engineer. Medical machinery. Makes sense, I suppose," he gestured once more, at Stamford, the sentence unfinished.

I hadn't imagined it would be possible to loathe Digby Smith more than I had before the evening had begun, but I had to give him credit: He'd proven me wrong.

"Pure fake, of course," he added. "I've read a few papers on her background."

"Mrs Stamford?"

"Mrs Stamford?" Now he was confused, then he laughed so loudly that even Karen Stamford's husband looked up momentarily from his phone.

"No," Digby explained, "*she's* alright. Company goes public soon, I hear, so she and the good Doctor should be very nicely off.

"I'm talking about the American woman. Makes out like she's a proud stage mother, like her daughter didn't grow up shifting from town to town every time the local law enforcement got wise to her scams. I've heard," he tapped his nose as though suggesting the past history of Francine Gerber had been the subject of confidential government reviews, "that the woman was run out of several states for running seances that were demonstrably nothing more than smoke, mirrors and ventriloquism."

I wondered whether he required a response, but was too busy trying to squirm away from him to do so.

"And the daughter's not much better," he added. "Virtually bankrupt now that the lawsuits about her quackery are coming out of the woodwork. I mean," he shuddered, "the obsession with," he gulped, as though biting back bile, "vaginas. It was bound to end in disaster."

I was momentarily dumbstruck, which was clearly all the encouragement Digby needed. "Tell me," he enquired leaning in even closer, "do you shoot much?"

"Excuse me?" I choked on the cognac, searing flames shooting up my nose, and tears coming to my eyes.

He blew a huge grey cloud of smoke from his mouth, his eyes glittering silver behind the veil, and smiled.

"Shooting." He stared at me as though simply repeating the word would give it meaning.

I stared back, wondering if I could fake a believable seizure and debating whether – if I could – anyone in the room would even bother to attend me.

"Well it's the whole point of the weekend, isn't it? Well, that and the fireworks, but those are mostly for the ladies, if you get my drift."

I didn't.

"Shoot?" Where I came from a weekend spent shooting was usually followed by a few days counting the loot and a week or so of internecine warfare wittling down the number of people who'd need to be cut in. "Shoot what?"

"Grouse," he answered, his pronunciation making the word rhyme with 'mice'.

I shook my head. "I don't shoot."

"Really? I find that hard to believe. I mean, your shoulders," he reached out and brushed an approving hand across my suit jacket, "made for a recoil. No hunting in your family?"

I shrugged, knocking his hand off my jacket. "My forebears may have been beaters."

"Nothing wrong with beating," he smirked. "Many a good shooter started off beating."

"I don't like destroying life. For sport."

"Oh," he smirked, his drink-sodden face not quite acting as a whole, "surely it's nice, sometimes, to get destroyed. For sport."

I gave him my hardest stare, which seemed to at least partially penetrate his cerebellum.

"I mean," he attempted to qualify, "surely life is struggle between the strong and the weak. Nothing else makes any sense. Oh Lord, you're not one of those 'lets all get on' types are you?"

I sipped my cognac and he tipped his head back and shoved the stogie in his maw, inhaling a tobacco plant's worth of smoke, which he held, his head slowly coming down level so that his eyes were staring straight into mine.

Smith turned his head to his right and exhaled another vast cloud smoke.

"Mind you," he smirked, trying once again, "I'm a fan of getting on. With all sorts of people."

And that was it for me.

I pushed back my chair and stood. "If you'll excuse me a moment," I said tightly, recalling Maximov's clear disdain for the men in the room and finding myself surprised at how fully I agreed with his feelings, "I have some business to attend to."

Digby Smith raised an eyebrow at me. "Hurry back," he said. "I'll be waiting. And I *will* get you shooting. I can be really quite persuasive, you know?"

I won't say I fled the dining room, but I certainly walked a lot slower when I was on the other side of the door.

I hoped Ali would still be in the kitchen and so I set off to find the stairs down to the kitchens, figuring that, as the food had arrived through the door I'd just exited the dining room by I had to be close to them.

I was standing in a corridor. Opposite me, the walls were entirely wood panelled, and every so often were doors stretching away. Turning to my left, I caught a glimpse of the entry hall I'd seen earlier.

I turned right, walking a little along the corridor til I found a narrow flight of stairs on my right. Just beyond them was a large, aluminium-framed dumb waiter, the open doors showing an empty box, and opposite the dumb waiter was an alcove in which I could see a trolley like the one that had just delivered a couple hundred grands worth of booze to the dining room.

I made to walk down the stairs and stopped dead.

Because I could hear voices drifting up from below me, and one of those voices was Sergei Maximov.

"Ah, but we both know otherwise, don't we? And besides, it makes no difference, surely? Scandal – the whispering, the unspoken knowing – it can often be more effective, even, than proof. And besides, there is her son. I mean, *his* death..."

The person he was speaking to said something. Their voice was low, I couldn't really hear, but for some reason I felt sure he was talking to a woman.

Maximov chuckled, his next words confirming my suspicions.

"Ah, lady. What I want doesn't matter at this stage. But when it does – when I let you know what I want – you," he paused, I held my breath though my heart was pounding so loudly I was sure Maximov had to hear it "you will know – we are clear now – what will happen if you fail to do give me what I want."

The woman he was menacing said something unintelligible, and I heard Maximov chuckle then – with shock – the sound of footsteps ascending the stairs.

I looked desperately around for somewhere to secrete myself and had just managed to squeeze past the trolley into the darkest recesses of the alcove when Maximov, his face impassive, his body language triumphant, came to the top of the stairs and headed towards the dining room.

I was about to release the breath I hadn't known I was holding when he paused, turned back, a frown on his face, then smirked, shrugged, and carried on his way.

I slowly exhaled and moved to squeeze my way past the trolley when I heard more footsteps coming my way. I froze once more, my heart dropping as a few moments later, Caz – her face set in an angry scowl – came up the stairs and followed Maximov's trail down the hallway.

FRIDAY

CHAPTER TEN

"Oh Lord, she's scented a rabbit," Caz said as Ellie bounded off into the trees.

I watched the glossy black haunches of the staffie-cross barrel away from us and, remembering her past life as a gangster's weapon who may or may not have eaten a dead man, hoped a bunny was the worst scent she'd acquired.

Caz stared through the dawn's halflight in the direction of the chasing dog a moment and then turned her face to me.

"Have I said thank you?" she asked, and my obvious confusion drove her on. "You agreed to come here and take part in my crazy idea which I would have had no heart for without you. So thanks."

I shrugged, about to mouth some generalities when she spoke again.

"To be honest, I'd forgotten what I was asking you to come in to."

"What d'you mean?" I asked, remembering her face when she'd come up from the servants quarters the night before.

Caz pursed her lips and issued a piercing whistle that was greeted seconds later by the sound of a solid muscly body charging to her through the undergrowth. She looked at me and raised an eyebrow.

"Danny, this is not a normal environment. Oh I'm alright," Ellie barrelled out of the undergrowth, ran in circles around her and barked once, as Caz dipped into her Barbour and extracted a treat which the dog sat for and gobbled before running off ahead of us along the track.

"I'm born to this." She nodded after Ellie. "Trained for it."

"They're just people," I said, and she stopped, seeming to shrink inside her coat.

"That's exactly what I'm sorry for. And exactly what I'm so grateful for you for." She waved a hand behind her in the direction of Dukes Halt. "They're not people; they're tropes. Some of them are trying so hard to be people. But they're stuck in the same net it took me a lifetime of struggle to escape."

I stopped, the silence of the forest enveloping me, the oily, decaying, mulchy scent everywhere, the quietness suddenly transforming into a symphony of creaks and whirs and snaps, and I sighed.

"I'm glad you escaped," I said, "but you are right: there are some truly bizarre people here this weekend. I think Digby Vane came on to me as soon as we were left alone together."

"Vane? Darling, he hasn't come on to anything since his wet-nurse introduced the bottle. Dreadful dried-up creature."

"Caz, I've met enough dirty old men in my time. I know when I'm being perved on."

"Really?" She stopped, her breath coming from her in clouds as the forest around us creaked and shushed.

Her attention, her genuine interest in my concerns, was touching. "My room," I said, "Was like an oven; they seem to have the radiator stuck on nuclear. So I opened a window. Only the draft kept rattling my door open, so I jammed a chair under the handle, and went to bed. Except I swear as I was going to bed someone rattled the door and would have come in if I hadn't had a chair jammed in front of it."

"So notorious homophobe Digby Smith turns out to be a – is 'closet case' an allowed descriptor these days?"

"Considering what he's done to so many people I'd say it's a kind descriptor. How was your evening?" I waited to see if she'd mention meeting Maximov.

"I had our Eastern European friend on one side and John Warren on the other," she said through gritted teeth. "Let's just say the conversation was far from glittering. And then afterwards when Pamela trouped us all off to the drawing room like we were the bloody Brontes or something, I got – well, to be honest, we all got – stuck with that bloody actress trying to sell us a retreat she's doing for the mega-rich.

"Honestly: I didn't have the heart to tell her that Pamela and I are as poor as church mice. She spent half the evening banging on about her exclusive Caribbean Island event – kept calling it a community, like it was a permanent settlement and not a bunch of over-privileged morons on a posh club Med getaway. Banged on about how they'd have a real Tibetan Yogi, at least I think she said Yogi. I dozed off at one point and I'm almost positive I heard her say real Tibetan Yeti, but that can't be true, can it?"

Ellie exploded from the undergrowth to our left, tail wagging, tongue flapping, stopped to check where we were, barked happily and dived into the undergrowth to the right of the path we were on.

"And when she twigged we weren't likely to bite on any of that, she started trying to pitch us on the benefits of her cleansing smoothies and rebalancing salt bath bombs, which frankly sounds like a recipe for disaster. And all this ladled copiously with references to The Sacred Feminine and the state of the world's vulvas.

"Ellie!" She paused, calling to the dog whose distant bark came from somewhere deep in the wood.

"Honestly," Caz continued walking as the sound of the glossy ball of muscle tearing through the forest approached, "I never fail to be amazed at the garbage that some people will pay good money for. Chapman came in once or twice and made it clear – through the medium of slamming everything down as though she were a high court judge and the coffee a gavel – that she disapproved; though whether she disapproved of the discussion of genitalia or the naked display of commerce, we shall probably never know."

She paused, and I took my chance: "Did you talk to Maximov much?"

"Maximov?" She frowned. "Only at dinner."

"Really?" Ellie, a few steps ahead of us, suddenly stopped, her ears perked up, her nose scenting the air, and barked. "I thought you'd spoken after dinner."

"Couldn't have," she said, "he was in the dining room with the rest of you butch alpha males until you all came in at the end and by that stage I was ready to head off to bed."

"I thought you went downstairs to chat to him," I pressed, realising that I might as well have come straight out and said, 'I saw him come up and you come after him.'"

"Downstairs? Oh, yes." Ellie barked again and darted ahead of us. "I went downstairs to talk to Ali, but she'd gone to bed. And while I was there I thought I'd have a go at figuring out what's been upsetting Lottie lately. What's changed around the place, what's likely to have destabilised her. So I asked Mrs Chapman, but the old bat told me to mind my own business.

Suddenly, a single gunshot echoed around the woods.

Caz stopped dead, tilted her head as though listening for the next shot.

"They've started early," she said as another shot rang out.

She frowned. "That's not rifle fire," she said, moving off the pathway and, with a whistle, calling Ellie back go her heel.

I too stepped into the undergrowth and mimicked her half-stoop, moving a dozen or so steps while another shot rang out before I straightened up, stopped dead and said: "What the hell are we doing?"

Caz turned to me with a quizzical look on her face as another shot rang out.

"Where I'm from, Caz, if you hear gunfire you run in the opposite direction. Can you tell me why we're currently walking *towards* the sound of gunfire?"

"Because you're not in Southwark any more, Dorothy, and I'm always intrigued to know who would get up at this ungodly hour and shoot a pistol in the middle of a wood."

"Wait," I called after her as she strode on. "What's more intriguing? People getting up before 7am or the gunfire?" But Caz had pushed into a wall of greenery that swallowed her up, leaving me with the option of staying here while there was audibly a gun-toting, possibly gun-crazed lunatic on the lose somewhere in the woods, or pressing through and catching up with her so I'd at least have company if whoever was out there came to pop a cap in my ass.

I pushed through the hedge, found myself amongst more densely packed trees, and caught up with Caz until we stepped out of the tree line and into a clearing.

The whole thing felt like a movie set.

Before us, but with their back to the two of us, a tall figure encased in a long, waxed overcoat was standing. A dark woollen beanie hat was jammed down over their ears, but a few stray tendrils of curly ginger hair poked out from under the hat and waved gently in the breeze. The figure's left arm was dropped casually to the side, the right arm pointed straight out, a large revolver gripped lightly in the hand and, as we watched, the figure breathed in, out, visibly relaxed across the shoulders, and the trigger was pulled.

The bullet thwacked into a target nailed to a huge old tree on the far side of the clearing and it was somewhat alarming to note that the target was a large man-shaped silhouette, a photo of Sir Phillip glued on top of the head.

The figure pointed the gun at the ground, flipped it open and tipped the used shells into their palm, dropping them into the left-hand pocket of the waxed coat before extracting, from the right-hand pocket, a selection of new shells.

Ellie, tongue hanging out and tail wagging enthusiastically, walked over to the figure and sat obediently.

"Hello there," the figure bent to offer the back of their hand to the dog and then, as if sensing there were other humans present, straightened, turning towards us.

It was a teenage girl, her tall slim figure almost drowned in the coat, her skin so pale it was almost translucent and her eyes a dazzling green.

She frowned at us, and I stepped forward.

"Morning," I said, as she slipped the pistol and the bullets into her pocket. "Lovely day for it."

"Hello." She was wary, nodding at both of us, and stepping away from Ellie, who took two steps and sat again, a look of adoration on her face.

Close to, I could see that she couldn't be much older than

Lottie, but her height and the clothing had hidden her youth. Caz stepped past me, walking over to the makeshift target and inspecting it. "Nice grouping," she said, indicating a trilogy of holes centred between Sir Phillip Warren's eyes.

"No idea who did that," the girl said, taking another step towards the edge of the clearing.

"I'm Danny," I said, stepping forward and offering my hand, a broad smile on my face. "Danny Bird."

She faltered, clearly taken aback by my greeting. Her eyes darted from me to Caz to Ellie, and eventually she sniffed, straightened her shoulders and took my hand, shaking it firmly.

Her hand was cool to the touch, and she shook twice, then released my hand and put hers straight back in her pocket. "I'm Gaia Kennedy," she said, the wariness flaring up as Caz approached.

"The gamekeeper's daughter," Caz said, smiling, and Gaia's face flushed angrily.

"Estate manager," she said brusquely. "Or should I say ex-estate manager, owing to the fact he's dead."

"I'm sorry," Caz said quietly, and the girl – as though taken aback by the genuine offer of condolences, faltered again, her bravado flickering off momentarily.

"Yeah, well, thanks." She shrugged. "I should be going."

"Where'd you get the gun?" I asked, nodding at her pocket.

"Gun?"

I gestured at the target. "We saw the last shot.

Gaia raised an eyebrow. "You were quiet. Normally I can hear people approaching."

"Risky," Caz commented, offering her own hand. "I mean if one of your bullets goes astray at the same time someone's walking through the woods. I'm Caz, by the way," she added, seemingly choosing not to mention the fact that she was actually Lady Caroline Victoria Genevieve Jane de Montfort.

"Walking through the woods?" Gaia shook Caz's hand and shook her head, chuckling. "That lot up there," she jerked her head in the direction of the house "haven't got out of their pits yet, let alone started tramping through the wood. And besides," she tilted her head slightly, a smirk flashing across her face, "my bullets never go astray."

She pulled the gun out of her pocket. At this distance I could see it was an ancient revolver. "War souvenir?" I asked, and she nodded, flipping open the chamber to check there were no bullets in it, then sliding gun into the rear waistband of her coat.

"My great grandfather's. From the first war. My grandad used to use it to shoot rats. My dad tried to teach me to use it," she pulled the gun back out of her jeans, held it flat in her hand and stared at it, lost in a reverie "but he was useless so my mum had to teach me how to hit a target."

"I wonder if you could help us," Caz said, and Gaia tore her eyes from the gun. "We were hoping to find a shortcut up to the folly."

The girl's eyes widened, and she shook her head. "You've come from the house?" she asked, her eyes darting to the target.

"Don't worry," Caz smiled, "I doubt you're the first person to want to use Sir Phillip for target practice. We won't tell."

Gaia exhaled, then shrugged laughing mirthlessly. "Tell away," she said. "He can't do much worse to me than he's already done."

"Meaning?" I frowned.

"Meaning my father dies. And my family – who have worked at Dukes Halt for over a century – is being evicted because I'm not a boy and my mother's not a man. I'm going to lose my whole life. What the actual fuck is that shit?"

I didn't understand and told her so.

"Every first son of the Kennedys has taken over the estate keeper job when his father was no longer able. We've worked this land more than the bloody Warren's have, and that old bastard thinks a woman and her daughter couldn't possibly be capable of taking over the place. I mean; who does he think was running his bastard estate for the last year while my dad was dying of cancer?"

I shivered, the mention of the word triggering the still-fresh memory of my mother's recent brush with the disease.

"My mum's keeping me shielded – or thinks she is," Gaia glanced back down at the gun in her hand. "But I heard her on the phone last night: He won't listen to reason. We've got a couple of weeks then we're homeless and my whole life is up in smoke."

~

Except, by the time we exited the woods, Ellie wasn't the only thing panting.

Caz – clearly bred to early morning yomps across the moors – was powering ahead while I – a city boy who's idea of an early morning hike was a coffee run to the Starbucks three streets away – staggered behind her, periodically receiving pitying looks and encouraging barks from Ellie.

"Not far now," Caz lied, her voice making me look up from Ellie's dolorous dark eyes.

I stopped dead.

Across the vast lawn, having seemingly just left the house, two figures were walking. I could tell that one of them was Lottie Warren, a fluorescent pink bobble hat on her head and a scarf wrapped around her neck, but it was the presence, beside her, of Sergei Maximov that disturbed me most.

The two were clearly walking together, his head bowed as he spoke to her, and I watched as she nodded, something about the definite jerk of her head telegraphing her absolute agreement with whatever he was saying.

From the front door, another figure came, this one moving directly towards us.

"Lovely morning for it," Francine Gerber called as she approached us.

For a moment, I thought she was referring to whatever it was that Lottie and Maximov were engaged in, then realised she meant for a walk in the woods.

Ellie barked, and tail wagging delightedly, ran to the woman who was clad in a knee-length waxed jacket and sturdy boots.

Caz called the dog back, apologising to Francine, who

laughed, shook her head and reached into the pocket of her coat.

"Always wanted a dog," she said. "But my life – as a kid and as an adult – has basically been moving around from one thing to another, so…"

From her pocket she extracted a bright yellow tennis ball and before I could question why she'd been carrying it, she showed it to Ellie, who barked happily, whirled around chasing her tail, and jumped up and down, her eyes never leaving the yellow ball.

"May I?" Francine looked back at Caz, who shrugged her permission, and the woman, lifting on to one foot, pulled her arm backwards and whipped it forward, her body rolling at the hips as well.

The ball – and Ellie with it – whipped away.

Far away.

Farther away than I had ever seen anyone throw a ball.

Cas whilstled in admiration, and Francine blushed, smiled. "Softball," she said by way of explanation. "Cudda been a pro, y'know. Sorry 'bout that."

I glanced towards Ellie- fifty feet away now, if she was an inch – and still running as the yellow ball arced downwards towards earth.

In my peripheral vision, I could see Lottie and Maximov.

She said something back to him and he laughed, his head tilting back and his mouth opening, though no sound reached me. And then, as he replied to her, he reached out and put an arm around the girl, who made no attempt to evade his touch.

I recalled, instantly, what Arianna had told me about this man; about what he'd done to her and her sister; about what she'd seen him do to other girls, to grown men, and I felt for a moment like I was watching a movie, some awful tragedy unfolding from a distance, something over which I had no control.

"Well," Francine said, turning towards the forest, "I'm told there's some gorgeous woodland trails so I'm going to get some walking in before we go out shooting. I'll see you both later."

And – before I could let her know that I'd rather boil my own hands than go shooting with this lot – she'd walked into the forest and vanished.

My eyes went back to Lottie and Maximov and, as I watched, something moved just over Lottie's shoulder and my eyes refocused on a figure standing in the drawing room window.

Even from this distance, I could recognise the shape of Pamela Warren, her statuesque athletic figure standing perfectly still, like an animal that's spotted a lion in the scrub by the waterhole. And as I watched, too far away to actually be able to see any detail, something about her – the way her arms were crossed loosely under her bust, the way her head was sat solidly, immovably, the way she seemed not to be breathing – suggested a fury that had been building a long time.

I tore my eyes away, afraid she'd see me watching her and – as stupid as it sounds – turn me to stone with a glare.

Did Pamela know her date's predilections? Or was she just aware that he was getting matier with her daughter than she wanted? No, I decided as I ran to catch up with Caz, this was more than an older woman resenting attention being paid to her daughter.

We eventually made it up to the folly, a vast ruined structure sprawled at the top of the hill, and I was standing in what was, at one time, the apse – or was it nave – of some vast Gothic church, a vast broken wall featuring a chunk of what I assumed, at one time, would have been a Rose window, all traces of the stained glass now long gone. Beyond the wall, fragments of pillars and arches were scattered around, and I was still trying to put into words how Pamela Warren had looked to me as Sergei Maximov headed off towards the wood with her daughter.

"This must have been some church," I muttered, craning my head backwards to take it in, and Caz laughed.

"It's a fake," she said. "There was never a church here. I

mean, why would there be? The family chapel is attached to the house, and the locals had a church in the village. This thing was built as a ruin by the fifth Duke in the late 1700s.

"It's basically nothing more than a vast movie set. That's what I wanted to see," Caz nodded at the farthest corner of the structure where a small wooden shed had been constructed."

She crossed to the structure and inspected the cheap padlock on the door.

"The fireworks," she explained to me, "for Sunday's display."

Having fingered the padlock, she nodded in satisfaction and we moved back out of the ruin that wasn't a ruin and away from the shed that was really a gunpowder store, and I was reminded of Lottie Warren's words about how nothing in this place was as it seemed, and the word came to me.

Murderous, I decided. The only word to describe the feeling I'd had when looking at the distant shape in the window was murderous.

CHAPTER ELEVEN

"You've got a fucking nerve!" Ali was clearly angry with me. Caz, for some reason, was simply nodded and sniffed at, while I was getting the full brunt of her not-inconsiderable anger.

"Me?" I looked around the vast kitchen as if expecting a chorus of support from the other people in it.

Caz had already flopped into a chair at the huge table and was helping herself to a piece of obviously cold toast from a pile of discarded plates, while the other person in the room – a pear-shaped woman with an oddly elongated neck so that, the neck and the rotund arse combined, she resembled nothing so much as a chiminea in a pinny – had her back to me and appeared to be trying to excavate a passage to the earth's core via the base of a Belfast sink so vast I suspected it could be used to drown horses in, if one felt so inclined and the sink in my bathroom was otherwise occupied.

No support came.

"What have *I* done?" I asked, as Ali tipped the cold toast from several other plates onto one, placed the leftover-laden plate close to Caz and started stacking the old plates into a dishwasher that looked like it might have been used to clear up the plates after the last supper.

No answer came from Ali, though her silence was far from comforting.

I glanced around the kitchen, the ancient flagstone tiles on the floor clashing somewhat with the more modern, though still somewhat old-fashioned units; the fifties cake mixer standing beside a state-of-the-art bullet blender. The place felt like people, over decades, had simply overlaid what was current without ever really disposing of anything or considering whether the place worked any more.

And then Ali, finished stacking the first lot of plates into the depthless maw of the dishwasher, turned to me.

"Done?" she whispered, her face a mask of injured outrage. "What have you done? 'Come to the country, Ali. It'll be like Upstairs Downstairs. There'll be fabulous parties and dashing bachelors.' And instead I'm nothing but a bloody kitchen wench for," she jerked her head at the rotund arse in the pale blue denims, "her."

"Oh." I sat, my mouth a perfect ellipse as Caz grabbed another leftover slice of toast and flicked through a discarded newspaper on the side. "Look, Ali, I'm fairly sure I was pretty clear that you coming wasn't a great idea. I seem to recall saying you needed to stay in The Marq to manage the talent show."

"Talent?" She spat, as though simply stating the word with outrage would convey the true depth of her fury to me. "Don't talk to me about talent. I was expecting cocktails and injured majors. Romance. Intrigue. Maybe a bit of the old how's your father."

I'd had enough. "Ali, you didn't get promised any of that from me. In fact the only person I know who might have promised you that shit was Georgette Heyer. And she's been dead for decades."

"Well I thought you'd at least have stood up for me," she hissed. "They sent me to the staff quarters."

"How's the plumbing?" I asked, and she squinted as though I'd asked her a trick question.

"Staff, Danny. I'm in the fucking attic. It's basically a barricade and a bald head short of being Les Mis."

"I know," I said, attempting placation. "But look: I'm a guest here myself. I don't really have the clout to demand you get moved. And I'm guessing Caz only had a plus one. Which was me."

"Ah yes," she said, fixing me with her steeliest glare. "You. The class traitor."

"The--?"

I got no further; the woman at the sink turned around, and

her jaw dropped.

"The hell you in my kitchen?" She demanded, her voice at least a dozen decibels louder than it needed to be.

Her hand went up to her ear, and she yanked out a white earphone, the tinny but unmistakeable sound of thrash metal drifting from it – all smashing drums and screeching guitars.

"Good morning," Caz smiled. "Any chance of a pot of tea?" She asked, adding – because I knew she loathed the stuff – "for my friend."

"Breakfast is upstairs," the woman said. "Kidneys, kedgeree, bacon, eggs, salmon" (this last pronounced 'Saul-mon') "and all the other," she paused, as though stopping herself using a word she knew was incorrect. Or impolite. "*Things* you English like to begin the day. Here," she cast a fierce eye at Ali, who flinched and hurriedly started collecting the rest of the discarded plates tipping the leftovers from them into a large bucket on the floor beside the table "we prepare dinner."

"Dinner?" Caz snatched at another piece of toast, discarding it at the last minute when she realised it already had teeth marks in it. "Lord, it's not nine o'clock yet."

The short woman drew herself to her full height, which wasn't very high. Her neck seemed to extend itself a couple of inches more, and she radiated umbrage. "Is a kitchen," she stated baldly, "not a day spa."

"Point taken," Caz, who knew better than to do anything that might interrupt a flow of free meals, shrugged, stood, and smiled. "Well I look forward to seeing what delicacies you prepare for dinner. But right now *I'm* starving, so I'm going to go and see what the gannets have left upstairs. Danny?"

"I'll hang out a bit," I said, receiving a raised eyebrow from Caz and an angry glare from the cook. "See if I can help."

"Suit yourself," Caz replied, and headed back upstairs.

"Help," the woman said and, when I offered my name and my hand, repeated the first as though testing how it felt in her mouth, and stared at the latter as though it might be diseased.

"I am Mila. Chef Mila," she said, indicating herself.

"It's a pleasure to meet you," I answered. "Your dinner last night was sensational."

"Was okay," she shrugged, trying – and failing – to hide her pleasure at the compliment.

"The tapenade on the Dover Sole was so wonderfully balanced. Salty but with a wonderful lemon-sharpness. And there was something else. A herb…"

"Is called čubar in my country. Savoury here. I add a pinch and it brings a taste of the countryside to balance the sophistication."

"Danny's a cook too," Ali, her body straining under the weight of all the dishes she was transporting to the dishwasher.

Immediately, the other woman changed. "A cook?" She said the word 'cook' as though, in the language of wherever she came from, it translated to killer-of-babies-and-ruiner-of-villages.

Her eyes squinted, her body language adopted a defensive posture, and she yanked the other earbud out, shoving both of them into her jeans as though to make clear she needed to keep her full senses about her.

"Well," I shrugged in what I hoped was a self-deprecating way, "I cook a bit. I run a pub."

"Runs a pub," Ali muttered, snatched a handful of cutlery and hurled them into the dishwasher with a force that suggested if she could have hurled them at my head and known she'd not have to mop up the resulting blood spillage she'd have done so.

This wasn't going very well.

"You come to steal my recipes," Mila, in full CIA interrogator mode now accused me. "To take the work of my life and bring it to your pub," this last word spat as though it befouled her to even say it. "To serve my dishes to customers and make fortune off my work? No," she shook her head, waved her hands as though shooing me from the room. "This will not happen. I will speak to Mrs Chapman, and you will be barred. I bar you from my kitchen."

I held my hands up in placation. "Honestly, I just wanted to help." I meant it. "I absolutely loved the food last night. But I'm not sure I fit in with the people up there," I jerked a thumb towards the ceiling, "and the idea of spending a morning with them when I could be here making food…"

I trailed off. The atmosphere upstairs at Dukes Halt was one of the weirdest I'd ever encountered. A bunch of people, half of whom were strangers to each other, all pretending to be having a wonderful weekend party while their eyes darted around like an ensemble in a silent movie. The Warren men had pretty much stayed in their corner all night discussing 'family business' in whispered tones, and when both sexes had gathered together at the end, Pamela and Henry had sat in a corner whispering while Sergei Maximov – ostensibly, I thought, Pamela's date – had chatted in a conspiratorial murmur with, at first, Francine Gerber and then with Lottie.

Which reminded me of the sight of he and Lottie heading off towards the woods first thing this morning. That was a development I did not like.

"And besides, they'll all be going off shooting soon," I added, "and I really want to avoid having to do that."

Mila looked me up and down. "You peel potatoes," she said. "And peel finely. No chunks of potato go into the pig bucket," she nodded at the galvanised steel bucket that Ali had now finished shovelling all the breakfast leftovers into.

"Lunch is good. They go shoot so we send them with picnic basket. Ali," she addressed my bar manager as though they'd been working together for years, "you go find that lazy bitch Samantha. Tell her to help you get the baskets and then fill each like that list," she pointed at a type-written sheet of paper pinned to the wall."

Ali, shaking her head at me as though I was personally responsible for every disappointment in her disappointment-filled life, moved to leave the kitchen.

"Samantha is village girl," Mila explained to me. "And lazy slut. Not like Ali. I like your staff."

I blanched, praying that Ali – who, by now, had left the

room, hadn't heard that last line. "Ali's not my staff," I explained, and, from the other side of the half-opened door she'd just left by, Ali's voice added: "I'm not his fucking staff."

"She's a friend," I added to a look from Mila that suggested she not only didn't believe a word, but felt also that I was too soft on my staff.

Before she could propose a place I could buy a cudgel to keep them in line, I stepped forward, my arms spread wide. "I should get an apron on," I said. Mila nodded, and within five minutes I was peeling a huge sack of potatoes as she continued to viciously poke a wooden spoon down what I assumed was a malfunctioning waste disposal unit in the sink.

"The American actress," she grumbled. "Her mother comes down yesterday. I find her poking around outside. 'What you want here?' I ask, and she tells me that the actress does not eat any of my food.

"'My food is most delicious food in whole county. Possibly whole country,' I tell her but she insist that the actress only eat some fucking macrobiotic high-fibre slop."

I remembered Sara's passing on all of the courses and how her main had been a bowl of something greeny-brown. I wondered how the 'traditional' plumbing of Dukes Halt was getting on with the results this morning.

"The shit was boil-in-the-bag. Boil-in-the-bag," Mila repeated as though it were the most outrageous thing she had ever heard, "and the leftovers went down here with a few other things. And I do not know what that stupid bitch is eating but it has set like concrete overnight. Mother- ah!" she grunted in triumph and the wooden spoon plunged into the machine as she broke through whatever had been blocking the mechanism.

"Here," I filled a jug with water and trickled a little down the hole. "Run the mechanism slowly."

Mila eyed me suspiciously but began to pulse the waste disposal unit as I poured water down to further break up and flush whatever had caused the blockage, and within minutes the machine was running freely.

She looked me up and down. "Thank you," she smiled, before switching back to angry Mila and turning to Ali and Samantha, enquiring how they were getting on with the picnic baskets.

As time was short, the four of us joined forces and filled a wicker basket up with thick-crusted pies, home-made pickles and chutneys, a cooked and sliced ham, a selection of cold vegetable dishes including a potato salad, a selection of dressed beans and a green salad along with a small bottle of dressing.

Several Thermos flasks of soup were added, along with a bottle of brandy and a second basket of cutlery, crockery and very expensive-looking crystal was assembled, all of the pieces held tightly in place by the use of straps, pockets, parcels and the judicious stuffing of linen napkins and a table cloth, and at length Ali and the hapless Samantha were tasked with hauling the two baskets out to the waiting cars that would transport sir Phillip and his guests to wherever they were going to blast the fuck out of the local avian population.

Left alone, I went back to peeling potatoes, while on the opposite side of the vast sink Mila began dicing a sackful of root vegetables.

"So you mentioned that at home the herb is called čubar. Where's home?" I asked.

She paused. "Serbia," she said after the flicker had passed. "I know what you're thinking: Bombs. War. Butchery."

For a moment, I saw Arianna, and I recalled a sense that even she had been at pains to explain that her homeland had not been the horror people like me had grown up imagining.

"In Serbia, after Communism – before the trouble came – there was such food." She stopped, the knife paused above the array of vegetables, her hand red raw but steady as an iceberg. "And such life. People mixed, food came from the country to the city. There were shortages at first, but when it came, it came as the sea to the shore. Wave after wave of such bounty. And nobody had the fear, the snobbery. Peasant food. Haute cuisine. All was – is superlative a word?"

I told her that it was, indeed, a word, and she sighed, relaxed her shoulders, tightened her arms and continued dicing the veg. "If the war had not come, I would have a restaurant. One that makes more than fucking soups and souffles the salade au fucking frisee that these people – who have been, once, to France and believe they have cuisine in their lives. If I had that restaurant I would make such food. I would bring the city together with the country. Herbs. Vegetables. Such food. But for a restaurant, you need money."

"You're an amazing cook. Did you learn at home?" I asked, remembering my mother putting dubious tubers into pots and telling my sisters and I that there wasn't a stringy cut of meat that couldn't be made delicious with slow cooking and a bottle of Guinness.

"Home? Ah," Mila chuckled. "You think, still, I am some peasant cook? I learn in my grandmother's kitchen? My mother teaches me how to make goatcheese souflee and lentil salad? No," she shook her head, "My mother could cook not for shit. There was no food to cook in communism anyway. But after, I learn – as I am now – in service. I worked in the kitchen of a hotel, and I pass exams to be a Chef. This title is not some bullshit glory. I am Cordon Bleu."

She stood, sticking her chest out, her neck extending in pride, then redoubled her efforts on the sofrito before her." My hotel – my employers, you understand – paid for this accreditation. They make me so I can do things with Zucchini – wait," she stopped herself, "Is courgette here. Back then, we learned all from America. Television, food, even the English language, all was American.

"And then – when war came, and America demolished the cities, and the hotel could pay me no more – in the kitchen of a hospital I learn to make soup and porridge in fifty-five variations. And I dream, always of my restaurant. One day."

My phone bleeped, and I put down my knife, wiped my hands on my apron and opened the text that had just arrived.

It was from Nick, and it read simply: *"KNOW THIS IS UNLIKELY, BUT HAVE YOU HEARD FROM*

ARIANNA. BIT WORRIED AS I HAVEN'T SEEN HER FOR A COUPLE OF DAYS."

I put the knife down. "Do you mind if I step outside for a bit?" I asked and crossed the kitchen to call Nick.

Outside, as I hit his number I saw a couple of black people carriers emerge from the woods and barrel towards the front of the house. I put the phone to my ear and strolled around towards the front of the house.

"Danny." Nick's voice came down the line, and – well, it's not possible to say this without it sounding sappy so I'm just going to say it – my heart skipped.

It's difficult to explain how hard it had been to discover, after spending a third of my life with my previous boyfriend Robert that he'd not only cheated on me but hadn't been that bothered when our relationship ended, and so when I'd met Nick I'd been wary, finally settled to accepting, and ultimately decided that the only way I wanted our relationship to proceed was without lies.

"Have you seen Arianna?" He asked, referring to the wife he'd pretended he didn't have.

The black people carriers pulled up outside the house, and various guests and family members – all clad in plus fours, waxed jackets and looking like the contents of the Bodum catalogue come to life – piled out of the front door and into the transports with much hilarity and laughter.

"Arianna?" I jerked back to Nick. "Why would I have seen Arianna?"

I choked, trying to figure out how to answer his question without getting into detail that would cause more trouble than I wanted to cause at this stage.

"Listen, Danny," he said, "I don't care what you talked about. But I've got a problem. She's gone."

"Gone? What do you mean gone?"

"I mean gone. She's not been in the house since the night before last, and she's not answering her phone."

"And what makes you think I would have seen her?" I brazened out.

"Well mostly because when I went into her room," he explained, "I found a flier for some talent show at The Marq on her bedside table."

He stopped dead, and I knew I was being interrogated.

"Well she might have gone there after I left. I can ask the twins, cos I've been here for a day at least."

"And where, exactly, is 'here'?" He asked.

"It's," I dreaded admitting my location, as though Nick would figure out my link with Arianna and then deduce that I had some involvement in her disappearance, "a place called Dukes Halt. I'm here with Caz."

"The thing is," he said, "Arianna and me have a meeting next week with the Home Office, and if she's not there she – not to mention me – is screwed. So I really need to find her. Look, Danny, I really don't need to know what Arianna visited you about, but if you have any idea where she's gotten to you need to let her know that she needs to be at that appointment next week or her visa status could be damaged. She could be deported, Danny, and I could get in serious trouble."

"Nick, I genuinely have no idea where she's got to," I said, though deep inside me a bell was tolling. I might not have known where she was, but something told me I had an idea where she was heading. Though how, I asked myself, could she be heading this way? Not even Ray and Dash had managed to twig that Maximov was at Dukes Halt.

Nick was silent again. "Well if you do hear from her, Danny, can you please pass my message along?"

I told him I would, expressed my wish that she'd be at home this evening, and we rang off. I knew Nick had married Arianna to get her away from a terrible situation, and that there was nothing romantic that I needed to worry about between them. But it still felt a little disconcerting to hear him so obviously worried about her whereabouts. I tried reasoning that his concern was based on the danger that a Home Office enquiry that went too deep might well identify the fact that the two lived separately, and that their relationship was a sham marriage the illegality of which would not only lose Nick his job but might also get him sent to prison.

But that reasoning didn't explain away the concern in Nick's voice.

Sighing, I turned and went back towards the kitchen, bumping into a green-looking Ali.

"Christ," she said, a hand over her mouth, "it's like a fucking horror movie in there. I'm done. Tell her highness that if she needs me I'm going back to my room." And she pushed passed me and was gone.

I paused outside the kitchen door and could hear Mila's voice talking. "Happy?" she spat, as though whoever she was talking to had offended her every sensibility. "Happy is not possible. I see bombs fall on weddings. Happy is passing. Money is macro paleo diets and a plate of slop for dinner. Money is getting to choose what you starve yourself of.

"These people; they think because they have money they have class, but I tell you – I could roll a turd in marjoram, poach it in cream and serve it garnished with caviar; it's still a shit on a plate. These people have money but no respect, no decency. No class."

Another woman spoke: "But that's the problem: They don't need to have decency or class, because they have the money; and the money is power."

I recognised the woman who had left the house when we'd arrived the day before, and whose daughter Caz and I had met that morning – Beth Kennedy. She sighed and carried on. "Don't get me wrong: I never had a problem with them before."

She paused and there was a grinding crunching noise.

"Here," Mila said, "you're doing it wrong. Let me show you."

A moment of silence followed, and then Beth Kennedy spoke again. "Back when Simon was alive they were fine. But this refusal to even consider I could do the job…"

She trailed off as I walked into the room and found that she'd been put to work pushing what looked like half a pig through a manual mincing machine while Mila sat now by the table, a pile of dead birds to hand and a large bucket full of bloodied feathers between her legs as she methodically plucked the game.

I made my excuses and left.

CHAPTER TWELVE

The rest of the day passed in the sort of fog that can only occur when one is a stranger in someone else's house and almost everyone else has gone out to shoot at anything that takes to the skies.

I found myself, at one point, back in the long gallery, the old oil paintings and ancient ceramics making it feel like I'd been locked in a museum after closing time. I strolled along the rows of ladies and gentlemen in powdered wigs, families portrayed in bucolic landscapes and stopped before the tiny selection of family photos, the chipped fire engine in place and the flowers of the previous day replaced with a new spray of multi-coloured freesia.

What sort of tragedy had hit this family, I wondered, that had left a mother dead, a son banished – excised even from family photos – and another son dead? Lottie had said that nothing was as it seemed here, that nobody was as they seemed, and I could understand her viewpoint.

But, looking at the photographs, at the altar arranged before them, I wondered if it was really true. Sometimes – especially when we're teenagers switching between terminal boredom at the smallness of our world and fearful excitement at the size of the world we're about to step into – we make things dramatic because the prosaic reality is too scary: The idea that when we grow up things will not be exciting and dramatic, but dull, and exactly as they seem.

Oh Lottie wasn't entirely wrong; the house was definitely full of secrets. Why on earth would Pamela Warren, divorced from Henry, bring her new date to dinner at her father-in-law's memorial to her long-dead mother-in-law? Why would Pamela have such clear disdain for the date she'd brought?

Why were the guests all virtual strangers to each other? And why was Sir Phillip so desperate to get Beth Kennedy out of her cottage and off the grounds?

Not to mention: why was Beth's teenage daughter prowling the woods with an antique revolver?

But those were veneers on top of the reality: This was a house in mourning.

Sir Phillip's presentation of his wife's portrait and, more importantly, of her ashes; his brusque personality, shaped to look like a rude aggressive old boor; even this temple to a family that said as much about who was obliterated from the record as it did about who was remembered fondly. All of this spoke of a man who was mired in grief and anger.

As if responding to my own thoughts, a voice, right by my ear, said: "There were happy times here once, you know."

I won't say my feet left the ground, but Mrs Chapman had approached so silently, and was standing so close to me when she spoke that I swear my heart skipped a beat and a small shriek of terror escaped my lips.

"You frightened me," I said, and a small turn of her lips suggested she knew, and that it had been her intent.

"You didn't shoot." She said it as a statement, but it felt like a request, and I nodded.

"I don't like guns. They're dangerous."

"In the wrong hands," she answered, the smile fading as she looked about her. "But then, in the wrong hands, anything can be a weapon."

I didn't know quite what she meant but it felt as though she were suggesting that mine might not be the right hands for whatever it was she felt I was doing. I nodded at the photos. "They look like happy times," I said, and she stepped around me and straightened the flowers.

"What happened?" I asked, and she confirmed my theory about the atmosphere in the house.

"Death came," Chapman said, her eyes staring at the badly truncated family grouping. "Death and deceit."

"Lady Marion?" I asked, and she nodded.

"And what happened," I pointed to the small boy in the photos, "to this boy?"

"Edward." She said the word, but her face took on the sort of look I imagine a religious zealot takes on when they call the name of their God. "He was a baby. No," she corrected herself, "nowadays he would be called a toddler."

I waited for her to answer the question.

"He fell," she finally said, something about the flatness in her voice, the way her whole body sagged, suggesting she was fighting to contain her emotions.

"It was the same week his mother died. To this day, nobody knows what happened. He was in one of the bedrooms. He shouldn't have been there. It was the summer, and the middle of a heatwave and windows were open, and-"

She stopped, staring once again at the photos.

"His death came three days after Sir Phillip had lost his wife, and it broke him. Dukes Halt has not been a joyful place ever since."

A silence developed. I figured I'd ask the question that had been bothering me since I'd first looked at these photos.

"The left-hand side of this photo," I gestured at the later family group, Lady Marion already looking unwell. "There seems to be someone missing. Wasn't there another boy? George?"

She straightened. "You're very well informed. For a last-minute guest."

I had no answer to that, so I drew her attention to where Sir Phillip's shoulder was cut off abruptly. "What happened to him?" I asked, and she looked at me with something that was like fury.

"Sir Phillip had three sons. One died in infancy. One grew to be Major Henry. And the third forfeited his right to be a Warren or a son of this house. Talk of him upsets the family. I would appreciate it if you avoided raising him – or his name – around Major Henry or his father."

And so saying, she turned her back on me and floated back along the gallery.

It was only when she'd gone that I realised what had been wrong about that look. It had been fury – outrage, I guessed, at my audacity in asking such personal questions – but there had been something behind it.

Something that one didn't expect to see from a woman like Chapman.

Fear.

~

I headed back to my room, closed the door behind me and leant on it, as though keeping out something that had been chasing me. A picture of the Warrens and their guests lining up, gun stocks pressed to their shoulders as they took aim at the sky came unbidden to my mind.

I really didn't belong here.

And yet I'd promised I'd help Caz with her mission, so here I was. Not to mention that now I'd seen Arianna's tormentor in the flesh I was reluctant to leave until I'd figured out what to do about him.

I needed to figure out what I was going to do about Nick as well. I'd lied to him. There was no way around it, though my heart whispered that I hadn't lied as such, simply omitted to mention some facts.

I was worried that Arianna might be on her way to Dukes Halt, but that seemed hihjly unlikely. The trail had gone cold for Ray and Dash, so how would Arianna have been able to find out where Maximov was heading when he left London.

No, I figured, Arianna was more than likely still searching the city and would be back at home by the end of today.

But I would still have lied to Nick, and that gnawed at me.

The world beyond the bedroom windows looked gray and damp, and realising that a long walk to clear my head was as out of the question as an afternoon spent laying around in the drawing room like some latter-day aesthete, I crossed to the corner of my room where an ancient and dusty book case sat, the shelves jammed with volumes that looked like they hadn't been read in decades.

A quick glance told me why: They were almost all kids'

books.

Had this been a boy's bedroom? And if so, which boy?

Not Edward, I realised as I ran my fingers along the spines of the books – Hardy Boys mysteries, Black Beauty, The Neverending Story. He'd died as a toddler and these books went up to the teenage years.

So Henry or George then.

And then my eye alighted on a trio of hardbacks: 'The Life of Da Vinci,' 'The Life of Rembrandt,' and 'The life of Picasso,' and I knew, instinctively, that the room I was staying in had been the one that George Warren had slept in in the years before his expulsion and banishment from Dukes Halt.

I ran my fingertips along the spines of the three artist biographies and stopped, running back to the Picasso and frowning at a strange bulge that made it sit differently from the others in the set.

The books on the bookcase were packed so tightly that they were almost a single unit, and when I slid my index finger into the space between the top of the book and the shelf above and tried to extract the Picasso, the other books on the shelf slid out too, until I had enough leverage to yank the Picasso away from the others and push them back into place.

It was a large hardbacked book, about A4 size, the cover a collage of famous works by the artist with a black and white portrait of him in his trademark Breton jumper and his signature printed in red.

Inside the front cover was inscribed 'To Georgie. Wishing you the happiest of birthdays from Mummy & Daddy.'

But the back cover bulged slightly, and I knew instantly that this was because there was something tucked into the book between the pages and the cover. I turned the book over and discovered that the book had been designed with a large envelope glued to the inside back cover to contain, it said, the reader's Picasso drawings.

I flipped open the envelope and from the envelope extracted a slim black notebook filled with a teenager's blocky handwriting

I put the Picasso book to one side, crossed to the bed, propped myself up amongst the thousand and one cushions and pillows strewn on it, and opened the notebook.

The first words I read brought me up short.

I blinked away a sudden stab of tears and read on.

GEORGE – 27TH JUNE 1986

I don't think my mother is going to get better. I really want her to, and she insists she'll be fireworking with us this year, but I don't think she's going to get better. C

School finished almost two weeks ago and I should have come straight home, but Henry had been caught cheating in his end of terms. Outage. Horror. All that noise, and long story short, he was forced to stay behind as punishment.

Except, of course, it wasn't just Henry who had to stay behind when everyone else had gone. Papa said that Edward and I couldn't take the train on our own, and it was 'a waste of money' to send a car, so we had to wait til H was ready to come home and then we could take the train back with him.

Which is a bit of a cheek, to be honest. I mean, H is seventeen and I'm fourteen, but I think between the two of us, I'm the one with more intelligence. I mean, I've never had to have extra tuition – or cheat - to pass an exam. I'm A's at almost everything (except Geography. If it was maps and stuff I'd be fine, but all they seem to want to teach us about is Rocks and shale and schist. And I tried explaining that that's, surely, Geology rather than Geography, but Aston, the Geography master just smiled that thin-lipped smile that makes one suspect he really misses the days when one could thrash a boy for insubordination and told me to just get on with the exercise). So anyways, if I'm smart enough to know Geology from Geography, and to get A's in English and French, History Mathematics Latin and Philosophy, I'm fairly sure I could get my baby brother on a train from York to Dukes Halt without getting myself lost or abducted.

But no; I had to wait for H to finish being punished for his own stupidity.

It was a bit weird being alone in the school after almost all the other boys had gone. Actually, it was VERY weird being alone in the school with only a couple of the overseas borders and a smattering of teachers.

I spent the time doing an art project. I'm getting better with sketching, so I decided to sketch as many of the remaining staff and boys as I could, except none of the staff wanted to sit for me, and most of the boys – when I asked – called me a weirdo pansy and walked off laughing.

Only Rohit – one of the overseas boys – was willing, and I suspect that's because – as nobody talks to him – he hasn't heard (or doesn't understand) the names they call me, so he didn't realise that he was supposed to say no and laugh at me.

So I sketched him again and again. He has interesting hands and a nose that's long and thin yet has a bulbous end that makes it look like an assemblage of two different noses on one face.

The great thing about him being younger than me and an overseas boy was that he didn't speak until he was spoken to, so I wasn't constantly having to shush him and ask him to keep his head still. I liked having him there, but I also liked the fact that we worked in silence.

Talking's dangerous. If one doesn't speak, one can't say the wrong thing.

And – of course – I had to keep an eye on Eddie, who had also been forced to await Henry's leave, and who had even fewer potential playmates, all the younger children having long gone. Edward's such a dunce, but I think he has a sort of crush on me because he's happy to do whatever I want to do and always follows me around like a lamb.

So I sketched Rohit and Edward drew terrible drawings of Spiderman and Batman with his crayons until H was ready to go home, and we made our way back to Dukes Halt.

Kennedy met us at the station and drove us home. It was late afternoon but the car was like a sauna, and with the three of us sandwiched in the back (because God forbid a Warren should sit up front with K) it was even hotter. I took off my blazer and undid my tie and H rolled a window down, and still I could feel my sweat-soaked shirt sticking to the leather seats.

I was fanning myself with my cap when we turned off the main road, rolled through the gate, and there was Duke's Halt.

Papa took one look at me and his face set. I knew immediately he disapproved of my lack of blazer, my tie askew and the fact that my cap wasn't on my head, but I didn't care, so I pecked his cheek, said it was nice to see him, asked if I might be excused to go to my room and freshen up, and – as he made a huge fuss of Edward - came up here.

I gave it a few minutes and – after Chapman had dropped my bag off – searched through it to find the sketches of Rohit and went to my mother's room.

She was okay last summer. We had picnics and she had Kennedy and Chapman help her and I carry some easels and water colours up to the Folly so we could spend a few days painting both it and the Halt, and she was funny and cheeky and lovely and all the things that a mother is supposed to be; but by the time we came home at Christmas she was ill, and spent most of the holidays in bed and in so much pain that Henry and Edward and I – apart from the times we tip toed in to see her and say good morning and good night – barely saw her.

I'd hoped she'd be back to herself by now, but when Chapman brought my bag she'd placed it on my bed and pointedly said "Now you're not to be bothering your mother. Lady Marion is far too weak to have children fussing around her," which was how I knew that my mother was still in her bed.

The room was bright, the curtains drawn and the windows propped open a little to let some warm dry air circulate, and mama was sitting up in bed, her glasses perched on the end of her nose as she read a book. I knocked and was in before she'd even asked who was there, and when she saw me her whole face lit up.

"Georgie," she said. "Oh my love, it's so good to see you."

I don't know if she registered my shock or not – she was so very thin, you see, her eyes were like huge blue pools in dark, sunken pits, and her nose was so thin, her cheekbones so sharp that my first thought was I wasn't looking at my mama but at a cubist portrait of her – but her next words were "I'm fine my dear, don't worry. I'm just tired."

She gestured at the bed as though the tiredness explained her presence there, then patted the covers beside her.

I'd missed her so much.

None of her letters all term had suggested that she was as unwell as she clearly is.

I was about to climb on to the bed when she was seized by a coughing fit that went on relentlessly til eventually she gestured, helplessly, at a jug and glass beside her and I ran around to pour her a glass of water, which she waved aside. Beyond the bedside table, I realised, hidden in the corner of the room, was a large wheeled tank of some sort with a mask clipped on to it and – as she continued to cough and gasp – I realised that this was what she was asking for so I pulled the mask free, rushed over to my mother, the thing held out in my hand and she took it, slipped it over her face and nodded back at the tank.

Realising, finally, that I needed to turn on the flow of whatever was in the thing I turned back. This was easy: there was only one wheel on the top of the tank. I turned it and a distinct hissing filled the room as my mama's gasps subsided, the coughing faded, and she lay back on her pillows, her– thin, birdlike little shoulders drooping.

"Should I call someone?" I asked, and the merest switch of her head told me No.

So – picking my scattered sketches from the floor - I climbed up on the bed beside her.

"I'm not very well," she said from behind the mask, her voice growing a little stronger as her breathing returned to normal, "but I'm going to get better."

"What's wrong with you?" I asked, moving closer. "Shouldn't you be in a hospital?"

She reached a trembling hand up and touched my face, her huge blue eyes looking deep into mine.

"Always worrying," she said quietly and shook her head slightly. "I want to be here, my darling, where your daddy and Chapman can take care of me and I get to spend as much time as I can with you all."

"But what's wrong with you?" I asked again.

"I- well you see my darling it's hard to explain. "My lungs are not very strong. They won't work the way they're supposed to."

"You had a cold," I said, remembering that when she'd taken ages to respond to one of my letters she'd explained that she'd had a very bad cold and hadn't been able to write sooner.

"Pneumonia," she said, lifting the mask from her face and placing it on the bed beside her even as she waved away my look of concern. "I'm fine. I didn't want to worry you by saying it in the letter, but I was quite unwell for a few weeks."

"And now you're better?" I asked, and she nodded.

"I'm getting better. Now," she tapped her cheek and I scooted over to place a kiss on it.

"Oh my baby; I have missed you so much," she said, and when I corrected her and said that Edward was the baby, she laughed. "Edward is the youngest, but you have always been my baby."

When I was born I was ill and – apparently – nearly died. I don't remember this, obviously, because I was a baby at the time. But my mama tells me often that this makes me somehow different. But in a good way.

Edward and Henry, she says, are strong in their ways, but I have a different strength. I – my mama says – have a will to live, and that gives me a completely different strength.

Well, she says that sometimes, but she didn't say it then. I must try to write this clearly – my teachers at school are always saying that I lack focus, and I suppose they're right, but I say that my lack of focus is only because the world is so huge and there's so much to see and do and how could anyone focus for very long on one thing in such a huge world?

Anyway, my mama spotted the sketches and asked what they were, and so I told her and showed her, and we were looking at them and laughing at the sketch of the back of Rohit's head – I'd got the proportions wrong so that, whilst I'd sketched the glossy black hair quite well I'd given him a skinny neck that made it look like I'd actually drawn a hairy lollipop on a stick - and we were both giggling when the bedroom door opened and papa was there. As soon as he saw me, his face instantly assumed a look of annoyance.

"Your mother isn't well," he said and mama waved it aside, telling him she was perfectly well.

He walked over to the bed as I squirmed to get away from my mother and off the coverlet, having realised too late that I still had my uniform – and, worse, my shoes – on.

"I'm sure your mother has enjoyed your visit," he said picking up the sketches from the bed, "but I really think she should get some rest."

His eyes glanced over the pages in front of him and he frowned.

"Come back later, my darling," mama said, her cheeks seeming a little pinker than they had when I'd first entered the room.

She held the sketch of Rohit's head out to me, and her hand was trembling, the tremor seeming to be shaking her shoulders too.

My father handed me the stack of paper, a look of disdain on his face, his jaw set, then reached over and snatched the other sketch from my mother's hand, shoving it on the bottom of the pile, and snapping, "Get changed. See what your brothers are doing and go play with them," and I was dismissed.

I was outside on the landing, their voices muffled by the closed door when I looked down at the pile of sketches, at the one on top that had seemingly so angered my father.

It was two studies on one page.

In the top left corner was a sketch of Rohit's *left eye, the almond shape almost perfectly executed, the lashes and brow feathery and gentle, while the iris was bold and staring, my own silhouette reflected in it.*

And under it, in bottom right corner of the page, were Rohit's *lips, full, parted, smiling.*

From behind the door I heard my mother begin to cough once more.

CHAPTER THIRTEEN

A loud rapping on my door startled me awake, the notebook falling from my hands.

At some point I'd fallen asleep, the airlessness of the room and the thermonuclear blast of the central heating lulling me to unconsciousness.

I snatched up the notebook, shoved it back into its hiding place, and jammed the Picasso book back on the shelf before scrabbling the door open.

"There you are," Caz said. "I wondered where you'd got to."

I was still sleep-stunned and managed to spurt the words, "You shot," with an imagined question mark at the end, and Caz half-shook her head in response to my half-verbalised question.

"I always shoot," she said, "but I make it a point of honour never to actually hit. How was your afternoon?"

"Surreal," I said, and she raised an eyebrow.

"Darling, this is Dukes Halt; Surreal is standard practice."

I was coming awake now, a slight tremor the last of the adrenaline that had shocked me awake, an all-consuming thirst telling me that the heat had dehydrated me, and I stepped back, ushering Caz into the room.

"I had the most horrific afternoon," she said dramatically, and dropped into the bucket chair in the corner as I dived into the bathroom, filled a glass with water and then splashed my face with cold water from the tap, turning it off just as the plumbing went into light percussion mode.

"I mean, I've been to house parties before but I've never seen a guest list as full of, well the only word that fits, really, is bastards."

"So the hunting went well?" I perched myself on the edge of the bed.

"Sir Phillip spent the day vacillating between pleasant to those who were in his favour and either ignoring or snarling at those who weren't.

"Which were you?"

"The former," she said, waving a hand in front of her face and crossing to yank at the sash window, "then the latter when he had a go at Lottie and I stood up for the girl. Lord, Danny, it's like an oven in here. That Stamford woman was a terrible snob and spent half the time on various phone calls to bankers about some IPO her company is about to launch. Sara Simone was still trying to sell us all space at some sort of new-age mega-rich hippy time-share while her mother – who's actually a really good shot – seems to think that losing her husband to a twenty-three-year-old Pilates instructor called Jesus means she gets a pass at low-level homophobia.

"Which, of course, meant she spent the afternoon cozying up Digby Smith."

"If she only knew."

"John Warren and Richard Stamford were pleasant enough, though I suspect that was more because both of them just wanted to be left alone. Pamela spent half the day squabbling with Lottie, who had clearly gone shooting under duress and made a point of missing every single shot."

"As," I reminded her, "did you."

"Ah yes, dear heart, but I always manage to make it look as though I'm really trying. I really need to give poor Lottie some tips on how to do that. The poor girl stormed off in the end. Claimed she had a headache."

"And how was the Russian?"

"Absent for a large part. Something was going on there because he and Pamela hardly spoke. The atmosphere was – well, tense would be underselling it. And he spent most of the time he wasn't actually shooting walking with Henry Warren, which – even I have to admit, and I grew up with this set – was a bit weird.

"I mean what sort of man goes for nice little chats with his ex-wife's new boyfriend?"

"Yeah," I tried to adopt an air of nonchalance, "on that: Where did Pamela and he meet?"

"Pamela and Henry or Pamela and Maximov?"

"The latter," I answered, and Caz shrugged.

"No idea. I suppose via work. I told you she's some sort of faculty head at Cheltenham ladies' college."

"Wait." I stopped her. "Where's she working?"

"I told you," Caz looked confused, "when she and Henry split she went to work at Cheltenham. Which is odd," Caz frowned, "as she never seemed like a particularly pedagogic type before. I mean she did languages and politics at Oxford, so why she suddenly decided to go and teach the daughters of the upper set how to Parlez Francais I'll never know."

"That's 'cos she didn't," I said, a light going on. "Did Pamela actually tell you she was a faculty member at Cheltenham ladies' college?"

Caz frowned, trying to recall exactly what she'd been told. "Well not in so many words," she finally said. "I think I asked her where the new job was."

"And she said Cheltenham," I said, and Caz nodded.

"Caz, the ladies' college in Cheltenham is only one of the major employers in the town. The other is GCHQ."

"GCHQ?" I could see the same light coming on behind Caz's eyes.

"The secret service," I clarified, in case she still hadn't arrived at my point. "Caz, your friend isn't a French teacher. She's a spy."

Caz giggled. The giggle stopped. "Oh you're serious?" She asked. "Danny, Pamela Warren likes fashion, shopping, shopping for fashion and occasionally acquiring jewellery to go with the clothes.

"She barely drinks and she doesn't even do yoga in case she cracks a sweat or breaks a nail."

"Not all spies are James Bond," I answered.

"She's not a spy, Danny. She's a language teacher."

"How many languages does she speak?"

The frown was back. "Four? Five." She counted them on her fingers. "French, obviously, German, Russian, some Spanish and English."

"Russia," I said flatly. "She speaks Russian, works in Cheltenham and turned up this weekend with a man who-"

I stopped dead. I'd not told Caz anything about Arianna or Petrovitch-Maximov. I'd promised Arianna I'd keep it confidential. But there was no way to avoid telling her what I knew about Maximov and how I knew it.

So I told her.

Afterwards, Caz sat in silence for a moment.

"I thought we didn't do secrets," she said.

"I told Arianna I'd keep it confidential."

"Danny, that man's been sniffing around Lottie all day."

"Pamela knows," I said. "I think she's watching him closely."

"But what on earth is she doing with him? I mean why bring him here?"

"I don't know," I said, "but I'm pretty sure of one thing: they're not dating. She's brought him here for a reason other than a nice weekend in the country."

"So is there anything else?" She asked. "Any other little confidences I ought to know about?"

I shook my head. "None," I said, my eyes flicking to the bookshelf and its hidden diary. Caz stood and brushed herself down, disappointment evident in her brusque manner.

"Well, then; I suppose we better get changed for dinner." she smiled and chucked me under my chin. "Perhaps someone will feed the awful Russian arsenic soup."

~

I was just out of the shower, my ears still ringing, when I heard a discrete knock at my door. I was convinced that Digby Smith had tried to get into my room the night before and so I was fervently praying, as I wrapped a towel around myself and carefully eased the door open a crack, that this wasn't another attempted visit.

It wasn't. Instead of Digby, Henry Warren stood outside my door.

"Ah," he was clearly embarrassed, his eyes shifting to the door frame. "Sorry to bother you old chap. Happy to come back later."

"No," I stepped behind the door, pulling it open, "just let me throw something on. Be with you in a second."

He entered my room and I darted into the bathroom, slipping back into my jeans and t-shirt and returning to the bedroom, where he was slumped in the bucket chair I hoped to sit in one day.

"Look," he was still clearly uncomfortable about something, "bit sensitive and probably nothing, but I was wondering if you'd seen Lottie lately."

"Lottie?" I was puzzled.

"Well, I mean, you weren't shooting," he trailed off as though that was an explanation.

I decided not to explain my absence at the shoot. "But Lottie was," I said and he nodded.

"Yes. Bit of a family – um – dispute. She left early."

"I'm afraid I was here," I said. "In my room. I was reading," I gestured at the bookcase.

"Oh," his shoulders slumped. "You see, the thing is, she didn't just leave early. She sort of stormed off."

"Well I'm sure she'll make her way home eventually," I smiled, wondering why Major Henry had come knocking on my door with this issue.

"Oh." His head came up. "Oh no, that's fine. We know she came home, because we've checked her room, and she's definitely been in it. But that's the problem."

I felt, suddenly, cold. "Problem?"

"Yes. She's taken a rucksack. And as far as her mother and I can see, she's taken some clothes too."

"She's run away?"

"Well," he held his hands out, palm up, as though to say, 'who can tell?'

"Well should you call someone?" I pressed, feeling more

concerned at Henry's uncertainty than I was at the idea of Lottie packing a bag and walking out of this place.

"Call someone?" He seemed genuinely puzzled, then nodded. "Police, you mean? Yes, possibly. Probably. But, well, we – that is Pamela and I – were wondering if she might come back."

"Well I suppose that depends on why she left in the first place," I responded.

"School," he said, in tones so despairing I was pulled straight back to George's diary and a sense that Major Henry had never found education all that enjoyable. "Lottie has decided she wants to attend a local school here. A village school."

I assumed that this was not the sort of thing a scion of the Warren's did and asked if that decision was problematic.

"Not problematic, exactly. Well, not for her mother and me."

"But for her grandfather?"

Henry was silent a moment. "You have to understand, my father wants only the best for her. He wants Lottie to have all the benefits that he can provide, and his worldview doesn't really include his granddaughter going to a village school."

"Well," I bit back a million comments I wanted to make, "what can I do for you?"

Henry nodded, as though acknowledging that we were getting to the point of his visit. "We – that is my, um, Pamela and I – were wondering. I mean we'd like to avoid police in the house if at all possible this weekend. Especially this weekend. We were wondering if you could maybe ask around, find out where she went. Maybe ask her to come home."

"Me?"

"Well we've heard so many great things about your ability to solve mysteries. To find people."

I glanced towards the window, where darkness had fully fallen, the night sky filled with fast-moving clouds so that the moon strobed through them. I was becoming used to solving mysteries in London, where the jungle was concrete and brick;

not here where everything seemed so alien.

But I was worried about Lottie. I couldn't shake the sight of her and Maximov this morning, of her mother looking at them as they made their way to the woods.

A part of me remembered the girl I'd met just a day before: cocky, cheeky, winding up the adults as only a teenager could.

And then I reminded myself that she was a child. One that – like her uncle George at a similar age – could use big words, and make themselves sound adult, but who underneath everything still needed protecting from a cold and scary world.

"I'll do what I can," I said to Henry, and he smiled his thanks.

CHAPTER FOURTEEN

Pre-dinner cocktails, on the first night had been a somewhat strained affair; understandably, perhaps as so many of the assembled party had been strangers to each other. But tonight – after a day spent out in the open air together – a more genuine rumble of chat was rolling around the drawing room when Caz and I arrived.

Sir Phillip was already in his place against the side table, the Stamfords were in conversation with Pamela and John Warren, while Henry Warren and Maximov were on the far side of the room with heads bowed together in conversation.

Digby Smith slimed up to me as soon as Caz and I arrived, and – whilst seeming to reach across me to get a drink from a tray held by one of the servers – whispered uncomfortably close to my ear "I missed you today. Maybe I'll get you shooting some other time."

I lifted my hand to adjust a stray hair and managed, accidentally, to knock Digby's hand so that the drink he'd just acquired was knocked from his grasp.

Sadly, none of it went on him, and one of the village kids came over to mop the spillage.

Digby retreated, a replacement drink in hand, and we went across to join the Stamfords, Pamela and John.

"No," Karen Stamford was saying when we arrived, "give me a new-build every time. I adore the history and age; but the plumbing." She shuddered. "I swear, when I turned on my faucet tonight, mud poured out."

I laughed. She had a point.

"Don't let Chapman hear you complaining about the place," Pamela smiled back. "She seems to think any criticism is a personal reflection on her. I made that mistake when I first arrived – pointed out that the fuse boxes downstairs were at least a hundred years old and we should maybe consider updating them before the place burned down.

"Honestly, you'd think I'd suggested throwing out the organ from York Minster and putting a banjo in instead."

We laughed, I sipped my martini, and glanced at Caz, whose eyes strayed over my shoulder as the colour drained from her face.

"Ye Gods," she gasped as the rest of the room – gripped by a sort of ripple of bemusement and outright horror – turned towards the door from the hallway.

Standing, framed as though in a proscenium arch, was Sara Simone.

She was wearing a cream silk mid-calf sheath dress, the spaghetti straps hanging languidly across flawless shoulders. Her face was so heavily made up that she looked entirely natural, only a pink glitter on her lips providing an acknowledgement of the artifice involved, and her hair – wet look and scraped back from her face as though she'd just stepped from the shower – glistened in the chandelier lights.

And around her throat was the largest diamond I had ever seen.

I glanced across at John Warren who appeared to have frozen in place.

From behind Sara, Francine appeared dragged up in a dress that looked like it had been constructed from the contents of Miss Havisham's wardrobe and overlaid with all the lace from the Baby Jane estate-sale.

"Is she wearing a wedding dress?" Richard Stamford asked.

"Well if she is," Caz said, her eyes still fixed on the stone around Sara Simone's neck, "it's more Vera Wrong than Vera Wang."

"Oh," Sara asked, a moue of regret on her face. "Are we late? I'm so sorry."

"All my fault," Francine said, her accent becoming more Foghorn Leghorn with each syllable. "Ah jest couldn't decide what to wear."

"So she wore it all," I muttered to Caz, who still couldn't tear her eyes away from the stone around Sara's neck.

"That's the Gianelli diamond," she gasped.

"The what?"

"Gianelli. Diamond. Sara bedded some Italian nobleman at some point, though God knows how; the man was ninety if he was a day."

I decided not to point out that Caz's own boyfriend was currently in a coma. She pressed on in a gossipy whisper.

"Anyways, the old geezer snuffed it this year and rumour has it that he died a happy man. He must have been very happy because he bequeathed Sara one of the world's largest and most accursed diamonds."

"Okay, largest I can see. Accursed?"

"Every owner – including the last one – died an unnatural death."

"He was at least ninety. How unnatural was that?"

"The rumours are he had a massive coronary and it took La Simone a good five minutes to realise the twitches and groans were not of advancing ecstacy."

"Ouch." I winced. "Point taken."

"Anyways, the family tried going through the Italian courts to nullify the will but no joy. He'd left the stone to her, and it's hers until her death, at which point it will revert to the family."

"Sir Phillip," Francine advanced on the aristocrat who looked as I imagine Belgium might have looked when the Wehrmacht made their advance in 1940.

"It's such terrible bad manners," she gushed, managing to contract the word 'terrible' into two syllables, one of which was an elongated 'u'. "Ah do hope you'll forgive us?"

"Why's she doing that voice?" Richard Stamford suddenly asked, and his wife shushed him. "Well she didn't come from Georgia at lunch time," he persisted. "It could be a stroke. Maybe I should go and check."

"A stroke?" Pamela Warren asked.

"Well they affect people that way sometimes," Richard

Stamford carried on as Karen tried to make him change topic. "Accents, personalities."

"Fashion sense," Caz muttered, and Pamela snorted.

And at that moment, a gong was struck, dinner was announced, and we all trooped into the dimly lit dining room.

The fancy fireguard sat in front of an even more meagre fire, so that I wondered whether it would be indecorous for me to pop back upstairs and put my coat on.

The room was freezing.

Where, the previous night I'd had my back to the French windows and Digby to contend with, tonight I was on the opposite side of the table facing Pamela and John. John was seated next to Sara. Beside Sara was Francine, who'd retained her position from the previous night, while Richard Stamford, looking like a rabbit in the headlights, sat beside Digby who'd been placed at the very end of the table, and did not look too happy about the fact.

Sir Phillip, at least, still had his position at the top of the table, and the side of the table facing the French windows consisted of Caz, then me, then Sergei Maximov (still fiddling with his mobile phone), Karen Stamford and Henry

Sir Phillip, when people had finally settled, glared around the room. "Is this someone's idea of a joke?" He demanded, lifting a small bell at his left hand and ringing it as his question triggered a general round of murmur and confusion.

A moment later Chapman appeared, her face as she registered where people were sitting, shifting from the usual calm confidence to confusion and then a red-tinted anger. She walked to Sir Phillip and bent her head to his as he demanded – in tones so low that they only barely reached me two seats away – to know who had butchered the seating plan.

"I laid the cards myself, Sir Phillip," Chapman insisted. "They were exactly as your instruction at six p.m."

"Well they're not exactly as my instruction now. Who's been in here?" He demanded and, when Mrs Chapman had no answer for him, rolled his eyes. "Carlotta."

"I'm afraid," Sir Phillip announced to the table "that

someone has played a rather childish practical joke and absolutely destroyed the seating plan we had prepared."

"I hope it won't ruin dinner too much, but I do apologise for the break in etiquette."

There was a general murmur that suggested nobody was that bothered anyway and then, as the first of the courses – a crab bisque with caviar garnish – began to arrive, the usual small talk commenced.

"So, Mr Bird," Maximov slipped his mobile phone into his jacket pocket, and turned to me, his spoon hovering over the bowl, "we have had so few opportunities to talk. Almost as though we avoid each other."

I smiled, mentioned he'd been out shooting all afternoon, as though that explained our inability to get together for a chinwag.

"Ah," he nodded. "I understand." Then he paused, looking around the table and frowning. "But the young lady – Carlotta – she is not here this evening?"

The hackles on the back of my neck rose. He knew something.

"I saw you walking with her this morning," I answered, deliberately swerving his attempt to question her whereabouts.

A twitch of the lips made it clear he knew exactly what I was doing. "We have so much in common, little Lottie and I"

I wanted to ask what he could possibly have in common with a teenage girl, then realised that that was exacly what he wanted.

"So did you have a good shoot?" I asked,

"It was…. Interesting." He smiled, lifted the soup to his mouth and slurped it. "You did not shoot today?"

"I'm not a fan," I answered, sipping my own soup." Proximity to him made my skin crawl even more than it had when – the previous night – I'd had to sit with Digby.

"Of guns?" He turned that 'I-know-something-you-don't' look on me, "Or of hunting?"

"I don't like killing things for sport," I said, and he smiled.

"Perhaps," he said, his voice rising a few decibels, "there is something which is worse than killing for sport."

A few eyes turned to him.

"Such as?" I asked, aware now that a number of other people were listening in to our conversation.

"Many people kill from greed, or hatred. Or cowardice."

The room had gone quiet.

"And many people, through their actions or inactions, cause death on a massive scale."

He smiled again, the performer knowing he had the room. "Take the Dam in Sri Lanka that the Standard Hydroelectric Company built in 2012."

"I say," Digby said, his tone anxious.

"Yes," Maximov turned the smile on Digby Smith, "the same Standard Hydroelectric Company you described prior to and several times since the Sri Lanka disaster as 'One of the jewels in Britain's industrial crown'."

"Tragic story," Digby muttered, and made some half-arsed attempt to move the topic away by asking how many birds Henry had bagged that day.

"And yet," Maximov continued, "this jewel in the crown seems unable to actually obtain contracts without the aid of friends like yourself, Mr Smith."
"What the hell does that mean?" Digby Smith growled.

"It means that during your time in the department for Overseas Aid and Development you put awarding contracts to Standard Hydro as a condition on awarding development contracts to at least seven countries, and in the course of delivering three of those contracts people – contractors, locals, and in the Sri Lanka disaster a school filled with fifty children – lost their lives."

"Terrible tragedy," Digby muttered again. "But nothing to do with me."

"Unless, of course, someone at Standard Electric was paying you to make their involvement a condition of the aid grants. Or blackmailing you. In which case those people – the fifty children that died when the dam burst in Sri Lanka and flooded their newly built school – would have died - indirectly, I'll grant - because of your greed or fear."

Digby spoke through gritted teeth: "I don't know what you're getting at, but I don't think I care for your tone, sir."

As though he hadn't even heard a word, Maximov looked around the table, all movement seemingly stilled, and smiled that shark-like smile. "I heard of a story," he said, "which took place not as far from here as you might think. A doctor," he gestured at Richard Stamford, "killed many many people. Not for sport."

"Bit off, old bean," John Warren said, and Sir Phillip shut him up with a glance.

"What happened?" Sara was wide eyed.

"A small hospital in a part of the world that I know well. A young doctor - idealistic. Hopeful. Ran the facility." As he spoke, his eyes moved around the table, checking he had an audience.

"Then the militia came, and demanded the doctor assist them in identifying every single patient of a certain type, separated the population, and put the identified patients into trucks."

"What happened?" Richard Stamford asked.

"The patients were never seen alive again," Maximov shrugged, as though he were discussing dry cleaning. "There were other patients to be considered, I suppose. Still: Seventy-five people were murdered that day." His eyes raked the table.

"And the doctor?" Sara asked? "What happened to him?"

"Oh the doctor survived," Maximov said. "And prospered. And it's hard to know why seventy-five innocent people died, but it was either for cowardice or greed, wouldn't you say?"

And at that moment, a sharp crack sounded from somewhere in the house, accompanied almost simultaneously by the sound of a woman – Mila, I think – shrieking, and then the lights went out and the house was plunged into darkness.

A sudden draft whipped around the room and from somewhere over by the French doors a deep, gruff voice said: "Hands up you bastards."

In the next instant, Sara screamed, Karen Stamford let out a cry of surprise, Digby Smith yelled “Don’t shoot”, Francine shrieked like someone was gutting her with a blunt knife, and Sir Phillip demanded to know what the hell was going on.

Then a shot rang out, and the screams got louder.

There was the sound of a scuffle, another shriek and a crash as the tablecloth was yanked and half the crockery and glassware on it fell to the floor.

And then, as though nothing untoward had occured, the lights came on and Eve Chapman stood in the doorway to the room.

“What on earth is happening here?” she demanded as everyone in the room looked left and right, desperately trying to make sense of what had just occurred.

At the top of the table Sir Phillip sat unmoved.

Digby Smith climbed out from under the table.

The French windows were wide open, the curtains billowing in the breeze coming through them, and the tablecloth was yanked to that side, most of the place settings on my side of the table now residing in the middle while what had been place settings on the far side of the table lay scattered and shattered on the floor.

Richard Stamford came rushing around the table to his wife, who sat rigidly, a look of blank shock on her face.

Digby sat down as though everything was normal, and held a hand-out to Francine, who was looking around in near hysteria.

Of Sara Simone there was no sign, until it became obvious that the scuffle, the shriek and the yank on the tablecloth had been Ms Simone attempting to prevent someone from pulling her from the room.

She’d succeeded; she was still with us, albeit she was lying dazed on the floor as Francine dropped to her knees murmuring something comforting.

And that was when Sara Simone started screaming.

“They’ve got my stone!” She screamed, her hand flying to where, only moments before, the diamond had rested.

"Those sonsabitches," Francine growled, and ran out of the French windows, shoving Digby – who moved to prevent her – so roughly that he staggered backwards and landed on his arse.

"You sonsabitches," Francine shrieked into the night, as Henry Warren bounded after her.

"Stop! They've got guns, Mrs Gerber," he shouted, returning moments later with a still furious but now somewhat tearful Francine on his arm.

"Oh my baby, my baby," she cried, dropping to her knees. "They coulda killed you."

"Mamma," Sara sobbed. "They got my diamond."

Francine shushed her, cradling the blonde head against her ample bosom and crooning while rocking back and forth for a few moments as the chaos settled to an absolutely stunned silence, at which point she looked up at the assembled and asked, "Well is anyone going to call the goddamned cops?"

CHAPTER FIFTEEN

The cops, as Francine put it, were called and duly arrived.

Everyone was searched. The room was searched. The grounds were searched – as well as they could be in the middle of the night – and not a trace of either the Gianelli Diamond or the thief was found.

Chapman confirmed that the powercut had been caused by a short in the fusebox which was downstairs by the kitchen.

I caught Pamela Warren's eye and waited for her to say 'I told you those fuse boxes were a disaster waiting to happen,' but she was clearly far too polite for that, so a small group of what some of my relatives might refer to as Local Busies (accompanied by Henry Warren, Caz and I) piled down to the narrow flagstoned corridor to inspect the fuse box and agree that the scorching and the small pile of half-evaporated plastic and wiring on the floor under the fuses suggested someone had rigged the system to short, which made it immediately obvious that – whoever the gunman in the doorway had been – he'd had inside help.

"Anyone been here who shouldn't have been?" One of the coppers asked, in tones that suggested he neither expected nor particularly wanted an answer.

In the end, they settled for slapping a load of Crime Scene tape over the fuse box, then locked and taped the doors to the dining room before, in the early hours of the morning, we were all sent to bed with instructions that nobody was to leave the house until statements had been taken next day.

Sara, by this stage had crossed the threshold from near-hysteria to full on last two reels in a silent movie, and was wailing, gnashing, twisting around in ways that I was sure would shred the lace of the dress she was in, and then finished by demanding whether anyone had, on their person, a cheeseburger.

Francine, who had absented herself for a moment to 'make some calls to L.A.' (the first one audibly being to an insurance company to report the theft and advise them to contact the local copshop) returned just as the plea for a cheeseburger was issued and looked around.

"She's clearly deranged," she said, "and I don't think her macrobiotic herbal remedies are gonna work tonight. Do any of you kind people have any really good Opioids?"

Richard Stamford said he had some sleeping shots in his bag that might help, before rushing upstairs to get them, the rest of us trailing along behind, with Henry and Digby supporting a loudly sobbing Sara.

She was taken to her bedroom and Richard Stamford administered a sedative, then the rest of the family and guests – still seemingly in a daze - drifted away until only Caz and I remained standing on the landing.

"Your place or mine?" Caz asked, adding "I've a very good Cognac in mine."

Which sort of made the decision for me.

George's Diary 28th June 1986

This morning, at breakfast, my father asked me to go over to Kennedy today. "There's some stuff he wants to buy for the fencing on Lady Anne's pasture," He said. "Over his budget so he needs me to check it and decide if it's money I want to spend."

I put down my slice of toast and tried not to blush. "Yes, sir," I said, though – unsure what, exactly, my father was asking me to do - I couldn't keep the question from my voice.

"I want you to take a look at the list and make a decision. So long as the total is under five hundred you're to say yes."

"And if over?"

"Then you say no to the excess and bring it back here for me to check," he said, a flare of irritation blazing and then being suppressed. "Use your common sense, George. Your mother says you have enough of it, so let me see how you use it."

I'd already decided that as Henry had a thing with numbers I'd been chosen specially to manage this financial task, but the last sentence sounded like he was offering me this task under sufferance.

I must have let my disappointment show, because my father's jaw set again.

"Problem?" he asked, and I shook my head.

"No sir, I answered, picking up my toast.

"Well off you go, then," he said. "You can eat breakfast when you get back."

Edward, of course, jumped from his seat. "Can I come too?" he asked hopefully, and I was opening my mouth to tell him no, he couldn't when my father lowered his newspaper once more and said "Edward. Sit down and finish your breakfast."

"But," Edward began to protest, and my father – his voice cold – told him to sit down.

I looked at my baby brother, his wide, enthusiastic smile shrunk immediately, and felt – for a moment – glad.

But as he sat and began playing with the cereal in front of him, his lower lip trembling like my mama's shoulders had the day before, I suddenly felt guilty. There weren't many people who wanted to spend time with me, so perhaps I should have been less eager to reject his company.

At that moment Henry, always a later riser than the rest of us, ambled into the dining room, cheerily wished us all a good morning and went to the sideboard to load up on bacon and eggs.

"I don't mind," I said to my father, and Edward's eyes – already filling with tears – perked up, found mine, and he smiled, putting his spoon down.

This time my father didn't move the newspaper.

"The boy doesn't move from this table until I tell him he may go," he said. "George, you have a task I have asked you to carry out. Why are you still here? And Edward-"

Edward turned his look back to the front and back pages of The Telegraph, a blush already crossing his face as Henry turned, went to sit at the table and – finally – sensed the atmosphere.

"What?" he mouthed at me, though he really meant 'what have you done this time?'

"Yes, papa," Edward – his voice wobbly – said to the newspaper.

There was a pause, then my father said "Finish your cereal and you can come with me to the village. I need to pick up something from Doctor Allen, and you can have an ice cream when we're done."

Edward's face lit up, his crown as preferred one back on his head.

I pulled a sour face at him, but he didn't even register it, so busy was he shovelling cornflakes into his mouth.

I glanced at Henry, who – the tension in the room seemingly broken – had commenced shovelling food into his mouth, and without saying a word I left the dining room and crossed the hallway.

Outside, it was already hot, the sky blue and cloudless and the sound of the crow scarer drifting from the distance where the rape seed was sown, the vast sea of yellow awaiting autumn's harvest.

Kennedy is our Estate manager, and he lives with his family in a cottage that's accessible via its own gateway. To get to it one would usually trek back down the drive at Dukes Halt, turn right outside the main gate and walk half an hour to the Estate cottage, but one can also – if one knows the way – cut through the woods that are to the right of the house. It's not necessarily a shorter route, but it is a less boring one. There are trees and birds and shade and as I didn't fancy being either bored to death or burned by the sun on the hike to the cottage I headed towards the woods and was soon wending my way through the dappled shade.

I don't know what's wrong with my mama, but the fact that my father is going to see Doctor Allen is worrying. Is there something wrong with him too? Might that explain his moods? Or is he collecting something for my mother? She seems so thin, I wonder if he's getting something that will help her gain weight?

I wonder if it's cancer. Freddie Newton at school had cancer. They said it was a rare one, and he was fine until one day he started to get giant bruises all over his body. I didn't see any bruises on my mama yesterday, but she did have a bruise on the side of her face at Christmas. She'd covered it with makeup, but one could see the shadow from the side of her left eye down to her cheekbone.

She said she'd fallen over – stumbled and lost her footing on the stairs – but I wonder. My father's never raised a hand to me, and he dotes on Edward. Even Henry – when he's being as insolent as he dares – is never threatened with physical violence. But could Papa have hit my mother?

Am I being melodramatic?

I was thinking these thoughts when I came into a clearing and – in the middle of it – there was another boy.

He was taller than I, his hair a sort of coppery colour, sparkling, like his chest, in the light filtering through the trees. His chest was sparkling because he was shirtless and sweating profusely and he was sweating profusely because he was chopping logs.

A pile of split wood, neatly arranged, was just beyond him on the other side of the clearing, and around his feet were the logs he had just cracked with the axe he was holding.

"Oh," he paused, his chest heaving, and I looked around me at the stacked logs, the pile of wood waiting to be cut, the muddy boots on his feet – despite it not having rained for weeks as long as I knew – and finally located something that had to be his t-shirt, slung over a branch on one of the trees by the pile of split wood.

"Who're you?" He asked, and I blushed as his words brought my gaze back to his green eyes and I saw an accusation in them.

"Me?" I straightened my back, did my best impersonation of my father and attempted to look down my nose at him, which wasn't particularly easy as he was at least six inches taller than I. "I'm George Warren. Who the hell are you?"

He blushed, his whole body – from waist to hairline – flushing lobster red, and gently put the axe down, rubbing his hands on the front of his jeans. "I'm sorry, sir. Your lordship."

He reached a hand forward. "I'm Simon. Simon Kennedy."

"I'm not your lordship," I said, unmoving as he stepped towards me, his hand still outstretched. "My father is Lord Newmont. I'm-" I stopped.

What, exactly, was I?

The second son. The spare in case Henry died, which – unless being not very bright became a fatal illness – was unlikely. The one my mother loved, because she so nearly lost me. The one my father, for some reason, seemed uncomfortable around, as though he had also realised I had little purpose in the family tree.

Simon Kennedy was still standing in front of me, his hand out, a slightly uncertain smile on his face, even as his eyes sparkled confidently.

And I put my hand out.

"I'm glad to meet you Simon," I said.

SATURDAY

CHAPTER SEVENTEEN

I was awakened the next morning by voices, the notebook slipping from my bed.

Beside me, the lamp still blazed.

I'd finally gone to bed having done my usual routine, so that the windows were open a crack, while a chair wedged the door closed.

I wasn't sure, at first, whether the voices I was hearing were real or whether a dream was still playing out in my subconscious. The words I was hearing made no sense, the sounds were quiet, with lots of soft 'j's and shushing sounds, but as I finally surfaced from sleep I realised they were drifting in through my open window, and they were a man and a woman speaking in a foreign tongue.

I dragged myself to the window, peeking out through the split where I hadn't fully closed the curtains the night before.

She was speaking, a long speech with a sing-song tone, and he chuckled occasionally.

Only when the woman clearly said the word "Restoran," which sounded too similar to restaurant to mean anything else, did I decide her voice belonged to Mila.

He said something to her, she chuckled, and then the tops of their heads appeared directly under my window.

From the angle, I couldn't see their faces, but I was shocked to see that the man with Mila – his bald head shining in the morning light – was Richard Stamford.

They walked a little way forward and then exchanged air kisses on each cheek before he said something to her, she answered, they both chuckled, they took a final drag from their cigarettes, and they parted.

I stood, still looking out at the day which appeared to have started bright and fresh, and then something off to my left caught my eye.

From the edge of the trees, a figure emerged.

Whoever it was halted momentarily, looked furtively around, and crossed to the house, vanishing from my view as the windowsill blocked them.

Something – the stealthy movements, the fact they'd waited til Stamford and Mila had left – piqued my interest, and I pulled up the lower sash window, wincing as it squeaked, and leant out looking to the left.

To the left of the ornamental fountain, Gaia Kennedy was furiously scrabbling through a flowerbed, pushing some evergreens to one side and another.

A knock came to my door. I glanced to it, then back. Gaia was still searching, but she was casting furtive glances over her shoulder now.

The knocking was repeated, louder this time, and I heard the handle rattle.

The chair I'd jammed the door with shifted but held.

Gaia shifted her approach, moved to the flowerbed on the opposite side of the fountain and searched again.

The knocking was now joined by Caz calling my name.

Rolling my eyes, I ran to the door, yanked the chair from its place and, as Caz stepped into the room asking what the hell I was doing, I said "Sssh. Take a look at this," and beckoned her to the window.

"What am I looking at?" She asked, peering out at an empty lawn, Gaia having clearly found whatever she was looking for and vanished back into the trees.

I told her.

"Wonder what she was looking for?" She mused. "And why are you naked?"

"Um-" I gestured at the rumpled bedding, "I was in bed."

"Well get dressed, or we'll miss breakfast."

"Breakfast?" I looked at her in bemusement. "Have you forgotten what happened here last night, or was it all a fever dream?"

“Darling, this is England. And more specifically the English ruling classes. Nothing stops mealtimes. It’s the only way these people know they’re still actually alive.” She paused, considered her last statement, added: “Though I suspect half of them expect there’ll be afternoon tea in heaven as well.”

“They’re assuming they’ll be going up there,” I answered, heading to the shower.

~

Some hours later, having breakfasted well in a hastily rearranged drawing room, Caz and I took Ellie out for another walk, passing the local constabulary, who had just arrived, their approach clearly being that here was no need to disturb the quality before breakfast.

I made sure we returned via the lawn.

The air was so still, the silence so total that the sound of a distant pop – Gaia practicing her aim, I assumed – drifted to me from the forest.

“I just want to see something,” I said as Caz rolled her eyes.

“Sweetie, whatever that child was looking for, she clearly found it. There’s no point digging around in the mulch at this stage. Far better to ask her directly.”

At which point Ellie barked, wagged her tail, and dived into the flowerbed to the left of the fountain.

I turned and presented Caz with a look intended to telegraph that even if she didn’t believe my hunches her dog did.

“What have you found there, girl?” I asked while gently pushing her snout out of the way and closing my hand around a huge, moist, soft mass.

I gagged, pulling back and waving my hand in the air.

“Christ, Danny,” Caz gagged, “I expect the dog to go for fox shit, but I thought you were smarter.”

“Fox?” I gagged. “Shit?”

“Hold still, for God’s sake,” Caz instructed, as though I were a truculent child and she a district nurse with the only remaining Polio vaccine for miles. From the bag slung over her shoulder she extracted a handful of doggie poo bags, offered them to my left hand, dived back into the bag, extracted a handful of wet wipes, swapped them for the poobags, and then produced an industrial sized bottle of Chanel number 5.

I was momentarily stunned. "I didn't know they did that in litre bottles," I commented, dropping the vulpine matter into the undergrowth while telling Caz that this was another reason I hated Nature, the Countryside, and Dukes Halt specifically, and slathering the slick wipes all over my hand.

"They don't," she said spraying my hand liberally with the scent before spraying it in an arc about my person as though I might have been possessed by the scent of fox shit.

"I don't know if Chapman would approve of you picking the flowers." I turned, and Karen Stamford, a puzzled smile in place, was crossing the lawn towards us her body huddled in a puffa jacket that went from neck to ankle and made it look like she was walking around in a repurposed duvet. "I get the feeling she views them – like everything here – as being her personal property." Her hands were jammed into the pockets of the coat as though she were freezing.

"Well she's welcome to this property," Caz muttered as she dropped the perfume back into her bag and held an empty poobag out for me to deposit the wet wipes in to.

Karen, closer now, paused, her nostrils flaring and looked from Caz to me to the fox poo filled baggies.

Ellie, barking happily and wagging her tail, came to heel as though saying 'see mistress, I find fox poo. Danny destroy it.'

Then something caught my eye.

"Hang on," I said, diving once more into the undergrowth. "What's this?"

"Badger poo?" Caz asked, every syllable dripping fear at what sort of excrement I was about to draw from the undergrowth.

"Not unless badgers excrete small bores," I said, holding up the gun I'd just found.

~

Caz and I marched through the front door of Dukes Halt,

Ellie straining triumphantly at her leash, Karen Stamford shuffling like a Geisha in her coat designed for an arctic winter, as I held the small gun in my hand.

"We've just found this outside," I announced to the startled constable, who recoiled - though whether from the lingering smell of fox shit, the sight of the gun or the grimy hand I presented to him was unclear.

"What is it?" He asked suspiciously, catching himself before I could respond and rephrasing it as "I mean I know it's a gun, but where'd you find it, and why'd you move it? That's tampering with evidence, that is."

"Evidence you failed to find last night," I snapped back as an obviously senior copper in an ill-fitting suit, the shoulders liberally dusted with dandruff, appeared from the direction of the drawing room.

"What's going on?" He demanded as Karen Stamford excused herself and, hands still jammed in the pockets of her duvet-coat, crossed the hallway and out of sight.

The officer, when I told him what I'd found, stiffened. "You shouldn't have moved it. That's tampering with evidence, that is."

"Yes," I nodded at the uniform, "we'd already ascertained that with your colleague. But I didn't want it to fall into the wrong hands, so I brought it to you."

I knew how lame my response sounded, but I was genuinely concerned that if Gaia Kennedy had been looking for the gun she might yet come back and remove it.

"Is it the one from the robbery?" The uniform asked, earning – for his troubles – a withering glance from the senior officer, who introduced himself as Inspector Dane.

"So where exactly did you find this?"

"I can take you there," I said, gesturing back where Caz, Karen Ellie and I had just entered. "C'mon then," he said, turning to the constable and instructing him to fetch forensics to photo the scene and see what they could find "That this gentleman hasn't already destroyed."

I winced as he turned back to me. "While we're on the topic

of the robbery last night, did you see the thief? Any ideas what they looked like?"

"Not really," I said, frowning. "It was dark, and all I could see was the door frame, with someone standing in it.

"Male or female?"

"Male. I think. Although," I paused.

"Go on."

I was wondering. Gaia Kennedy had a deep voice. Could she have deepened it and pulled off a jewel robbery?

And that was when we heard the first gunshot.

It came from behind us, a loud bang that sounded more like a large pistol than a shotgun, matched a second later by a rat-tat-tat that could only have come from an automatic weapon, and responded to by a couple more loud bangs that sounded like whoever had the large pistol was trying to cut down the shooter of the automatic weapon.

"What the hell?" Dane snapped, turning towards the front door as Henry and Pamela charged out of the drawing room.

"What on earth is going on?" Pamela demanded.

Behind her Sir Phillip came shakily from the room, leaning on Henry's arm.

"What's going on?" Francine – a note of hysteria in her voice - came from somewhere in the back of the house, John Warren beside her as Sara Simone and Richard Stamford came charging down the stairs.

"Are we under attack?" Karen Stamford, coming from somewhere at the back of the house asked, and Francine, in her clearest Bronx drawl announced to everyone that it was "Probably terrorists. The Goddamn Arabs haven't forgiven my daughter for starring in that remake of 'Not without my daughter.'"

I had to agree that – if Al Qaida had hated Sara's work on that film half as much as I had, then it would be the first time I had anything in common with them. But I somehow doubted that they'd display their dislike of the movie by staging an all-out armed assault on Dukes Halt just to get their point across.

The banging continued as the assembled huddled together in the middle of the hall and then did what people always do when faced with the sounds of violence and conflict.

The stupid thing.

We moved towards it.

"What the hell are you doing?" Dane demanded as we all rushed towards the front door. "Get back into the centre of the house and take cover."

Henry Warren reached inside his jacket and withdrew a small gun – not much bigger than the one I'd discovered and which Dane was still holding in a Ziploc bag – and waved at everyone else to do as Dane advised.

I looked at Caz, who raised an eyebrow at me.

The noise coming from outside suggested that a dozen more armed assailants had joined the gang. Bangs, accompanied by the whistles of ricochets, echoed around the hallway as everyone ignored the instructions to move away from the fracas and – in unison - crawled slowly back to the front door, which was standing open.

From here the smell of gunpowder drifted in on the wind, and it took a moment for the scene outside the house to register on most people.

The light was wrong, the daylight seemingly augmented by flashes and sparks, and the air itself was smoky and heavy.

"Fireworks," Henry snarled, stepping outside the front door as the last of the fireworks exploded, a roman candle whizzing across the lawn and towards the trees. "Bloody fireworks."

"Who the hell set those off?" Sir Phillip demanded as the rest of us looked at each other in stunned silence.

And then, from behind us, somewhere deep in the house, another loud bang sounded.

I looked around the assembled.

"Where's Maximov?" I asked, and everyone looked at each other in confusion.

"Where'd that shot come from?" Karen asked.

"Drawing room," Pamela Warren responded, the

assembled moving, once more, towards the sound of a gunshot.

The drawing room was empty. Henry and John stopped dead in the doorway, the rest of us colliding with each other, peering over their shoulders until Inspector Dane forced his way through the crowd and into the space.

Dane's entry seemed to break whatever spell had frozen the rest of us so that we all followed him into the long, elegantly furnished room, some people checking behind sofas and swishing curtains to one side as though whoever had fired the last shot was hiding behind the furniture, but it was quickly obvious that there was nobody in the room who hadn't entered with the rest of us.

And then, almost as one, all eyes moved to the door to the dining room, still locked and with the 'Police. Do not cross' stickers in place.

Henry Warren pounded his fist on the door, twisted the handle as though to test it was still locked.

"Maximov!" He shouted, then listened at the door.

"There's someone in there," he said, and turned to Dane. "Do you have the key?" He demanded, and Dane reddened.

An idea occurred to me.

I ran from the drawing room, across the hall, out the front door, along the front of Dukes Halt and rounded the corner, heading for the steps up to the Dining room.

And as I rounded the corner I could already see that one of the doors was open, swinging lazily in a breeze that was making the trees around shush and sigh.

I pelted across the gravel, already hearing signs of a struggle coming from within the room, and – again, without really stopping to think whether barrelling into a room from which a gunshot has just been heard – bolted through the open door.

And stopped dead.

From the other side of the door, Dane and Henry continued to hammer.

The doors of the sideboard under the portrait were yanked open, piles of napkins and table cloths torn from the cupboard and scattered all over the floor. Several of the chairs were toppled on their sides, the seat cushions discarded haphazardly. The ornamental fireguard was lying on the same Persian carpet where, a few feet away, Maximov was sprawled on his front.

The back of his head had a deep dark hole in it, and from it glistening blood was spreading down over his collar and shoulder to pool around his head.

Standing over him was a blonde woman, holding a revolver.

"Arianna."

She froze, the gun still in her hand, and turned to face me.

"I can't find it," she said, panic – mixed with despair - clear in her voice. "I've looked everywhere and I can't find it."

I stepped forward, my hands raised and palms open to show her I had no weapon and was no threat. "Put the gun down. Please."

"Gun?" As though noticing it for the first time, she looked at the pistol and relaxed her hands, dropping it.

As it fell, I realised I'd seen it before, not far from this house.

"You have to help me find it," she said.

"Find what?" I asked as the pounding on the opposite side of the door became a solid thud.

"The book. His black book. Without it I'll never find Klara. Oh God Danny," she sat back, noticing for the first time that in her panic to search the corpse she had gotten his blood on her hands.

"He must have hidden it. He must have realised that you'd comc to find him and hidden it."

I didn't have the time or the energy, right then, to tell Arianna that Maximov and I being in the same space had been nothing but cruel coincidence and that it was unlikely the man had even registered my existence.

She stared at her bloodsoaked hands, her whole body slumping as though every last drop of hope was draining away, and then tore her eyes away from the gore to look straight at me.

"Oh God, Danny. What have you done?"

And then, with an ear-splitting crack and a splintering of wood, the door burst open and Inspector Dane and Henry Warren, followed swiftly by what seemed like the entire population of Dukes Halt, burst into the room.

CHAPTER EIGHTEEN

Dane was furious.

"Give me a reason," he demanded, "why I shouldn't lock you up with your crazy girlfriend?"

"Firstly," I said, "cos she's not crazy. Then cos she's not my girlfriend. And lastly cos I didn't murder anyone. And I don't think she did either."

"Didn't murder anyone?" He looked across the interview room at the uniform who was doing a studied impersonation of one of the denizens of Madame Tussauds, and, as though despairing of receiving a word of sense from anyone in the place, rolled his eyes to heaven.

"She was standing over the body. Her fingerprints are all over the gun. The place was ransacked. The door was locked. And I repeat: the only people in the room were your girlfriend, a Russian and yourself.

"And as the Russian had a sizeable hole in the back of his head and you're insistent you had nothing to do with putting it there I think it's fair to say – and I have to be honest here: I'm only an 'umble copper your lordship," he tugged his forelock in mock deference. "But even I can see that if you didn't shoot him, it seems fairly clean cut that the crazy blonde did. What I want to know is: What was your part in the whole thing?"

I sighed. "Right. First off, again: Not crazy. Arianna was close to hysterical. She was tearing that room apart looking for something that the dead man never left off his person."

"Shame she didn't check he had it before she put a round through his skull," Dane muttered. "What the hell was she doing there anyway? And why him?"

"She knew him," I said, and he tilted his head to the side,

no longer playing the permannoyed copper, his demeanour instantly serious.

"How?"

I paused, uncertain whether what I had just said was likely to help or hinder Arianna's case. Unsure how much more would be safe to say.

"Arianna had history with Maximov," I admitted. "Years ago. He was a trafficker, a pimp. He forcibly separated her sister and her, and she was convinced he knew where her sister was. But he'd vanished for years until she stumbled across him in London, only to lose his trail again. Which is when she asked me to try to find him."

"So you trailed him to Dukes Halt," Dane interrupted, and I held a hand up.

"Do you want me to tell you the story, or would you rather tell me?"

His lips pursed angrily. "Go on."

"I was invited to Dukes Halt as a guest of the family. I had no idea that Maximov would be there. When he arrived, I was shocked by the coincidence."

"Yeah," Dane muttered disbelievingly. "Coincidence. So how did Mrs Fisher end up in Dukes Halt? You call her?"

I shook my head. "I've no idea how she found him. But she's a smart woman. I suppose she figured it out somehow. You'll have to ask her."

"Oh we will," he said. "As soon as she starts talking."

"Starts talking?"

"She hasn't said a word since we arrested her. No explanation, no denial. Nothing."

"Her whole life has been based on finding Maximov, on making him tell her where her sister is. And then today she finds him dead, and the black book he keeps all his secrets in is nowhere to be seen. The only thing that kept her alive for years is gone. Her her chance to track down her sister is gone."

"Because she put a bullet in his brain," Dane said again, lifting a paper cup from the desk and putting it to his lips.

"Nope," I shook my head. "It makes no sense: Arianna

wanted her sister."

"What? She didn't want revenge on the bastard who split them up?" Dane smirked in disbelief.

He had a point.

I remembered her equivocation in The Marq.

"Anyone would want revenge on that bastard," I said. "But she's spent years tracking him down. You're suggesting she managed to locate a gun, tracked him down, made her way to Dukes Halt, then found him in the one room in the house he shouldn't have been, confronted him and shot him? That's your theory?"

Dane raised an eyebrow, lifted the cup, sipped it again.

"Oh," I added, "and that cup's been empty for the past ten minutes, so if you're going to keep the NYPD Blue act going could you at least ask Dixon of Dock Green over there to pop out to Starbucks and get you another. I'll have a pumpkin spice latte while he's at it."

"Sharp, aren't you?" Dane crushed the cup in his fist, hurled it into the corner of the room. "Okay, the facts aren't knitting into an easy quilt. So what do you think happened?"

"I don't know," I admitted, "but I'm more interested, now, in the gaps between what I do and don't know."

"So talk," he said.

"First: We know that Arianna somehow or other made enough connections on her own to lead her to Dukes Halt. Then she sees an open door.

"At the moment she finds the open door, there's a huge commotion out front. Everyone's distracted. So she enters through that door."

"Could be she started the commotion," Dane mused. "Figured the distraction would give her time to get in kill him and get out."

"Except," I reminded him, "Maximov shouldn't have been in that room. Your coppers supposedly sealed it the night before. So how did he get in there? And why was he there in the first place?"

I paused. Dane regarded me in silence. "Look," I carried

on, "Arianna had no way of knowing when she stepped into the dining room that the doors leading from it to the house were locked. That the only way in or out of the room was by the door she'd just used. And there was no way she could have expected Maximov to be in that room."

"Unless she'd watched him enter by the same door she did."

He had me there.

"But why would he go in there?" I asked myself aloud. "And what happened to his killer?"

"Well we'll never know the answer to the first question," Dane – tiring of my confusion almost as much as I was – answered, "but the answer to the second question is clear: She's sitting in my cells downstairs."

"I know she didn't kill him," I said as much to myself as to the Inspector. "We were – all of us – standing in the front hall when we heard the shot. Except we can't have been. Someone else had to have been in that room."

"Let's say you're right," Dane said. "Some mysterious X follows Maximov into the dining room for some secret assignation away from prying eyes. I'll rent that story for now. It makes as much sense as any I've heard lately. This mysterious X follows him into the room, shoots him, we all hear the bang and go running to the door.

"Within seconds you're back out across the hall out of the house and around the corner to enter through the dining room window and there is your lady friend with – as we've said before – a smoking pistol and a deceased Russian. Let me ask you a question: How come the woman in the cells downstairs has yet to tell me who she saw follow Maximov into that room? How come she's yet to say who she saw coming out through the French doors? She'd have to have seen them; I mean, she was in the room holding the gun and tearing the place apart for this mythical black book within seconds. Am I wrong?"

I shook my head. There was something I was missing.

"Well if I'm not wrong," Dane finished, though his tone

was less triumphant than I might have expected, "then unless the person who murdered Sergei Maximov was capable of teleportation there's only one possible explanation: much as you don't like it, and much as I dislike the degree of chance and uncertainty that my theory has, Arianna Fisher shot and killed him."

And then it came to me.

CHAPTER NINETEEN

"Secret tunnels?" Dane was still looking at me as if I'd said 'Treasure map,' but we were, regardless of what he thought about me, in a police car heading back to Dukes Halt.

"I need to interview the rest of them anyways," he'd said when I'd blurted out the two words, "and the bigwigs want them to be given the courtesy of having statements taken at the house rather than dragging them all down to the station. But seriously – secret tunnels?"

"Maybe passages is a better word," I said, though the look he gave me suggested he found it no less Boys Own Adventure than the previous phrase. "They've got a priest's hole," I offered lamely, the words drying on my lips as Dane turned a look of warning on me.

"Listen, I'm willing to buy that you didn't have a hand in killing the Russian. I'm still not entirely convinced you didn't tell the killer where she could find him, mind. Which would put you in the frame – at least – for accessory. But if you make me look like a tit here, I will make sure you're charged with everything on the books."

~

We arrived back at Dukes Halt shortly after a burst of static on Dane's radio had told me that there was a code 12 at Dukes Halt and officers had been dispatched.

I looked at Dane, who kept his eyes studiously fixed on the road ahead.

"Are you going to tell me what a code 12 is?" I asked, and his answer caused my heart to sink.

"Minor missing," he said flatly. "Everything I needed right now."

So Henry and Pamela had finally decided that bringing the

rozzers in on the fact their teenage daughter hadn't been seen since yesterday afternoon wasn't such a bad idea after all.

The Major himself was at the door as we pulled up.

Dane told him that specialist officers were en route, and then gestured at me before explaining that I had a theory on how the murderer got in and out of the room without being seen.

"Secret passages?" Henry Warren looked at me as though I'd just suggested his house contained the Holy Grail.

"Or tunnels," I added, lamely. "Lottie showed me," I said, dashing for the stairs. "Up here."

The two men followed me, both huffing as we sprinted up the stairs along the landing and then on up more stairs until we reached the long gallery.

I charged the length of the long gallery and lead them through to the sitting room at the end. "She said there was a priest's hole here," I said. "That the house was riddled with secret passages."

I pushed the sofa aside, pressed where Lottie had pressed.

And nothing happened.

I looked at them. Henry looked concerned, as though I were a friend who had suddenly become delusional. Dane looked angry that he hadn't charged me with conspiracy when he had the chance, but marginally comforted by the fact that he could always do so at a later date.

I padded the wall again, and the panel clicked, slid, and the space was exposed.

"There," I waved triumphantly. "There's the priest's hole."

"Oh." Henry Warren looked at the space.

Looked at Dane.

Looked at me.

Looked back at the space.

"Danny, that's where we keep – or used to keep – the vacuum cleaners. It's a storage space. Lottie- well, she likes to imagine things. But this house is not riddled with secret passages."

Dane coughed. "So: No secret panels means no way for

Maximov to have gotten into that room – or for any third party to have left it – other than via the door Mrs Fisher went in through. That leaves us back where we were: either she saw him go in and followed him, or she would have had to have passed the killer as she was going into the room herself.

"And as she hasn't mentioned seeing a single soul exiting the room, it would appear that we have the killer in custody."

"It's too neat," I said as Henry pushed the cupboard door closed and straightened.

"Neat?" Dane chuckled. "If you'll excuse my levity sir, I've a foreign businessman with a bullet hole in the back of his head, a completely mute murderess, a houseful of dignitaries; I still have a missing diamond that the insurance report that hit my desk this morning values at about twenty million quid, and, apart from Mrs Gerber's description of a tall muscular figure in black last seen fleeing into the woods, no sign of the thief, the diamond or their escape method. And now I have a missing child.

"I should like to know what you consider neat."

"She didn't kill him," I shook my head for emphasis. "No way. I can't stress this enough: She wanted him to suffer, but she wanted that black book first. She wanted her sister."

"Black book?" Henry's tone was suddenly sharp. I explained, briefly, the situation with regard to Arianna.

"But this woman hadn't seen the victim in years," Dane said, and I nodded tightly.

"Well if Mr Maximov was the sort of person you describe, that black book would have been the size of an encyclopaedia by now, surely?"

"Unless it wasn't a book any longer," Henry mused, adding in response to our puzzled looks "he had a mobile phone. Black cover. Looked like a notebook. I saw him with it several times. I'll have his room searched, see if it's there."

"I'd rather my people did that," Dane said flatly, and Henry – looking for a moment as though he might be about to argue – shrugged, then said "Inspector, perhaps you and I could talk in private?"

Dane raised an eyebrow. "Well I need to take statements, sir. Where would be a good place to do that?"

"My father's study," Henry said. "He's already vacated the room. It's yours as long as you need it."

Dane nodded. "I'll start with you, if you like, sir. Then do the rest of the family. Mr Smith. Miss Simone. Her mother. Who else is here?"

"There's the Stamfords," Henry answered. "Dr Richard and his wife. Mr Bird and his friend Lady Caroline. Their driver Carter."

Ali would love that description.

"And then there's Chapman. And Mila, the cook," Henry finished.

"That it?" Dane asked, and Henry nodded.

"The rest of the house staff are locals who don't normally start til mid-morning. None of them – so far as we know – had arrived by the time the," he coughed discretely, "event occurred."

"Fine," Dane turned. "I'll have my sergeant take notes. If you could ask someone to gather the people you've mentioned." He crossed to the doorway and turned. "Oh, and Mr Bird: don't go anywhere. We will talk again."

~

I went looking for Caz and found Pamela Warren in a small room behind the main stairway.

The walls were papered in dusty pink, another large ornately framed portrait of Lady Marion Warren hanging over an empty fireplace, the room feeling cold and abandoned.

Pamela was sitting at a small bureau opposite the door tapping furiously at a laptop.

"Sorry," I apologised, and her head snapped up in alarm. "I was looking for Caz," I said, stepping into the room and adding, as the fact that she'd been crying registered on me, "are you okay?"

Another millisecond passed, during which she reset herself, and I wondered whether the Warrens took classes in this fitting of bland placid masks over any and all emotions.

"Caz?" she asked, notably failing to answer my question. "She's in the woods. Looking for any signs of Lottie."

"Has anyone checked the local train station?" I asked. "I mean, if she's run away she might have gone to London."

Pamela rubbed the back of her neck. Regarded me coolly a moment longer, then seemed to deflate.

"First thing I did. Used some contacts to get the CCTV downloaded, and there was no sight of her at all."

"So if she left Dukes Halt where could she have gone?"

"Anywhere she went would have involved walking along the main road into the town and we've asked everyone, There were no sightings of her yesterday."

"Which means she might still be on the estate."

"Somewhere in the woods," Pamela replied, nodding miserably.

"Can I ask a question?" I asked, and then went ahead and asked it anyway: What did you think about her request to attend the local school?"

"Me?" she shrugged. "I don't really have a say any more. I left my daughter here. Her upbringing is no longer something I have much input to."

"You're still her mother," I said.

"All I've ever wanted was for Lottie to be happy."

"The why did you leave?" I pressed, and she stiffened momentarily.

"Living in Dukes Halt. Living with Sir Phillip and with Eve Chapman. Well," she paused, considering her words, "it was difficult at the best of times. I wanted to move, get our own place, but Henry wouldn't hear of it. I loved him dearly but he seems to be afraid to leave his father. And then my," she took a deep breath, crossed from the window to a large powder pink chesterfield sofa against one wall and sat down, perching on the edge and crossing her legs demurely. "My brother died suddenly. He was on a trip to China. I was asked to step in and take over the family business.

"It would require a lot of travel. Lottie was a toddler, she couldn't come with me. And besides, it wouldn't be safe to bring her to some of the places I'd be going to. So it was decided – I mean I decided – that a move away from the family, just for a short time, would best allow me to focus on what I needed to do. Only the short time became longer, and, while I was away, Lottie grew into a young woman. And now I'm not really anything to her."

"I don't think that's true," I said quietly.

"The family business you went into: Caz thinks you're a school-teacher."

Now Pamela's eyes tightened, the moment vanishing and a smile being slowly rolled out for my benefit. But the eyes remained cautious, suspicious. "Not quite," she said, and returned to silent mode.

"I saw you yesterday," I said. "When Lottie and Maximov were going for a walk."

This, at least, elicited a sigh.

"That man," she said, brushing invisible lint from her skirt. "That *awful* man."

"Who you brought here as your date," I said, and she laughed bitterly.

"Yes. Not the first boyfriend I've brought to Dukes Halt. Where my husband and my father-in-law are so accepting of them and me. And where my daughter is treated like a piece of furniture to be ordered around."

"You're not a games mistress, are you?" I asked, and she looked up from the inch of skirt she'd been studiously observing.

"And Maximov wasn't just a date, was he?" I added.

The spell was broken almost immediately. "I'm afraid I don't know what you mean," she said, a slight catch in her breath. "But if you'll excuse me," she gestured back at the laptop, "I really need to get on with contacting all the people I can think of, in case Lottie's staying with them."

She stood, crossing to the desk and opening the lid. "I have to find her. She's the only good thing that's ever come out of this place, you see."

CHAPTER TWENTY

I bumped into Eve Chapman after Pamela had so clearly given me the bum's rush and asked her the way to the Estate Manager's cottage.

"Why do you need to go there?" She'd asked, suspicion coming from her in waves.

"Caz – Lady Caroline, that is – has gone looking for Lottie. I thought she might start there since it seems to be the logical place for someone to run away to. I mean, it's got a roof and a kitchen I suppose, and you know what teenagers are."

"Well if you'll forgive me saying so, there's far too much toleration shown to teenagers these days. In my day you kept your mouth shut and your eyes down until you were married."

"You're Mrs Champman, aren't you?" I asked. "Is there a Mr Chapman?"

Her lips pursed so tightly they went white. "He died. Car accident. I moved here and I've spent my life time ensuring that this family is safe from scandal, that their home works efficiently and comfortably. And not once have I ever thrown it over on a whim.

"Girls these days: Expelled from schools. Trouble at every step. Arguing. Mobile phones. Computers. Boys, no doubt."

I wanted to stop her before she got on to mentioning that votes for women was the start of all the trouble, but I also wanted to see where this would go.

"What scandal?" I asked, as she stopped for a shallow breath.

She squinted at me, and her lips tightened even further.

"You mentioned that you've spent your working life making sure the family is safe from scandal."

I was remembering, now, Maximov speaking to a woman

two nights ago. A woman I had thought was Caz. But what if the woman had been Chapman? That sort of made more sense. Maximov was a collector of secrets, of scandals, and I already knew that something scandalous and secretive had driven George Warren from the house over thirty years ago.

"The world is full of evil," Chapman said, her composure restored. "People who are only too willing to believe the worst of good people."

What was it Maximov had said? Something about how scandal can be more effective than proof? Then he'd said something about a son. But which son? George? Edward? And then I was reminded of something Lottie had said to me on the first day: How her grandfather had murdered her grandmother.

And now Maximov, a man who might well have been collecting secrets and scandals about the Warrens, and who had clearly been letting a woman – Chapman, I was convinced – know that he had something on the family – was dead, and Lottie was missing.

"And that evil must be defended against."

"Expelled?"

"If necessary," she said quietly.

"Do you mind if I ask where you were this morning when Mr Maximov was killed?"

I figured there was no harm in asking it flat out; any attempt to beat around the bush with Chapman would doubtless have been met with the disdain it deserved.

Her lips curled at the edges. "Do you suspect me of murdering him?"

"I was just wondering why the noise of the fireworks going off didn't bring you running to the main hall like it did everyone else?"

"Ah, but it didn't bring everyone running," she said, pressing the smirk from her lips, but not quite wiping it from her tone. "And I was upstairs. There'd been a complaint about the way some of the rooms were cleaned yesterday and I wanted to oversee the work this morning. I didn't need to come charging downstairs to the entrance hall because I had a perfect view of the display from the bedroom windows upstairs."

I wasn't sure I loved the idea of Chapman poking around my room while I was absent.

But she did have a point: Not everyone had been in the hallway when Maximov was murdered. Chapman had been missing. Lottie. Who else?

I put the question to one side as a realisation struck me: The smartly dressed, proper-to-a-fault woman in front of me was lying: Henry Warren had told Dane and I that the servants and chamber maids were locals who hadn't arrived by the time the fireworks went off. So Chapman couldn't have been overseeing them.

"Surely you had more pressing things to do than overseeing teenage girls making beds," I asked, unable to avoid the cheap jibe.

Chapman bristled. "I was up before six a.m. As I am every morning. I prepared Sir Phillip's diary for the day. Typed up some letters he wanted to send. When the post arrived, I opened and arranged the correspondence. Household bills I manage directly; personal correspondence I organise for Sir Phillip."

"Personal correspondence like letters from his sons?"

The eyebrow went up. "Sir Phillip – as you well know – has only one son."

"But he did have three, at one point, didn't he?"

Chapman was silent now and almost completely still, a slow blink the only indication that she'd heard – but chosen not to respond to – my question.

"And now," I said, wondering just what secrets this woman had kept, what scandals she had hidden, and what she might do to protect a family – and a man – that I suspected she held more than a professional regard for, "there's just Henry. And Sir Phillip. And you."

"And Carlotta," she said, drawing herself to her full height and looking down her nose at me.

"Who seems to have gone missing."

"Ah yes," Chapman smiled, the curved lips seeming superimposed on a face of cold fury. "You mentioned something about looking for her. Let me tell you how to find the estate keeper's cottage."

And so, following Chapman's instructions, I'd made my way down the drive, along the road, staying as close as possible to the high redbrick wall that surrounded the estate as the sound of someone far beyond the Warren estate shooting a shotgun at something carried on the frosty air.

I pulled my phone from my pocket and dialled Nick, hoping that I would find the words to tell him what had happened, and praying that he would understand why I'd kept Arianna's secrets.

The phone rang. Rang. Rang twice more, then went to voicemail.

"Hi," his voice – the same trusting smile he always had almost audible in his tones – came down the line. "Nick here. Sorry I'm unavailable, but please leave a message after the beep so I don't spend the rest of the day wondering who it was who called and didn't speak."

Then there was a beep.

And I hung up.

What else could I do? Say "Hi Nick. Your wife – y'know, the fake wife – well, she's been arrested for murder. And I sort of knew that she was hunting the man she's accused of shooting dead, but I kept it from you. Still: I'm sure it'll all work out in the end. Gimme a call when you get this."

I put the phone in my pocket, and sighed deeply, the foggy air seeping into my bones.

This was not good. Not good at all.

After half an hour, I turned in to another gateway, along a narrower drive than the one that lead up to Dukes Halt, this one surrounded on both sides by dense forest.

The ground underfoot was unpaved, mulchy, and after another ten minutes or so of walking, I realised that the only sound I could hear was my own breathing, the squelching of my own footsteps, the slow death-rattle clacking of branches filled with already dried leaves as the wind passed almost tenderly amongst them.

It was another couple of minutes later that I discovered the smart new-build on my left, passed beyond a huge farm gate and onto a pebbled driveway where a large 4X4 hulked silently.

I walked up to the front door and pressed the doorbell.

A moment passed, then Beth Kennedy, a striped butcher's apron over her jeans and sweatshirt, opened it.

"Forgot your keys again?" she asked, the smile on her face dying as she realised I wasn't who she'd expected me to be.

"Oh," she stopped, half closing the door so as to prevent me looking past her and into the house. "Hello. What can I do for you?"

"Hi." I smiled, decided not to offer my hand just yet. "We haven't formally met yet, but I'm staying at the Halt," I gestured vaguely behind me, realising as I did so that I was no longer really sure where I was in location to the house, that the walk and the forest had disorientated me completely.

"Yes," she nodded, her body language becoming impassive. "I remember you from yesterday."

"I'm Danny," I said, offering my hand. "Danny Bird. I'm," I paused. What was I, really? "A friend of a friend of the family, I suppose," I finished lamely.

"That's nice." She nodded again, made it clear that she wished I'd state my business and be gone.

"Look," I shrugged, "I'm officially here to see if you've seen Caz – Lady Caroline de Montfort. She's out looking for Lottie Warren. But there's something else I wanted to talk to your daughter – to Gaia – about."

That triggered a reaction. She shrunk back behind the door, pushing it even further closed, jamming herself into the sliver of space that remained, as though hugging the wood and hoping the doorframe would support her. "Gaia's out," she said. "She's with your friend. Said she'd help her look for Lottie. Gaia was so upset when Lady Caroline told us what had happened."

"Were she and Lottie friends?" I asked, and Beth Kennedy shrugged.

"Not so's you'd notice. I mean they don't really mix in the same circles if you know what I mean."

I pondered what sort of circles two teenage girls stuck in the middle of nowhere with families in crises for different reasons might mix in but chose not to voice my thoughts aloud. "Look," I stepped forward as she made to close the door, "maybe you could help me. It's a simple question really."

She paused. "I don't know that I could," she said, smiling apologetically and jerking her head behind her. "I've baking on. Need to keep an eye on it."

"It's about the gun," I said, and she froze, as though the whole world had hit pause. Only the rattling of the trees behind me told me that it hadn't.

"Gun?"

"The one I saw Gaia practicing with yesterday. Family heirloom, I understand."

Beth frowned, shook her head, though I noticed her grip on the door had relaxed, and it had opened a little further, allowing me – as she leaned against the door frame – to see a sliver of a clean, magnolia painted hallway.

"I don't know anything about a gun," she said, her eyes looking straight into mine.

"Really?" I stepped forward, lowering my voice. "Only Gaia told me that because her father was a terrible shot she'd learned to shoot the thing from you."

She slumped now. "What do you want?" she whispered fearfully.

"Truly," I answered, "and genuinely to talk. That's all. Just to ask some questions."

Beth Kennedy sighed, the fight seeming to flee from her, as her eyes scanned the space beyond me to make sure I was alone, and then she stepped to one side, flung the door wide open, and gestured that I should enter the house.

“Well, you better make it quick,” she said, “I’ve cakes to make.”

CHAPTER TWENTY-ONE

The hallway was long and brightly lit. To the left was a door that I assumed led to the living room. Beyond that was a flight of stairs that lead up to the first floor. To my right, just inside the door, was another doorway – a downstairs loo, I supposed – and then a long expanse of wall on which were a selection of small, framed pencil sketches. Trees. A very young Gaia. A younger looking Beth holding a baby. A series of studies for eyes and hands.

"My husband," Beth Kennedy said when she saw me looking at them. "My *late* husband. He loved to draw."

For a moment I was reminded of the Long Gallery at Dukes Halt, the majority of the pictures feeling impersonal, cold, bought or inherited and thus of little personal value to the current inhabitants.

Except for the tiny selection of photographs and toys at the end.

"Go through to the kitchen," Beth ushered me forward, wiping her hands on her apron.

The kitchen took up the whole back of the house, the L-shape housing a dining space with a long dining table which was covered with cardboard boxes into which, it seemed, Beth had already started packing the contents of a large Welsh Dresser which stood against the wall.

In the kitchen space proper stood a gargantuan table on which was a selection of bowls and a huge food mixer, the space filled with the scent of cinnamon and spice.

"Christmas cakes," she explained. "I normally make them later than this," she gestured at a seat and I pulled it out and sat at the table.

"But I won't have much of a kitchen after next week. And

they'll keep til Christmas. God knows, there's enough booze in them to keep them til New Year. She began sieving flour into a vast ceramic bowl."

"And where will you be after next week?" I asked.

"I have a flat in the village. But if I can't find work then I might have to move in with my suster in London," she said. "D'you want a cuppa?"

I shook my head no, thanking her for the offer anyway, and she began sifting flour into a large basin.

"You heard about the robbery last night?" I asked, and she nodded.

"Why on earth anyone would wear millions of quids worth of jewellery to eat dinner in that drafty old pile is beyond me," she said.

"And I suppose you've heard about what happened today?"

She stopped what she was doing and nodded. "I don't want to sound cold, but I'm being evicted from this place by that lot," she jerked her head in what I assumed was the direction of Dukes Halt. "So I'm trying to care less about what happens to them and focus on what happens to Gaia and me."

I said nothing.

Sieving done, Beth Kennedy added butter to the mixer bowl and switched the machine on.

"D'you think they're connected?" she asked. "The robbery and the shooting."

I shrugged. "Doesn't look like they are. But the dead man was known for holding secrets. It's possible, if he knew who the thief was, that he overplayed his hand and they decided to get rid of him. But it's all a mess," I admitted, then switched to the reason for my call.

"Where was Gaia," I asked. "Last night?"

"Gaia?" The alarm in her voice was clear. "What the hell does that mean?"

"I wondered – if she was in the woods she might have seen or heard something that might help the police. Y'know: with their enquiries."

"Well she wasn't in the woods," her mother said. "She was

out with a friend til about eight, then came home. Went to bed early."

That meant she was supposedly in bed when the stickup occurred, but didn't mean she couldn't have crawled down a drainpipe or snuck out the back door and made her way back to Dukes Halt.

But I knew she hadn't. I'd found the gun that had been used in the robbery the previous night, and it wasn't the gun that I had seen Gaia playing with the day before.

That one – that family heirloom – was the one, I was now sure, that Arianna had been holding when I'd come through the French windows this afternoon.

"So: The gun," I said to Beth Kennedy.

She sighed. Dropped into a chair opposite me. "That bloody gun. I told her this morning, it had to go. All I needed was for some busy body to mention that she had one, and the police would be through here like Stormtroopers. I was terrified they'd find the bloody gun. Like I don't have enough trouble on my plate already.

"Simon's dad got it from his dad. It was just a thing they used to shoot at vermin. But nobody ever had a licence for it.

"Nobody ever needed one. Til last night there was a stickup, a gun was fired, and I knew that if the police turned up here we'd be in real trouble."

"So what happened?" I asked. "To the gun."

Beth shrugged. "She took it up to the house at first light."

The phrase 'at first light' had a slightly vague, almost medieval hint to it.

"And how early is first light?"

"Five. Five thirty. I heard the police sirens last night, made some calls. Found out what had happened and told her to get that bloody gun out from under this roof as fast as she could.

"She said 'how?' and I said 'take it to the house. Let those bastards deal with it. Simon's granddad got it fighting in a batallion the bloody Warrens led. Let them explain why the gun is in *their* house.' So we waited til it was beginning to get light and she went. I figured there's always someone awake in that place, even that early in the morning."

And at that moment, from the other end of the hallway, there was the sound of a key in a lock, and the door opened.

"Mum," Gaia Kennedy called, "Can I get dinner and-" she walked into the room and stopped. "Hello," she said to me, and I smiled back.

"Hello again," I replied. "We were just talking about you."

She glanced at her mother. "Them cakes smell awesome," she said, rounding the table and pausing only to plant a kiss on the top of her mother's head. "It's a shame we won't be here for Christmas."

Gaia crossed to the kettle, clicked it on, and extracted a mug from the cupboard before scrabbling around in the tea caddy for a bag. Her figure – tall, slim, and clad in a long waxed man's coat that I suspected had belonged to her father – moved stiffly, as though she were trying to figure out how to look calm while feeling anything but.

"Your gun," I said, and she sat down, cradling her mug.

"What of it?"

"Your mum was telling me you got rid of it."

"Was she?" Gaia sat at the table and regarded me over the rim of her mug as she blew gently on clouds of steam. She turned her eyes, momentarily, to Beth. "She really should be careful what she says to strangers."

"I saw you with it in the woods the other day," I said, and Gaia sipped the tea, shrugged. "And?"

"Who'd you give it to?"

She looked at me. Puzzled.

"This morning," I said. "When you got rid of it. Who'd you get rid of it to?"

Gaia looked once more at Beth and put the mug down on the table. "I took it up to the Halt. Went up first thing this morning – half five, six. Something like that. My mum was having kittens all night. Panicking about what would have happened if they ever found the gun. Though to be honest, they never would have."

"Why's that?"

Gaia smiled. "It wasn't here. I haven't had it in the house for a very long time."

"Well where was it?"

She picked her mug up and sipped the tea. "Hidden." Gaia put the mug down and gestured airily behind her. "It's a big forest. I know places to hide anything."

"Like guns?" I asked, and she smiled again.

"What about people?" I pressed, and the smile faded. "Lottie Warren is missing."

"I know," Gaia said, her face serious. "I just took your mate and the dog all over the forest looking for her. No joy."

"How close are you to Lottie?" I pressed. "Any idea where she might have gone to?"

Gaia paused. It was a flicker, nothing more, but it registered with me. "I like her," she said at last. "She's not as stuck up as the rest of that lot, and she doesn't want my mum to be sacked just cos my dad got sick."

"Did you give the gun to Lottie?"

"Lottie?" Gaia frowned. "No. Why would I give it to her?"

"So tell me what happened when you got to the house."

"Listen, I got rid of the gun, okay? That's it. What's this all about?"

"You heard there's been a killing today," it was my turn now to gesture vaguely in the direction of Dukes Halt. "Up at the house?"

She nodded. Beth Kennedy watched her – and me - intently.

"Your friend – Lady Caz – told me," Gaia said.

"A man was shot dead," I said, "and a friend of mine is in the frame for his killing. She didn't do it. I don't know who did. But I do know – and right now I am the only person who does know – that the gun he was murdered with was the one I saw you shooting in the woods yesterday afternoon."

A stunned silence fell on the table.

"So who," I asked once more "did you give the gun to?"

"Fuck," Gaia breathed, her eyes huge and shining.

I waited.

"I didn't," she finally said. "I went all the way up there trying to plan it in my head: I'd knock at the door, someone – probably that dragon secretary of Sir Phillip - would answer, and I would tell them I'd found it in the woods.

"They wouldn't believe me, of course. Then I played it where I told them the truth, except I could see that bitch then using the fact we'd had an unlicensed firearm as another nail in my mum's coffin. I didn't know what to do for the best.

"I'd basically decided on the lie – as obvious and stupid as it was – by the time I got to the house. Except I didn't need to knock. Cos the door was open."

"Open?" It was my turn to frown. There'd been an armed robbery at Dukes Halt the night before. I would have assumed – human nature being what it was – that security would have been redoubled, not that the front door would have been left unlocked.

"I assumed someone who didn't have a key had gone for a walk and left it on the latch so they could get back in when they came home," Gaia explained, and my mind went to Caz and her comment that she and Ellie had been out at the crack of dawn.

"Only now I'm wondering if Lottie left it open when she left the night before."

I knew that was impossible: Lottie Warren had been long gone before the house settled down for the night.

"Any idea why Lottie might have left?" I asked and Gaia laughed mirthlessly.

"What? Apart from the fact that her family are a bunch of warped bastards who want to send her to school in bloody Switzerland?" She shook her head. "Best thing she could do is get the hell away from the Warrens. They're warped. Even my dad used to say so."

"Gaia," Beth warned, clearly remembering that I was a guest of the Warrens and thus, perhaps, not entirely to be trusted.

"No," Gaia shook her head at her mum, "I don't care. My dad used to say that the Warrens would do anything to maintain their perfect little world, and they didn't care who they hurt to do it. Said they'd even destroy their own to stop their dirty little secrets leaking out."

"What did he mean by that?" I asked, images of Lady Marion – dead of mysterious causes – and little Edward – dead so soon after his mother – running through my head.

Gaia shrugged. "Who knows? Who cares?" She was silent a moment, staring at the table, running a fingernail lightly along a chip in the wood, then looked back up at me, suddenly back at Dukes Halt this morning.

"So I let myself into the Halt, then realised I was basically walking around a house I shouldn't have been in. I panicked a bit. Wiped the gun and put it on the hall table and left it there."

"Just the gun?"

"There was a box of shells too. They were useless without the gun, so I left them on the table as well. I figured Chapman or whoever found it would hand it in."

Except, of course, they hadn't.

"So you left the gun and the shells and what? Came straight home?"

"Where else would I go at that time of the day?" Gaia was putting on a brave face. "Listen: are we in trouble? I mean, if that gun was used to kill someone."

It was my turn, now, to pause. "I haven't told anyone," I admitted. "And it's an old gun. My guess is they'll never trace it back to you."

"We should say something," Beth murmured quietly, and before Gaia – whose face was already darkening angrily – could speak I held up a hand.

"Hold off. Just a while. Let me try to figure this out. Right now, the only reason you know it was your gun that was used is because I came and told you. If you have to fess up you can cross that bridge then."

I was back on the doorstep promising to keep them informed if Lottie showed up when a thought occurred to me. Here I was protecting these women, and Gaia hadn't told me the full story. I turned to her.

"Gaia, did you go back to the Halt later?"

There it was again: That flicker of calculation. She shook her head "No. Why would I?" She was lying, of course; I'd seen her return with my own eyes. But if she'd already handed in the gun, why had she returned a couple of hours later?

CHAPTER TWENTY-TWO

I tried Nick again, went to voice mail again, and didn't bother to leave a message, though I was really worried. If he didn't already know that his wife had been arrested for murder by now, it was only a matter of time, and much as I really did not want to be the bearer of such bad news, I also did not want him finding out from someone else then putting two and two together and realising I'd been keeping secrets from him.

I turned out of the Kennedy driveway and rambled to my right. At least, I reasoned, I hadn't actually lied to him. I mean, when he'd called to ask if I knew where Arianna was, I'd said I didn't know, and I hadn't known. There was no way I could have known that she'd somehow managed to track Maximov to Dukes Halt and was en route.

But I could, I supposed, have told him that I had an idea why she might have vanished.

Except I'd promised Arianna that I would keep her confidences.

So I hadn't lied; I'd simply kept confidences, and now Arianna, Nick, and most probably me, were in various degrees of what the philosopher Hegel once referred to as 'die Scheiße.'

And Caz was somewhere in the woods hunting for a missing girl while a jewel thief was roaming free.

I stopped, the deep impenetrable silence seeming to grip me, and realised I'd gone the wrong way.

Instead of heading back to the main road I had accidentally turned and started walking through the forest. I looked around. The afternoon was already fading, the light in the forest was dim and dappled, but it seemed mostly to be coming from behind me, which meant I was heading East.

I thought.

What am I, a forest ranger?

I looked behind me, realised I'd come further than I'd thought, and stood a moment longer debating whether to turn back to the Kennedy House or carry on the way I was heading. Then suddenly, the hair on the back of my neck stood up, and a shiver ran down my spine.

I looked around me. I seemed to be totally alone, but I knew with absolute certainty that there was someone else here. Someone who was watching me from the dense foliage.

Or at least I hoped it was a someone; with my luck that dysenteric fox had probably tracked me down for a second round.

I put a foot forward, all my senses straining to note any movement in the forest that might suggest the location of who or whatever was tracking me, but no noise came from the wall of greenery, no sign of any shifting foliage.

Nothing.

I carried on walking the way I had been heading, grateful that I was at least on a fairly well-cleared trail, the age and regular usage of the pathway giving me comfort that it had to lead somewhere. My paranoia at being outside of a city, however, reminded me that whilst that would probably be Dukes Halt, it might also be a stone circle with a fucking massive wicker man in the middle of it.

I picked up the pace, conscious that the light was fading and dreading the idea of bungling around in this stupid forest in the dark. I mean: Who has a fucking forest on their property? What's wrong with an Alpine rockery and a water feature?

From behind me, somewhere to the right, I heard footsteps pushing through the undergrowth. Big footsteps.

My pursuer was no badger or fox; it sounded like an adult-sized human, and they had picked up their pace too.

Which was enough for me; I sprinted forward, shards of amber light bursting through gaps in the canopy above and momentarily blinding me as I barrelled onwards, aware that one misstep on the mulchy shifting earth underfoot could have me jamming my foot into a pothole, a set or a bear trap, or piling head-first into a centuries-old English Oak.

Something – the adrenaline rush, the sudden shock to a system that can only come from unanticipated physical exertion in close proximity to nature – had caused me to break out in a cold sweat, the combination of flashing lights, heart-pounding and sweating serving to completely disorientate me so that I blundered into the undergrowth, leafless branches snatching at me like skeletal fingers.

And still, whoever was behind me powered relentlessly on.

Breath catching in my throat, I burst into a clearing and realised that I had long abandoned the pathway and was trapped, a wall of trees and dense, decaying vegetation surrounding me. I froze, like a cornered animal and turned to leave the clearing I'd blindly charged into, only to discover my exit blocked.

By Digby Smith.

Digby. Bloody. Smith.

I bent double, gasping for oxygen as the bulky member of parliament for the fifteenth century, his corpulent person clad in sweatshorts and a Black T Shirt, his feet encased in the sort of trainers that would get him knifed on the streets of Southwark for crimes against footlocker.

"Digby. What the fuck are you up to?" I was so breathless that what I'd intended to come out as a furious demand ending up sounding more like the last words of a consumptive chainsmoker.

"Well hello," he smarmed, entering the circle and lifting his tshirt to wipe sweat from his eyes, exposing a white belly overlaid with a pelt of dark hair.

I straightened up, my heart still pounding in my chest, and glared at him.

"I thought it was you," he smiled, stepping into the clearing and closing off any escape route for me. "Out for a run." He gestured, entirely unnecessarily, at his getup. "You too? Not really dressed for it."

He moved forward and I involuntarily retreated. "Look, Digby," I started, still out of breath and thus still rather breathy.

"I've been watching you," Smith said. "Watching how you keep avoiding me."

"Avoiding you?" I should have been avoiding Digby Smith the way Catholic Nuns avoided Satanic Sex Midgets, but I couldn't for the life of me imagine how the man with whom I'd dined for two nights on the trot, who I'd nodded to at breakfast, and who had been able to bend my ear any time he'd wanted in the house could have come to the conclusion that I was avoiding him.

"My eyes," Digby Smith clarified. "You don't look me in the eyes, Daniel. And I know why."

"Look," I said, taking another step backwards as he took two towards me. "I don't want to be funny Mr Smith." "Digby," he smiled, his cheeks dimpling, his chest puffing out as he inhaled deeply. "Call me Digby. Please."

"Digby. Right. Look-" I got no further; Digby Smith was clearly not the sort of person who allowed someone else's thoughts to interrupt either the forming or the vocalising of his own.

"You won't look me in the eyes, Daniel, and we both know why."

I didn't, really, but I had a horrible feeling that Digby Smith thought he did. I took another step back. And discovered my back was pressed against a large and immovable oak tree.

"Sex." Smith said, stepping towards me, his cheeks reddening.

"Sex?" I asked, and he giggled like a schoolgirl.

"Well only if you insist," he joked, and my stomach flipped.

"Look, Digby," I tried again, "I don't want to be funny – or rude – but the thing is-" I was scrabbling for a polite way of saying 'I think you're a vile creature.' I settled for, "I don't think we have a single thing in common."

"We're men, Daniel. Or can I call you Dan?"

"Digby-" He was right in front of me, his chest heaving, his eyes sparkling dangerously. And so I went for it: "DIgby," I straightened my spine, made the eye contact he'd been convinced I'd been avoiding, and said: "You've voted against every pro-Gay proposal that has come before parliament. You've said horrible and hateful things about Gay men and Women and you voted to block measures that would stop Trans people being deported back to regimes that would kill them."

He paused, confusion flickering across his face.

"Well yes, but what's that got to do with you and I?"

"What?" I was choked. "Digby, you're gay! How can you vote the way you do? How can you even think of doing that?"

He stopped dead at that one, and laughed, his dimples deepening, his curly, sweat moistened hair glistening in the half light. I could see why so many Tory Ladies had voted Digby Smith again and again, but I could also see past the physical to the really rather worrying darkness inside.

"Gay?" He shook his head, an eyebrow too perfect to be purely god's own work raised in shock. "I'm not Gay. I'm a man, Daniel. And as a man I'm a sexual being who can see when there's an attraction to and from another sexual being."

"Okay, Digby," I knew there was nowhere else for me to go so I tried placating the delusional bigot, "maybe you're bisexual."

"Look," his eyes hardened, and he leaned forward, planting a hand on the tree, to the left of my head. "I'm not gay or bi. I'm not one of those freaks. I'm a man."

"Who just suggested having sex with a man," I answered, unable to keep the panic from my voicc.

"Hey," he drew back momentarily then replanted his hand by my head, "it was you who suggested it."

"But you hate me," I said, wondering at what point I'd entered the twilight zone. "You vote against my interests, you try deny me equal rights."

"Not true." He shook his head, the smile softening as though he were about to impart a long-hidden truth to me. "I don't hate you Daniel; I hate people *like* you."

I felt, at first, like I'd been stunned with a brick, then wished I had a brick handy to stun Smith with. "You what?" I asked.

"I love people," he said. "People are really rather fascinating, aren't they? But," he paused, as though considering, then savouring the next word, "*Concepts*. Concepts aren't people, Danny. Gay. Lesbian. What are they but concepts? I stand for individuals, for people. I'm standing. Right now. For you."

I felt the bile rise at the back of my throat. Words failed me, though it transpired they were unrequired anyway.

Digby pressed on. "But I cannot – and will not – stand for or with the activists, the gangs, the special interests. The people who make being gay all that they are. They're the ones I'm voting against Daniel. Not you. Not me."

"Are you fucking serious?"

That stopped him. For a moment. "Daniel, has anything a politician ever done impacted you negatively?"

"Yes," I said. "I still remember section 28. I still remember school kids calling me a faggot and teachers looking the other way. That was politicians."

"Was it though?" He tilted his head in mock concern. "Wasn't that just bullies and lazy teachers? Wouldn't those things have happened even if the politics had been entirely absent?"

"No," I shook my head. "You voted to empower those bullies and bigots; to tell them it was acceptable to treat me like shit."

He chuckled as though I were a silly boy and he the wise and pedagogic elder. "I'm not old enough to have voted to put Section 28 on the books, Daniel."

"But you voted against repealing it," I shot back, my familiarity with his voting record (thank you Google) throwing him for a moment. "And you voted against equal marriage again and again."

"And who did you want to get married to, Daniel?"

"Me?" I thought of Robert, who I'd spent ten years 'engaged' to despite the fact he knew we could never get married and of how, when I'd discovered his philandering, Robert had been more worried by the idea that I might – because the laws had changed – be entitled to half his fortune than he had been about the ending of our decade-long relationship.

And then I thought of Nick, who had never mentioned marriage and who rarely mentioned love, but who made me happy.

And I wondered whether he and I might ever be married.

"I'm waiting," Digby sing-songed.

"Nobody," I said, "but that's not the point."

"So you admit that you'd have been bullied with or without Section 28, and-"

"I admitted no such thing," I interjected, but – as usual – Digby Smith wasn't listening.

"And you openly recognise that you're not in need of gay marriage and yet you feel my voting record – against large blocs of special interests who are not seeking equality but seeking to overthrow the existing order – is a reason not to give me at least a kiss."

"Give you a what?"

He leaned forward. His other hand came up on the other side of my head, and he leant forward. "A kiss," he said.

And smiled.

And leaned further forward, planting his fat wet lips on mine.

I was stunned, for a moment, then outraged. I pulled my head back and knocked the back of my skull against the bark of the tree behind me and still Digby powered on, his fleshy slug-like tongue now pressuring my firmly closed lips like a burglar's jemmy against the safe at Fort Knox.

I struggled, twisted myself out of his reach, caught a flash of something behind him, and he was on me again, the full weight of his body this time, his chest pressing against mine, and I lifted my hands and forced them against his shoulders as he shifted at the hips and moved to grind himself against me.

So much went through my head in that millisecond: Polite boys do not punch members of parliament in the face. I had to spend the rest of the weekend with this man, and if I smashed him in the nuts it would make for rather uncomfortable post-dinner engagement. I shouldn't be in this situation. In fact, perhaps I wasn't in this position. Maybe-

"No!" I swung my knee up, catching the top of his thigh. Digby seemed to find my resistance an aphrodisiac, redoubling his efforts to get his tongue into my mouth and his crotch pressed to mine. My words had come out, even to my own ears, as a mumble that he might have heard as an entreatment.

But they hadn't been, and Smith's relentless determination to snog and frot me against both a tree and my will had my anxiety turning into outrage.

Years ago, in order to put those schoolyard bullies in their place, my older brother Paddy had taken me to a boxing gym just off the Old Kent Road, and from the men and boys there – who didn't care who or what I was, only that I trained, worked, and was as diligent as them in committing to becoming the best fighter I could be - I'd learned that I wasn't a very good prize fighter, and that when an opponent in the ring was pounding me, restricting my movement, pressing me into a state of panic, I should stop trying to fight against them, let them think I'd given up, and draw them in…

I withdrew, went limp, relaxed.

Waited until Smith, sensing my acquiescence, pulled back, a look of smug triumph on his face.

And I headbutted the bastard.

He didn't shriek. I think – in hindsight – I'd been half expecting him to shriek and collapse. Instead he grunted, jerked back, the smugness transformed into confusion that was quickly morphing into fury.

"The fuck?" He demanded, his body moving backwards as I realised the movement was leaving his most vulnerable parts exposed and I drove home my advantage and – with better aim and a clearer angle this time - my knee.

And as Dudley Smith bent double I looked over his body towards the entrance to the clearing and there – staring right at me with a mixture of sadness and disgust – was Nick Fisher.

I shoved the now-moaning and grunting Digby Smith to one side and ran after Nick, who'd turned from me and vanished into the woods, but as soon as I got outside the clearing it became obvious that he was nowhere to be seen.

It didn't matter: I was in panic mode. I didn't know what he'd just seen, or how it had looked from his viewpoint. The fact he hadn't come to my rescue suggested it hadn't looked like the attempted sexual assault I was now becoming aware it had been, and as I ran through the unforgiving walls of leaves and branches calling his name I wondered how the hell he'd found me, then wondered if he had actually been looking for me.

But of course he couldn't have been looking for me.

He'd clearly come down to Dorset on getting the news about Arianna with no idea that I was anywhere in the locale and had been scoping out the surrounding area when he'd stumbled on…

I stopped, gasping, his name coming from me but in a whisper this time rather than a shout.

I was lost.

In every sense of the word, I was lost.

I didn't know where I was, had no idea how I was going to get back to Dukes Halt, how I was going to find Nick, and how I was going to fix this shitshow.

How was I going to prove that Arianna was innocent of Maximov's murder? And what I was going to say to or do about Digby Smith?

"Nick!" I shouted his name once more, at the top of my lungs. "Let me explain."

Let me explain.

I stopped, sighed deeply, turned my face up to the sky, almost violet now, with some of the bigger and bolder stars already beginning to show themselves, and swallowed the profanity that had been about to shoot out of me.

Then I heard movement off to my right?

Smith coming after me? I held my breath, tilting my head towards the sound.

No, definitely Nick. I don't know how I knew, but something about the gait, some sixth sense told me it was him.

I turned and followed the sound, and in moments could see his back, shoving through undergrowth, clearly lost.

"Nick," I called. "Wait, Please."

He stopped, froze, and turned to face me, his face angry.

I caught up with him, gasping for breath. "You're fitter than I thought," I said, wanting to say something light, to make him smile, to banish this horrible darkness between us.

"What the fuck," he gestured behind me in the direction of the clearing, "was that?"

"That?" Instinctively, I glanced behind me. "You mean Smith? He's a lowlife lech who's been pressuring me all weekend. I'm fairly sure he even tried to get into my room the other night. I've been sleeping with a chair jammed under it ever since."

"Well it looked quite cosy when I found you."

"Cosy? I'd just headbutted the bloke."

"I didn't know what was going on," he said. "And when I saw you. When I saw your face. I just," he paused, "lost it."

Now, I was angry. "How long were you standing there?"

"Not long," he answered. "But long enough. You looked to be flirting."

"Flirting? Are you out of your mind? He was assaulting me. He was fucking assaulting me and you just stood there and watched?"

"Why are you even here?" Nick snapped back.

"I could ask the same of you," I shot back.

"Well I can answer that one," Nick said. "I'm here cos the local cop shop called to say my wife had been arrested on suspicion of murder. I came straight here and then they mentioned that they'd had someone in earlier for questioning. Some bloke from London who carried on like he was the one in charge of the case.

"And I knew. You lied to me."

"I didn't lie," I said, "I just," my shoulders slumped. I didn't even believe the words I was about to say. "I just didn't tell you everything that was going on."

"I asked at the house," he said. "They send me here. I got lost." He chuckled bitterly.

"I got lost is a bloody good metaphore for all this really, isn't it?"

"Nick," I tried again, "Arianna's innocent. The truth is-"

"No." He held a hand up to stop me. "Don't bring her in to this. This is about you and me. This is about you lying to me. Putting me up to my ears in the shit."

"I didn't mean to," I said, hating the wheedling tone that had crept into my voice.

Nick shook his head. "You never do. But Danny: I could lose my job. I could go to prison. Arianna could be sent back to Albania. If she goes back there, she's dead. And all you had to do was give me the heads-up. Give me a chance to figure out a better way to handle this than the clusterfick we've ended up in."

"And what was back there?" I demanded. "You standing by while that bastard tried to shove his tongue in my mouth? What? Punishment?"

"You seemed to be doing okay when I left. By the sounds of it you broke the bastard's nose."

"I hope I did," I spat back and Nick sighed.

"And if he presses charges? Claims you attacked him?"

"I have a witness," I said, gesturing at Nick.

"Yeah," he smiled sadly. "'Cos I'm expected to step up for you. Do the necessary to stop you getting into the shit."

He shook his head. "One call, Danny. That's all it would have taken. Look: I need to sort this out. The local guys are letting me sit in. They shouldn't, it's a total conflict of interest, but they're a decent lot so they've said they'll keep me in the loop.

"I think I need to get back to them. Figure out how I stop this from becoming any worse than it already is."

“Nick,” I held a hand out. “Talk to me. We need to work this out together.”

“Together?” He shook his head. “No, Danny. I need to do this on my own. You’ve done enough damage.”

And so saying, he turned away from me and pressed on through the woods leaving me alone and lost.

I had no explanations. No ideas. Nothing.

But I was going to get some.

I’d had enough of the politesse and veneers of Dukes Halt.

My mind was made up: I was heading back to the house and sorting this shit out for once and for all.

CHAPTER TWENTY-THREE

"Lord," Caz – Ellie by her side like a sleek, sedate Cerberus – said. "You look like Tarzan. What've you been doing."

As I stalked further into the entry hall, my head no longer blocking the decaying sunlight behind me, her impassive look faltered.

"You two," I pointed at the couple behind her, who'd been crossing the space from the drawing room to the more private spaces of the ground floor. "I want to talk to you both. Now."

Henry and Pamela Warren paused, their heads – bowed together in communion – uncoupling.

"Our daughter is missing." Pamela announced, her annoyance at my interruption clear.

"She'll live," I answered, still smarting at how easily Lottie had convinced me that her family house was a hive of secret corridors. "But we need to talk."

They looked at me, their thought that I was an annoying guest with no right to confront them writ plain on their faces.

"I know who Maximov was," I said, passing Caz and Ellie (who, as she'd got my scent, had become less Cerberus, more waggy ball of recognition and adoration) and crossing the hallway, my trainers leaving flat, brown prints all across the William Morris tiling, "and I know *what* he was," I added, as they came within earshot.

Did I imagine it, or did they both straighten, then almost instantly resume their previous postures?

"And we're gonna have a chat now," I said, arriving at the two as Caz and Ellie arrived behind me. "Here, or somewhere more private."

"What on earth are you talking about?" Henry- his equilibrium restored – demanded.

"Where are the police?" I asked, my voice still louder than it needed to be, considering our proximity.

"Police?" Pamela, now, frowned.

"More precisely," I added, "where are they not? Cos in the last two days, you've had a jewel theft, a murder and a child go missing, and I've just walked in through your front door, and not one person has stopped or questioned me."

I stopped in front of them. Their eyes sought each other, and something communicated between them that suggested the gig was up.

"To be honest, I know where they're not, and I think I know why they're not, and I really think we need to talk, 'cos I'm tired of the subterfuge."

"We should go to the salon," Henry said, turning away from me and heading back the way he and Pamela had just come through.

We followed them through the archway, down a dimly lit hallway and through a door into a large room, this one furnished in shades of green and brown, the fireplace surmounted, this time, by a huge portrait of someone who – despite the almost overpowering walrus moustache – was clearly a Warren, albeit one whose domineering glower was somewhat tempered by a squint the artist had tried and failed to hide.

"Why was Sergei Maximov here?" I asked, even before I'd sat down.

"He was a guest," Henry Warren said. "My father likes lots of people her to celebrate my mother's birthday each year."

"Bullshit." I gave him my best, most polite, smile as Ellie stirred, turned her head and licked my palm as though in encouragement. "Your father didn't even know Maximov was coming here until shortly before he turned up. You see," I leaned forward and Ellie leaned forward with me, "I know who – and what - Maximov was. So there's really little point in fucking around with me folks."

I glanced past Ellie to Caz, who was managing to layer a look of mortification over a foundation of fascination, like a

HGV driver passing a five-car pile-up on the Watford bypass.

Henry looked at Pamela. Again, no words passed between them, but I knew that the words she spoke next were a script they'd both, somehow, agreed.

"What do you think he was?" She asked.

"Know," I repeated. "Sergei Maximov was a secret seller. A blackmailer. A pimp. A procurer. Someone who bought and sold children into slavery, corrupted businessmen and politicians. And somewhere in that stew is a reason why you," I nodded at Pamela, "brought him here this weekend."

They looked, once more, at each other.

I sighed.

Caz leaned forward. "Look," she said. "far be it from me to suggest you're out of your depth, but he knows this stuff, and he's absolutely relentless."

The two of them looked at her in slack-jawed amazement.

"I'm not bigging you up," she smiled at me. "Just telling the truth. I don't know anyone who can figure out messes as well, or see through lies as easily. So unless you want him strolling out the door and going straight to the press with what will probably prove to be pretty much verifiable facts," this back to Henry and Pamela, still regarding us with something beyond confusion but not quite wonder, "I'd fess up to whatever you know. Now."

I turned back to them.

"You don't know anything," Pamela said flatly.

"I think I know where your daughter is," I half-lied, and she cracked.

"Is she safe?"

I nodded. "She's safe. I think. I don't have her," I added hastily, lest they think I'd stolen their daughter, "but I think she's with friends."

"Friends?" Henry shook his head. "Lottie doesn't have any friends."

"Is what you think? But what do you two – so wrapped up in secrets and espionage – know about your daughter?"

Again, they exchanged a glance.

"Stop looking at each other," I barked. "I know what you people are, what you do; and I know you love Lottie. I also know that you two never broke up. Not properly."

Their absolute stillness told me I'd hit a gaping nerve.

"Your brother," I nodded to Pamela, "died and you felt obliged to do something to carry on his work. But he wasn't a games master at a school, was he? He was a spy."

I felt ludicrous. But I knew I was right.

"My family have been in service for decades," Pamela finally said, "and Michael was the last in the male line and – frankly – the best of us. And when he died, I was desolated.

"But there was a spot – no notice, no delay allowed, either yes or no – to step into an event he'd been involved in, and to make a difference."

"So you abandoned Lottie," I said, and her shoulders dropped.

"This life only works if you have nothing that can be held against you. I left Lottie with Henry. I went undercover."

"As a games mistress in a girl's school?" Caz asked, receiving from Pamela and Henry, looks of confusion and from me one of consolation.

"Caz, when Pamela leaked that she was going to work in Cheltenham, she didn't mean the ladies College; she meant General Command Head Quarters. And – if I'm right – ever since then, she's used her placing there and her acceptance in the Warren family to bring people with secrets to sell to the house under cover of them being her dates."

"Henry knew what each of them was," Pamela said, not even registering that her daughter - excluded from the scheme – might have assumed her mother and father were simply in some sort of unstable relationship.

"And then, a week ago, completely out of the blue, Maximov got in touch," Henry announced. "Said he had evidence that an establishment figure has been working with a foreign power against British interests."

"And was he known to you before this approach?" I asked.

Pamela shook her head. "Once the approach was made, I

did some checking. One gets a number of cranks, disaffected members of the intel community, double agents."

"Lord, it's like a Le Carre," Caz breathed.

"And your checks?" I pressed, and Pamela, her lips clamped together, cast a glance at Henry.

"Let me guess," I answered my own question: "Not Russian. Probably not even originally called Sergei Maximov. But known for having intelligence for sale since the 90s."

She raised an eyebrow. "You're very well informed. For a barman."

"I'm a good barman," I answered.

"A very good barman," Caz added. "And like all good barmen, Danny hears things."

"So what was the deal?" I pressed.

Pamela paused, as though measuring once more who I was and how much could safely be disclosed to me. She sighed. "Maximov said he had to come to Dukes Halt this weekend. It had to be here and now or there was no deal," she answered, and something went off in the back of my mind.

"Why here?" I asked. "Why specifically this weekend?"

They shrugged, looking back at me with no answers.

"Okay, well do we think Maximov had anything to do with the events of last night?"

"The robbery?" Henry frowned and Pamela shook her head.

"Not his style," she said. "Not based on the intel I have. Unless you know something else."

"So…?" I asked, waiting their verdict on the theory.

"We file that as a possible – but unlikely - explanation for Maximov's presence here this weekend," Pamela answered.

This was getting us nowhere. "Okay," I tried another tack, "is it possible that the establishment person Maximov had detail on was also here this weekend? I don't think it's beyond him to auction his secrets off against buyer and seller. So who was here, and why?"

Henry began counting the guests off on his fingers. "Sara Simone is here because John Is enamoured with her. Her mother is here because Sara is."

"And the Stamfords?"

Henry shrugged. "Richard Stamford was – originally- the point of the whole weekend. He's up for recognition."

"I'm assuming you mean some sort of award and not a Blue Peter Badge."

"Some of the people in front of the committee are sent for a face to face with the head of the honours committee."

"Jesus," Caz breathed, "you're not saying Sir Philip is the head of the committee that awards knighthoods."

Pamela shrugged.

"So to be clear," I said, "Maximov insisted he had to be here this weekend, and the only other outsiders were Caz, me, Sara Simone, Francine Gerber and Digby Smith."

"Actually Digby was here because he's on the awards committee too."

"That explains a lot," I added dryly. "So Maximov came down under cover of being your date, Pamela?"

She nodded, and Henry carried on: "He arrived and told me he wanted ten million transferred to a Swiss Bank account before he'd let me even see the evidence he had. I was awaiting further instructions from Vauxhall when he was shot."

I realised that by his reference to Vauxhall Henry was referring to the offices of MI5, and not to The Royal Vauxhall Tavern, a notorious and long-lived drag bar close by.

At least, I assumed he was.

"Wait," I leaned forward in my chair, "are you saying he had the proof with him?"

"Had being the operative word," Henry nodded. "I had his room searched, and there was nothing there."

"That's because his mobile was gone. Taken by whoever killed him."

"His Phone?"

"By the sounds of it, the man has enough dirt to fill a library. It's probably cloud-based. And accessed via his phone. You still haven't found it?"

Henry shook his head. "Not in his room either."

"A figure within the British Political Establishment?" Caz mused. "That could only be Digby or John."

"Or," Henry replied sadly, "My father."

"Or me," Pamela added. "Or you, Henry; we're all establishment figures."

Henry nodded his acknowledgement. "But then Maximov was shot by that woman, so we'll never know for certain."

"Okay," I held a finger up, "bear with me: What if she didn't kill Maximov? What if she's telling the truth: She arrived, saw an open door, stepped into it intending to use it to gain access to the rest of the house and look for Maximov. Only on stepping in, she finds him dead."

Henry shook his head. "We heard the gunshot. She'd brought a gun. It had to be her." He paused, frowned.

"Something else?"

"Well, I noticed a while ago that there are some scratches around the lock of the gun cabinet."

"As though someone were trying to pick the lock?" I asked, and he nodded. "But that couldn't have anything to do with Maximov's death, because the woman who killed him came with her own gun."

"Okay, look," I said, "Arianna had no access to the house beyond the dining room. All the doors out of the dining room were locked and sealed after the robbery. And I happen to know that the gun – the one that was used to shoot Maximov – was left on the hall table early this morning. Whoever shot him had planned the murder. They'd stolen the fireworks last night and set them to go off and cause a distraction. They'd been trying to get a gun when fortune put one right in front of them. And as Arianna was trapped in the dining room with Maximov, she couldn't have been the one who found the gun, let alone set off the fireworks."

"But the rest of us were at the front door when the gun went off," Pamela insisted, and I shook my head.

"Not everyone." I closed my eyes and tried to remember who had been in the hall when we heard the gunshot.

"I was with Caz and Karen Stamford when the first

firework went off. We were talking to Inspector Dane, and then you, Pamela, and Sir Phillip came out of the drawing room with Henry."

"We'd been discussing the situation with Richard Stamford," Pamela explained.

"Okay, so that's me, Dane, Caz, Karen Stamford, both of you and Sir Phillip."

"Then the Gerber woman came in hysterical along with John and her daughter," Pamela said, and I nodded.

"And Richard Stamford came down the stairs. Which means we don't have Chapman, Lottie, or Mila," I finished, opening my eyes and looking at the Warrens.

"So: One of our missing people has been missing for 24 hours. Another was down in the kitchen – a room with easy and direct access to the dining room. And the third has keys to pretty much every door in this house."

CHAPTER TWENTY-FOUR

Mila was not exactly pleased to see us.

In fact, as Caz and I walked into her kitchen, Ellie clicking along behind us, her habitual scowl deepened and she pointed at the dog. "You two," she said, before pointing a bony finger at Ellie and adding "No animals in my kitchen."

Caz, making as though she was completely oblivious to the complaint, crossed to the huge table, pulled a chair out, gestured to me to sit, and then removed the capacious Gladstone bag from her shoulder, settled herself in a chair at the top of the table before extracting from the bag a hip flask and two brandy glasses, pouring a good slug of brandy into each, sliding one in front of me and then gesturing from me to Mila as though to suggest the floor was mine.

Mila watched all of this with a glower that approached incendiary levels.

"Thank you, Helen Keller," I muttered to Caz before lifting my glass, sipping, savouring the really rather fine Cognac, and deciding that Caz had clearly been liberating more of Sir Phillip's cellar.

"Mila," I said, "I was wondering if you could clear something up for me?"

"I cook," Mila snappedback. "If you want mess cleared you speak to the woman upstairs." I assumed, by this, she meant Chapman. "She will have one of those brats from village clear your mess."

"No," I smiled, "that's not what I meant. I meant that there's something that puzzles me. Something that I was hoping you could explain."

Mila became, immediately, cautious, her eyes focusing on a point not quite in my eyeline.

"What," Caz demanded, as though she were the bad cop in a bad cop-good cop double act she'd neglected to inform me we would be performing, "have you done with Ali?"

"Ali?" Mila was destabilised. I didn't know what she'd been expecting to be asked, but it clearly hadn't been to explain the absence of my friend. "She goes into town. Takes car. The butcher calls this morning and tells me he has a side of beef going cheap but has to be collected today as he has no freezer space."

Caz blanched. "Car?" She lifted her brandy glass and drained it. "My car?"

"Paolo's car," I reminded her and she swatted aside the detail.

"She's collecting a large quantity of still-bloody meat and transporting it in a hundred- and fifty-thousand-pound Ferrari like it was a Tesco home delivery van."

"I'm sure it'll be double-bagged," I smirked. "And let's face it: It's not exactly the oddest item that's been transported in that car this weekend."

"My item," she snapped back, "was far less likely to bleed all over the upholstery."

Which was a fair point, but not the topic I'd intended to discuss. "Mila," I tried again, "I was wondering why you didn't come running when you heard the gunshots."

"Gunshots?" Mila's wariness was back. "Which gunshots?"

"Exactly," I stood, crossed to the long workbench that she was working on, and cast an eye over a selection of vegetables and meat in various stages of prep. "Do you want a hand with any of this?" I asked, moving to the vast Belfast sink and rinsing my hands under the tap without waiting for an answer.

"Carrots," she grumbled, the wariness almost cast iron now. "Batons."

I nodded, "Yes chef," lifted a huge sharp knife from the block in front of me and set to batoning the already peeled bowl of carrots at one end of the workstation.

"The gunshot I was referring to," I said, as I chopped and Mila went back to peeling potatoes, "was the one last night.

The one when Sara Simone was robbed. You were here, right? I mean, it was at dinner so I'm assuming you were down here cooking and serving the dishes?"

"You think I make dinners for those village brats to reheat and serve?" She demanded, professional pride flaring up and momentarily dislodging her caution. "Of course I was here."

"And yet you heard gunfire – as, surely, you did today when the Russian was murdered – and you didn't scream, didn't come running up the stairs to see what was going on."

"Mister," Mila finished peeling the potato in her hand, dropped it in a bowl of iced water, placed the peeler down, and turned to me. "You think I am an idiot? Look at me. I tell you last time: Where I grow up, bangs, shouts, screams, gunshots," this last said with an annunciation that suggested she was mocking my pronunciation, "are things you run from, not to. I hear the screams.

last night, and I stop what I am doing, and I wait.

"And when I hear the gunshot," she gestured at the table we were sitting at, "I get under that and I wait until I hear the police arrive."

"And this morning?"

She was furious now, her eyes no longer absently focussing on some vague space but staring into mine with righteous anger. "What did you do this morning?"

A cold smile curved her lips. "This morning," she said quietly, "I write my letter of resignation."

"You're leaving?"

"Oh, so now I should be staying? At first you are suspicious because I am not scared enough, and now because I have had enough?"

"But what did you think this morning?" I asked, "When the explosions started outside."

"Explosions?" She looked at me as though I were a small child who had said something unbelievably stupid. "I was in apartment once. Third floor. A rocket – American made – hits the building and turns floors four through six into rubble that is still falling like rain when I get down the three flights of stairs and away from the building.

"I know explosions. This morning was fireworks. Toys for children. Distractions for the rich. I tell that policeman: These things do not frighten me. Dying alone and poor," she nodded definitively, "this frightens me. But the policeman, he thinks I should be," she searched for the word, then came up with "alarmed. By fireworks. I tell him what I tell you: when you have almost died alone and penniless, when a whole building has been blown up above you, these things are not frightening."

"And what are you going to do if you leave?" Caz, from her place at the table, asked.

Mila's face split into a beaming smile. "I think, perhaps," she announced, turning towards Caz, "the time is right for me to open my restaurant. Yes," she nodded, "I have had enough of you crazy English. I find investor. I go home. I open my restaurant. And I cook what I love."

~

Mrs Chapman appeared to be tidying up what a small bronze plaque on the door named 'The Gentlemen's smoking room.'

The room was small, wood panelled, and contained two huge leather chesterfield sofas and a trio of matching high-backed winged leather club chairs, and Chapman was standing ankle deep in a sea of cushions that she appeared to have pulled from the furniture.

"Filthy habit," she said when I raised the fact that it seemed so strange to me to have a whole room dedicated not just to the act but to the act as practiced by a specific gender. "And dangerous too. Look at his," she held up a cushion. "Cigar burn. The whole place could have gone up like a tinderbox."

She tutted, discarding the offending soft furnishing to one side and turning her attention to us.

"Can I help you, my lady?" She enquired of Caz, choosing to completely ignore me.

"Well," Caz smiled, gestured at me, "I – or rather my esteemed friend here – were hoping we might ask you some questions. About," she glanced at me, clearly at a loss as to what exactly we wanted to talk about, and I smiled my most ingratiating smile and stepped into the breach.

"Nocturnal movements," I said, receiving, for my effort, a withering glare and flared nostrils from Mrs C. This was good; she didn't like me, and I didn't like her, so at least we were equal.

"Specifically," I added as she made like she'd not heard a word I'd just said and turned back to the cushions, "last night's movements in the house."

"Mr Bird," she straightened up, drew herself to her full height and looked down her nose at me, "I'm afraid I have absolutely no idea what you are talking about. If you could, please, clarify?"

"I'm assuming," I said, "that you remained awake until the police had finished their initial investigation after the robbery last night."

"I am the housekeeper," she said flatly. "I'd hardly be keeping it very well if I took to my bed whilst an army of strange men marauded all over the place."

"So who was up by the time you went to bed?"

"Who?" She frowned, remembering. "Major Henry was still up, obviously. He'd sent Sir Phillip to bed. His father is an old man and in need of rest. Plus, the excitement of the evening had left him in a state of some anxiety. Obviously."

"Anyone else?" I asked, and her lips pursed in annoyance.

"Sir Henry was on the stairs behind me. He and I locked up the house together. There was a young policeman left downstairs to monitor what was – before it became a crime scene – the dining room. That's-" she paused, then carried on. "That's all. Everyone else had already come upstairs."

"You recalled something," I said, and Caz, before the housekeeper could opine on my rudeness, spoke:

"He's right, you know, Mrs Chapman. You paused. I saw it."

Chapman's face clouded, her desire to vocalise exactly what she thought of jumped-up nothings like me clearly challenged by the fact that this jumped-up nothing was being backed up by one of her betters.

"You asked who was still up when I came to bed. And I have given you my answer," she said.

Caz dropped to a squat and rubbed her hand behind Ellie's ears, causing the dog to adopt the sort of dopy look I'd seen on Nick's face once or twice. At the memory of Nick, my heart sort of stopped. I had to get hold of him soon. I had to fix this mess, because already the thought that I might have damaged our relationship terminally was breaking my heart.

"Mrs Chapman," Caz looked up from her squat, "someone left this house last night, climbed to the folly, and stole a batch of fireworks."

Again, the conflict between arrogance and servility flitted across Chapman's face.

"The doctor," she finally announced. "He was still up. He left his room as I was passing along the landing, said he was going to check on Ms Simone. Make sure the sedatives had worked, and she was sleeping okay."

"Alone?"

"He doesn't travel with a nurse, and as his wife was already asleep in her room, yes."

"They have separate rooms?"

Again, the basilisk stare. I shrugged.

"So you went to your room. Henry to his."

"*Major* Henry went to speak with Mrs Pamela Warren." Chapman said, her anger at both my familiarity and my audacity increasing exponentially each time I spoke. "The evening – as you are well aware – was a rather fraught one."

"So you don't know – after he spoke to her – whether he went straight to bed or, perhaps, left the house?"

"I'm also unaware of whether the good doctor retired immediately after he'd checked on Miss Simone."

"So who else left Dukes Halt," I pressed, "during last night."

Chapman managed, without seeming to move a muscle of her body, to give the impression of a vast Gallic shrug. "I have no idea."

"I've heard you described as many things," I said, and there was a flicker of confusion across her otherwise impassive face. "And one of those things was as the eyes and ears of Dukes Halt. You've been working here for so long. How many years is it?" I asked and before she could remember to apply her disdain filter, Chapman's natural pride at her position kicked in.

"Almost fifty years," she smiled.

"And you really expect me to believe that you can't tell – even when you're asleep – that someone has opened the front door and left the house?"

She smiled, and the air temperature in the room dropped about twenty degrees. "I don't expect anything from – or of - you, Mr Bird. But I slept soundly last night, and that, I'm afraid, is all I can tell you."

And she turned back to her cushions.

"One last question, Chapman," Caz asked, her tone deliberately clipped, and the housekeeper's head came back up.

"Where might I find Sir Phillip?"

She stopped dead. It was as though the air in the room had simply evaporated, and I know if I had asked that question I'd have received a variation of the 'do not disturb the family' line I'd received the day before. But this was Caz asking, and so Chapman forced a smile on her face.

"Sir Phillip is in his study, ma'am. But he's asked not to be disturbed."

"Thanks," Caz smiled. "I'm sure Mr Bird will be the soul of discretion."

"Mr-?" Her eyes darted to me.

"Yes. Sweetest, I've just remembered something I 'd almost forgotten. I'd like to check it out, so are you alright to talk to Sir Phillip without me?"

Chapman's mouth got so tight I swear I heard teeth cracking, and I smiled at Caz.

"Well, now I know where to find him I'm sure I'll be fine."

"Good." Caz, who at some point had transferred from a

squat to actually sitting on the floor playing with the dog, pulled herself effortlessly to her feet, thanked Chapman for her help and, me following behind her and Ellie, we left the room.

~

Sir Phillip was in his study but not, as I had expected, behind his desk.

The room was a large space, a huge walnut desk at one end, a solid leather-backed chair behind it and two smaller reproductions of the chair in front of the desk.

Off to the side, a smaller desk – Chapman's, I assumed – sat empty.

I'd been expecting a vast library but was surprised to discover that this room was devoid of books and stuffed, instead, with greenery – from small ceramic bowls containing delicate succulents to vast palms embedded in heavy glazed pots.

And amongst them, after I'd knocked twice and been ordered to enter by the man himself, I found Sir Phillip dozing in yet another huge, high-backed club chair.

I coughed.

He stirred, and – without so much as opening an eye – said, "I'm busy."

"I just had one question to ask. And then I promise I'll let you get back to whatever you're doing."

He sighed deeply, and theatrically, and hauled himself upright.

"They've let you out then." He smiled, the smile looking like someone practicing something they'd only heard described by telephone, and gestured to yet another vast overstuffed leather chesterfield sofa opposite him.

It crossed my mind to ask how many cows had actually died to furnish this house. I didn't ask. I suspected he'd know to the last head and take great pleasure in explaining the history of tanning and upholstery in Dukes Halt. I'd never been a fan of those people who regularly throw everything they own into a skip and redecorate their entire house from the latest trendy store so that the whole place has a history that goes back no further than the credit card bill in question. I liked my home to have a mix of old, new, borrowed, bought, inherited and found, but I was finding Dukes Halt, with its insistence on the value of history unsettling.

"I wasn't exactly helping them with their enquiries," I smiled back at him, settling myself into the sofa.

"Must make a nice change," Sir Phillip said dryly.

I was thrown for a moment. His smile had vanished but in its place was a more genuine sort of smirk, as though I amused him in some way.

"It won't last. They're doubtless drawing up my arrest warrant for something as we speak."

"Oh I do hope not. The Chief Constable is my brother. It'll make for such a trying Christmas if I have to give sanctuary in the family chapel to a ne'er do well. I'm told Digby Smith came back from his run today with a broken nose and some very painful bruising."

I said nothing.

"Said he stumbled. Ran into a tree. Odious little man. Wouldn't have him here if I didn't have to, but politics, you know."

Did I imagine it, or did his smirk turn somewhat apologetic?

"Still, though I can never officially state anything of the sort, it was rather pleasing to see a tree that finally fought back."

"Has he gone back to London?" I asked hopefully, and Sir Phillip filled his cheeks and expelled the air in a disgusted blast.

"Not bloody likely. The man's got the self-awareness of a loofah. He'll be at dinner tonight – wherever Chapman manages to arrange it – looking like a panda that's feeling sorry for itself and waiting for me to make some decisions on which of his nasty little cronies I'm going to allow to go to the CBE committee.

"You have a lot of power."

Now, he actually chuckled. "Had. The old order passeth, and all that. I'm assuming the whereabouts of the bruised member of parliament was not the question you wanted to ask me."

"No," I paused. This was the point of no return, really. I still felt like Sir Phillip had a greater degree of power – and knowledge – than anyone in this house, but it felt stupid asking the question. Still, nothing ventured.

I leaned forward in the sofa, dropped my voice, and said "I was wondering if you knew who murdered Sergei Maximov?"

"I understood it was a deranged young woman whom the police currently have in custody. May I ask: Is there a reason why you're interrogating me in my own home?"

"Have the police?"

He paused, a slow smile crept across his face, and he nodded. "Touché, young man. They were rather ermine struck. The title tends to do that to some people. But not," he added dryly, "to you."

I mirrored his nod. "The woman in custody is neither disturbed nor a murderess."

"And yet," he noted, "she was found in a locked room with a gun and a dead man."

"It wasn't locked," I said. "I got in. And if I could get in, someone else could have gotten out. Having shot the dead man."

"But we were all standing in the hall when the gun went off."

I shook my head. "Not all of us. Only the guests."

"Sir Philip chuckled, shook his head. "You're suggesting the servants murdered him?"

"He was nominally Russian," I reminded the aristo before me. "The servants did a lot worse than shoot the odd blackmailing pimp in 1917."

Sir Phillip's eyes tightened. "Where were you schooled?"

"Saint Agatha and Saint Lawrence RC Boys school Peckham," I said, and he winced.

"And your degree?"

"Paper communication delivery; I left school and became a mailroom boy. But you already know all of this; you checked up on me, remember?"

"And there's that much detail on the web? How fascinating."

"There is on the webs you use. I've spoken to your son and his wife."

"Ah." He templed his fingers in front of his face and regarded me inscrutably. "In my day, of course, one would have consumed cyanide before fessing up to – no offence meant – a mailroom boy from a state school who made some lucky guesses."

"None taken," I assured him then, before he could resume the irritated but dotty old aristo act he'd been putting on since I'd arrived at Dukes Halt, asked again: "So: Who killed Sergei Maximov?"

"My dear young man," he smiled, his ice blue eyes twinkling, "I have absolutely no idea."

It was my turn, now, to regard him silently. And changed tack.

"What happened to your son?" I asked.

Sir Phillip frowned.

I waited.

"He was always lazy," Sir Phillip finally said. "He's improved with age, but there's still no real back bone there. It's why I suggested his wife was a better candidate for," he smiled sardonically, "the family business."

"I meant the other one."

"Young man, I think I've been very generous with my time. But really, I fail to see what the topic you're now approaching has to do with recent events in my house."

"On my first night here," I dropped my voice again, "while you, Major Henry and John were discussing 'family business,' I overheard Maximov threaten someone. He was talking about your wife's death, and about your son's death. He suggested he knew something that would give him a hold over your family."

"My wife was sick. She died. My son Edward was a small boy. He should not have been left alone. The house was in mourning. He was spirited but, I think, a little lost. He fell," Sir Phillip gestured vaguely behind and above him, as though the exact location of the spot from which his six-year-old son fell to his death was uncertain.

"He was left unattended. Someone should have been looking after him, but my wife's death," he cleared his throat, the emotion of the history he was reliving seemingly disturbing him, "caused such turmoil. She was sick for a very long time, you see, and I'd become so embedded in my own fear, my own sadness, that I was in no fit state to manage a household this size.

"And so Edward," his eyes teared over, "who was a really quite remarkable boy, was left alone. His death was an accident. A tragic, but faultless accident. But there was nothing about it that could possibly have provided Maximov – or anyone else – with a hold over anyone in this house."

He sat back in his chair, a cloud flickering momentarily across his face, as though he were reliving that period. Or recalling something he'd previously forgotten.

"And your other son?" I asked, knowing as soon as I did so that I'd overstepped the mark.

"I'm tired," he said. "I've enjoyed our chat, Mr Bird, but I really need to rest."

"Why was he banished?" I pressed. "I promise, I'll leave now. But why?"

"He was sent away to think about his actions. He has never come back," Sir Phillip said, already drifting, or feigning the drift, into sleep. "Still, there's time. Maybe one day…"

CHAPTER TWENTY-FIVE

Sir Phillip Warren has no idea George Warren is dead.

The thought ran around my head as I softly closed the door behind me and stood in the hallway listening to his gentle snores from the other side of the door.

Or does he? Maybe he was just choosing to pretend otherwise. But why would he do that, I wondered, as Lottie's words came back to me: *They were terrible people, really, my ancestors: Disloyal, treacherous. They were spies and turncoats and thieves. And I'll let you in on a secret: We're as bad today as we were then.*

How could he not know his son was dead? I looked around me, at the silk-lined walls, the gilt-framed paintings of people who'd been dust for centuries and of landscapes untarnished with motorways or high rises; a world devoid of pension schemes, NHS hospitals or workers' rights, where the only thing that mattered was *The Family Business*; and I found myself wondering how easy it would be for people in this place to evade, by choice or circumstance, anything outside their bubble.

I was still pondering the situation and wondering whether I should have told Sir Phillip the truth about his son when I walked into the great hallway and was grabbed by Caz.

"Fancy a walk?" she asked, making it clear that we were leaving the house.

I glanced at the fanlight above the door where the sky was dark and raised an eyebrow at her.

"I'm not a fan of new exercise-crazed Caz," I said darkly, and she pointed at Ellie.

"Blame my new companion," she said. "She's been drinking way too much water."

"Not a comment anyone has ever made about her mama," I replied.

"Yes, well we can discuss that, or we can take Ms Ellie here for a widdle before she drains herself all over the hall carpet. Your call."

"Let me get a coat," I said, and Caz looked at me as though I had suggested I pop upstairs and get a map of the continent of Atlantis tattoed on my back before we went out.

"Pourquoi?"

"Because it's nearly November," I said, as though explaining to a small child.

"God," she sighed theatrically, "it's still mild. Where I'm from we don't dig the coats out til the first snows. And even then, we kept the floor-length minks til there was an actual blizzard blowing. Anyways," she nodded at Ellie who trotted to the door, paused, and looked back expectantly, "you don't have time."

Ellie whined, as though the entire manoeuvre had been rehearsed.

"And minks?" I asked as Caz opened the door and ushered me out into a barely-there twilight.

"Calm your jets, cowboy: Those minks were dead before Queen Victoria. And I'm assured they died of old age." She paused as a voice drifted towards us from somewhere outside.

"Goddamit, Damon. I *pay* you to keep a lid on this sort of shit." Sara Simone, by the sound of it, was not a happy starlet.

"Well do *something*. I don't know. Pay the judge. Fake a seizure. Pay the judge to fake a seizure. Just stop it from going forward. If she's not stopped," La Simone said, the panic in her voice audible, "it's game over. I'm finished."

We stepped out, Ellie bounding past us towards the darkness, and the cold night air immediately made me shiver.

Sara was at the end of the house, seemingly unaware that her voice was carrying. "I don't care what you do, Damon, but do something. 'Cos I'm not going down without a fight, you hear me?"

She looked up. Spotted us. "I'll call you back," she growled into the phone, then switched on the smile that had earned her twenty million dollars a movie.

"Evening folks. Nice night for it," she kept smiling as she squeezed past us and into the house, slamming the door behind her.

"Well speak of the devil," Caz said.

"What have you got?" I asked, wrapping my arms around myself and stamping my feet in a vain attempt at keeping warm.

Caz looked pointedly at the recently closed front door, "First a question: Which of our fellow guests has been the victim of a jewel robbery lately?"

"Sara Simone," I answered, puzzled by the question.

"Indeed. But which of our guests has been present at a jewel robbery lately? Apart, that is, from the one we've all been witness to?"

I didn't understand the question. Ellie had run off into the middle of the lawn and was clearly performing her doggy ablutions, whilst Caz and I stood some way off and observed the clouds skidding across the face of a still rather large moon.

"John Warren, sweetest. I'm talking John Warren. I knew there was something about the whole thing that rang a bell, and it came to me today. I remembered Whitney Onway talking about it during the summer at Suki Van Standt's Henley regatta ball."

"Okay, first things first: should I have a clue who Whitney Onway or Suki Van Standt is? And what was discussed at this regatta ball? And also: regatta ball?"

"It's a party. To celebrate a regatta. Lots of young men with very broad shoulders and long legs trying to get overly familiar with ladies like Whitney Onway and Suki Van Standt, who have trust funds bigger than the GDP of Norway, and bodyguards hired expressly to prevent young men with very broad shoulders and long legs getting overly familiar with them. But that's not relevant. What *is* relevant is what was discussed:

"Suki was at a weekend event. Some oligarch had rented

Sicily for a party attended by a thousand of his closest friends."

"And I get Dorset in November."

"October, dear. And you wouldn't have liked the Sicily affair. Your conscience would prick you every time you ate one of his oysters and considered how corrupt his money was."

She was right. I still feigned outrage. "I'm quite happy eating with the Warrens. Who probably evicted my ancestors from their small holdings at one point or another."

"Quite different. That was well over a century ago, and you can personally see how miserable the whole lot of them are, which has to salve both your guilt at eating their mousseline de coquilles St Jacques sauce crevette, and your anger at the actions of their ancestors. But are we – oh, good girl," she broke off as Ellie, tail wagging and tongue hanging out, came bounding over. "Shall we walk this way?"

"Aren't you going to check?" I gestured at the lawn.

"Check?"

"Well she might have, y'know," I searched for the correct phrasing, "laid an egg."

Caz raised an eyebrow. "She'd have barked."

"Barked?"

"Yes. You know: woof woof."

"You've trained her to bark when she takes a shit?"

"Well obviously. She's not an animal. I mean, she is, but, well, a lady doesn't leave that sort of thing for the groundsman to discover, so whenever she," Caz paused, "delivers something from Harrods, she barks. Don't you girl?"

At the end, her voice went up a tone, and Ellie, looking over her shoulder, seemed to take it as permission to go berserk, and went charging off into the darkness, her panting and the crashing of vegetation audible to us even as we kept to the driveway.

"I'm lost," I said, and Caz went back to the beginning. "Suki. Sicilly."

"Oligarch," I added, confirming I had found my place.

"Well, on the Saturday night there was a grand party at which tout le monde wore their finery. Jewels. Gold. Platinum bangles and the hautest of couture. And the ladies dressed up too, I'm told.

"Except, come the morning, at least one of those ladies found it difficult to lay her hands on the tiara – diamonds and sapphires with two perfect twin emeralds that the empress Eugénie had worn at her coronation. So the lady in question – the contemporary one, not the dead empress - on waking from her slumbers, discovered – as I have spent some time now trying to explain – that the tiara was no longer in her possession.

"Or, a search of the villa determined, in the house she was staying in."

"Pinched?"

"Well unless the empress Eugénie came back from the other side and repossessed it, one is forced to that conclusion."

"You mentioned John Warren?"

"On the guest list. I called Suki to check. She'd not mentioned it before – no reason to, really - but this is where it gets rather interesting."

"*This is where it gets interesting?*" House parties, in my experience, usually ended up with tears and recriminations, but the fact that – to Caz – a house party ending in the theft of an antique and hugely expensive tiara with a shadow falling on all one thousand guests suggested she had a different definition of interesting than I.

"Well, when Suki told this story she was responding to Whitney Onway's original tale. South of France. Cannes film festival. That actress – you know the one: her bosom acts more than her face?"

I named the actress. Caz nodded.

"Well, she turns up on the red carpet wearing a Dior gown and a ruby the size of a baby's fist. And guess what?"

"The ruby goes missing," I said, in a tone that suggested her attempt at drama had fallen as flat as the actress's brow.

"Indeed. She wakes up the next morning with her date from the night before still snuggled against her Oscar-deserving bosom, and the ruby – which she'd persuaded Garrards to lend her - has vanished.

"And that date? The one nuzzling her best supporting actors?"

A cold breeze blew from somewhere, carrying with it the scent of fires and decaying leaves. "John Warren?" I guessed.

"Two Jewel robberies. And at each, John Warren was present. Once is bad luck."

"Twice an unfortunate coincidence," I said.

"So do we think thrice is evidence of a pattern?"

I sighed. "I have no idea what I think anymore. But I do wonder who – or what - John Warren really is."

"You've met him," Caz said. "You tell me."

"The Warrens are spies. They've been spies for – well," I shrugged, "forever. Sir Phillip doesn't seem entirely convinced about Henry's abilities, but he seems almost ignorant of John. I got the feeling Digby Smith," who's attempted assault on me, I suddenly realised, I hadn't mentioned to Caz, "is here because he has to be, and John is here only because he's Smith's secretary."

"More to the point," Caz explained, "John's father is a policeman."

I recalled Sir Phillip explaining his brother was Chief Constable.

"Do we really think the son of the local Chief Constable is an international jewel thief who's pulled a job not only on daddy's patch, but amongst his own family?"

"When did he meet Sara Simone," I said, lowering my gaze from the starlit sky above to the impenetrable darkness ahead.

"Well my source tells me they met at Cannes."

"Whitney?"

"Variety, actually. But it was well known, even before the met that after Cannes La Simone was heading to Italy and might possibly end up – if the court case went her way – with the Gianelli stone."

"So what? John seduced Sara and brought her to Dukes Halt so he could set up a jewel robbery?"

"Cocktails are being served," a voice behind us announced, and we both jumped, one of us, not Caz, emitting a brief shriek.

We turned.

"Dress is casual, and cocktails will be served in the Ladies' lounge," John Warren added. "Which is sort of understandable in light of recent events. Lord," he smiled, "you both look like you've seen a phantom. Come in when you want, but if you want a Negroni don't leave it too long; Sara's mother seems to have attacked the gin like a shark on flesh."

And – as he chuckled and we wondered how much of our conversation he'd heard – he went out of the darkness towards the brightly lit entrance of Dukes Halt.

George's Diary 29th July 1986

Mama was a little better today, some colour back on her cheeks, and she said that it was having her boys back that had raised her spirits.

She came down to breakfast, her movements unsteady, a brittle smile on her face, kissed us all good morning and sat, asking Chapman to bring her a tea and some toast.

Henry and Edward told her all about school and what they'd done yesterday on the first day of the holidays and I was watching my father – watching how his eyes looked everywhere except at her – when my mother asked me a question and I zoned back in just in time to see an expectant look on her face.

"I'm sorry, mama?" I asked, and she laughed.

"My Georgie. Always a million miles away. I asked what you got up to yesterday."

"I-" I blushed, stammered.

"I asked him to run an errand for me," my father – clearly bored with the conversation or perhaps with my inability to plainly respond to the question provided.

"That's right," I said, and I saw my mother's eyes dart to my father, a puzzled look coming over her face, and then a smile – something sort of triumphant – crossing her face.

"Well," she smiled as Chapman put the tea and toast before her, "isn't that nice."

"Well it would have been," my father muttered, "if he'd actually done as I asked. Straight after breakfast, George, you go back and do what I asked you to do yesterday."

I really enjoyed meeting Simon yesterday.

By the time we'd trekked through the woods to the cottage we were both sweating and a little breathless as we'd talked all the way. His t-shirt, which he'd put back on before sheathing the axe and putting it over his shoulder had dark patches under his arms a long dark streak down his back, and a Van Halen logo on the front.

I couldn't understand how we hadn't met before but he insisted we probably had at some time or other. "Just not in the middle of the wood when I was swinging around a lethal weapon," he smiled, and I found myself blushing. Nobody ever makes jokes with me. Most of the time people either tease me or ignore me.

"Most of the time you're away at school," he said. "And when you come home, I guess I'm in town with my mates. I'm only here today 'cos the rest of them have gone on some stupid day trip to see a concert in London. You only come home for Christmas and Summer, don't you?"

"Sometimes half term," I answered, "but the past few years we've gone skiing at the Michaelmas and Lent half terms, and we've gone to London or Paris with my mama at the Summer half term."

He chuckled.

"What?" I bristled.

"Mama," he mimicked me, almost perfectly. "I call mine Mam. Amazing what an extra 'a' can do to elevate how it sounds."

He said it again now, in his own voice, then shook his head.

"Nah, doesn't work when I say it."

"I think mine's dying," I said, and he stopped immediately.

"Oh shit. I'm so sorry." The air around us was hot and still. The whole forest seemed to go silent.

"It's okay," I shrugged, wanting the moment to last, but not wanting to jinx my mama, "she might not be. I just-"

What? What was I going to say?

"I just worry," I finished lamely, and he nodded, clapped me on my shoulder and turned, pressing on through the trees.

"I hope she's okay," he said.

Nobody has ever taken my worrying so well. At home, my mama will tell me not to let the world bother me, while my father will bluster that I'm wasting my energy on nothing whatsoever, and at school everyone – the students and half the staff – laugh in my face if I ever them how I worried about almost everything.

I try not to, but I can't help it.

There's the nuclear bomb, the state of the planet, prisoners behind the Iron Curtain, the famine in Africa, Chernobyl, the Space Shuttle explosion, so much to fear.

And all so worthless when I think of what life will be like without my mama.

When we got to the tiny cottage, Kennedy and Mrs K had gone out, so Simon let me in to the house and asked me if I wanted a cold drink.

For a moment I thought of asking for a beer, because I didn't want him to think I was a little kid; at the same time, I was there on business for my father, and didn't want to look like I was being unprofessional, but then Simon sorted my dilemma by offering me a lemonade or a ginger beer, and I had the ginger beer.

"They'll be back soon enough," he said, handing me the glass. "You can wait if you like."

"I'm just supposed to look at a list of stuff your father wants for the fencing on Lady Anne's pasture. Has he left the list?"

Simon blushed now. "He might have, he said," swigging from his glass.

"If I could take a look at the office I might see it."

"You're not allowed to," he replied, a look of mild panic in his eyes. "Nobody's allowed in there except my dad. It's private business."

"Only it's not," I smiled back. "It's my family's business."

I knew, as soon as the words came out of my mouth, that I'd blown it.

Stupid, stupid, stupid George. Why hadn't I left the paperwork, waited for Kennedy to return from wherever he'd gone to? I could have spent the intervening time drinking ginger beer with Simon and sitting at his kitchen table.

Instead, I'd pulled rank.

He blushed deeply.

I wanted to say that I was sorry. That I hadn't mean it. But it was too late; I'd said what I'd said.

"He locks the door," Simon said, his whole demeanour changing, as though shutters were dropping behind his eyes. "Whatever he needs, the list will be in there. And – now I think about it – I've no idea when he'll be back."

"But you said-"

"Well whatever I said," he shut me off, "I was probably wrong. He might be hours. Why don't you come back later?"

My heart sank.

"I could wait."

"I need to get back to work," he said, draining the glass. "Logs to chop. But I'll be sure to tell him you called."

CHAPTER TWENTY-SIX

I'd washed my hands and splashed my hands in the downstairs cloakroom (Czech & Speake toiletries that made it feel like I was experiencing an Ottoman Hamam; plumbing that made it feel like I was experiencing the bombing of Dresden) when I followed the sound of voices and found my way to the Ladies' Lounge.

Caz (who, in the time it had taken me to splash and wash, appeared to have managed to change into a beaded dress and arrange her hair in an effortless chignon that still required at least twenty hairclips and a bare-faced defiance of gravity, shoved a large tumbler at me.

"Drink," she ordered as, from somewhere behind her, the sound of an orchestra playing a somewhat funereal arrangement of 'Anything goes' by Cole Porter issued. "And drink heavily," she added, leaning in as though to adjust my non-existent bow-tie. "It's what these people understand."

I lifted the pink-tinged glass and sipped it.

Gin. Neat, almost undiluted gin.

"Negroni," she said, leaning in to add, "I have sources Mrs Gerber can only dream of annexing."

The aforementioned woman was sat on the far side of the room in what looked like animated conversation with Digby Smith, whose back was mercifully to me.

Between me and her was the duo of Richard and Karen Stamford, stood like the pillars of Hercules on either side of the arrangement of sofas (rich brocade this time, the decorators having obviously run out of cows to skin) and gripping their drinks as though they were talismans against the horror that his enoblement had dumped them in to.

I sipped my drink and stepped forward.

"Shocking," I said apropos of nothing.

Apropos of nothing, it seemed, was all that was required.

"Horrifiying," Richard Stamford said, and to be honest I was unsure whether he was referring to the fact that a man had been murdered today, in the dining room, or to the fact that we were having cocktails in the Ladies' Lounge.

Karen lifted her glass – a large martini giving off the blue-green tinge of vodka married with vermouth – and toasted me. "A lesson to everyone on the fragility and value of life."

I toasted her back. And took my chance.

"You're sleeping at the front of the house, right?"

Karen Stamford's face set in a puzzled smile.

"I wonder if you heard anyone leaving the house last night?"

Richard looked at Karen, who smiled back at me, her smile looking as natural as her buttercup tresses.

"My husband slept soundly," she said, though Chapman's disclosure that the duo had separate bedrooms in Dukes Halt reduced the reliability of her statement. "And I was on a video meeting with some colleagues in North America until the early hours of the morning. I had earphones on, and my focus was on the conversation, I'm afraid, so I didn't hear anyone leave."

"So you must have slept late," I asked and Karen Stamford shook her head.

"Up with the birds," she said. "I find it hard to sleep in the mornings, but it's fine; I have business to attend to."

I remembered Digby's comment on the first night: Mrs Stamford was involved in some big business deal. If it came off, she'd be richer than Croesus. Hence, I supposed, all these late-night calls and early morning starts.

"So did either of you hear anyone out and about early?" I asked. "I mean those fireworks didn't set themselves."

"Oh. I see," Karen looked, somewhat pointedly, at Richard, who suddenly found his Old Fashioned of great interest. "Well I slept until just before I came down for breakfast. Richard?"

Her husband looked at her, at me, back at her, and lied.

"I slept til at least ten," he said, despite the fact I'd seen him talking to Mila before eight. "Didn't hear a thing."

"Interesting," I said, pressing past them both and moving on to the middle of the space.

George's Diary 30th July 1986

Why do I end up ruining every friendship I make?

I really like Simon, and my own crass behaviour yesterday ruined everything.

I went back to the cottage this morning. I couldn't not go. My father had insisted.

I wonder if he'd asked me to run the errand just so he could watch me fail.

I'd been wracking my brains trying to think of some way to make the visit less embarrassing. Part of me wondered whether I might be able to visit at a time when I knew Simon was out of the house, so I wouldn't have to see him, but I couldn't really think of a foolproof way of ensuring his absence, and besides – I really did want to see him.

Then, at breakfast, it had hit me: Henry was slathering marmalade on his toast while humming some tune he'd heard on the radio when my father lowered his newspaper just long enough to advise him that we were at breakfast, not at a coral evening, and that if he was unable to dine without making 'that infernal racket' he was welcome to consume his breakfast in his room.

Henry stopped humming but stuck a tongue out at the re-risen newspaper, eliciting a smile of complicity from our mother.

And that's when I had the idea.

George has a record player in his room and a small collection of records, and I was fairly sure he had a couple of Van Halen singles.

I was out of my room, along the corridor and outside his in moments, an ear pressed to it when Chapman appeared at the other end of the corridor.

"What are you doing there?" she asked, suspicion obvious in her tone, and I wished I could say the words to let her know her place, but blushed instead and said I'd thought I heard George call my name.

I knew, as I said it, that the excuse was stupidly weak, and Chapman made no attempt to pretend she considered it anything but contemptible.

"Aren't you supposed to be running an errand for your father?"

Blushing, I muttered something about needing to just go and use the bathroom, then rushed back to my room and – as the door closed behind me – cursed my stupidity. We have a shared bathroom between our rooms.

Now that I knew George was downstairs, I could use it to get into his room, find a record to bring as a peace offering to Simon, and then come out of my own room, and if George ever went looking for the record he'd assume - because he had so many split between the house and his rooms at school – that he'd left it back there.

And anyway, I figured, as soon as I could get to a record shop I would buy another copy of the blasted record and replace the gap in his bloody collection.

I was out of the house, my bag slung over my shoulder, when Edward caught up with me. I didn't want him anywhere near me today, but I couldn't think of an easy way to get rid of him, so as we dipped into the trees I took him into my confidence.

"Look Edward," I said, squatting down to his level, "Can you keep a secret?"

"Secret?" He was confused, so I told him. "I've borrowed something. It's a gift for my new friend, but I don't want anyone to know that I've borrowed it."

"Borrowed?" He was puzzled.

I sighed. "Taken. I've taken something. But I promise I'll replace it."

"You shouldn't take things that don't belong to you," he said, his wide-eyed innocence almost comical. "It's naughty."

I considered my response. "Yes," I put my hands on his shoulders, looked into his eyes as though taking him into my deepest confidence, "It would be very naughty if I was stealing it. You know what stealing is, Edward?"

"Very naughty," he said with utmost seriousness in his little face.

I nodded. "Yes. Stealing is very naughty. But this is borrowing. Do you know why that's not so naughty?"

He shook his head, a little tentatively.

"Because I'm not going to keep what I borrowed. I'm going to replace it. You see: I'm going to put it back, so it's alright to borrow it."

He considered this for a moment then his face split in a beaming smile. "Borrowed," he said, accepting the truth I'd fed him.

Simon wasn't in the clearance, and my heart sank a little. What if he'd gone to town, or been sent on an errand? What if I came all the way to the Estate manager's cottage and he was nowhere to be found?

I shifted the bag on my shoulder.

"I'm hungry," Edward whined beside me.

"You've just had breakfast," I said, rummaging in my bag and finding a banana I'd been saving for later.

"Don't want a 'nana," he said, "I'm thirsty too."

"It's a banana, Edward," I said through gritted teeth. "Only babies say 'nana'."

"I'm not a baby," he snapped sulkily. "And I'm thirsty."

"Well there's nothing I can do about that," I said, shoving the banana back in my rucksack. "Maybe when we get to the cottage they'll have some lemonade."

This seemed to perk him up and in no time at all I was knocking on the door of the cottage.

Kennedy's wife answered. She's a large jolly woman and always seems happy to see us. She smiled at us, and gave a special welcome to Edward. I wished, for a moment, that we could swap – send Chapman to live in the cottage in the wood like some sort of fairytale witch and have Mrs Kennedy to look after us in the house. Maybe she'd bring Simon too and I wouldn't be so friendless.

I told her that I'd been sent to look at the list of requirements her husband needed for the fencing on Lady Anne's pasture, and she explained that he was out but was due back imminently.

"Would you like to wait?" She asked. "I've just made some shortbread. And there's fresh lemonade in the fridge."

Edward's eyes lit up and she smiled, stepping to one side and ushering us into the house, Edward darting straight away, his nose indicating where the kitchen was.

And there was Simon.

He'd come out of the living room drawn, I suppose, by curiosity to see who was at the door.

He was wearing a different t-shirt today but I saw with relief that it was another Van Halen one.

"Oh," he said as his mother followed Edward into the kitchen. "It's you."

"Simon," I stepped forward, "I'm sorry. So very, very sorry, if I was rude or insulting yesterday."

He blushed again. "Don't know what you're talking about," he said gruffly.

"I'm talking about me being so gauche."

"Gauche?" His blush was back, his puzzlement once more putting a barrier between us.

"I mean," I said, stepping forward again so that I could drop my voice, "that I'm sorry for behaving like a tit."

He laughed.

"I was stupid and rude," I said.

"You were rude alright," he said, smiling, "but it's okay."

It was my turn to blush now, to feel my cheeks redden and my heart hammer.

"I brought you something," I said, scrambling around inside the bag. "To say sorry, to – I hope – seal our friendship."

I grabbed at the record, and pulled it but as it came free of the bag it caught the loose pages of my sketchbook and they flew up from the bag, cascading around me on to the floor.

I held the Van Halen record out to thin air. Simon was on his knees picking up the sketches, looking at them and frowning.

"These are good," he said, holding up one of Dukes Halt that I'd sketched from the Folly the previous day, and lifting from the floor a page that had landed with the sketch face down.

He glanced at it and laughed out loud. "Really good."

It was a picture of my father, but I'd made his eyebrows even more extended than they were, his creased angry brow more furious, his hair a deranged whip of sliver-streaked fluff, the whole thing looking like some sort of angry bridge troll.

I laughed too. "Oh I should probably burn that one. If he ever sees it I shall be disinherited."

Simon stood. "You're a really good drawer." He offered me the sketches back and I took them, offering in exchange the Van Halen single.

I shrugged. "No future in drawing."

"Picasso didn't think so."

"You know Picasso?"

"Well believe it or not Your Lordship," he said, his voice acquiring a sort of yokel tone as a cheeky grin played over his face, "even folks as like us have heard of old Pablo." He shook his head to stave off my furious apologies. "I'm joking. I like art at school. But I'm no good at drawing.

Can't draw a circle, me."

"I bet you could," I said, stuffing the sketches back into my bag. "It's really all about focus and confidence. Most of the time I have neither – I'm bright, but I hate Maths and only like English when it's composition. But when I sketch, or when I write I'm sort of not there any longer. I'm so focused on the work that all my doubts fade away and all that matters is the light and shade, the next line, the moment after this one and the moment after that.

"And I'm no longer thinking about whether people like me or not, or what I'm going to do with my life, because none of that matters."

He looked at the record, a tinge of the blush back on his cheeks. "Thanks," he said.

"You don't have it?" I asked, suddenly afraid I'd gone to the trouble of stealing George's record for nothing.

"No," he shook his head. "I really like it. Do you want to listen to it? I've got a record player in my room."

The air in the hallway was stuffy and scented with vanilla and suddenly it was also still. Still and silent like the world.

"I'd love to," I said, and he smiled.

"I wish I could draw like you," he said as he led me up the stairs.

CHAPTER TWENTY-SEVEN

Dinner was a buffet.

Now don't get me wrong: I've been to buffets, and few of them featured veal cutlets, wasabi crusted short rib, carrot soufflés and horseradish pea salad. But I could still imagine that – despite Mila clearly pulling out all the stops and delivering her entire repertoire - a meal served on a table in the Ladies Lounge, and consumed on hastily arranged card tables in the ballroom at Dukes Halt had to be a first.

"How are you all holding up?" I made my way over to Sara Simone, who was sitting nibbling at a large bowl of what looked like alfalfa, John on one side and Francine Gerber on the other.

"Oh, you know," John said, a smile on his face that the word dopey was invented for. "Just getting on. Sara wants to go back to London tomorrow."

"So soon?" Caz asked. "But you'll miss the fireworks."

"I think we've seen enough fireworks for a lifetime," Francine said morosely, lifting her glass and realising – after she'd tipped it to its apex – that it was empty. "Robbery. Gunmen. Murder." The last one made her shudder. "Should have never come here. I mean getting robbed wasn't the worst? We have to be half-murdered too?"

"Mama," Sara put down her knife and fork, "you're drunk. Maybe you should lay off the sauce."

"Drunk? Christ, Maureen, we're sharing dinner with a murderer. You think I should, maybe, be sober and making small talk?"

"My name," Ms Simone said, through gritted teeth, "is *Sara*."

"Well I named you Maureen, Maureen; so I think I know

what your name is." She shook her head. "Named you after my aunt. Her name was Maureen too," she added unnecessarily. "My mother told me it was bad luck: To name a child after someone who was still alive. Like tempting God," she said, pointing a finger skywards and looking wildly around. "Where are those waiter kids?"

"Mother," Sara-slash-Maureen said, a dark tone very clear in her voice now, "lay off the gin."

"I shudda listened to my mother," Francine carried on. "Should never have come here."

"Your mother warned you off coming to Dukes Halt?" Caz asked, receiving for her puzzlement an equally puzzled stare from Francine Gerber, who seemed – until that moment – not to have noticed we had joined their table.

"My mother died in 98. She was eighty-two years of age. Fell off a horse."

"She was riding at eighty-two?" Caz was impressed.

"Well I say horse," Francine corrected herself. "It was a statue. Bronze. On a plinth, you know. Between the horse and the plinth, the drop was about sixteen feet. Wudda killed a woman half her age, they reckoned."

I didn't want to – I really didn't want to – but I found myself asking the question that at least three fifths of the people at the table had to be thinking: "Mrs Gerber, what was your mother – your eighty-two-year-old mother - doing on a statue of a horse?"

"Tryn'a communicate with Robert E Lee," Francine slurred. "He was also on the horse. Well, a statue of him was on the statue of the horse, if you get my drift. She had the gift, y'see."

The gift and, clearly, a degree of flexibility and stamina that few octogenarians could lay claim to.

"Right." A silence descended on the table as we all, I supposed, considered our reactions to the tragic – and surreal – story we'd just been told. "Ladies," I suddenly asked, "where are your rooms located?"

They looked at each other, Francine appearing to have

semi-sobered up, as though I'd asked which Swiss Bank they were currently using to hide income from the IRS.

She squinted at me.

"Why?" Sara asked, toying once more with her alfalfa.

"I'm wondering," I said, "If you heard anyone leaving the house last night. Or coming back in this morning."

"Last night?" Sara looked at me like I was deranged. "Last night, after I had been robbed and shot at, that lovely doctor gave me some pills that sent me to sleep til the early morning. A chorus line could have high-kicked through my bedroom and I'd have slept through it."

"And you?" I turned to Francine.

"Didn't sleep a wink all night," she said, "and never heard a thing outside my room."

CHAPTER TWENTY-EIGHT

I went to bed.

I brushed my teeth, but before I brushed my teeth, I pulled out the book from the bookshelf, and extracted the diary from within.

I called Nick. I told him I wanted to talk, and that I hoped he'd call me.

Then I opened George's diary.

George's Diary 5th August 1986

I've been teaching Simon to draw.

It's been a little less than a week now, but he's a good student, though he struggles with shading. He was entirely wrong about his inability to draw a circle; he has a steady hand, and he can outline the shapes of the things he sees, but he hasn't quite got the focus or the confidence yet.

I wonder if, perhaps, he has less need of escaping the world and so is never entirely consumed by the work.

My mother has spent most of the last week back in bed.

Doctor Allen has been around a couple of times, and yesterday I followed him out to his car. I was going to demand he tell me what was going on, but Chapman – who has taken to acting as a nursemaid to my mother – came out of the door as I was approaching him and stood as though waiting for me to finish whatever I wanted to ask before she proposed her question.

It was supremely awkward. I really did not want her to hear my question so I asked some stupid one about whether there was anything I could do to help with my mother's recuperation.

"What a kind boy you are," he smiled as, over his shoulder, I saw Chapman frown suspiciously. "I think," Doctor Allen gestured at Chapman "that your mother's in the very best of hands right now. But you must be a good brave boy and leave everything to the grown-ups."

I wanted to tell him that I was sixteen years of age. Hardly a baby. But Chapman had already started talking to him about needing more drips or something and I stomped into the house in a bad mood.

It was only when I was in the woods trying to show Simon how the light coming through the canopy made the branches look like they were half solid and half shadow as Edward – my constant companion these days – scribbled crayon colours into a colouring book he'd acquired from somewhere, that a thought came to me.

Brave.

Why did I need to be brave?

CHAPTER TWENTY-NINE

I was not liking the shift in the diary.

I glanced at the heavy velvet curtains, pulled tight against the dark night, and let my eyes roam around the room, trying to imagine George here that summer, feeling, as he must have, that things were spiralling out of control.

In George's case, it was his family. In mine it was Nick, Arianna and everything that had happened in the past few days.

I needed to repair the damage that had been done; to put right the mess.

But I had literally not one idea where to start.

George's Diary 9th August 1986

I think Chapman and my father have been poisoning my mother.

It seems like a crazy idea, but once the question of why I would need to be brave occurred to me, the thought was like a germ mutating. I've been awake all night trying to make sense of why I would need to be 'Brave'.

And there's only one reason, of course: Because Doctor Allen knows that my mother is going to die soon.

I asked Simon what I should do, and he frowned and cast a glance at Edward, who – as always – was oblivious, satisfied just to be in our presence.

"That doesn't make any sense," he said, putting his pencil down.

"She's been getting weaker and weaker for a long time," I attempted to explain, and he shook his head.

"No, not that. What doesn't make sense is that Old Allen would know about it and do nothing."

"Well what could he do?" I asked, still clinging to my hypothesis. "My father owns the village, probably owns the building that Allen's surgery is in. One word from my father and-"

Simon chuckled. "It's not the nineteenth century, George. I mean once upon a time the Lord of Dukes Halt could probably have gotten away with murder but Allen would be guilty too. He'd go to prison if he knew they were poisoning your mother and did nothing about it. He'd be a whatsit – an accomplice."

"Well maybe he's in on it," I said.

He considered this, nodded thoughtfully. "I suppose he could be. But then why would he warn you? Why say 'Be brave,' at all?"

Now I mused on his point. "But if it's not that," I said at length," what is it? Why did he say, 'be brave'?"

Simon put the sketch book down. He sat, like some forest creature soaking in the heat and light while I watched him, my pencil moving as though by itself until he lifted his head upright again and opened his eyes.

"This is a horrible thing to say," he said looking solidly at me, "and I really hope it's not true. But maybe you're partly right. Maybe Allen knows your mother is dying and is just telling you that – when the time comes – you're going to need to be brave."

It didn't even take a moment. I shook my head.

"There's something else going on," I said. "I don't know what. But I know that she was bright and so full of – well, everything – last year and now she just sleeps all day while Chapman and my father meet and whisper and plot. And the only visitor to the house is Doctor Allen."

"So what are you going to do?" he asked.

"I'm going to find out," I said. "One way, or another, I'm going to find out what's happening.

George's Diary 10th August 1986

"Edward tells me that you've been spending your days with the Kennedy boy," my father said at breakfast this morning.

I froze, something about his tone triggering an alarm inside me. On the opposite side of the table, Edward – oblivious to the glare I shot him - was eating toast, the bread cut into fingers and pasted with marmalade that was already smeared around his lips.

Henry, at the opposite end of the table to my father, was reading his own newspaper and seemed oblivious to the conversation.

"I'm teaching him to draw," I said, for I felt a justification of some sort was necessary.

"I'd rather you didn't spend so much time with him."

"But he's my friend," I said, realising how whiny my voice sounded, knowing that the tone would antagonise my father even more.

"He's the estate manager's son," he replied. "And you're mine. His father knows his place, and you should too."

"My place?" Tears came to my eyes.

"George. I know you're probably bored. Other years you would have been on holiday somewhere and there would be things to do and adventures to be had. But this year-"

"What exactly is my place?" I spoke over him.

"If you're bored I can come up with some things to keep you busy. We can maybe find a cousin or something that you could go and stay with."

Now the world tilted. "You want to send me away?"

"I don't want you spending your days with that boy."

"Why?" I demanded.

"Because I don't," he answered, a menacing tone clear in his response.

"And if I don't stop seeing the one friend I have in this? If I don't ignore him and treat him like he's part of the furniture? What will you do, father?"

He paused, I saw him struggle to contain his temper.

"He's the one friend I have," I said, no longer caring how wheedling my voice sounded. "And you want me to end our friendship because he's – what? beneath us?"

"This has nothing to do with him," my father said.

"What? It's me?" I laughed bitterly as Edward finally looked up, his

mouth agape at my tone. "Why do you hate me so much, papa?"

"Hate you?" now he was angry. "I'm your father, George."

"Well start acting like one," I snapped back, all inhibition gone now. "All you ever do is give me orders: Go here. Do this. Don't do that. I see you at breakfast and at dinner, and…" I was furious now, looking for barbs to throw at him, "you would have known that Simon was my friend if you had bothered to talk to me the past few weeks."

"George," my father said, "I know things have been difficult. Your mother."

"Don't you dare make this anything to do with her."

And then it dawned on me: He wanted to send me away so they could do whatever they wanted to do to my mother and I wouldn't be around to see it or stop it.

I looked at Henry, who had lowered his newspaper and was studiously tucking into a plate of scrambled eggs.

Edward had resumed playing with his toast.

"You can't send me away," I said desperately. "I won't go."

"George, stay away from the Kennedy boy."

I looked around the room. The sunlight was streaming in through the windows, beyond which a vast expanse of cloudless blue sky seemed to stretch forever. And here, in the dining room at Dukes Halt, everything felt tight.

My father could do whatever he wanted to do. I knew that. And he knew I knew it.

But I would be damned if he would end my friendship with Simon.

I pushed my plate away from me.

"May I be excused, please."

"Finish your breakfast," my father said, reaching for his newspaper.

"I'm not hungry," I said, struggling to contain my fury.

He paused, stared at me, then shook his head slightly and waved a hand in my direction.

"Then you're excused," he said. "Oh, and this morning I want you to give Kennedy the money to pay for that fencing. He's expecting you. The money is on the desk in my study. Don't stay there. And George: Stay away from his son."

"Why do you hate me?" I asked, and at last Henry looked up from his newspaper.

My father frowned. "Hate?"

"Nothing I do is good enough. Nothing I say or do. And now I'm not to have a friend. I'm not even allowed that. What have I ever done to you?"

His frown deepened. He picked up his newspaper. Put it down again. "You are my son. George. A Warren of Dukes Halt. You're not some village boy who can just do what he likes and be what he likes. You are a Warren of Dukes Halt."

"You've said that already," I replied coldly. "And surely being a Warren of Dukes Halt means I can do whatever I like. We're rich, and titled. People like us can do what we like."

His face became thunderous. "You think so? You think we own the world because we have money and privilege? We have standards, George. Precedents. We have a Name, dammit," he said, capitalising the word 'name,' as though it were some sort of holy mission, The Warrens of Dukes Halt venturing out to civilise the world.

"You think our money is all that matters?" He laughed dryly. "George, the Warren name – the standards, the precedents. These are not easy things to live up to. People without those can do what they like, because they have nothing to lose. You are a Warren. And with that name comes Dukes Halt. And with that comes duty. And I am sick to the back teeth of you behaving as though that duty were a forgettable irrelevance."

It was the longest speech he'd made to me in my whole life.

I was shocked to silence. For a moment.

"And you hate me because I won't be this obedient duty-bound thing you want?" I couldn't help it – I cast a glance at Henry, who was sitting open mouthed, staring at the scene unfolding.

"You're my son," my father said, as though reading from a script. "I love you George, as I love all of you. But you have to listen to me: There's been enough stupidity. Enough sketching of trees and flowers and other boys. It's time to grow up and be a man."

"And be friendless," I said.

"You'll make new friends."

"As I say," I said, folding my napkin and putting it on the table, "I'm not hungry. If you'll excuse me."

I stood.

"Take that money to Kennedy and come straight back, George. I want you to help me with the planning for harvest. Perhaps you might visit with your cousins in Dorset before then. If you're bored here."

Only when I was out of the room, the door closed behind me, did I let my panic kick in.

It was impossible, of course, that I should never see Simon again. He was my best friend – my only friend in the whole world.

I ran straight to my mother and barrelled into the room, all my fear and frustration spilling from me.

Something was wrong.

Three things hit me instantly: The room was in almost total darkness, the heavy brocade curtains still closed.

And there was a metallic tang in the air, as though all the chemicals my mother was being fed had finally begun leeching back out of her body into the room.

Then I heard the noise. A scratching sound like rats scurrying inside the walls.

I could see her shape, lying on her back in the middle of her bed, the pillows behind her propping her into an almost seated position, and I gently closed the bedroom door before running over and clambering on the bed to sit beside her as I had done so many times before.

She groaned, an awful wheezing sound, and I realised that the sound I'd heard was her breathing.

'Mamma," I lay next to her, my face close to hers, and the barest curve of her lips told me she'd heard me. She opened her eyes and turned her face slightly towards me.

"Baby," she said, her voice a whisper, "my Georgie."

"Mama," I wanted, so badly, to tell her everything – what had just happened, how I was feeling, my fears, my suspicions, but her eyes closed again and her head rolled back into the valley in the pillows where her body lay, and I realised that what I had dreaded my whole life was looming ever larger.

So I kissed her and told her I loved her, and I left the room and went back downstairs.

The money was in an envelope in the study with Kennedys' name written on it in my father's clear bold handwriting, the flap tucked into the back of the envelope. I stared at it for an age, the rest of the house moving and shuffling and groaning around me.

I hate this place. I hate it so much. It's poisonous.

I left the house, making sure to slam the front door behind me, and stalked across the lawn towards the tree line, hoping I might meet Simon in the forest and trying to think of what I would say to him.

Because I was sure of one thing only: I would die before I would obey my father.

I didn't meet Simon as I made my way through the trees. There were no sounds of wood chopping, just the hushing of the trees, and a cacophony of birdsong, and I had decided, by the time I came out of the forest, that I was going to tell him nothing. I was going to pretend nothing had happened and I was going to figure this out without his involvement.

I walked up to the cottage and knocked, and Simon opened, and suddenly there were tears in my eyes again, and he frowned and pulled me into the kitchen.

"What's wrong?" he gasped. "What's happened?"

"It's-" I struggled, grasping for words to explain but knowing, somehow, that I couldn't risk telling him what 'it' was. "It's my mother. She's really ill today."

He put an arm across my shoulder. "It'll be okay, George. You'll see. Have some lemonade. Take a breath."

He led me into the kitchen, dropped me on a kitchen chair and went to the fridge.

His parents were out. They'd gone to the Cash & Carry in Kenford.

"How bad are things?" He asked, putting two glasses of lemonade on the table and sitting beside me.

"I don't know what's going on," I said. "She can't speak. Can't breathe. She should be in a hospital. But he's just left her there in her room with the curtains drawn. He's left her to die, and now he wants to send me away too."

"Away?" Simon's eyes widened.

I bent double, dropped my head into my hands and moaned. "It's all ruined," I said, and he came closer to me and put a hand on my back.

"Why?" He asked, and I laughed, softly at first and then with something approaching hysteria.

"Because he's a bully, and a snob, and he hates me."

"But I've heard him talk about you to my dad; he says you're the

brains of the family. He seems really proud of you."

I straightened up. Simon was really close to me, but he didn't pull away again. "Proud? Of me? He's ashamed of me, Simon. He wants to send me away and forget about me. What could he possibly be proud of? I'm a disappointment."

"You're not," Simon said. "You're smart and funny and generous." His words stopped mine. "You're an artist, and you care about things. And you're my friend, George."

I kissed him.

Everything sort of stopped.

All the air seemed to be sucked out of the kitchen, the cottage, the world, and I leant forward and put my lips on his.

And he jerked backwards, shoving me away from him at the same time.

His movement jerked the table and the glasses of lemonade tipped over.

"What the fuck?" he said, his voice a sort of strangled sound and I looked at his face and saw a sort of surprise mixed with disgust.

"I'm sorry," I said, the tears pressing once more against the back of my eyes, my heart hammering, my whole body blushing as I reached out a hand to him and he shrunk away.

I dropped my hand.

"Listen, George," he said, his face still darkened by a frown, "it's alright, but I'm not- I mean, I don't feel that. You're a mate, that's all. But it's okay." Now, he reached a hand out to me, and it was my turn to shrink back.

"I'm sorry," I said again. "Sorry. Please don't tell."

"Is this why he wants to send you away?" Simon asked.

"Sorry," was the only word I could speak, though in my head other words were shrieking. Words like destroy, disappointment, ruin, shame, faggot, homo, queer.

Then Simon's face darkened again and I thought for a moment he was going to hit me but instead he turned.

"Shit," he said as the tipped over glasses, the spreading pool of lemonade now dripping off the edge of the table and on to his leg registered.

As he watched, one of the glasses rolled to the other side of the table and off it, landing on the flagstoned floor and showering slivers of glass all over the kitchen.

"Shit," he jumped up, grabbed for a cloth.

And I ran.

"I'm sorry," I said once more. "Please don't tell anyone, please."

I stood and ran from the room.

"George," he shouted after me, but I'd fled the room, fled the cottage, and escaped into the trees.

Then, just inside the trees, I stopped.

He would tell. He would tell people what I had done.

My mother would die knowing. Believing.

My father would have all his disappointment confirmed. He'd hate me. He'd be so ashamed of me.

Henry would never speak to me again and I'd be sent away, never to see Edward again either.

It was ruined, it was all utterly ruined.

I was dirty and stupid and foul, and I had destroyed the one bright spot in the whole world, and Simon would tell his parents.

Then they'd tell my father.

And he would tell my mother. He would want her – as ill as she is – to know just how right he'd been and how wrong I was.

And everything would be destroyed.

I could deny it, of course, say he was lying, but I knew that they would believe Simon, not me.

It was hopeless.

I was hopeless.

And then I had an idea, and before I was able to rationalise it, before I could realise how wrong it was, I stepped back out of the forest.

CHAPTER THIRTY

I turned the page.

This one was almost blank and was undated. Was it a continuation of the day I had just read?

Or had time passed?

On the page, George had written five words.

They sent a chill through me:

I have done something unforgiveable.

SUNDAY

CHAPTER THIRTY-ONE

The rapping at the door was accompanied by a scratching and wheezing that I knew could mean only one thing: my best mate and her furry black shadow were at my door and Caz was doing her best to rouse me from what, I suppose, she imagined was slumber.

I glanced at the clock, then back at the notebook.

What did you do, George?

I flipped over the page and could see immediately that there were only a few more pages of writing in the book.

The rapping came again, more insistent this time.

"Go to sleep," I said, keeping my voice.

"Open the door you idiot," Caz shot back. "Quick."

I sighed, opened the drawer on my bedside table and slid the notebook into it, then padded across to the door.

The chair under it tonight was more out of habit than necessity; I'd figured, somehow, that Digby Smith's attempts at nocturnal visits were a thing of the past, but had still unthinkingly made sure that nobody else could join me in the middle of the night.

Or perhaps, I thought, casting a glance back at the bedside table and its secret cargo, I'd been trying to make sure I could read George's diary undisturbed.

"Caz," I sighed again as I yanked the door open. "It's gone one in the morning. Can't this wait?"

"Look out your window you idiot," she said, breezing into the room. "No, it can't. And nice t-shirt. Shame you didn't bring any pyjama bottoms. Or boxer shorts," she added, passing straight to the window and pulling back the edge of the heavy drapes.

I grabbed my jeans from the chair I'd slung them over

before retiring and pulled them on as Ellie made brave attempts to lick my legs.

"What the hell's going on?" I asked, coming up behind Caz.

"Turn the lamp off," she hissed, and something in her tone told me that something serious was happening.

I switched off the lamp and joined her behind the curtains, the cold air beyond the window panes chilling the space.

Outside, semi-visible in the half-light cast by a moon that seemed to be engaged in a battle-to-the-death with a bank of thick clouds, the lawn of Dukes Halt stretched away to a deeper darkness that was the woods in which Beth and Gaia were sleeping.

But Caz was directing my attention away from that part of the estate.

"Look," she said, pointing to the distant right of the scene.

I looked.

More half-imagined lawn stretching, this time, to the denser darkness that was the hill to the west of the house, on top of which the folly, with all the fireworks for tomorrow night's display, stood.

"What am I looking at?" I asked, and Caz shushed, me, holding a finger up, as though to say 'wait for it'.

A moment passed.

"There," she said. "Did you see it? There."

"Are you on meds?"

"There's someone up there," she whispered.

"What? Up at the Folly?"

She nodded, her eyes still fixed on the distant space with absolute conviction.

And then I saw it.

The darkness was almost impenetrable but, as I stared, a flicker of amber streaked from right to left, vanishing at various points as obstacles between it and us blocked the light.

"A fire?" I asked, and Caz shook her head.

"A fire would be growing. This was there and then gone, and now back."

"Lottie?" I wondered. "I have a feeling she's not gone far."

"Or our murderer back to the place they stole their diversionary fireworks from last night?"

"That's not a bad idea," I admitted, wondering whether the police had even bothered to check the hut where the fireworks were stored. What if the killer realised they'd dropped something incriminating and had returned to collect it?

And as that thought ran through my mind, I realised Caz was wearing a thick waxed jacket and a pair of Wellingtons.

"We're going over there, aren't we?" I asked, thrashing my way back through the maroon-coloured velvet curtains and pushing my feet into my trainers, which were still mud-encrusted from the afternoon's adventures.

"Would you be able to sleep if you didn't?"

"What about madame?" I nodded at Ellie, who had already curled herself up in the dead centre of my bed, the residual heat from my body lulling her to a softly snoring snooze.

"She'll be fine there. She hardly ever wets the bed these days," Caz said, tossing my coat to me. "And bring your phone. For the torch," she explained to my puzzled look.

We crept along the landing and down the stairs, then Caz opened the door, the chilled night air poured in, and she turned to me.

"Hurry up," she whispered, and we stepped out into the night.

At first, we hugged the outline of the house, making our way as stealthily as we could towards the folly which – now we were outside – was occasionally visible during breaks in the slowly drifting clouds.

"What's going on?" Caz hissed at me as we reached the end of the house and stepped onto the spongy grass, the dampness immediately soaking through my trainers.

I aped puzzlement and she paused, shook her head at me, and kept marching inexhorably towards the folly.

"You. You've been distant since we got here. And tonight. You were awake. Your light was on. At gone one in the morning."

"What? I'm supposed to be abed by ten now?" I was overly

defensive, but I really didn't understand what Caz thought could be achieved by choosing now – as we stalked towards who-knew-what in the folly – to ask me about my mental and emotional state.

"You were distant."

"You've said that already," I answered. "I'm here, aren't I? And we still have you-know-who stashed in your bedroom. And I've had dinner with a homophobe, and been brought in for questioning, and been lied to by your goddaughter, and barked at by the cook and treated like an oik by the family, and menaced by the fucking housekeeper, and – oh yeah – almost raped by the fucking homophobe.

"Oh, and my boyfriend thinks it's my fault his wife is under arrest for murder. I can't imagine why I might appear distant."

"Digby made a pass at you?"

"No, Caz." I stopped dead in the middle of the darkness, forcing my voice to stay at a whisper, and clenched my fists in frustrated fury. "I've had passes made at me. He cornered me in the woods. And assaulted me."

"You called the police, right?" she asked, and I laughed bitterly.

"What's the bloody point? That lot," I gestured behind me at the house, "know who he is and what he is and seem to have been covering up for him for years. So long as he does what the right people want when it comes to voting, he gets to be a fucking hypocrite."

"Wait," Caz said. "The black eye?"

"I'm not a push over. But it was still fucking scary."

"I can imagine." Caz sighed. "We need to think about this. Digby's going nowhere for now. Not until after tomorrow night anyway – well, tonight I suppose, seeing as how it's now tomorrow, if you see what I mean."

I shook my head. "Just leave it. He knows now that I'm not up for grabs. That's as much as I can hope for."

The clouds cleared momentarily, and her eyes sought mine out. Her lips pursed, and she reached out and grabbed my hand. "And Nick?"

I shrugged. "I get his point. But he saw Smith making a move on me."

"He what?"

"I know. I think, for a moment, he actually thought that whatever was happening was consensual."

"Nonsense. Nick's smarter than that."

"I thought so," I said, dropping my voice even lower as I suddenly realised there was another figure off to our right, indistinct but definite, and heading the same way we were heading.

"Who's that?" I whispered, bringing Caz's attention to the figure.

She paused as, from our left this time, a voice came across to us.

"Who's there?" Richard Stamford called, his voice loud and clear.

Caz and I turned immediately towards the place his voice had come from as a bright light came on and shone directly into our faces.

"What the hell are you doing?" Caz demanded, holding a hand up to shield her eyes. From behind us the sound of footsteps stomping through the wet grass approached.

"What on earth is going on here?" Mrs Chapman – for it was her – demanded.

"Switch off the bloody torch," Caz hissed, and Richard Stamford's voice came in response.

"What are you lot doing out here at this time of night?"

"We might ask you the same thing," Chapman replied in a tone that suggested she'd had enough of his shit. "And as her ladyship requested, would you mind turning off that light?"

"What?" The light wobbled, and Stamford, as though realising for the first-time what light everyone was referring to, shone his torch upwards and then downwards, then towards his face, cursing all the time that the blasted thing wouldn't switch off.

But of course, eventually, it did, and the four of us stood in the silence and even deeper darkness that followed the light's extinguishing.

"There's someone up on the hill," Stamford said, and both Caz and Chapman responded as one.

"We know," they said.

"We were hoping to creep up and catch whoever it was unawares," Caz said, and Chapman snorted.

"No chance of that now," she muttered.

"Shall we still take a look?" I asked, and the four of us – silent now, our path illuminated only by the sporadic blasts of moonlight – continued on towards the folly, the stark, broken shape appearing as a more solid darkness against the navy blue of the night sky.

At length – with Stamford huffing and puffing and explaining loudly that he clearly wasn't as fit as he'd thought he was – we arrived at the summit of the hill.

"Have to do some more Stairmaster when we get back," he explained, and Chapman gifted him with a look so sour that – even in the gloom of the night – I suspect it would have curdled cream.

"The light seemed to be mostly coming from over there," Caz whispered, though I suspected her caution was misplaced; anyone who was creeping around the ruin would have scarpered long before now. Still, as one, we moved cautiously through the broken arch of a doorway.

One end of the construction had the remains of a high stone balcony, while the other end was a couple of low steps up to an expanse of white marble and the skeleton of a rose window – a half circle devoid of glass, the whole thing looking like a set for a movie.

And in the middle of the expanse of white marble something was piled up. Something that seemed to be spreading, multiplying, the edges of whatever it was expanding, their dark shiny tendrils glistening menacingly in the minimal moonlight.

Caz lifted her hand and shone the torch, and the shape was exposed, immediately, as a body.

The feet were facing us – a pair of trainers shining white in the light from Caz's phone.

"Hello," Stamford called, stepping forward as the rest of us followed.

"Are you okay?" I asked, realising as the words came from my mouth what a stupid question that was.

"This is private property," Chapman announced with her usual authority frayed only at the edges by a trace of uncertainty. "Whatever you're doing, you can't do it here."

I'd stepped around Stamford, whose progress had slowed as we neared the steps up to the 'altar', and suddenly the clouds broke and the whole altar – as opposed to only the thin sliver illuminated by Caz's torch – was visible.

And I knew that whoever they were, something was terribly terribly wrong.

Because the dark shiny tendrils glistening menacingly in the minimal moonlight weren't tendrils growing from the thing on the marble slabs; what had been spreading, oozing, glinting, was blood. Blood that was coming from the body on the altar.

I charged forward.

"She's been stabbed," I said, unable to tear my eyes away from the gash that had opened up the throat of the woman on the marble.

The other three caught up with me seconds later and Stamford let out a cry of terror and dropped to his knees to check for a pulse while shouting for someone to staunch the flow of blood as he began attempting CPR.

And still I stood perfectly still, staring down at the wound, even as Chapman pulled a scarf from around her neck and applied it to the darkly shining mess.

I stood as Caz attempted to explain to Richard Stamford that the woman on the floor was dead and that his attempts were pointless, staring at the bloodied hands on her chest where she'd obviously raised them in an attempt to staunch the flood of blood that had poured out of her throat, at the viciously sharp knife I'd seen in the kitchen at Dukes Halt the day before, and into the face of Mila, who made the most amazingly delicious food, and who had dreamed of owning her own restaurant, and who had survived having a building blown up on top of her only to die in a fake church on a windy hillside in England with a look of absolute surprise on her face.

CHAPTER THIRTY-TWO

"If there are any prints on that, they're probably mine," I said to Dane, who hoisted the evidence bag the weapon was in and looked at the knife as though he might actually see my dabs with his naked eye.

"I used it earlier," I said. "To cut carrots."

In case he thought I was confessing.

Dane and his team had arrived quickly, the Inspector sporting the sort of bed-head and grumpy demeanour that suggested he'd been awakened by the call. And wasn't happy about the fact.

"And what were you doing stomping around here in the middle of the night?" He demanded.

"We saw lights," Caz answered. "As, I suppose, did Doctor Stamford and the house keeper."

"Lights." He said the word with – I thought – a little more sarcasm than was strictly necessary. "And none of you – considering everything that's been going on here - thought to call the police?"

"We were afraid that if we waited, whoever it was would get away," I answered.

"And how'd that work out for you?" He asked.

Busted. "I suspect they heard us approaching and went down the other side of the hill, doubled back around and were tucked up in bed before Chapman and Stamford even called you.

Dane handed the evidence bag to a uniform. "So you think whoever did this came from the house?"

"It seems – considering everything that's been going on here – likely," I said staring him down.

"Could be some passing loony," he said, though his tone

suggested that even he didn't believe it.

"Who – what? – lured Mila to the folly in the middle of the night and killed her? No," I shook my head, and then something came to me. A picture of Mila this afternoon, an odd excitement in her eyes.

"She survived the Bosnian war, you know? Was in a building once when a bomb dropped on it, and Mila walked out unscathed."

"Everyone has their time," Dane said, running a hand through his dishevelled hair and glancing ruefully down on the body as the flash of a photographer's bulb lit the scene in almost pornographic detail.

"All she wanted was to have her own restaurant. She'd handed in her notice here today."

"You think one of them," he jerked his head towards the house, "killed her cos she'd quit?"

"Well a good cook is a nightmare to find," Caz murmured, "but 'if I can't have you, nobody can' seems a bit excessive. Even for the Warrens."

I shook my head. "She quit because she was going to open her restaurant. She'd found an investor."

Dane blew his cheeks out. "An investor?"

"Out of the blue."

"Well, there's a lot of money down there," again he jerked his head in the vague direction of Dukes Halt, "so no shortage of potential business partners. She make any suggestion as to who this money man – or woman - might be?"

I shook my head, and a memory of Mila, her eyes shining with excitement, her fingers twitching for a cigarette break ran through my head.

"But I have an idea," I said, suddenly. "Is everyone at the house awake?"

Dane nodded. "Whole house is up by the looks of it."

"Good." I looked down on the body of Mila as a sheet was finally thrown across it. "I expect you'll want to interview everyone. Shall we head back there?"

~

I got a surprise when I entered the Drawing Room at Dukes Halt.

The family and their guests were gathered there. Sir Phillip was in a high-backed chair with Pamela and Henry on either side of him. Francine and Sara, her head nestled on John's shoulder, were on a sofa that was really only large enough for two of the three people squeezed onto it. Richard Stamford and Karen were sat on another sofa, Richard looking pale, Karen looking exhausted, and Ali was slumped on a delicate Louis Quinze sofa, Chapman beside her straight-backed and with a look of disapproval on her face, while Digby Smith – his eyes glittering angrily from behind a set of purple-yellow bruises – was sitting alone in a chair.

And Nick Fisher – the Metropolitan Police's sexiest young DS – was standing in front of the fireplace, under the portrait of the late Lady Marion, and glaring at Smith's injuries.

My heart actually swelled when I saw him. Yes, I know that makes me sound like I'd drunk the nineteeth century kool aid of Dukes Halt and become one of those heaving bosom heart-swelling people that always end up in Drawing rooms and Austen novels.

I don't care. My heart swelled.

The sight of him, his very presence, just made me happy. Made me believe that things might be reparable.

They all quieted as Dane entered the room, Caz and I behind him.

"I regret to confirm," Dane announced to the assembled, "that the cook is dead."

"Well, cereal for breakfast it is then," Smith announced laconically, adding – in response to the gasps and glances of opprobrium he received – "I was heading back to town today anyway. This has not been the most enjoyable weekend."

"Don't worry," Sir Phillip announced clearly, "you won't be coming back. I've spoken to some people in Whitehall. You're being removed from the committee."

"I'm being what?" Smith's whole face bulged with fury. "You can't do that!"

"It's done," Sir Phillip replied flatly. "The committee has been concerned about your behaviour for some time. We do have *some* ethics you know. And your actions this weekend," Sir Phillip glanced pointedly at me, "your frankly ungentlemanly behaviour towards guests in my house, was the final straw. You'll be replaced on Monday."

Smith's hands gripped the arms of the chair and it looked like he might be about to pull himself to his feet, but then the fight sort of evaporated from him and instead he turned a look of pure hate at me. But even that faded quickly as he realised it was his own actions, his own behaviour, his own hypocrisy and entitled attitude that had brought him to this.

Still, I'm sure he consoled himself, there'd be a vote soon – women's rights, gay rights, something positive, that he could take great delight in voting down. That would salve his current fury; but I had a feeling that being kicked off the committee he'd just been ejected from was not just a massive dent to his pride, but also to his career.

Maybe that – the knowledge that sooner or later actions *do* have consequences – would encourage Smith to think again before he pushed himself on to the next young man.

Or maybe not.

Either way, I could see Nick glancing from Sir Phillip to Digby Smith to me, and his eyes lighting up as he began to figure out what had just happened.

"We have Detective Sergeant Fisher here," Dane announced. "DS Fisher is with the Met and is here as a professional courtesy."

Which made it seem like the locals either didn't know that Nick was Arianna's husband or – more likely – knew but were giving him the benefit of the doubt.

Dane gestured me forward into the heart of the semi-circle. "And Mr Bird here," he said, in tones that suggested he expected everyone's attention, "has some thoughts on tonight's events."

I stepped forward, feeling every eye on me. "Mila," I said, though I felt sure everyone in the room had to already know, "was murdered."

A rumble went around the room. Clearly, even though either Chapman or Stamford had already said as much, there was still a shock value in hearing the fact stated unequivocally.

"And I think her murder was linked to an attempt she had made to blackmail someone in this house."

This time, the rumble was louder, people looking suspiciously at one another and Digby Smith finally hauling himself out of his chair.

"Inspector, is there a reason why this civilian is being allowed to sling around libellous accusations?" he demanded in his best droit de seigneur tones.

"Because I'm interested in seeing what his theories are and where they lead us, sir. Do you have somewhere to be?" Dane replied, gesturing that Smith should resume his seat.

The bruised and bulging MP finally, reluctantly, lowered himself into his seat and I continued.

"I wasn't sure if the blackmail was linked to the jewel robbery the other night," I gestured at Sara, whose hand went instinctively to where the stone had been nestling on her the night it was stolen, "or to the murder yesterday morning of Sergei Maximov."

This time, I nodded at Pamela, who frowned, almost as though she were trying to decide whether to return the nod, or whether to do so would look incriminating.

"And then, of course, there's the case of Lottie Warren. A young girl missing since some time Friday night. Was the blackmail linked to that?"

"Who says it was blackmail?" John Warren asked as Francine nodded.

"Yeah," she agreed. "We've only your word that the cook was a blackmailer. She could have been killed by a sex maniac."

"She was not," I assured her, "murdered by a sex maniac." And then I went through the logic that I'd explained to Dane up at the Folly.

"But why does that have to be blackmail?" Karen Stamford

asked. "She was an amazing cook. Maybe one of us just genuinely thought a restaurant with her in the kitchen would be a good investment."

I considered her words. "That's a good point," I said. "So: Does anyone want to own up to being that person? The one who promised to let Mila have the money to open her restaurant?"

There was more side-eyes and a couple of people muttered that they hadn't done any such thing and when it became clear after a few moments that nobody was going to own up to being the investor, I nodded.

"So Mila believed she had money coming from someone.

"Someone who arranged to meet her in the folly and who – instead of paying her off – murdered her."

"But who?" Henry asked, looking around the group and then back at me. "Who was it?"

I caught Nick's eye across the room. He raised an eyebrow as if to say *you're doing it again, aren't you*? And I felt my heart flip a little.

"I wasn't sure who it might be," I said, "til I remembered Saint Ives."

Another series of puzzled glances.

Digby Smith groaned, "Just get on with it," and Nick shot him a look of pure venom.

"You might know the nursery rhyme. Well Mrs Gerber and Ms Simone may not; I'm not sure how well it's known outside of Britain. But the rhyme goes

As I was going to St. Ives I met a man with seven wives,
Each wife had seven sacks, each sack had seven cats,
Each cat had seven kits: kits, cats, sacks and wives,
How many were going to St. Ives?"

"Charming," Chapman said dryly. "But it is rather late. Could you, perhaps, get to the point a little faster?"

I nodded in acknowledgement. "The point of the nursery rhyme is that – despite all the references to other people –

only the narrator was going to Saint Ives. Everyone else was coming back from it."

I looked at a sea of blank faces. "Caz – lady Caroline – and I left the house together after we saw movement at the folly. We were making our way across the West lawn when we noted you, Mrs Chapman, also approaching the hill, and we had just identified you when Doctor Stamford here called out to us all."

"I actually only called out to yourself and Lady Caroline," Stamford corrected me. "I hadn't spotted Mrs Chapman at that point."

"Quite." I accepted his correction and turned my attention to him. "You said you were also coming to investigate the lights, but you seemed to be crossing the west lawn from a far more southernly point. Almost as if you'd been hugging the edge of the forest."

"And?" he shrugged. "What of it?"

"Well, that would have meant you exited Duxes Halt, crossed the main lawn, got to the edge of the forest and then turned left towards the folly, turning right again and reversing your journey to the edge of the forest only when you were halfway across the west lawn. Which seems like a somewhat roundabout route to take, surely?"

"I didn't want to alert whoever was in the folly," he answered, a confused look on his face.

"And yet, when you spotted Lady Caroline and I you shouted to us, shone your torch and created an atmosphere of confusion so that we couldn't really tell where you were coming from. Or going to."

He clenched his jaw. Stamford was no dummy; he was ahead of me. "You think I was coming *from* the folly?"

"Having murdered Mila," I confirmed.

"You're delusional," he shook his head. "Utter poppycock. Why would I be doing anything of the sort? I'd never even met the woman."

"Our lawyer will have a field day with this," Karen Stamford snapped, pulling a phone from her dressing gown pocket and beginning to type a number.

Richard reached a hand across and put it over hers. She stopped what she was doing.

"Why?" He said, an almost amused look on his face. "What possible reason could I have for wanting to murder the chef?"

"To your first point," I felt a dozen pairs of eyes boring into me, "you say you never met Mila. But you did. I know you did because I heard you speaking with her yesterday morning."

Stamford shook his head again, and he laughed disbelievingly. Then a light came on. "I was having a cigarette. So was she."

"You met," I said, "and you spoke what I'm assuming was Serbian."

His smile faltered, flickered out for a moment and was then replaced. "I'm a doctor. I save lives, I do not take them."

"But you did know her," I said, "and you knew enough Serbian to suggest a familiarity with the country. That's the first of your lies addressed."

"Lies?" He stood to his feet now, anger flaring up on his face. "I've had enough of this. We're going up to our rooms and packing. And," he turned to Sir Phillip "you can stick your bloody knighthood. Since I got here I've had disturbed sleep, armed robberies, hysterical women, murders, and now I'm being accused of being – what? – a murderer. Just because I passed a few pleasantries with the bloody cook?"

"I would ask, sir, that you refrain from leaving the premises until we have had a chance to take formal statements," Dane said solemnly, and Stamford turned on him.

"Fuck your statements."

"Hear hear," Digby Smith said, and Dane nodded to a couple of uniforms who had been idling just inside the door.

"We can take the statements tonight, sir, and you can be on your way in the morning. But I would like to get the paperwork done before you drive back to London."

"So tell me," Stamford turned his fury back on me, "why did I kill her? What was my dirty little secret that she was blackmailing me for?"

"You killed her," I said, "because she knew you'd murdered Sergei Maximov."

His reaction was almost hysteria. "I did what? Why?"

Stamford dropped back on to the sofa as though he'd been hit with a brick.

Karen Stamford put her hand across and took his in hers.

"Enough," she said. "Richard was in the hall when Maximov was shot. You saw him with your own eyes."

She had me there. "But he spoke Serbian," I said, faltering slightly.

"So what?" Digby Smith spoke up. "I speak Russian. Doesn't mean I offed the Russki."

"You were a doctor in Serbia," I addressed Richard Stamford directly. "You worked at a hospital."

He seemed almost to have shrunk. When he looked at me, his eyes were confused and he had lost the fury that had been there moments before. "In Serbia? Yes," he gestured at Sir Phillip.

I looked at Sir Phillip, who nodded. "I'm afraid I'm at a loss to understand where, exactly this is going," he said, his eyes showing no emotion.

"Maximov told the story," I said. "The night of the robbery. About the hospital where the doctor in charge rounded up the patients and delivered them to the militia."

Stamford sighed, running a hand through his hair. "Jesus," he laughed, and his wife put her arm around his shoulder and shot a venomous look my way.

"You think that was me? You think I killed Mila to stop her telling you I killed Maximov, and I killed him to stop him telling anyone that I had effectively murdered dozens of my own patients?"

"Richard," Karen put her arms around him and kissed him on the cheek. "They can't make us stay."

Stamford seemed, suddenly, to come to his senses. He pulled himself erect, then stood upright, Karen rising with him.

"You're right," he said to her, then turned to me.

"The first time I went to Sarajevo was in 2002. The war had been over for years. I went because," he pointed at Sir Phillip "that man asked me to go and help rebuild some of the medical infrastructure his bastard of a son," this time his finger moved to Major Henry "had bombed to fuck. I was not in Serbia before or during the war.

"So unless I masterminded this handing over of sick patients to a bunch of murdering fascists by remote control your whole story has as much relation to reality as her claims," this time he pointed at Pamela "to be a fucking school teacher. Now *we're* going to bed," he turned to Dane, "and in the morning we're going home, and if you want a statement you can contact my solicitors who," he turned on me, "will be hearing from me tomorrow with instructions to sue *you* for slander. Me?" he waved his arm around the room, "you slander *me* when this lot include war criminals, career spies, hypocrites, deviants, bankrupts and thieves. And me, you slander?"

He stopped, suddenly, some of the angry colour draining from his face, and Karen Stamford squeezed his hand, her eyes filling with tears.

"And now," Dr. Stamford added, regaining the level of righteous outrage that had momentarily drained from his eyes, "unless anyone else here has any more insane theories to kick around, we're going to bed, and in the morning we're leaving Dukes Halt, and we're never coming back."

And so saying, he and his wife stormed from the room.

"Well," Digby Smith smiled, "that was fun. Can we go to bed now, Inspector Dane? Or is there a self-immolation for afters?"

CHAPTER THIRTY-THREE

I stayed where I was while they filed past me, some with downcast eyes, some with eyes that accused, some in bemusement and at least one who seemed to be loving my discomfort.

Only as Sir Phillip hobbled from the room, paused, and looked back over his shoulder at me to say "It happens," before being helped away did I break.

Which was when I ended up sitting on the edge of the fountain, the cold stone soaking through my jeans, watching Caz – who had walked out there with me and attempted to console me – passing Nick in the rectangle of light that was the doorway of Dukes Halt.

From the distance, a fox shrieked, the sound so like a woman's scream that my heart raced for a moment before I willed myself to calm down, watching as Caz and Nick exchanged words and he walked – crunching at first across the driveway then silenced as his feet hit the lawn – towards me.

I'd relied on instinct and some disconnected facts to make my case against Richard Stamford, and it had failed, but I was still certain that there was truth there.

"Well that didn't end well," Nick said, arriving before me, his words issuing as white clouds in the night air.

"You reckon?"

He sighed, turned and sat beside me, and we both looked at the flat broad front of the house as lights went on and off across the upper floors until there were only two lights remaining.

"Why do you insist on doing this?" He asked at length.

"Insist?" I turned to look at him, then made myself look back at the house, as though not facing each other would limit the impact of the storm I felt was coming.

"You know what I mean. The local police are perfectly capable of the job. Why try to make everything an episode of 'Murder She Wrote'?"

"Because they wrongfully arrested your wife," I said, turning again to look at him.

"Who was only here because of you," Nick replied, the last four syllables strangled, as though he'd got halfway through his statement then realised – too late to stop – where it was heading.

"I had nothing to do with Arianna being here. She found Maximov without my involvement," I said tersely.

"Mate-" Nick, in my peripheral vision, turned to me.

"Mate?" I was alarmed, turned my face to him briefly, then turned it back.

"Danny. Baby. Listen. You should have called me. The minute she came to you, you should have called me."

"'She'?"

He shook his head. "Don't make me the bad guy here."

I was gripping the side of the fountain. "I didn't know there needed to *be* a bad guy here."

Nick moved across, found the hand nearest him, and squeezed the fingers. "There doesn't. But I don't understand why it always ends up like this."

My shoulders dropped. I wanted to turn my hand around, grab his, lock our fingers, fall backwards into this fountain, and never come up again.

I sighed. "Why did you have to marry her?" I asked.

"Marry?"

"Arianna. I know the reasons you've told me. Woman in danger. No alternatives. Blah blah blah."

"Blah blah blah? Did you really just say that?"

I was embarrassed. "I just want everything to be okay."

"Danny. Listen to me. Look at me," I turned my face to him.

"There has never – in the history of man – been a point where *everything* has been okay. Look," he said, "I know this hasn't worked out how either of us might have wanted it to. I married Arianna because it was the only way that I could think of to get her to safety. And because of that we – our relationship – has been stilted."

"You're still not out at work," I said. "You're not out anywhere. As far as the world is concerned, you have a lovely wife and I'm smuggled in and out of places like some sort of guilty secret."

"Well it's not as though you haven't had your secrets from time to time."

That stung. "I told you about Robert, told you how he lied to me. Told you how I was never going to be lied to again. And you lied to me."

He laughed briefly, the sound almost like the bark of the fox that I knew was probably sitting at the edge of the forest watching us, and rephrased his own accusation: "And *you* have never lied to *me* since?"

I was offended, but Nick pressed on: "Don't do that. Don't pretend you haven't once obscured fact or kept stuff from me since we started."

"Started what?"

He stared up at the night sky. "Since *we* started," he said baldly.

I followed his gaze up and then tore mine down to the ground.

"I remember the first time we went to your house," I said. Then, as the silence developed: "Your curtains were shockingly bad."

He actually turned his whole body towards me at that. "Curtains?"

"The first time. The first time we went to your place. I remember thinking your curtains were shocking. They were purple with a sort of sateen sheen to them. And you had no cushions. I mean," I gave him my most disbelieving look. "*No cushions*. What sort of animal has no soft furnishings?"

"I thought we were having sex, not auditioning for ideal homes," Nick smiled.

"Yeah." I dropped my head. "I thought we were doing something else."

"No," he shook his head, "what you thought was 'here's something I can fix.'"

I looked at him again, his whole face steely blue. "And is there so much wrong with that?"

He smiled nervously, moved towards me.

I moved away.

"Not everything in life is broken, Danny. Sometimes things just are as they are. Not perfect, but not crying out for a correction."

I looked at him. "I trusted you."

"I trusted you."

"And then you married her. And you left me wondering what I was."

"You know what you are," he answered. "And I have always trusted you despite you repeatedly lying to me."

"Me? Lying to you?"

"Oh Danny," he smiled paternally, and shook his head in a way that had my blood instantly boiling. "you keep secrets. It's what you do, until you're ready to disclose them."

"I keep secrets?" I stood, the coldness suddenly wrapping itself around me like a shroud. Now I laughed bitterly. "I didn't take you home, tell you we might have a future, then go off on a business trip and come back with a wife I hid for months."

Nick shook his head, "Don't do that, Danny. I'm not the villain here."

I dropped back on to the edge of the fountain, my head in my hands. "Nick, why are you here?"

"Because – in case you'd missed it - my wife – Arianna – has been arrested for murder. A murder you might have been able to help me head off if you'd called me when she called you."

"She asked me not to tell you."

"You know, it feels sometimes like you only obey those sort of requests when they're about keeping information from me.

I bet Caz knew everything."

"She knew nothing," I said. "So leave her out of this."

"But I should have known. Why would Arianna have wanted me kept out of the loop?"

I straightened up, stared at the house where only one light apart from my own still shone.

"Think about it Danny," he pressed me. "Why would she have wanted me left in the dark?"

"Because…" I started, then the words ran away from me.

"Because she planned – once you'd found this man – to do something she knew I would disapprove of."

"Disapprove? Jesus, Nick. You've only been here a few hours and you're already sounding like it's 1895. You don't get to approve or disapprove of the actions a woman plans against a man who beat her, raped her, sold her into slavery and then stole her sister from her. That's not your call."

"So what? I enable? Blindly? Even where her actions might be criminal?"

I froze. "You think she did it. You actually think she murdered Maximov."

He tilted his head back, stared up at the night sky. I turned my head away, let my eyes drift to the Folly where lights still blazed, the crime scene officers of the local constabulary still attempting to make sense of the mess of blood and footprints that had framed the snuffing out of Mila's life.

"I know she couldn't have," Nick said eventually. "But that doesn't mean she wouldn't have, if things had been different. And think how that would have worked out. For all of us."

I glanced up at the sky, then briefly at the granite chippings around the fountain, and then at him. "But she didn't," I said.

"You should have told me what she was planning to do," he said.

"She asked me to find him. She told me a story I couldn't repeat without breaking her confidence. And why should I have done that?"

"Because I thought you cared about me," he answered. "And because I cared about you."

'Cared.' Past tense.

Suddenly, I was colder than I'd ever felt. Above us, the vast sky stretched, the clouds skidding across it as quickly as my heart was beating, the moon there, then hidden, then there, then obliterated. Gone. Almost all light banished from, it seemed, the world.

The silence stretched on and was broken eventually by the same fox-shriek. The clouds moved again and the moon reappeared, feeling cold, too bright, and uncaring of whatever was occurring below.

"I cared about Robert," I finally said. "And I thought he cared about me. Til it turned out he'd been lying to me for years.

"And then I allowed myself to fall in love with you. Except you lied to me."

"Lied?"

We were back to this thing; this grain of truth. A grain I'd tried so hard to accept, to understand, perhaps even to forgive, but which had grown over time into a boulder that I couldn't get around.

"You married her, Nick. I know why you did it. Fuck knows I applaud why you did it. But you still messed up everything I had. And now you have the nerve to complain that I've lied to you. And I didn't lie; I just didn't come running to you like a good boy to spill every secret Arianna told me. 'Cos it seems I trust her more than you do."

He stood up and he shoved his hands into his trouser pockets.

"You're losing sight of the facts," I pleaded with him. "Whoever murdered Maximov murdered Mila. And since Arianna was in jail when Mila was killed, it can't have been her."

"No," He said. "You're assuming facts that fit your hypothesis. You know nothing about Mila. There could be a million reasons why she's dead, and none of them connected to anything else that's gone on here this weekend. Boyfriends. Husbands. Ex-boyfriends. Ex-husbands. Debts. Addictions.

You're assuming that her death is part of a chain that starts with Arianna seeing Sergei Maximov. When really, you have absolutely no way of knowing."

"There's a link," I said. "I explained it in there," I nodded at the house.

"When you accused a man who was entirely innocent of the crimes," Nick said. "Danny, sometimes, the truth is simple and messy, but you insist on making it clean, even if doing so requires you to twist logic til it's more fantasy than reality. Let's just leave this," his head dropped.

"And just so we're clear: When we met, I didn't need – I still don't need – fixing. Life's a shitshow, Danny. I know you think your job is to fix it, but it's mostly unfixable."

"I thought my job was to find someone who could be truthful enough with me to help me figure out what was fixable."

"And that could have been me," he said sadly, "if you'd picked up the phone and called."

"I wouldn't have had to pick up the phone," I answered, "if I'd felt like I was something more than just an appointment in a calendar."

And I stood, hurt, angry and knowing that I wasn't so much burning bridges as incinerating a landscape I had hoped would be my home for the rest of my life. Then, clenching my fists so tightly my fingernails dug into my palms, I started walking back towards Dukes Halt.

CHAPTER THIRTY-FOUR

I opened the notebook. Ellie stirred on the side of the bed she'd annexed.

My intention had been to put my head down. Sleep. Try to let go of the fact I'd just falsely accused Richard Stamford of murder; try to forget that Nick and I were probably over.

But I'd slid under the sheets and – despite the horror that had unfolded that night – the last words I'd read came clearly to my mind.

I have done something unforgiveable.

What had George done, and why did I feel so absolutely positive that it was still ringing through the empty spaces of Dukes Halt.

The page I was looking at – like the last one – had no date appended. George had clearly stopped trying to capture dates.

George's Diary August 1986

My mother died last night.

I don't know what time it was.

I mean, it's not like I was asleep; I spent the night staring wide-eyed at the ceiling, hearing every creak and groan in the house, and waiting for Kennedy to knock at the door.

After dinner we – Henry and Edward and I – were asked to visit her in her room.

I didn't go. I lied and said I felt sick, and when my father insisted I go I told him I had the shits and asked whether he wanted me to explode all over the bedroom.

So Henry and Edward sat with her and I could hear their laughter from my room where I sat in silence and wondered when the accusation would make its way from Simon to my father and on to my mother.

I wondered if it might be easier to just creep to her room at some stage and get some of the pills they give her to sleep, and end it all.

Perhaps, if I had gone to her room, I would have been there to save her.

Maybe, if I'd been trying to kill myself she would have lived.

Maybe, if I hadn't kissed Simon Kennedy yesterday she would have lived.

I know that's not logical – that's not how things work. But I still feel, somehow like this – what's happened up to now, and all that's going to happen from here on in – is my fault.

Chapman woke me this morning to tell me. I don't know when I finally fell asleep, but I still felt like I was in a dream as I walked down the hallway to my mother's room and went inside.

The room was still dark, and that metallic scent was still there, but it was fading already, and the scratchy wheeze had been replaced instead by a snivelling coming from Edward.

They'd brought the six-year-old in to look at his dead mother.

Henry and my Father stood on the far side of the bed on either side of him.

I stopped on the nearest side, looked down on her, so still, so small, knowing that this wasn't my mother, but knowing – at the same time – that it was.

I don't remember much of what happened after that.

I don't want to.

The writing stopped there, midway through a page. I turned the page and the handwriting – precise, clear script – carried on. I guessed that the choice of a new page indicated a new day, but again the page was undated.

Edward came to my room earlier, and I was horrible to him.

The funeral is in a few days and my father had told me I was being sent away.

My father knows everything.

This morning, I watched him and Chapman going into her room with black plastic bin liners and collecting all the medications they could lay their hands on before shovelling them into the bin liners and creeping – their voices still, frightened whispers – back along to the hallway and downstairs.

I heard the front door open a minute or two later and saw my father putting the two bin liners into his car.

Removing the evidence. Hiding the records of just how much medication they'd given her; just how fast and easily they had finished her off.

She should have been in a hospital. She said she didn't want to be, but if my father had cared about her he would have made her go somewhere where there'd be doctors and nurses and twenty-four-hour care.

Instead he kept her home where he'd given her a deliberate overdose of the pills he was now shovelling into the boot of his car.

And he'll get away with it. Doctor Allen will sign a death certificate. Pneumonia. Heart problem. Whatever. And they'll bury my mother and I will be alone here with just Henry and Edward and him.

Except, I won't be here any more. Because he's sending me away.

Kennedy telephoned this morning, spoke to my father.

I knew nothing of this, of course, and came down to breakfast as heartbroken as my brothers, each of us looking at the food on our plates as though it were ashes we had to force down our throats.

"Eat up," my father said gruffly to the three of us. "There are trying times ahead. You need to stay strong. So eat."

And, as though he were the captain of a ship that had sprung a leak (Instead of one that had lost its sails and rudder) that was it.

Edward was still crying, sniffing and trying to hold back strangled little sobs. He's been doing it off and on since the day before yesterday when – despite him having near hysterics – he was made to kiss her goodbye.

"Edward," my father said, "please stop crying."

I sighed heavily, stood and – carrying my plate – moved my chair next to Edward and put an arm around him.

"You need to eat," I said, bending down towards him and lifting his fork, scooping some scrambled eggs up. I didn't look at my father; didn't want to see his disapproval. Edward was six. By my father's reckoning he should be in complete control of his emotions, and the fact that his little heart was as broken as all of ours hadn't even crossed the old bastard's mind.

So I fed Edward, and soothed him, told him we'd play games later on, managed to get most of the eggs and a grilled tomato into him and then ate my cold eggs and sausage.

And while I was doing this, Chapman was searching my room.

I knew, as soon as I went up to it after breakfast, that someone had been moving my things around. The bed was made and usually I have to make my own, my father having decided at some time in the past that character in a boy consists of an ability to make one's own bed and never cry, even when one's mother is dead.

Clothes that had previously been scattered on the floor were now folded and placed on a chair. A drawer in my chest of drawers was sticky and never closed properly. But now it was flush with its brothers, proof that someone had opened and shut it firmly.

It seemed odd but – at the time – I assumed it was just someone tidying up.

And then Chapman knocked on the door and told me my father wanted to see me in his study.

And everything fell apart.

I'm not being sent away for being a pansy.

I'm being sent away for being a thief and a liar.

I needed to stop Simon telling anyone. But I knew I couldn't. I knew he would tell them and it would destroy everything and it wouldn't matter if I denied it because my father already looked at me like he was trying to work out what was wrong with me and this would explain – prove – what was wrong with me.

So I needed to make Simon a liar. Needed to make it easier for me to say he was lying and give a reason for why he might want to make some terrible accusation about me, why he might want to direct attention towards me.

So I'd stopped at the edge of the forest, opened the envelope with Kennedy's name on it – the one my father hadn't bothered to seal – and taken two fifty-pound notes from it, tucked the envelope shut again, crept back to the cottage and put it back on the hall table.

And then I'd come home, sure that if I was accused of kissing Simon I would have the comeback that the envelope was short and Simon had stolen the money and his lying about me was a smokescreen to hide his theft.

This boy I loved.

The only friend I had, who laughed with – never at – me, and who let me be his friend.

I was ready to throw him away.

But I never got the chance, because he didn't say anything.

By the time Kennedy and his wife got home the smashed glass was in the bin, the sticky lemonade spill was wiped up, and Simon was out chopping logs once more.

And there was a hundred pounds missing from the envelope.

Then – I don't know how – the records came out. I'd taken some more of Henry's records – after he'd failed to note the absence of his Van Halen single – and given them to Simon, and his parents found the records and – at first, I suspect – assumed he'd bought them with the missing money.

Or maybe they didn't. Maybe they knew their son was too honest to ever steal money and waste it on stupid records.

Whatever happened, they called my father.

He realised that the only person who didn't entirely have his trust in the chain was me, and so Chapman was dispatched to search my room while I was busy at breakfast.

And she found the two fifty-pound notes where I had absent-mindedly shoved them into the pocket of my jeans.

And I considered lying, saying I didn't know how they got there, but really by this stage I was past caring.

None of it had worked. She was dead, he hated me, and none of that was going to change now no matter what I did or said.

So I told him I'd taken the money and assumed Simon would be blamed, and my father just looked at me with this weird look. I thought he'd be furious. But the look he gave me was sort of empty.

And then, when I'd come back to my room, Edward barged in waving a comic book around and wanting me to read him a story.

I told him I didn't feel like it, and he chattered on about drawing and Superman and to be honest I can't really tell whether he wanted me to draw Superman for him or whether he wanted to draw Superman for me or whether he wanted me to read him a Superman story, so lost was I in my own misery.

And finally I snapped. "Listen Edward," I said, "please just leave me alone. Go away and leave me alone."

And he did the thing I was most dreading: He put his arms around my waist and – still clutching the comic book – he hugged me. He hugged me so tight that I nearly snapped, nearly hugged him back. But I was so sad and so angry that I pushed him away.

"He's sending me away Edward," I said. "Papa is sending me away and I will never see you again."

"No!" Edward rushed back at me, his arms wide as though he could hug me and stop them sending me anywhere. "You stay here. You play with me. Draw. You have to stay."

I stepped back, as his tears began to flow and – God help me – a little part of me was pleased to see someone else in this house in pain.

"He won't let me stay," I said, and I wanted to tell him that I would come back and take him away with me, but I couldn't. I could lie to my father but lying to Edward – the only good thing left here – was a step I couldn't take.

"But why?" He was on the edge of hysteria now and he tried again to hug me and I – once more – backstepped. "Why can't you stay?"

And what could I say? 'I can't stay because I'm a thief and a pervert and because our father can't bear to look at me any more'?

And so I said, "I can't stay because I know Papa killed mama."

His breath caught, his eyes going wide. Only six. A small boy no bigger than most four-year-olds, and Edward had been babied by everyone at home and at school his whole life, but he knew what I was saying.

"Mama got sick," he said. "Mama died."

Anger flared up in me. "Oh grow up Edward. If she was so sick why wasn't she at a hospital? He kept her here. Kept her away from doctors. Only let Doctor Allen in to see her once a week. And he controlled all her medications."

His whole body was shaking now as though the explosion of emotions inside were too much to keep inside his tiny frame.

"No!" He shouted, the tears returning.

"He left her in her room," I shouted. "Left her there to die. Alone. In the dark."

At this, Edward started sobbing.

"He left her and she died because he left her there in the dark with nobody to take care of her. He murdered her, Edward."

"You lie," he screamed, his face red and angry. "You're a liar and I'm going to tell on you."

"Tell," I shouted back, my fists balled up in fury, wanting to destroy the whole stinking place. "Go on!"

And he threw the comic book on the floor and barged out of the room.

CHAPTER THIRTY-FIVE

And that's where the notebook ended.

I flipped through the rest of the blank pages, held them to the light above my bed, wondered if the whole thing was fake, then dipped my head back on to my pillow and, as Ellie shifted, glared accusatorily at me, farted and went back to sleep, I dozed, and dwelled on the things I'd read, until Caz knocked at my door.

"Couple of things," she said brusquely. "Three things. Four things actually."

I backed into the room as she barrelled past me and Ellie, every bone in her body waggling, jumped from my bed and welcomed her.

"George has gone missing," Caz announced, sliding over to my open suitcase, "and La Simone's companies have declared bankruptcy in LA in the wee small hours."

She dived into my suitcase.

"More importantly." She asked. "how'd it go with Nick? And why, despite my comment last night," she dug out a pair of knockoff 'Kalvin Cleens' my mother had bought for me the preceding Christmas, "are you still answering your door like a life model on a day off?"

"Because I'm not used to being barged into before my Batman's got me into my silk pyjamas," I answered reflexively, then reset:

"Wait. George? What?"

"Missing. Pants," she flung a set of underwear at me. "And more importantly, as he's dead and Nick isn't: Nick?"

"Disastrously," I said, pulling the pants on. "I think we're over."

"Oh Danny. That can't be. He adores you."

I slumped into the seat in the corner of the room. "If he adores me so much why doesn't he ever say so."

"He's that type, isn't he?"

I shook my head. "I say it. I say, 'I love you' all the time, to all sorts of people."

"But you're *that* type," she answered. "Okay: What, exactly, did he say?"

So I told her the gist of our conversation.

"Yes," she said in a considered tone. "Well. That does sound like – if it's over – it's because you ended it."

I'd dropped my head into my hands, but it jerked up at that. I wanted to ask why she was taking his side, but realised she was right. I'd walked away.

"What a mess," I groaned.

"Life's like that, sometimes," Caz said. "The question is: what are you going to do about the mess?"

I laughed dryly. "Missing child. Jewel robbery. Maximov's murder. Mila's murder. Nick. Arianna. And now George. I don't even know where to start any more. Wait," I counted on my fingers. "You said four things."

She looked at me as though I'd just spoken in Medieval French and her O Level French studies were struggling to make sense of my words.

"When you walked in. 'Couple of things. Three. Four actually.'"

"Oh I did," Caz said, her memory coming back.

"Well George and Nick makes two. My lack of underwear – which is perfectly allowable when I am in my own in my own room, and which I could have rectified if you hadn't barged straight in – makes three. So what's four?"

"Well to begin with," she answered, "I did not barge in. Ladies do not barge into rooms. I," she scrambled for an excuse, "I thought I heard you calling me. Telling me to enter."

"Really?" I raised an eyebrow. "That's the best you can do? Whatever," I waved the issue away, "what was the fourth thing?"

"Oh," Caz brightened a little, then remembered what she had to tell me, and assumed a sombre look. "La Simone's website has gone bust. The candles, the throw rugs, the cushions with cute slogans, the biodegradable vajazzling. Kerput."

"Ah," a gong went off somewhere in the depths of my memory. "That must have been the argument we heard yesterday."

"The one begging for another couple of days?" Caz nodded. "Seems like she ran out of time."

"And – to go back to my earlier question – George?"

"Does that signify that you've finished discussing the situation vis a vis Nick," she asked, her head tilted in that way that said she felt there was a lot more that still need to be said and analysed.

"Well I have if you're taking his side," I answered tartly and she shook her head slowly.

"Sweetest," Caz rested a hand on each of my shoulders and stared into my eyes. "You know that the only side I am ever on is yours. But sometimes, you need to be reminded that you don't always act in your own best interests. Still makes me on your side. Just stops me being a sycophant."

"I could go off you, you know?" I smiled back. "Now, for the last time: George?"

"Well," she flung her hands up in despair. "I put him where I put him," she gestured at me as though she couldn't quite bring herself to say exactly where the earthly remains of her friend had been placed.

"In the back of the wardrobe," I nodded. "I remember."

"And I – well, I sort of left him. I mean I have my plan," she nodded towards my bedroom window. Well, had my plan. Til last night. And so, plan sorted, I didn't really see much point in checking in on him every couple of hours. I mean, as I've said, he's gone somewhat beyond needing a nurse to check in on him. And he wasn't going anywhere."

"And yet."

"And yet. Indeed," she sighed. "I checked this morning –

the party is tonight, so I suppose it was playing on my mind. And he wasn't there. Well at first, I thought I'd made a mistake – checked the back left corner when I'd put him in the back right, you know? – but no. I've checked the wardrobe, the chest of drawers, under the bed and in the bathroom cupboard.

"And he's vanished."

I sighed deeply, my brain running through the possibilities I could think of and discarding them all until only one remained.

"Okay," I pulled on my jeans and slipped a shirt over my t-shirt. "Can you wait here for me? I'll be back in a few minutes."

~

Sir Phillip was already in his study. I knocked on the door and it was opened almost immediately by Chapman.

"What do you want?" she demanded.

"I was wondering if I could have a few moments with Sir Phillip," I said, and she actually bristled at the request.

"Sir Phillip is very busy this morning. Perhaps later, after lunch."

"Who is it?" Phillip Warren's voice came from within the room, and Chapman raised an eyebrow, pursed her lips and glared at me before half turning her head and speaking into the room.

"It's Mister Bird," she said. "I've told him to come back later."

A moment of silence followed, then Sir Phillip said "Show him in."

I saw Chapman's neck tense, the muscles working as an angry flush ran up the side of her face.

"The accountants are due next week, Sir Phillip," she said flatly and, after another momentary silence she turned back to me, stepped aside and with a look of barely concealed fury, gestured for me to enter the study.

"Not too long," she instructed. "He really is very busy."

Sir Phillip gestured at the chair on the opposite side of his desk and told me to sit.

So I sat.

"Sir Phillip," I opened, "I really cannot apologise enough for last night."

"Which bit?" He asked dryly. "Finding my cook with her throat cut, or wrongly accusing one of my guests of being the murderer?"

I opened my mouth, but no words came out. Sir Phillip raised an eyebrow. "I mean, accusing Stamford of murder when the man's incapable of swatting a fly might be unforgiveable if you hadn't previously given that nasty old letch Smith a good smack. Still, it's going to take some work on my part to calm the good doctor down. He really does deserve the gong, you know. Man's a genuine hero. Saved lives. Made a difference."

"I should apologise directly to him," I said and Sir Phillip considered this for a second or two then nodded definitively.

"He deserves it, I think. I can see where you were coming from, but I still think Maximov's death – and, if it's connected, Mila's – are linked to Maximov's reason for coming down here in the first place."

"The traitor in government," I said, and Sir Phillip's lips turned upwards in a mysterious smile.

"I see my idiot son's been telling tales again."

"I'd sort of worked out that the cover story was nonsense. Pamela and Henry are still clearly very much in love, and even if they weren't, Maximov and Pamela made no sense to me whatsoever."

"Risk of reusing cover stories," he smiled. "Chapman," the woman looked up from the paperwork she'd been reading, a pile of correspondence open on the desk before her, "could you give us a few minutes?"

She blinked, puzzled, then collected the stack of letters and – oozing disapproval - she nodded at him, conspicuously ignored me, and left the room.

As the door closed, Sir Phillip turned to me. "You do understand, young man, that you currently know enough to make it very easy for me to instruct certain people that you're never to be allowed to leave this house?"

"A lifetime in captivity here," I answered, "would have been – until Mila's demise – more attractive than threatening."

At that, he laughed. "Ah, you've caught it too, have you? I grew up here, and I think I was about twelve when I brought a friend back from school and watched him fall under the spell of this place.

"I never understood why so many people over the centuries had lived and died for Dukes Halt. Til I saw it through the eyes of my schoolmate."

"It's a beautiful place," I agreed, remembering the thing I had shoved into the back pocket of my jeans. "But I think also a sad place."

The smile that had been playing around his lips died. "The house has had," he considered his words, "its fair share of sadness. Over the centuries."

"I was thinking of more recently," I said, pulling George's diary from my pocket. "I found this," I said, "in the room I'm staying in. I think the room was your son George's."

His face flickered from confusion to sadness and on to a sort of bland mask that I figured someone in his profession would have perfected over the years.

"This was George's diary," I said. "For that last summer." I held it out to him, but he made no movement towards it.

He seemed to be considering his words, and when he spoke the flat blandness was mixed with something approaching emotion. "I don't know that I want to read something that can only bring pain back to this house."

"It raises some questions," I said, and he tilted his head querulously. I put the book on the coffee table. "I'll leave it. It's up to you, I guess, to decide what you do with it."

He glanced at the notebook then, as though deciding the topic was closed, turned his attention back to me. "Do you have any news of Lottie?"

"Well," I paused, suddenly aware of how my certainty the previous night had led to such public humiliation, then went for it. "A couple of questions for you first, if you don't mind."

He indicated with a nod of his head, that I should ask them. "When Maxiov was killed, the mobile phone he never let out of his sight went missing."

"I can neither confirm, not deny that statement," he said, the smirk back in place.

"Sir Phillip: I found the body, remember."

"And your other question?"

"Oh that was a statement, my first question is: Whilst everyone was being questioned by the police, you had someone – or someones – search our rooms. I'm assuming you were looking for the phone. My question is: Something was discovered in Lady Caroline's room. May we have it back?"

Now he frowned. "Discovered? What?"

"Ah," I nodded. Whoever had George clearly hadn't told him. "It doesn't matter what, but I would be appreciative if you could instruct your people to return it forthwith." I moved quickly along to my second question. "In the diary," I said, and his eyes turned slowly and – this time – with an obvious interest in them – to look at the slim notebook on the table.

"Well," I said, "it's about your son's friend, Simon. But first, I said, an idea coming to me, I was wondering if I could ask a favour of you…"

~

I left Sir Phillip still sitting by the coffee table looking at the notebook.

I had no idea whether he would read it or throw it onto the feeble fire in the grate, but I knew that the man I'd come to know over the past few days was not the monster George had drawn in his diaries and, once again, I was reminded that nobody at Dukes Halt was who they appeared to be.

But then I banished the thought. George's diary was written over thirty years ago. The period it covered was a period when Sir Phillip, by the sound of it, knew his wife was seriously ill. The stress of this – along with the scandal of Henry having been caught cheating – might have made the father adopt a more severe style. And George – well, I tried to remember what I was like as a teenager having to come to terms not just with how hard growing up and finding my place in the world was - though admittedly George might have had a slightly better start than me on that launchpad - but with my sexuality as well.

I remember being frustrated and confused a lot of the time, and being angry and depressed some of the time, and I found myself wondering whether some of George's descriptions of his father as a cold, overbearing archaic figure were really just some form of what the psychiatrists would call projection.

Then I recalled how, less than two days ago, the old man had ordered that his granddaughter attend a boarding school when all she wanted was to visit the local school, and I finally decided that whilst the diary might not be an entirely objective sketch of Sir Phillip, there were certainly some elements of truth in it.

After all, thirty-some years had passed, and the old man had cut his son out of his life. So perhaps he was presenting a good face to me.

Whatever, I shrugged as I made my way back upstairs. I'd delivered the diary. That was one thing done from a long list of errors that needed correcting.

Also on the list was apologising to Nick. All a part of me wanted to do was hunt him down and beg him to give us another go.

I knew that there was fault on both sides, but I also knew – because it was a lesson I'd learned from my parents – that one side has to make the first move, and I wanted him so badly that I was willing to swallow my pride and be that person.

But first, I'd shower, hunt down Stamford, apologise profusely, then – with the directions Sir Phillip had just given me - go in search of Lottie.

Something was gnawing at me, but I couldn't figure out what it was. Something Sir Phillip had said, or something someone had said that morning. But what was it?

I was so deeply lost in my thoughts that the appearance of Francine Gerber – her head encased in a scarlet turban, her ample figure swathed in a silk leopard-print wrap dress, her face oddly tight as though she'd fallen asleep with a face mask still on – completely threw me.

Seriously: All that was missing was the monkey on a lead and the instruction that she was ready for her close-up.

"Mrs Gerber," I tried to mask my discombobulation with a pleasantry, and her tight face seemed to tighten further.

"Mister Bird," she said, in a way that made it clear I was about to get far more than a simple morning greeting. "I want you to know that the way you treated that nice Doctor Stamford was an absolute disgrace."

She glared at me as though expecting me to spontaneously combust.

After a moment – during which I didn't so much as smoulder – she sniffed, squeezed herself around me and made her way down the stairs, muttering something I couldn't hear but which I comforted myself probably referenced the fact that it was the pictures that got small.

I turned, heading along the landing to my room, and stopped again.

Karen Stamford was standing outside the door to her husband's room.

As I watched she knocked, and called his name.

Something alerted her to my presence and she turned her face towards me.

"Mrs Stamford," I said, walking quickly along the landing, "I wanted to apologise to your husband. And to you."

"To me?" she frowned, her hand still raised to knock on the door again.

"For last night, I meant."

Her hand dropped slightly then came up and knocked again. "I know what you meant," she said. "I was there, you know. When you accused the sweetest, kindest most placid man I've ever met of," she shook her head as though the thought was still unbelievable, "of murder. Richard," she turned back towards the door, "it's me. Listen," she turned back towards me, "you made a mistake. I genuinely cannot understand how. I mean a few minutes research would have told you that Richard wasn't even in Srebrenica until years after that terrible war ended."

"It was a heat-of-the-moment thing," I said. "I saw Mila, recalled seeing him speaking to her, meeting him as we were en route to the crime scene."

She turned towards me and held her hand up. "Please. You explained your rationale last night. In excruciating detail. But surely you must see now that the story about this doctor, the horrible story Maximov told that night was exactly what most of us saw it as – a story. He was taking so much pleasure in tormenting everyone. Sir Phillip about his children. Major Warren about his war record. The whole family with suggestions that they or their ancestors were looters and criminals. He made comments designed to upset or outrage almost everyone at that table. And they were all designed to sound offensive without any of them being based on truth."

"No smoke without fire," I said quietly and she nodded.

"I want to talk to my husband. He was distraught last night, and I want to see if I can't calm him down, get him to stay at least until you have the opportunity to offer him a proper apology."

She knocked again, called his name and opened the door, adding to me "or at least until you have a chance to talk him out of suing you for slander."

She walked into the room, chatting to her husband, and I heard the sound of the heavy curtains being pulled apart, all soundtracked with her bright breezy voice, the sound of a nurse trying to cheer up a depressed patient, and as I went to pass by the room to my own, her chatter stopped, an odd silence descended on the room, and her voice came back low and urgent.

Then there was a strangled sound, a sort of choked cry and, as I drew level with the open doorway, Karen Stamford appeared in it, her face leaden, her eyes red rimmed, and her lips moving as though they had begun to move before her brain had processed what they needed to say.

And then she locked eyes with me, and she spoke.

"My husband's dead," she said, her voice clear and loud, as though she were asking when she'd be able to get new towels.

"My husband. Richard," she faltered, stammered, and then – as my own shattered brain made sense of what she was saying, she said it again. "My husband is dead."

And she began to shriek like a thing possessed.

CHAPTER THIRTY-SIX

Later, of course, I realised that the first thing I should have done is to get myself as far away from that room as I could, on the assumption that the last words Stamford had spoken to me were a threat to sue me into oblivion.

If anything dodgy had happened, me being present at the event would not be helped by the fact I'd gone pawing around the crime scene and left my dabs on everything.

But on the other hand, if he wasn't dead – if Karen Stamford had made a mistake – then I might be able to help.

And on the other hand (yes, I know: Three hands. Stay with me) or was that back to the first hand? Whatever: If Richard Stamford's death was suspicious I wanted a look at the crime scene and it was either now or – once the rozzers arrived – I'd be back at the station and so far away from the room that by the time I got back Chapman would have redecorated and put a bowl of begonias on the window sill.

So I pushed past the still-hysterical woman and crossed to the bed where Stamford – seeming to have shrunk unbelievably overnight – lay in bed, the covers pulled up to his chin, his face waxy and almost silver blue.

I didn't need to disturb him, didn't need to get my fingerprints on anything.

One look at him and at the syringe sitting on his bedside table was enough to tell me that Doctor Stamford wouldn't be instructing his legal team to take me down today.

Or ever again.

"Oh God," Karen moaned behind me.

I turned, and she was leaning against the chest of drawers. Her mobile phone in her hand. To her right a small writing desk – a selection of Dukes Halt notepaper and pens positioned as though Chapman had used a spirit level to test their straightness – sat unused, and beyond that a small vanity unit with a Dipthyque scented candle sat with a small kettle and a Nespresso machine.

Stamford had clearly been entitled to an upgrade from the untouched kids' rooms that Caz and I had been parked in. Not for him tired old furniture and a selection of kids' books for entertainment.

But then, I reasoned, neither Caz nor I were up for knighthoods.

People – drawn by Karen's hysterics – had arrived, and the first to enter the room was Digby Smith, his request for her to tell him what on earth was going on transforming, when he saw I was present, to a demand of me to tell him what the hell I had done.

Sara Simone came next with John Warren, and Caz with Ellie wasn't far behind, all crowding into the room and stopping dead when they saw what was lying on the bed.

I crossed to the widow Stamford, who was still staring at her phone.

"I heard the buzz," she said, lifting shocked eyes to mine. "I was asleep, you see? But I heard it and I just assumed it was something to do with the IPO. My company, you see: We're going public this time next week."

She was still staring at the phone.

I leant forward.

One of my skills – honed when I was a mailroom boy at a now-defunct fashion magazine and often had to deliver sealed messages to senior editors – is an ability to read upside down.

The email on her phone screen didn't really challenge the skill too much. It was hardly the Gettysburg address.

"I'm sorry," it said. "I can't do this any more."

I looked up at her. The blood had drained from her lips.

"If I'd read it," she said. "If I'd seen it and come in here straight away."

"Don't do that," I said, reaching out to put a hand on her arm.

"Get your bloody hands off that woman," Digby Smith – in full flight as the spirit of virtuous Justice – moved towards me, a snarl on his face that faltered only when I turned towards him as – I assumed – memories of what I'd done to him the previous day crossed his mind.

I stepped back immediately, hands up in supplication as John, Sara and Caz were joined by Henry and Pamela.

"I really think someone should call the police," I said, and pushing past them all, proceeded to do just that.

~

"I'm thinking of putting you on speed-dial, Mr Bird. I mean I might as well not bother calling the station any more. We could have a Whatsapp group and you could tell me what major crimes have been happening on my patch while I've been trying to grab an hour's sleep and get breakfast into my daughter."

Dane was his usual joyful self, his morose attitude compounded by the fact that he didn't appear to have had time to shave since we'd first met, and thus – on top of his usual air of disgruntlement - was dark-cheeked and generally dishevelled.

I shrugged and attempted to look innocent. I hoped nobody had reminded him what Stamford had threatened to do to me hours before he'd taken a one-way walk into the land of Morpheus and provided the blandest response I could give.

"I guess I've just got a talent for being in the wrong place at," I considered my phrasing, "quite frankly the wrong time."

"I'll say," he snorted. "Though my daughter described you and your latest discovery as a pest and a pain. So the dead Doc's threat to sue you for every penny you have wasn't a factor in you being in his bedroom today?"

I cursed his preternatural powers of recollection.

"I was passing and thought a more formal apology than the one I gave him might be the thing to do."

"Formal? While he was still in his pyjamas?"

"I didn't get as far as the door. Or the discovery of what he was wearing. Mrs Gerber delayed me, and by then I discovered Mrs Stamford outside his door. And in case you were wondering," I added, "I have precisely four hundred quid in my savings account, a credit card debt substantially higher than that amount, and last time I checked, no further assets. So Dr Stamford bankrupting me in a libel case would have been a mercy, to be honest. I had more reason to keep him alive than to off him."

"Slander," Dane sighed deeply, his demeanour becoming more bloodhoundy by the second. "I hate it when people mix the two up. If you wrote a letter to the papers calling him a murdering fascist sympathiser who'd sent a busload of young men to their death it would be libel. If you only said it out loud, it would be slander.

"And if it was true, it would be neither."

We were in the pink salon that I'd found Pamela Warren in a day earlier, and Caz had been silent so far, picking at a croissant and flipping through a copy of Vogue so old that none of the women in its pages were hatless.

"True?" her head jerked up and Dane turned slowly towards her voice like a vole discovering that the fencepole in the corner was ambulatory.

"But it wasn't true," I said, and his head turned just as slowly back to me.

Caz soothed Ellie, who'd been awakened from her slumber by the alarm in her mistress's voice and was now snarling at Dane in a way that might have been menacing if her rear end weren't wagging joyously.

"So it was just slander then. Still a reason for you to want him in a place his legal team would be unable to negotiate fees with him."

Caz snorted. "You clearly don't know many London lawyers. Bastards would use a Ouija board if they thought it would get them billable hours."

"Look," I started explaining the rationale behind the accusations I'd laid at Stamford's feet the night before and, within a sentence, Dane had his hand up.

"Hard as it may be for the likes of a big city," he coughed, "amateur detective to recall the minutiae, I was present last night when you did that speech." Dane cast a concerned glance at Ellie, who had stopped wagging and was now watching him as though at any moment he might distress Caz and need his throat ripped out.

I tilted my head back. "Yeah," I sighed. "You were, weren't you? So you heard Doctor Stamford's rebuttal."

Dane raised his eyes. "Rebuttal? It's like we're on Law & Order or something. I heard him say he didn't turn up til after the war was over."

I glanced at Caz, who flared her nostrils at me, flicked a page in the September 1959 edition of Vogue and distractedly petted Ellie on the rump.

"And your point is?" I asked.

"He took a shot of some very strong stuff a few hours later and emailed his wife that you were right."

"So it *was* suicide?" I asked, and Dane considered the idea for a moment.

"Her name's Gail," he finally said. "My daughter. Though right now she's insisting my husband and I call her The Princess Gailette."

My confusion washed over me like a wave, and – like a wave – left me cold and more aware than I had been before.

"Husband?" I asked.

Dane caught my realisation and smiled slightly. "Yes, Mr Bird. Not everyone in the countryside is straight out of Thomas Hardy Central casting. In the same way that not everything that looks like a suicide is necessarily a suicide."

~

"I'm not entirely sure Columbo meant you could tramp merrily across the county when he said you could go," Caz bitched as a switch of leafless branch slapped back and snagged in her bouffant.

"He said I was free to go. And he's gay, Caz. A gay cop with a husband and a daughter and a relationship that hasn't destroyed his career. And he's in a regional rural force."

"Okay, then, "she sighed, *Gaylumbo*. And before you go

getting all hero-worshippy, may I remind you he said you were free to go *for now.*"

"Well like he said," I added, "this isn't Law & Order."

"I didn't think it was the Lord of the bloody Rings either," she grunted, slapping into a low hanging bough. "And why's it got so cold?"

Ellie paused, looked up at Caz and, realising there was no danger imminent, slapped a pink tongue out, waved a tail wildly, and skipped a few paces beyond both of us, but not so far that we couldn't still hear her breathing and pawing at what she doubtlessly considered potentially menacing piles of leaves.

"You don't need to be there, you know," I said. "In fact, it might be good if you weren't."

Caz finally tore a length of some half-dead vegetation from her hair and stood upright. "Balls, Mr Bird. It may be more appropriate if you deal with initial approaches. But she's my responsibility. And I know it might look like this whole place – including me – have skirted their responsibilities for way too long. But in my case I'm owning up that it's been entirely my fault. And the fault gets addressed here and now. Though I do wish you'd asked if they had a flamethrower. Or a machete, at the very least."

"It's not far," I smiled, reached forward and pulled at a wiry fern that she'd missed. "And I dread to think what use a flame thrower – or a machete – would have been put to this weekend if they'd been available."

It had been the descriptions of the Estate Manager's cottage in George's diary that had – earlier this morning – alerted me to the idea.

In George's diary, the family lived in a tiny ancient cottage, which had not matched up to the modern build that was now described as The Estate Manager's House.

It had taken til today for me to realise that the cottage referred to was a different – and possibly extant – building to the one Beth and Gaia lived in today, and it had taken a conversation with Sir Phillip to confirm my suspicions.

"It's somewhere here," I said, not entirely sure where the cottage was. Sir Phillip had explained where the cottage was in tones that confirmed he knew his land in detail, but which made it clear that if you were not 'Of' Dukes Halt you would forever be an outsider.

"I think that was the lighting-struck elm," I said waving vaguely behind me.

"Lightning-struck what?" Caz, belatedly realising my lack of clear map co-ordinates, staggered behind me as I shoved a curtain of leaves forward and stepped forward into a tiny clearing that the forest was determinedly trying to reclaim.

In front of us was a cottage that seemed to have been carved from the forest that surrounded it.

Ivy, together with various other climbers, had wound their way around the small low building, and on the opposite edge of the clearing the forest itself appeared to have conquered the construction so that the cottage seemed to be growing out of the woods.

I pushed my way into what was left of the clearing, and squelched my way across the space, realising as I did so that I was looking at the back of the cottage.

I stepped towards the back door and paused for a moment before hammering on the wooden frame.

"It's me," I called out. "Danny."

Silence – apart from the cries of disturbed birds and the scratching of the wind through the trees.

I looked at Caz.

She looked at me, and we both looked at Ellie who, sensing our attention, stopped snuffling in the patch of undergrowth she'd fixed on and turned a genuinely concerned look on us.

At which point a figure, cradling a shotgun, came around the left side of the building and stopped dead.

"What are you doing here?" Gaia asked.

"Hoping to speak to Lottie," I smiled.

Gaia frowned. "Lottie? Why on earth would she be here?"

"Why would you be here?".

Gaia shrugged. "I was just exploring the woods. Literally

just came across this place. Was looking for rabbits."

She was fast on her feet; I had to give her that.

"I'm not going to tell them where she is," I looked in the direction of Dukes Halt, "if she doesn't want me to. I just want to talk to her."

"She's not here," Gaia said, still straight-faced.

"How d'you know? You've literally just come across the place. So how would you know who is and isn't here?"

She tore her eyes from mine and cast a quick glance towards the cottage. "Place looks deserted, don't it?"

"I saw you yesterday," I said, and in response to the confusion that washed across her face, I added "in the garden. When you came to pick up her message. She didn't have a mobile phone, so that's how you'd been communicating wasn't it?

"Smart, but unsurprising. Lottie comes from a long line of spies. Using a dead letter drop would doubtless make some of her ancestors very happy."

Gaia shook her head. "Listen," she said, with obvious tension in her voice, "I don't know what you're on about, but I've got to get going. You have a nice day, okay?"

She went to move off. "You knew about the threat to send her to a Swiss School," I said.

Gaia stopped, her back to me. "I don't know what you're on about."

"When I came to your house yesterday afternoon. You said that her family were 'a bunch of bastards who want to send her to school in bloody Switzerland'. Switzerland hadn't even been mentioned until hours before Lottie went missing. So how'd you know about Switzerland if you hadn't seen her since she went missing?"

"Bugger," she sighed.

I tilted my head towards the back door. "You got a key?"

"Not for the back," she said. "We'll have to go around the front."

CHAPTER THIRTY-SEVEN

The hallway this time was the tiny space George had written about in his diary, the whole cottage encased in encroaching vegetation and dirt felt gloomy and secret.

"She's upstairs," Gaia said, removing the cartridges from the shotgun and standing them like sentries on a small shelf just inside the door.

The gun itself was leant against the wall.

"Will you wait in the kitchen while I fetch her?"

The phrasing felt archaic somehow as though the inter-war atmosphere that Sir Phillip tried so hard to project in the Halt itself had infected even the likes of Gaia.

"You're not going to help her squeeze out a window and down the drain-pipe are you?" I asked as she headed towards the stairs.

"Well not now I'm not," she muttered as Caz, Ellie and I made our way into the kitchen.

The table was still here, the whole room still furnished more or less as George had described it, though the overhead light – when I tentatively flicked the switch – remained resolutely dark.

Shortly Lottie Warren came tentatively down the stairs and into the dimly lit kitchen, her eyes darting nervously around. Gaia was close behind her.

"What do you want?" Lottie asked, and Caz crossed to her and took the girl's hands in her own.

"Firstly," Caz said, "to congratulate you. This was a smart bit of subterfuge. You know they've had people checking the ports and the railway stations around. Nobody thought to look for you here. And secondly," Caz let go of Lottie's hands and folded her own arms angrily, "to tell you how disappointed I am in you. Your parents have been worried sick."

"Really?" Lottie tilted her head. "Only they don't appear to have even looked for me. I mean were they leading the search parties? Oh wait," she held a hand up. "There haven't been any search parties, have there?

"Not really fair, Lottie; they've got a lot on right now. There've been two murders and a suicide that might be a murder since you left, you know."

"I know," she said, reaching back and pulling Gaia forward. "Gaia's been keeping me up to date on what's been going on."

I sighed, stepped forward. "If you really wanted a search party," I said, "I can suggest they organise one. Lots of worried locals stomping all over the forest looking for your lifeless corpse."

Caz frowned at me, her displeasure almost tangible.

Lottie, however, laughed. "You know what I'd like? I'd like someone to give a fuck about me."

Gaia stepped forward, put a hand in the small of her back where she thought I couldn't see it.

"Someone other than Gaia," Lottie corrected.

"Look, Lottie," I shrugged, "there's no nice way to say this: Your parents aren't awful people. But they are *terrible* parents."

"Danny," Caz turned a shocked face on me. I held up my hands placatingly.

"That doesn't mean they don't love you," I said. "It doesn't mean they don't give a fuck about you. I know even the old man loves you. But I think your problem is that they've seen how strong you are. So they don't think you need reminding that it's Okay to be a bit lost. It's okay to want a hug."

"A hug?" Lottie gave me the same look my nephews give me every time I refer to The Web.

If I'd started the conversation feeling old I was being aged faster than a Hollywood actress in a decade-spanning mini-series.

"The thing is," I pressed on regardless, "Your parents and your grandfather live lives that don't really leave much room for you. Their drive is stuff that happened in the past.

"They do what they do because they feel that the past – the Warren ancestry, your uncle's death in service – is a road that needs to be respected and followed. And I'm so sorry that that's meant they forget that you – here, now – matter more. But hiding isn't going to help move this on."

"It's better than being made to sit there like furniture while they decide my life for me," Lottie said flatly. "I'm tired of it; of being pushed around to one school or the other; of being shipped off whenever they have one of their secret squirrel meetings. Of being either shut out or drowned in fake concern."

"Plus," I said, "you're in love."

Her eyes widened like saucers, and her whole face blushed.

I looked behind me at the kitchen table. The place where Lottie's uncle had fallen in love with Gaia's father, and considered, for a moment, whether George's ghost would have been satisfied by how neatly the circle had been closed.

And then I remembered, in the hall of the Kennedy house, the framed pencil sketches, and realised, with a shock, that they were the sketches George had done of Simon. Simon, who hadn't loved George the way that George wanted, but who had clearly loved him as a friend, and who had kept the sketches his whole life.

And I wondered if Simon had been as hurt by the blunt, brutal way that George was sent away and by what appeared to have been a severing of all communications from George.

Gaia put an arm around Lottie's waist. "Do *they* know?" Lottie asked, her voice a whisper.

I smiled at her. Christ, I wanted to put my arms around both of them, tell them that it would be no shame if their parents did know, but instead I shook my head. "Nobody knows. And nobody needs to know until you're ready to tell them."

"It's all screwed anyway," Lottie said, tears in her eyes. "Even if they don't send me to Switzerland, Gaia and her mum are being kicked out of the house soon. They've found a flat in the village, but unless Gaia's mum can find some work they'll have to move away and then it'll all be over anyway."

"I'll never let that happen," Gaia said fiercely. "You can move in with us."

Lottie laughed sadly. "Oh yeah? How's that gonna work when your mum has no job and no income. Do you really think she's going to want to have another mouth to feed?"

"We'll figure something out," Gaia said.

"We could run away," Lottie said. "Just go to London. Get jobs." She looked at me with something like desperation in her eyes, as though she knew, even as she was saying it, that what she was suggesting was impossible, but desperately wanting me to tell her it was a good plan.

"But I don't want to go to London," Gaia frowned, a glance at Lottie making me wonder if this was how I looked at Nick when he said something that made me question what we had in common.

Lottie Warren wasn't starting from nothing. Her family, her position, would surely buoy her up, and Gaia at least came from a family where her mother obviously loved her, and where whoever she was and however her life panned out, she'd have a cheerleader.

But even as those realisations came to me I remembered myself at their age. Life so vast before me, and everything unknown; how desperately I had wanted my life to start whilst fear gnawed away at whatever confidence I had.

And I realised that it made no difference where they started from: Lottie and Gaia were pain-in-the-arse teenagers, but both of them were as scared and as lost as each other.

And I suspected they felt like - for the most part – each other was all they had.

"Look," I said, already dreading the looks they'd doubtless give me when I'd finished, "I know it feels like a disaster right now. But it will get better."

They didn't disappoint. Their looks of withering disdain would have shrivelled a cactus.

"He's not wrong," Caz said, moving over to Lottie and

hugging her. "Life is shit. Your parents are nightmares. None of this is fair or workable."

She let go of Lottie, took a step back and glanced over her shoulder at me.

"But he missed out some stuff. Mainly, I suspect, because he thinks you're a spoiled brat who needs telling how hard the world is."

"He's not wrong, you know, about the spoiled brat," Gaia smirked and nudged Lottie playfully in the ribs.

Lottie squirmed from her but directed her distrust and animosity squarely at Caz and I.

Caz continued: "He forgot to mention what will happen next. You hate your life right now – with," she gave a fond smile to Gaia, "certain exceptions."

The two girls turned their heads towards each other in almost perfect synchronisation. As one, they giggled, stopped the giggle, smiled and forced the angry blandness that has forever been the façade of youth onto their faces.

"But what my clever and kind friend forgot to mention," Caz gestured towards me, "Is that not all of this is going to remain constant."

"It's not a phase," Lottie said, her face moving towards anger. "I love her."

"I know," Caz, not even acknowledging the flare up, continued. "And for the avoidance of doubt: I know what a phase looks like."

She smiled. "And I know what love looks and feels like. But the things beyond you. The things you can't control. The things that matter right now: They are so very, very impermanent. The feeling that being in love and alive and convinced that the most important thing in the world is this moment? That will last.

"How you feel – who you are – I'm not trying to persuade you this is not important. But what I want you to know is that whilst where you are now is hard, the truth will stay the same while the rest of the world moves off elsewhere."

She widened her arms and hugged Gaia too.

Gaia squirmed uncomfortably.

"Are you on one?" she asked. "Only, if you start fitting there's no way the paramedics'll find you out here."

Caz ignored her.

"My mother left when I was a child." Caz was talking, but I couldn't tell whether she was talking to Lottie, Gaia, me or to herself. "She was there one day, and the next," her fist, held in front of her face, exploded like a dandelion, became a hand and was waved in the air.

"Gone. Leaving me the daughter in a family of boys, none of whom knew what to do with me. And all I knew was that I didn't want what I had or what seemed mapped out for me."

"What happened?" Lottie asked.

Caz shrugged, came back to the moment from wherever she had been. "I had a miserable childhood. Unseen. Uncared for. Mostly unloved. But the world rolled on. I lost myself for a bit.

"And if you ever find yourself lost all I can do is tell you to remember this: You will both," she held a hand up to stop the smirks that flickered across their faces, "I was not about to say *grow up*. Quite frankly, I wouldn't wish that on my worst enemy let alone on two young women I'm fond of. No; you will both move. On. Up. Away. Sometimes, maybe – and I hope so – back to here where it all began.

"And on your journeys, wherever they lead, I just pray you'll both meet friends who make your life richer than you ever dared believe it could be. I hope you meet smart clever mailroom boys who laugh at your jokes, whose love for you makes you realise how deserving you are of love, who stand by you when the world turns against you.

"I hope you will both meet friends who don't just accept you for who you are, but who celebrate you. Both."

She glanced at me once more. "Because Danny's right: Life is a bit shit. Fuck it," Caz said, making even me gasp, "Life is sometimes *a lot shit*. But the opposite of love, as complicated as love is, isn't hate. It's apathy. It's death. It's having nothing and nobody to make you realise how wonderful life can be.

And friends; The right friends," she smiled in my direction, "friends you never thought you'd have, and never dared to dream you'd deserved, are there waiting to make life wonderful. They transmogrify shit into whatever the opposite is."

"Joy," I said, wiping a tear from my eye. "How can your father have spent so much money on your education and you don't know that the opposite of shit is Joy?"

"Sweetie," she turned to me with a smile, "my education was in how to manage the housekeeper and disguise a black eye. For the minor stuff like reminding me what joy is, I have you."

"Can you two get a room?" Gaia asked, and I actually laughed out loud, so easily and completely had she killed the moment.

"Okay," I said, still glowing from Caz's words, "you really can't stay in this cottage. The power's off for a start."

"Don't I know it," Lottie grumbled. "I've had to sit here in the dark without a book to read or even a phone to watch Netflix on."

"My heart bleeds," I said. "But when you get back to the house the first thing you need to do is put your foot down. You need a phone. I mean, how does a teenager know what parts of themselves to hate if they don't have Insta or TikTok."

"Fuck that," Lottie, suddenly straight backed and tense, replied. "First: I don't do social media. All the bitches at the last school were obsessed and I don't ever want to touch it. And also: I'm not going home. And you can't make me."

I didn't want to point out that as she was still on the Dukes Halt estate she'd never, technically, left home; or that I could easily summon a phalanx of the county's burliest coppers to hoist her up and haul her back to the entry hall with its dusty armour and unnecessary antiques.

Instead, I said "What if I could fix everything?"

They looked at each other.

"Didn't she just say the world was fucked and unfixable?"

Gaia asked, nodding at Caz.

"And that we should pray to get a time machine back to nineteen hundred and fuck knows so we can meet a sassy mailroom boy?" Lottie added.

I looked at Caz, who had the good grace to appear sheepish at her description of me as a magical blue-collar character in my own story.

"She's never been right since she fell of her pony," I said. "I have some ideas. It's not going to be easy to pull them off. And it's not guaranteed. But I think it's Just, and all we can hope is that Justice prevails."

"Oh Lord," Caz addressed Ellie, "he's off again."

I ignored her. "But I think I might be able to work something out. Something that lets Gaia and her mum stay here and lets you," I nodded at Lottie, "go to school where Gaia does."

"I told you they were drug fiends," Gaia said to her beloved. Then, to me: "How are you going to work all that out then?"

"Ah," I smiled. "I'm glad you asked. First, like I say, you both need to come back with us to Gaia's house where I can have a word with her mum. And then, Lottie, you need to come back to Dukes Halt with me."

"They'll ship me off to Switzerland as soon as you're gone," she said distrustfully.

"They won't," I said. "And if they do I'll come to Gstaad or wherever the hell you are and rescue you. But I promise, you'll go to school where you want."

She looked at Gaia, at Caz and finally at me. Even in the dim light of the kitchen, the desperation in her eyes was obvious.

"You promise?"

I smiled at her, and nodded.

And even as the two of them held hands and moved towards the door, I could hear Nick pleading with me to stop my need to fix everything.

Caz Ellie and I followed them out of the cottage and made

our way through the trees to Beth Kennedy's house, and I prayed I hadn't finally made a promise I couldn't keep.

CHAPTER THIRTY-EIGHT

From the edge of the forest we watched Pamela swoop on Lottie. As she approached, I saw the girl lift her arms up and run towards her mother, the two of them embracing tightly before Pamela released her and rained kisses on her forehead.

We watched Lottie and Pamela go in through the door of Dukes Halt. Caz stood to one side, eyes downcast as though the display of mother-daughter love embarrassed her. ~~I knew otherwise~~.

"Are you okay?" I asked, and she sighed deeply.

"When does it stop?" She asked, and I knew she didn't require a response.

"My mother walked out when I was twelve. I was at school – another boarding school I absolutely hated – and when I came back for the half-term break she was gone. And I never saw her again."

I reached out for her hand, but she made no move to take mine, as though she weren't even there, couldn't even see me.

"I miss her every day, and I wish I could tell her that it's okay. That I understand why she couldn't stay with my family any more." She smiled sadly. "God knows there were – and still are – times I wish I could remove myself from them. And then," she gestured vaguely at the door that Pamela and Lottie had gone through.

"Pamela walks out; Lottie hates her boarding school. Nothing changes."

I wanted to tell her that George's story had been revised in Lottie and Gaia and that this time there was a happier ending, but I couldn't: it wasn't my story to tell.

Instead, I said "It's not always the same story you know." I nodded, myself, at the house. "This time mother and daughter are reunited. There's time for them to reconnect. There might still be time for you," I said, and she chuckled dryly.

"Ah Mr Bird. Ever the cockeyed optimist. No," she shook her head. "My mother's made her wishes crystal clear. I'm a De Montfort. She's not.

"I used to hope she was dead, you know? That she was dead and buried in an unmarked grave. That would explain what happened to her, why she abandoned me so completely. But she's not. She's just good at staying hidden."

I didn't know what to say. So I said nothing.

"What's that song?" She suddenly asked. "All the lonely people? You know that? I Used to wonder if she was alone. Miserable. I wanted her to be. Because I was. Only I'm not alone, am I? Not any more."

Caz smiled at me, looked for a moment like she was going to cry, then dropped to her knees and snuggled Ellie, asking "Who's the bestest doggie in the world?

"And you," she said looking up at me, two tears running down her face. You're not bad either, mister bird."

She stood and hugged me.

"What?" I asked, "I don't get a snuggle and a 'who's the bestest barman-cum-detective in the world'?"

"Don't push it," she smiled, and looked over my shoulder. "Oh," she said, her smile widening. "You have a visitor. I'll see you inside later."

I watched her, Ellie by her side, heading towards the house, then I turned, and there was Nick, standing by the fountain.

"Oh Jesus," I walked towards him, "you haven't been here all night, have you?"

He smiled "Not quite. Dane let me join him. They're still working on the," he nodded towards the house "scene."

"So they think Stamford's death a murder then?" I found myself stopping some way from him.

Nick shrugged. "There's enough questions to make it worth looking at."

"Aren't there always?"

"Well," he smiled, shifted his body as though inviting me

closer, "when you're around, there usually are. I'm sorry," he said suddenly.

I stepped forward.

Stepped again and, now, the thought ran through my head, we were close enough to kiss.

"No," I said. "I'm sorry. I'm jealous and stupid and not proud of either trait."

He chuckled now, put his hand out and laid it firmly on my arm, halfway between the elbow and the shoulder.

For a moment I feared I was about to be arrested. And then he squeezed my tricep. Leaned in.

"You're an idealist. And the smartest person I know. And I am sorry for last night."

I paused. I wasn't ready to revisit the acrimony but I also wasn't ready to let go of all my anger. But I still wanted – as Nick had so correctly pointed out – to make everything right.

Yet I was no longer willing - especially after I'd seen Gaia and Lottie and their openness and love – to bury any of myself in order to make this work.

We had to love each other entirely or not at all.

"I don't think I've said sorry enough," Nick said. "I mean, for messing everything up."

And now I was apologising though a tiny, buried, part of me resented the act. "You did what you did because it was the right thing to do. In a way, you're as determined to make the universe right as I am."

He paused, raised his eyebrows and smiled, nodding again. "Thing is, there's something else I don't think I've said; or – if I have – that I've said often enough: I love you Danny Bird. I love that you try to fix the world, but I worry that it will hurt you terribly one day when the world refuses to be fixed."

I glanced over at Caz.

She tilted her head, as if to ask whether I needed her to stay. I smiled, shook my head.

"I know," I said. "Sooner or later. But I'm going to do what I can as long as I can. Because I hope on that day I'll have the people I love by my side."

He smiled and suddenly there were tears in his eyes. "I've been thinking about this all night. There's obviously paperwork to be done and some other stuff, but in a while Arianna will not need to be married to me to stay here. She can be safe and single.

"And I'm sick of you being in your place and me in mine, and of everything having to be furtive and-" Nick reached out and took my hand, dropping to one knee.

"And when this is all sorted. As soon as we can. Danny, will you marry me?"

The world stopped.

I took a half step backwards, wanting to carry on moving backwards and realising only when I felt the tug of his hand holding mine that I couldn't.

"Is this cos we had an argument?"

Nick shook his head. "No. Well, yes, but only because it made me realise what matters. You drive me mad, Danny Bird: your need to make everything right. And I hope that never changes.

"But I also know that right now we're floating, getting by. I don't want that. I want to be going somewhere, heading towards a future. With you."

"And you think getting married will do that?"

His smile faltered, and then went back on. "I think it will make me very happy to be able to tell the world that you're my husband."

I could feel a cold sweat bursting out all over my body. Why wasn't I just saying yes, and rushing into his arms? What was wrong with me?

"But what will you tell work?"

He chuckled. "Jesus. You're still at it. Fuck work, Danny. They'll be told, and they'll deal with it. Just say yes. Cos this gravel is cold."

I wanted to say yes.

I wanted that more than anything.

He was the most straightlaced man I knew. His determination to do the right thing had nearly ruined us.

I'd been hurt by the last man I'd committed to.

But I wanted to say Yes. To move from being Danny to being Danny and Nick.

And yet.

If I said yes, what would happen? I'd been one half of Robert and Danny for years, and discovered too late that I'd been mugged off, used, abused and cheated on, and that what I'd felt for my uptight lawyer was nothing like what he'd felt for me.

What if, the minute I said yes to Nick, the universe got to work on ways to fuck this up as well?

I wanted, so badly, to say yes, but what if I didn't deserve this? What if good old-fashioned conventional romance wasn't for me? What if this relationship ended up as fucked up as my previous one?

Was I overthinking this? Of course I was: Overthinking is what I do, what I've always done. I wanted a home to run to, a safe haven to rest in, but I wasn't a child any more. I wanted someone who would be with me forever, in a world where things break, people get sick, love dies. I wanted perfection, but nothing is ever perfect.

I was standing in a cold, bedraggled field in Dorset and worrying about how this would end in five, ten, fifteen years.

Unbidden, an image of Mila popped into my mind, of her grousing about where she was and how much she hated cooking for the people Sir Phillip brought to Dukes Halt; how perfect her life would be when she got her restaurant.

But nothing is ever perfect.

I looked around. A watery sun the colour of old dishcloths was filling the sky, painting the whole scene a dingy yellow, and a gentle breeze was wafting the uncut grass on the lawn, blowing Nick's hair into his eyes, and rippling the water in the fountain, the sun's vague reflection fracturing and sparkling like glitter.

And suddenly everything was clear.

I reached down and grabbed his other hand, pulling him to his feet.

"Yes," I said, and my heart was going mad. "Yes, oh yes. Yes. How could I have been so blind?"

The blissful smile that had burst across his face was crossed with a puzzled frown for a moment til I leant in, planted a smacker on his lips, pulled back and, still holding him by the shoulders, beamed.

"I need to talk to Sir Phillip. Can you do me a favour: Stand here. Stay right here. Don't let anyone – *anyone* – near this fountain.

"Can you do that for me?"

His smile was bemused rather than joyful now, and his confusion was understandable, but Nick smiled as though acknowledging I was a hopeless case, and sat down on the edge of the pool.

"Thank you." I knelt down, kissed him again, and, throwing an "I really do love you, you know, but don't sit on the edge; you'll get piles," I ran at full tilt towards Dukes Halt.

~

"Everything alright?" Caz asked as I powered across the hallway at Dukes Halt.

"Fabulously," I beamed. "I've just got to have a word with Sir Phillip. Oh, and I think I'm getting married."

She was still staring open-mouthed at me when I reached the study door, knocked and – without waiting for a response from within – entered.

Chapman's outraged gasp was quieted by a look from Sir Phillip, who stood up from behind the desk and gestured at his factotum to move from her seat opposite him and retire to her desk.

This she did in silent but obvious fury.

"Sorry to bother you," I started as Sir Phillip moved towards me, hand outstretched and took mine.

For a moment I had a flashback to Nick out by the fountain and hoped he wasn't about to propose to me as well.

Instead he shook my hand enthusiastically. "I won't ask how you managed to do it but thank you for returning my granddaughter to the fold."

"I'm not sure she's back in the fold," I said, "but listen: There are a few things I need to talk to you about, and some favours I need to ask."

I crossed and – unbidden – sat in the seat that Chapman had just vacated.

Sir Phillip resumed his seat on the other side of the desk. From behind me I could feel Chapman's eyes burning into my skull.

"You've done my family a favour," Sir Phillip said. "Name your price."

"First," I said, "Have you located the item I asked about earlier?"

"Not yet. I've asked all my people, but as you are well aware, there have been some strange goings-on around here lately. It may have been acquired by someone who is not part of my staff or family."

"Please try to locate it. It's important."

He nodded. "I will. Next?"

"How skint are you?" I asked, and he bridled as, from behind me, a sharp intake of breath indicated that Chapman was listening to every word we said.

Before he could answer, and sensing the answer would be a prevarication of some sort, I added some observations to my question.

"Sir Phillip, despite keeping the shutters closed in the long gallery upstairs, the sun has bleached the silk on the walls. I can see where some of the larger paintings that once hung there have been replaced by smaller ones. I guess they've been sold. The only decent pictures remaining in the house are those of your late wife - and I'm guessing you'd part with those on pain of death – and that ludicrous sea battle in the dining room, the absence of which would be impossible to hide.

"There are – with the exception of Mrs Chapman and – until recently – Mila, no permanent staff for a house of this size. The food has been amazing but Mila was not exactly shy about the challenging budgets she had to work with." I didn't mention the disfunctional hearing or the meagre fires in the various rooms.

Sir Phillip straightened his back, looked down his Patrician nose, and gave me his best Johnny Gielgud. "All houses like ours are struggling."

"What if I told you I'd just spoken to someone who has ideas that could generate a million a year in revenue."

"I'd say, firstly, that they were talking rot."

"It's a big house," I said. "A huge estate. But it hasn't come into the modern day. There are blockages that prevent any modernisation really taking off."

"Modernisation." He said the word as though it was ashes in his mouth.

"Adapt or die," I answered. "I get it: Some things are immutable. Love. Loyalty. Decency. Truth. But the world beyond these walls is changing and the saddest thing is that as much as you might resist that change it's hitting you. It's killing Duke's Halt. The negative impact of that change has left you close to broke. Another few years with that change going on and you *will* be broke.

"But there are parts of the change beyond the wall that could be used to benefit you. To offset the negatives."

He straightened a pencil. "What?"

"Ah," I smiled, "that's something you'd need to discuss directly with the candidate I'm thinking of."

"Candidate?"

"For the position. Of Estate Manager, though the role would expand to include management not only of the grounds but of the house itself."

"Sir Phillip," Mrs Chapman finally spoke, her tone arctic, "Perhaps I should absent myself."

Sir Phillip glanced at her, alarm on his face.

"What? No, Chapman, not at all. Stay, please. Mister Bird," he turned back to me. "The management of this house has been in Mrs Chapman's hands for forty years and her role-"

"Has brought you to the edge of bankruptcy," I said. "Well, her role and the fact that it matches so perfectly with your preferences and prejudices. A role like Estate Manager needs to be the opposite of simpatico. They should challenge you, push you out of your comfort zone, as should you to them."

Sir Phillip shook his head. "No, I'm afraid I really cannot consider anyone but Mrs Chapman managing the running of the house, though I will admit that I do need a new Estate Manager. Kennedy's recent death has left me with a vacancy in that position. May I ask who the candidate you mentioned is?"

"The incumbent," I said. "Beth Kennedy."

"Kennedy's widow? Oh no," Sir Phillip shook his head. "Absolutely not. She's been here already pleading her case. He glanced at Chapman. I turned around to follow his gaze and found the housekeeper staring at the blotting paper.

"And you rejected her?"

"Her ideas. Shooting weekends. Nature preserves. Farmers' markets. Nonsense, all of it."

"Why nonsense?"

"Strangers tramping all over the place. Stag parties. Gangs of braying city bankers."

"Sir Phillip, I don't wish to be rude, but this weekend you've had Americans and Russians you barely knew along with a member of parliament who attempted to assault me on the grounds. I can't see that allowing a few more people to visit the grounds on select weekends when you yourself could be off the premises – and when those visitors would be paying a substantial amount of money to be here – would be so offensive."

"And that's because you have never had the responsibility of a place like Dukes Halt," he said, the coldness tempered somewhat by a sadness in his face. "We don't own this place, you know. Oh, I know the deeds have the Warren family name on them, and I know that what little rent is paid is to my bank account, but my father and his father before him strongly held that rather than merely owning the place and – as so many landowners had done before – raping it for as much financial gain as we could, it was our job to guard and safekeep it."

"Commendable ideals," I said, and let a silence fall for a moment before adding "and ones your son will doubtless remember when he's forced to sell the whole lot off to a developer who turns this place into a block of luxury flats and bulldozes the forest to build five thousand identical luxury family homes."

Sir Phillip actually went green at the thought.

"Look," I said: "Beth Kennedy is a local. She's from the village. Her husband's family have been in Dukes Halt for generations and have a love of the place almost as great as yours. Her daughter is heartsick at the thought of having to leave.

"But Beth knows that changes are going to be necessary to ensure the future survival of the place; that keeping the gates closed and the walls fortified will not stop the outside world from storming Dukes Halt. And isn't it better to have a welcoming environment that brings people here? "They don't need to be Investment Bankers and Americans; there's a huge movement in eco-tourism, in retreats for people who want to write, learn to cook, practice yoga; people who would spend money just to be here, but whose presence would be in line with your ideals, and whose cash would benefit the estate."

He made to object and I kept talking. "Visitors who would become an even more valuable asset to the estate: a group of people who would go back to their communities and preach the value of a place like Dukes Halt so that it would be far less easy for the barbarians to storm the ramparts."

Sir Phillip's brow furrowed. I took my chance.

"Look," I said, "you won't find anyone with the experience and the knowledge of Dukes Halt for the money you're paying Mrs Kennedy. Letting her go just because she can't promise you that doing the same things you've been doing forever will produce different results is," I searched for the right word; one that would clearly articulate how dangerous the old man's stubbornness was without insulting him in a way that would damage my case. "Unwise."

I glanced once more over my shoulder. "It's time you had some people around who told you no, and who told you the truth."

"Oh now I really cannot allow this to stand," Sir Phillip – loyal to a fault – finally objected to my clear disdain for Chapman. "Mrs Chapman has never shied away from having difficult conversations with me."

"Never?" I said, and his frown deepened.

"You know I'm very grateful that you recovered my granddaughter," he said, clearly making ready to return to whatever he'd been doing when I'd barged in, "but-"

"What happened to Edward?" I asked, and he stopped speaking, his mouth continuing to move silently for a moment as a deep red blush moved inexorably from his collar to the roots of his swept back hair.

"He fell," Sir Phillip finally managed, and I held a finger up to silence him.

"I wasn't talking to you," I said, turning around in my seat so I could look Mrs Chapman straight in the eye. "I was asking you."

"Me?"

I looked back at Sir Phillip. "You read the diary?"

He blinked, cleared his throat. "It was… painful. I can see why George hated this place and all it stood for."

"But he didn't," I said. "He stayed away because he loved all it stood for, and because he'd shamed himself and you. Not by being gay, but by trying to frame Simon Kennedy for theft. By being caught. And by being so lost in his grief that he failed his little brother and – George felt – sent him to his death.

"He wrote, when he was dying, asking to come back. I'm told your response made clear he could never return. It was his dying wish, and he received a letter from you telling him he would not be welcome."

Now tears came to Sir Phillip's eyes and ran down his cheeks. "He never wrote," he whispered, his hands shaking as he opened his desk drawer and withdrew the slim notebook.

"I have every reason to believe he wrote," I answered. "By

that time he knew Simon Kennedy was dead and that he would not have to face him. He wrote, but you never got the letter. Or, to be more precise, the letter was received – as so many others had been over the years - and responded to without your knowledge."

He lifted his eyes. "But that would only have been possible if…"

I asked the question again, turning directly to Chapman. "What happened to Edward?"

"Sir Phillip," she stood and came around her desk, her face flushed, her own hands shaking. "This person's a liar. Last night should have shown he makes outrageous and baseless accusations."

Sir Phillip reached into the inside pocket of his jacket and withdrew a long, slim wallet, opened it and, with shaking hands, removing something.

I knew at once what it was; in the long gallery upstairs there was a family photo, framed and hanging on the wall. I'd commented on seeing it at how bluntly and obviously it had been cropped to remove George from the composition.

And now I saw why: For years, George, cut from that frame, had been in the old man's wallet, close to his heart.

He laid the photo on top of the notebook, his trembling fingers caressing the face gently.

I cleared my throat. "Lady Marion had Huntington's disease, didn't she? I assumed it was cancer, but I asked Lady Caroline what killed George, and when she told me I knew. It's hereditary. She wasn't going to better. She knew that far worse was coming."

Chapman glared at me. "You're not fit to say her name," she hissed.

"I think she decided, at some point, that she wanted to spare her sons seeing the worst. Especially as she knew there was a good chance that at least one of them might have the genetic disease themselves.

"One of the side effects – rare, but not rare enough to be invisible in the data – of that disease is suicidal thoughts. I think you knew her plans which was why you were so angry and depressed that summer."

Sir Phillip's head dipped. "I tried to talk her out of it. I begged her. But she said she was going to do it. That she wanted to see the boys one more time and – when they'd gone back to school – that she'd take something and go to sleep.

"I begged her. I argued with her. The last few months were hell. There were days when she was so depressed that I feared she would do it there and then. I watched her like a hawk."

"George," he tapped the notebook, "misconstrued it as cruelty on my part. It was desperation. I wanted her to go to a hospital; she refused, said she wanted to be here so she could see the Folly from her window. Said she'd take an overdose immediately if she had any inkling I was going to move her. Please don't think badly of her," he looked me in the eyes.

"She loved this place. Loved her sons. Loved me.

"My wife, Mister Bird, loved life. But the disease was erasing her piece by piece and she couldn't bear the indignity she knew was coming. The brain rots away. The jerky movements, the loss of co-ordination, all of these were cruel enough, but she knew that she would eventually be unable to speak to, then see, her boys; that dementia and death would come but that her boys – and I – would see her destroyed. And she wouldn't allow that. I told her it was the easy way out, but I knew that that was a lie. The easy thing would be to do nothing because the fear of action was more terrifying than the certain knowledge that paralysis and death was coming."

"So she killed herself," I said.

He looked at me, the colour suddenly draining from his face. "My God, I've been watching the rot creep across this place since she died and doing nothing. I've been so scared to act – so scared of losing what was left – that I…"

He trailed off.

"And the next day," I said, bringing his attention back to me by patting George's diary, "Edward fell."

"George was supposed to be looking after him," Mrs Chapman spoke.

Sir Phillip nodded. "Edward followed George around like a puppy. But they had a falling out." He put his hand on the notebook. "I now know why, and Edward seems to have left George's room and somehow got into one of the other rooms."

"A window was open," Chapman – as though taking on the responsibility for saying the words she knew would bring pain to her employer – spoke.

"And he fell," Sir Phillip said, more tears coming to his eyes.

Silence.

Sir Phillip coughed, dipped into his pocket and extracted a handkerchief into which he blew his nose.

"But we know that's not true," I said, and as Chapman visibly bristled, Sir Phillip lifted his head and glared at me.

"Not true?"

"You've read the diary. You know what happened between George and Edward. You know the last words Edward said to George."

Sir Phillip's eyes met mine, tears running slowly down his cheeks. *"You're a liar and I'm going to tell on you."*

I nodded. "But who was he going to tell?" I asked. "It didn't register with me until Lottie came home just now and ran straight into the arms of her mother. But Edward couldn't tell his mother. And he wouldn't have run to you because you scared him.

"He'd have gone running to the only other maternal figure in the house."

I looked back up at Chapman. "So I ask again: What happened to Edward?"

CHAPTER THIRTY-NINE

There was a silence so deep it felt like the whole world was holding its breath.

Chapman pulled herself upright, her whole body bristling with outrage.

"I'm not going to stand here," she said to me, "and be slandered by the likes of you."

"He came running to you, didn't he?" I asked. "You were upstairs. In your room. It was summer, and there was a heatwave, so all the windows were open."

"Sir Phillip," Chapman turned her face towards her employer. "I really must protest."

"Answer him," Sir Phillip said, his eyes looking from her to the torn photo of George on his desk. "Tell him what you know."

"Marion – Lady Marion - was in so much pain," Chapman said. "And so very unhappy. I begged her to stay strong. For the boys. For Sir Phillip. But she didn't want the indignity of a long, drawn-out death. She preferred them to remember her as the beauty with the big blue eyes and not as something penetrated by tubes and wires."

She stopped, as though her mind was running back to the scorching summer when the boys came back from school late because Henry had been caught cheating.

"But Sir Phillip controlled her medication. He wouldn't let her ever have enough to stockpile. So I helped her."

A sound like a sob came from Sir Phillip, whose eyes hadn't lifted from the picture of George all the time that Chapman had been talking.

"You have to understand: It's what she wanted. She begged me."

"You had access to Sir Phillip's study," I prompted her.

"He kept the pills – the ones she wanted – in his desk drawer. I waited til everyone was busy elsewhere and stole a box."

"I knew we were a box short," Sir Phillip said. "I thought the error had been made at the doctors. Went back into town to ask why the prescription was a box short."

"You gave the pills to Lady Marion," I said as Chapman's whole body slumped.

"I gave her the pills. And then, in the night, I went to her room and cleaned her up so that when Sir Phillip found her he would be," she paused, "less distressed."

I looked at this woman, this woman who could have had a life, a family, but who'd given it all away to clean up messes for someone else's family, for people who would never look at her as anything more than an employee, and I felt a deep sorrow wash over me.

Then I remembered my theory about what had happened in the days that followed, and I realised that she had spent the intervening years ensuring that George and Sir Phillip would never again meet so that her secrets wouldn't be uncovered, and instead of lessening, my sadness deepened.

Lottie had been right: This place was cursed.

"And when Edward came to you to tell you that George was claiming his mother had been murdered?" I asked.

"I was in my room. The boy burst in. He was hysterical. I tried to calm him but he was so confused and angry. He didn't notice at first: I had the night dress Lady Marion had been wearing. There was some – she'd been sick," Chapman said, pausing as though struggling for breath. "And the box of painkillers. I'd planned to put it all in the furnace, but because of the heatwave there was no way to do that without bringing attention to myself, so I'd been cutting it up into strips. I don't know why. You have to understand that I was as mad with grief as the rest of the house.

"But then Edward saw them, and he became even more hysterical. The window was open. I feared someone would hear and come in. I was panicking and I went to the window to close it, but he came after me screaming 'why are you tearing up my mummy's nightdress,' and I was so scared that I slapped him."

She stopped, staring into a long unfixable past.

"But I hit him too hard, and he sort of staggered. He put his hand out to stop himself, but of course the window was still open, and he put his hand into air."

A single tear broke the line around her right eye and began slowly to make its way down her cheek. She lifted a knuckle and stopped its progress. I couldn't help wondering how many tears she'd shed, alone in her room in the attic of this vast house in the thirty-something years since that blisteringly hot day.

"I grabbed for him, but it was too late. He didn't even make a sound as he fell. Absolute silence, as though he couldn't believe this was happening. As though he'd realised there was no point making any noise."

The silence in the room was broken only by a thin brittle crackling from the fireplace, the hollow thunk of scorched logs settling, their movement sending a shower of fluorescent sparks up the chimney.

"What happens now?" she finally said.

Sir Phillip lifted his eyes from George's face, found mine and, without even looking at her, said "Now? I think it's time you moved on.

"I think," he added as she gathered herself, bowed her head in his direction and made to move away from the desk, "that it's time we all moved on."

The door closed almost silently.

"What are you going to do?" I asked him, and Sir Phillip put the photo back in his wallet before sliding the diary across the desk and into the drawer.

"About Chapman?" He inhaled deeply, as though resetting himself, packing his emotions back in the velvet-lined box they'd been resigned to for decades. Then he straightened himself and regarded me with the bland disinterested look he'd been wearing all weekend.

"What can I do? Marion wanted to die. I've long suspected Chapman had a hand in it. And Doctor Allen – though I'm sure he too had his suspicions – signed the death certificate. Natural causes."

"But what if Lady Marion didn't take the pills knowingly? What if Chapman fed them to her surreptitiously?"

A sad smile cracked the edges of his lips. "What ifs are of little use to us now, Mister Bird. My wife has been dead for almost four decades. Any evidence of what might have happened is gone. My son is in an urn with his mother on the mantle in the drawing room. What happened-"

He faded out for a moment, his eyes looking down the same long tunnel that Chapman had been staring down moments before, and he was silent for a long time before clearing his throat and refocussing on me.

"What happened then, seems less important to me, at this point, than what happens next."

"Ah," it was my turn to clear my throat. "On that: Any chance you could get everyone outside?"

"Outside?"

"By the fountain, preferably. I think I've worked out how the jewel robbery was done, and who did it. And I need a favour from you."

He asked what the favour was and I told him, at which point he tilted his head back and actually laughed. "You really are wasted as a barman, you know. I've some friends in the services who'd happily offer you a job if you ever need one."

"Thanks," I stood and headed towards the door, "but I'm not sure the world's ready for me with a licence to kill just yet."

~

Nick was still standing by the fountain, though he'd been joined by Ali Caz and Ellie, who was now encased in a rather fetching bespoke Vuitton doggie coat while Caz appeared to have acquired a bottle of Veuve and some glasses from somewhere.

Well, I say 'acquired'; it's perfectly possible, knowing my best friend, that she brought them with her to Dukes Halt in case she fancied an impromptu champagne after midnight.

Caz shoved a Baccarat crystal flute into my hand and toasted both Nick and I.

"I think you're awful people and you deserve each other," she smiled as Nick smiled shyly at me and held his glass aloft.

"I'll have to get a hat," Ali beamed, necking her glass in one and holding it out for Caz to top up. "Here; you doing the reception at The Marq? Only, y'know, we'll have to start figuring out how to keep Chopper's lot apart from," she jerked her head at Nick "the groom's lot."

"It's not going to be for a while yet," Nick rushed to calm their jets. "I mean, there are one or two things we need to sort out first."

"What?" Ali asked, "like getting your wife out of chokey and then figuring out how you break it to her that she's not really your type? Or are you gonna go all bigamist."

I shook my head. "She's taking the piss, Nick. She's fully aware of the situation with you and Arianna."

Nick's blush faded. He smiled shyly at me. "Are you – are we – okay?" He asked, and I beamed back at him.

"You're brilliant," I said. "I'm – well you called it really, DS Fisher: I'm someone who needs everything to be fixed and I know that that's not always possible, but I think spending the rest of my life with you is as close to fixed as I can imagine."

"He means yes," Caz clarified, clinking glasses with Nick and I in turn. "Though why he always feels the need to say it in so many words is a mystery to me. So," she turned back to me, "when's the stag do? And are you planning to wear white to the ceremony, or do you have some scruples left?"

We laughed. "It's going to be a while off yet," I said, shyly catching Nick's eye and nodding at Ali. "Like you say, there's the matter of proving Arianna didn't kill Maximov first."

"Well that's obvious," Caz answered, topping up our glasses as from the direction of Dukes Halt a loud and persistent wail began to issue.

"Christ," Ali frowned, "has that bloody housekeeper discovered we've nicked the champagne?"

I looked at Caz, who had the good grace to look slightly chastened. "All property is theft," she said, staring straight in my eye.

"Well thank you Carole Marx. That noise," I replied to Ali as the first group of people began to make their way out of the front door and over towards us, "is the sound of the fire alarm. We should have everyone out of the house fairly soon."

"Arianna can't be the murderer," Caz returned to the topic. "She was in prison when Mila copped it, and if Doctor Stamford's death was murder too then Arianna definitely didn't have anything to do with that. Ergo, she didn't kill Maximov."

"Not necessarily," Nick frowned. "I know Danny made a good case last night for Mila's death being linked to the Russian's. But like Stamford said: Prove the connection. Without a connection, Arianna is still the most obvious suspect to have murdered Maximov, and her being locked up when the chef and the doctor died doesn't put her in the clear for the one she was found standing over."

Somewhere in the back of my mind, a bell went off.

But then the first of the group were on us.

"Oooh, Champagne. Is this a party?" Sara Simone smiled at the glasses and Caz turned, uncovering the picnic hamper that she'd clearly lugged out of the house with a selection of glasses and another three bottles, and offered glasses to Sara, her mother and to John Warren , handing glasses to Pamela and Henry as they arrived, and offering one to Karen Stamford, who waved the glass aside, and shoved her hands deep down into the pockets of the floor-length duvet-like puffa-coat she was wearing.

Beth Kennedy and Gaia walked out from the treeline at that moment and were beckoned over, Gaia and Lottie nodding shyly at each other and then gravitating towards one another as glasses were filled and handed around.

Inspector Dane, who appeared to have taken up residence

in the house was – along with a silent and ghost-white Mrs Chapman – the last to arrive, and both refused a glass of fizz.

"What are we celebrating?" Lottie asked, holding her hand out, and Caz raised an eyebrow at Pamela, who shrugged and held her thumb and forefinger up to indicate a small glass would be allowable.

"We are celebrating the fact that two of my favourite people just got engaged to be married," Caz said, pouring a half glass of champagne and putting it into Lottie's outstretched hand.

"Well that's nice," Francine Gerber smiled, looking around as though wondering who the two people in question were. "But couldn't we have celebrated indoors? It's gotten cold today."

"I thought we might all enjoy a chance to get some fresh air and talk about," I held up my champagne glass, the façade of Dukes Halt refracted and distorted through the bubbling liquid and the crystal surrounding it, "things that sparkle."

"Say, sweetheart," Francine addressed Caz, "how many has he had?"

"We've had an eventful weekend." I put my glass on the side of the fountain and turned back, gesturing at Dukes Halt, bringing their attention to the building.

"Eventful?" Karen Stamford shook her head. "My husband's dead. Whatever this," she pulled her hand from her pocket and indicated me, the group, the building beyond, "is, can I please go back inside and start packing? I need to go home. I want to go home."

"Just as soon as the paperwork's complete," Dane murmured. "I still need to formally get your statement."

"I wanted to talk about the first bit of excitement," I said. "The jewel robbery."

Sara Simone's hand went, almost instinctively, to her throat where the diamond had sat. "Do we have to?" She murmured. "This has been the worst weekend of my life, and I'm in no hurry to relive it, to be honest."

"I sympathise," I said. "It can't be easy losing such a

valuable piece of jewellery and having your businesses declared bankrupt."

She bristled at that. "The diamond was more than a piece of jewellery. And my businesses are still in negotiations with their creditors. If we can hold off anyone pulling the trigger before next week we may be able to negotiate some new funding."

"Really? Only I thought the New York Times said the trigger had already been pulled."

"You shouldn't believe everything you read in the papers," she snapped.

"Hasn't been a great weekend for you either, has it?" I turned to John Warren, who had the good grace to blush. "But then you must be used to this sort of thing. Having," I explained to his puzzled look, "been involved in so many previous jewel robberies."

"Me?" John's frown deepened as though he were struggling to recall the series of jewel robberies he'd been present at this summer.

I decided to help him out. "Sicily. July. Weekend party. And before that, Cannes in May. Ring any bells?"

"Oh those." His face split in a sheepish grin and he ran a hand through his floppy fringe, pushing it back from his forehead. "Well I wouldn't say I was exactly involved." He sipped his champagne and shrugged. "Just around."

"Around? You were sleeping in the same bed as the ruby that was stolen from the actress in Cannes. That's something more than vaguely 'around,' surely?"

"Johnny?" Sara asked, a frown on her face.

"Snookums," he smiled, put an arm around her, "it was before we met."

"To be precise," I corrected him, "a day or so before you met. Because you were there too, weren't you Sara? I mean it's an international film festival and you – even more than Mister Warren here – had cause to be in Cannes that weekend."

"I-" she stiffened, smiled the smile that had charmed audiences the planet over, and leaned into the one-armed hug that Johnny Warren was providing, "yes, I was there. Some producers wanted to talk to me about a new movie they were looking to finance with some German banks. But I don't know anything about any rubies."

"So you two met in May in Cannes," I moved the conversation on, "which means that when John went to a certain party in Sicily later in the summer you were already an item.

"Ah, but we know you were in Italy at the same time," I smiled before either John or La Simone could speak, "because that's when you finally acquired the Gianelli Stone. It was news all over the world."

Sara nodded. "I was in Italy. What of it?"

I ignored the challenge in her tone. "Let's move on to the day of the robbery."

CHAPTER FORTY

"Listen," Francine piped up, "I don't care what we move on to, but can we do it inside? I'm freezing my tukas off out here."

"Just a little longer," I smiled at her. "I was wondering about the fuse box. Who could have set the charge that caused the power surge that created the pitch darkness into which the jewel thief could step.

"I think we all agree that that part – at least – had to be an inside job."

There was a general uncomfortable shuffling.

"Well I suppose any of the family could have come and gone without comment. As could Mrs Chapman."

Chapman's gaze didn't move from the ground where it had stayed since she'd been forced to join us on the lawn.

"Because the fuse box was close to the kitchen, so if anyone unusual had been messing around there they'd have been seen and possibly challenged by Mila, wouldn't they?"

I let that idea settle. "But you were there earlier in the day, weren't you?" I turned to Beth Kennedy. "I saw you in the kitchen with Mila."

"Me?" Beth laughed dryly. "Why would I pull off a jewel robbery?"

"Perhaps because you were about to be homeless and unemployed?" Chapman suggested, her face still expressionless but a spark of hatred in her eyes.

"Thanks to your poisoning Sir Phillip to any idea I put forward," Beth snapped back. Then she nodded. "But tell me this: If I was going to steal something, why would I steal a bloody great diamond the size of my hand? What would the likes of me do with that? Take it to the pawn shop in

Dorchester?"

"She has a point," I said. "The only way to turn the Gianelli stone into cash would be to have a decent fence with access to the tools to recut it, maybe reset it and resell it. So who else might have had the opportunity to rig the fuses?"

"Well you said it yourself," Karen Stamford said sulkily. "Any visitors – any strangers – would have been spotted by the cook and challenged."

I nodded my agreement. "But that does not mean that none of the visitors had access to the fuse box. I myself spent a while in the kitchen chatting to Mila and Ali. Ali, you were there with Mila. You could have had access to the fuse box."

"'Ere," Ali drew herself up to her full five feet two and exuded umbrage like a skunk exuding stink, "I'm a good girl, I am. And besides, I didn't even know she," she pointed at Sara "was gonna be there, let alone that she'd be wearing that bloody diamond."

She also had a point.

I let it lie in the cold air. "Maximov was down there as well," I added, "the night before the robbery. Two nights before his death. I heard him threatening someone. A woman. I suspected it was Lady Caroline," I gestured at Caz, who mimed surprise, "but I know now who he was talking to. It was you, wasn't it Mrs Chapman?"

Chapman turned her Medusa eyes on me. "He'd done his research on the family," she said. "Had a number of half-baked theories and innuendos. Was trying to threaten me."

"To what end?" I asked, knowing now what those theories and innuendos consisted of.

"To the end of frightening me," Chapman answered simply. "I think Mr Maximov was someone who liked having power over people, even if he had – at that time – no use for the power. He wanted me to know he knew things that could embarrass," her voice caught, cracked, "the family. He knew I'd do anything to avoid embarrassing The Warrens."

"So Maximov was down there, near the fusebox, as well as you, Mrs Chapman."

"Hang on a minute," Ali piped up. "Doesn't what she just said give her a motive for Maximov's murder?"

I smiled. *That's my Ali.* "It does indeed," I admitted, "but – in light of last night's events – I'd like to hold off discussing Maximov's murder just now."

"What?" Francine snarked, "In case you slander any more of us?"

"So," I looked around the assembled, "almost every single one of us had the opportunity to go down to the fusebox and tamper with it. But, apart from the family, any one of us ran the risk of being challenged and uncovered."

"Unless the cook was in on the robbery," Dane said.

I pointed at him. "Good point, and one which raises the question of whether Mila's death was linked not to the murder of Sergei Maximov after all, or whether it was more closely connected to the jewel robbery."

"Oh here we go again," Karen Stamford snapped. "You seem determined to make that man's killer anyone but the woman they arrested."

In the distance, Sir Phillip walked out of Dukes Halt, down the steps to the drive, and held a hand up. A moment later, the bell stopped ringing.

I smiled. "Ah," I said, I see the alarm is over. Shall we head back in? Perhaps we could finish this conversation in the drawing room?"

Grumbling and moaning, the assembled began to move off, Caz and Ali leaving Nick to close and hoik the heavy looking champagne hamper as they scuttled on ahead, glasses in hand, clearly aiming to get decent seats at what they suspected was going to be an entertaining show.

I held back, put a hand on Inspector Dane's arm and said a few words to him.

He raised both eyebrows. Even his droopy moustache seemed to move skyward.

"Are you serious?"

I nodded.

His shoulders began to shake. His eyes screwed up as

though he was in some discomfort and – as I wondered whether it was trapped gas or perhaps a mini stroke – he made a noise and I suddenly realised he was laughing.

"My god," he said after several seconds (by which time the last of the crowd had gone into the house) "I want to know how your mind works. You really want me to do this?"

"Please." I said. "You'll know fairly quickly if my hunch is right."

Still chuckling, Dane shook his head and then shrugged. "Well I'll hang on here, then.

Good luck."

He was still chuckling when I turned and made my way back to Dukes Halt.

CHAPTER FORTY-ONE

The drawing room, where I had first laid eyes on many of the assembled, seemed fuller than it had been at any point that weekend.

Lady Marion still hung above the fireplace, her doleful smile filled, in light of what I now knew, with meaning I'd missed before. And arrayed in a semi-circle around the fireplace on various sofas and chairs, were the family and visitors to the place.

Sir Phillip was in a high-backed chair next to the grate, though this time not even a miserly fire flickered. Next to him on a sofa sat Pamela and Henry, Lottie between them. Beside them sat Beth Kennedy, Gaia perched on the arm of her chair.

Caz and Ali had commandeered a small chintz-covered sofa that was at the apex of the curve, while Nick perched on a foot stool just in front of Caz and was stroking a snoozing Ellie.

Sara Simone and John Chapman were seated on an Art Deco love chair, while Francine and Karen Stamford were squeezed on to a slightly-too-small sofa, as though each had nabbed it at the same time and neither was willing to give up their place, while Digby Smith occupied another wing-backed chair.

Mrs Chapman, her whole being exuding a combination of misery and anger, stood just outside the circle, as though ready to run for the doors as soon as she was able.

I stepped into the middle of the circle, nodding at Sir Phillip, who returned my nod, his lips twitching briefly, and I resumed my story.

"Now," I asked, "where were we?"

"Freezing our asses off on the lawn," Francine drawled,

tilting her champagne glass back and realising she'd already drained it some time ago.

"Ah yes," I nodded. "Considering who could have tampered with the fusebox and not been challenged. Another point worth considering," I added, "is the dinner itself. Or rather, what happened when we went in to dinner."

"The place cards," Digby Smith said, his tone bored and irritated.

"Indeed. I have to be honest," I nodded at Lottie, "Like a lot of people, I half assumed that you'd deliberately shuffled them up as some sort of prank. It wasn't, of course," I added, before Lottie could protest her innocence. "But the fact remains: Someone deliberately rearranged the table setting, and it's my contention that it wasn't done purely from anger, but that there was method to the madness.

"Mrs Chapman?" The housekeeper ignored my call at first and then – as though zoning in from far away – raised her face and stared silently at me.

"Do you have a record of the original table plan for the dinner that night?"

She nodded. "I keep – kept – all plans and dinner menus in case Sir Phillip wanted to refer to them in future."

"And would it be fair to say," I asked, "that in the original version Miss Simone and her mother were seated with their backs to the fire. That is to say on the opposite side of the table from the French windows?"

She frowned in concentration then nodded. "Yes," she said. "They were towards the top of the table, but on the opposite side to where they'd been the night before."

"So: someone deliberately moved them so that they would be by the window."

"Well that seems fairly obvious," Karen Stamford piped up. "If the insider could doctor the fusebox they would certainly want at least Sara by the window so their accomplice could grab the diamond without having to walk around the table and risk being tackled either on their way in or on their way out."

I looked around at the assembled, all considering this point, several of them nodding in agreement.

"That seems to make sense, right?" I asked, and there was a general mumble of agreement. "But tell me this: Why?"

"Why?" Sara Simone asked. "Because of the diamond. I don't understand where this is going Mr Bird, but-"

I cut her off. "The thief had a gun. They had an inside man or woman, but one assumes the person who actually broke into the house, stole the diamond and discharged the gun would have been a stranger to us all – or could have been masked in a way that made them hard to identify.

"And they had a gun. So why plunge the room into darkness and then tell us they had a gun when we couldn't see it. Why not leave the lights on and show us the gun?

"I think it's fair to say that none of us – faced with a gun – would have done much more than sat meekly while they helped themselves to the diamond."

"Well maybe they wanted to do more than steal the diamond," Pamela shrugged. "Sometimes pointing a gun at someone, as terrifying as it is, isn't as disconcerting as darkness and menace and threat."

Knowing what I knew about Pamela's day job, I assumed she knew what she was talking about.

I waggled a finger at her. "That's a variation of what ran through my mind," I said. "This was a robbery that could have been so simple: kick the door open, point the gun, snatch the stone, vanish. Instead we had the room plunged into darkness, the doors flung open, screams, cries, a gruff voice telling us they had a gun, a struggle – all under cover of darkness – and a gunshot rings out.

"It feels," I paused as though searching for the right word, even though I had the word on the tip of my tongue, "theatrical, somehow."

"Like a really bad old movie," Lottie said and I nodded, smiling.

"You told me once that nothing in this place was entirely real, and that robbery seemed like someone who'd never actually committed a robbery imagined one would feel. But I propose another reason for the darkness," I added as Inspector Dane, the cuffs of his jacket much darker than the rest of his suit, walked into the room flanked by two uniformed policemen.

He nodded at me.

"I propose," I said nodding back, "that the darkness was deliberately designed to prevent us really seeing what was going on."

"You mean the inside man was involved?" Digby Smith asked.

Ali, glaring at him in a way that told me Caz had shared news of my recent contretemps with her, added "Or woman."

"Or woman," I acknowledged her correction. "Yes. Though I think we're making the mistake we were always meant to make. You see, there was no outsider. There was no accomplice. There was only ever Francine Gerber and her daughter, Sara Simone."

A momentary silence fell while people processed what I'd just said then a rumble of voices rose as all eyes turned towards the two women.

"Oh now look," John Warren stood to his feet, "this has gone on long enough. It's bad enough you accuse me of being a jewel thief, but now you're accusing Sara of – what? Stealing her own jewels? Why on earth would she do that?"

"Because the Gianelli diamond," I responded, "is worth a fortune. And Miss Simone's businesses were about to crash and burn."

"Well if I needed money that fast," the actress demanded, "and I'm not saying I did – I could have just sold the goddamned stone. Why would I go through the charade you just described?"

"Because you couldn't sell it," I said, and she laughed as though I were crazy, but under the ridicule there was a thin, distinct layer of anxiety.

"The diamond was left to you by Prince Amadeo di Lorenzi. His children have already made attempts to have that section of the will nullified, but failed. I guess old Amadeo wanted you to have something beautiful to remind you of him. But he wasn't stupid, was he: He made a clause in the will that prevents you from selling or disposing of the diamond."

"Bullshit," she snarled, and I dipped into my pocket and withdrew my phone.

"My Italian is a little rusty, but the story made it from Corriere della sera to the New York Post. The Post's reporting was a little less florid than Corriere, but they both quoted the Prince's daughter – would she be a princess?" I looked around the room for confirmation of the lady's title, but getting none, went back to the news article I'd been referring to.

"The prince's daughter – who may, or may not be, a Princess - mentioned a clause that ensures the stone comes back into the family on your death.

"'The offense is not that this ancient jewel has effectively been loaned to this harlot,' the possibly-a-princess said, 'but that whilst in her possession it will be subjected to the most outrageous of indignities and the most vulgar events imaginable. I know my father would not have wanted this and thus we are suing for the return of this ancient and venerable diamond.'"

"Stuck-up bitch," Francine growled.

"Mother," Sara said, a clear warning tone in her voice.

"So you could wear the stone, but you couldn't sell it, And if you couldn't sell it you couldn't use it as collateral for a loan. And so you had to come up with another plan. One which was inspired by the jewel robberies you'd heard about this summer, and one which you had already worked out before you even arrived in Dukes Halt."

"And how, exactly, did my mother and I manage to steal the diamond and make it vanish without trace?"

"Sara, sweetheart," Francine growled, her glare never leaving my face, "don't say another word to this crazy sonofabitch. Not content with driving that poor doctor to his death last night he's clearly trying to add us to his score."

"Miss Simone, you didn't eat the same food as the rest of us at either of the dinners."

"I'm on a special macrobiotic keto diet," she answered almost instinctively and then, as though realising she'd not been meant to speak to me, blushed and jerked her head dismissively.

"Yes," I considered this. "Mila commented on how frequently you, Mrs Gerber, were up and down to the kitchen with instructions on what food Sara could and couldn't have, and instructions on how it should be prepared and served.

"And my guess is that after a while Mila would have stopped registering your presence; you came, you went, you came back. She would not have noticed if, the second time, when you left the kitchen you found out where the fuses were and if, on Friday afternoon you came back from shooting, popped down with some more dietary instructions and again, instead of going straight back upstairs, popped into the cupboard under the stairs to set the timer on the device that would then blow the fuses later that evening.

"So: the stage is set. And as you said, Lottie, it was very much a stagey robbery. The seating has to be adjusted so that the two women are sat exactly where they were the night before – the only two people, apart from Sir Phillip, who were. The timer on the device downstairs kicks in, the lights go out, there's general confusion and noise during which Francine opens the French doors while Sara deepens her voice and puts on a somewhat alarming cockney accent."

"I thought that was a bit Dick Van Dyke," Caz said.

"Sara removes the diamond, hands it to her mother who then, as the thief 'leaves' the room, lets off a random shot and, as they had planned, chaos ensues. And then the lights come back on."

"So where – if my mother had the diamond when the lights came back on – is it?" Sara demanded, a triumphal look on her face.

"Now?" I said as the crowd leaned forward awaiting my response. "You mean where is it right now?"

"I mean where was it when the lights came on, where was it when the cops searched every last one of us, and – yes -

where the hell is it now, you smarmy limey bastard," she snapped.

"Well right now," I smiled sweetly, "the diamond that was taken from round your neck two nights ago is sitting in Inspector Dane's pocket."

Dane stepped forward, dipped into his jacket pocket and withdrew an egg-sized stone, the facets a little dull, but the sparkle still present.

As one, all those in the room gasped.

"After Maximov's death," I explained, "everyone's room was searched. The police," I glanced at Henry and Pam, "were looking for an item of vital importance to national security but if the diamond had been in the house it would have been located during those searches.

"The fact that it wasn't seemed to support the theory of an 'outsider' who got away with it, but something has always bothered me about that theory.

"When the light came back on, Miss Simone here was lying on the ground in a highly emotional state, and most of us rushed to help her while her mother, seemingly outraged at what had been done to her daughter, raced out after the thief.

"It was mere moments before you, Major Henry, had chased after her, but that was time enough for her to toss the pistol that had been used to cause maximum chaos into the flower bed where I discovered it the next morning, and to hurl the diamond into the fountain."

"From the patio outside the dining room?" Karen Stamford asked disbelievingly. "That's got to be sixty feet."

"Ninety feet, actually. I've checked. And a couple of days ago, Mrs Gerber, I witnessed you throwing a ball for Ellie. You threw it the whole length of the house and when I mentioned what a good throw it was, you told me you'd been a star softball bowler in your youth. What was it you said?" I asked and Francine Gerber glowered at me.

"Still got it," she snarled.

"Major Henry," I asked. "When you got out of the door and onto the patio outside – moments after our supposed outside man had fled – there was no sign of anybody crossing the lawn, was there?"

Henry considered this for a moment then shook his head.

"It's ninety feet to the fountain and about another ninety beyond that to the forest edge. A hundred and eighty feet and the mysterious outsider managed to cross that space in seconds."

Henry nodded. "You're right. It was a cloudy night. Dark. But a figure running across the lawn should have been visible."

"So let me get this straight?" The scorn was back in Sara Simone's voice. "I needed money. Fast. And I had a diamond I couldn't sell. So I arranged to make it look like it had been stolen. Then, once it had been stolen, I had my mother hurl it across the lawn with pinpoint accuracy into a fountain?"

"The throw we've already addressed. And the fountain bowl is at least fifteen feet in diameter. It just needed to go in, and I'd imagine that's a far greater target than most softball games."

Sara shrugged. "So: We've robbed the stone, hurled it into the fountain. Now what? I mean, it's useless to me sitting in a goddamned pond in England. What was I gonna do? Surreptitiously drain the thing?"

I considered her point. "That's a really good question," I said, "and one that bothered me. The only way Inspector Dane was able to find the stone today was because Sir Phillip here – under cover of a fire alarm – activated the mechanism to drain the bowl."

"And there," Dane held the stone aloft, "it was."

"My first thought was that you'd planned to go back the next day and retrieve it, but that Maximov's death and the fact that the house has, since then, been overrun with Police had prevented you.

"But then I realised – as you note – that this would have been an impossible task. Somewhere in the fountain is a stone that would have been impossible to locate. Which was when I realised you didn't want to retrieve it."

Sara Simone shook her head.

"You're a goddamned lunatic," Francine muttered, rolling her eyes like a silent movie actress.

"Because you didn't need to retrieve it," I explained. "Because that," I gestured at the thing that Dane was holding aloft as though he was a gameshow hostess and it the star prize, "is not the Gianelli diamond."

There was another round of muttering, and when the rumbling had died down, Sara Simone stood and gave me a slow and contemptuous round of applause.

"So the old bastard left me a paste rock?" She asked, her accent moving closer to her mother's than the refined smooth one she'd had since I met her. "You can't prove that that's not the one I collected from the lawyer in Milan. And you sure as hell can't prove that my mother and I staged any goddamned robbery."

"You sold the Gianelli stone, didn't you?" I pressed. "As soon as you could. And that was your one mistake."

Her expression – part outrage, part triumph – faltered.

"Because the person you sold it to was someone you were put in touch with by someone you'd met on the Riviera. And that person - willing to buy diamonds no questions asked – must have been very happy when you saw something pretty in their shop. Something you used some of your newly acquired funds to buy.

"Something pretty for yourself."

I nodded at Sir Phillip, who reached into his jacket pocket and withdrew the two emerald earrings that La Simone had been wearing at dinner the first night.

"You see, you're quite right about it being difficult for us here and now to prove that you knew that the stone you arranged to have stolen from you was a fake. But I'm fairly sure the Italian lawyer would have had various assessors and authorisers who could state unequivocally that what you received in Milan in the summer was a genuine diamond.

"And while we wait for that confirmation, Inspector Dane has a nice cosy cell for you."

"A cell?" Francine almost shrieked.

"On what charge?" Sara demanded, her outrage dialled up to eleven.

"Possession of stolen goods," I said, nodding at the earrings which Sir Phillip – under cover of that very useful fire alarm – had liberated from Sara's room.

"I bought those earrings from a dealer in Italy," La Simone said, stopping herself before she could say any more.

I nodded. "Indeed. But before they were earrings, those emeralds were part of a tiara that had once been worn by the empress Josephine. A tiara that was stolen from a house party in Sicily. You see the person who introduced you to their friendly jewellery dealer was introducing you to the person they themselves had been using as a fence, so the earrings you bought from that dealer were the proceeds of a robbery that person had already committed."

The blood drained from her face, and she turned on John Warren. "You," she gasped. "You thieving, lying, stupid sonofabitch."

John Warren at least had the good grace to look sheepish. "They really did look very pretty on you, you know," he smiled as Dane gestured at the uniforms, who took Francine Sara and John into custody.

I figured one of the trio would squeal first and before too long they'd be singing madrigals over each other.

As the trio were read their rights and lead from the room, Sara Simone turned back, her eyes blazing. "Just so we're clear," she said to me, "I might have done everything I had to do to keep my business going, but I'm not a thief, and I had nothing to do with murdering Maximov or the cook."

"Oh I know that," I answered, and the assembled looked once more at each other.

"Well then who the hell killed *them*?" Henry Warren demanded.

"Well Doctor Stamford, of course," I answered, and Sir Phillip shook his head.

"Unless you've got the motive entirely wrong, that's

impossible. Richard Stamford didn't arrive in Serbia until long after the event Maximov referenced."

"That's true," I admitted, "but I'm not talking about Doctor Richard Stamford. I'm talking about Doctor Karen Stamford."

CHAPTER FORTY-TWO

"The fact that Richard didn't arrive in Serbia until after the massacre – and the fact I didn't check up on that fact before I made my stupid announcement last night – has caused me much sorrow. Because if I'd known about that fact, Doctor Richard Stamford might still be alive."

The room had stilled.

Even Dane and his two uniforms – all still holding on to their arrestees – remained where they were. Only Karen Stamford seemed not to have been turned to stone.

"Well if my husband's lawyers were going to have fun with you," she said, smiling coldly, "mine will eviscerate you."

"I think," I replied, "they'll be busy trying to get you off a murder charge."

She shook her head, her face stony. "You have no idea how much pain my people will put you through."

"I was almost right last night," I said, speaking directly to her as the rest of the room seemed to fade away.

"So much of what I said was right that it must have caused you some concern all along the way until I named your husband as the killer. You did so well not to show your relief. But while I had some of the picture last night, I'd been looking at it the wrong way.

"Sergei Maximov was a blackmailer. He'd been a lot of things in the past, but he'd realised some time ago that selling children, pimping, facilitation were all rather dangerous activities. Profitable, but each brought their own risks. And so he'd moved full time into something that had been a sideline all along: Collecting and monetising secrets.

"It was, supposedly, one of those secrets that brought him here this weekend: He contacted British Intelligence and told them that he had details of a traitor that he would be willing to disclose, but that his debriefing had to be done here, in Dukes Halt this weekend.

"It didn't occur to me to wonder why. He was in London. MI5 headquarters are in London. He could have gone in there, detailed his secrets, had his money and vanished again. And then, today, I realised: the secret was not the point. It's possible there wasn't even a traitor. What mattered – what was vital to his plan – was that he be here in Dukes Halt this weekend.

"Maximov was a late addition. Mrs Chapman herself noted this fact. He was added on after the rest of the guests had already been decided and his addition messed up her table plans.

"Which means he knew who'd be here, and he wanted to be here with them. He collected secrets, and he sold – or suppressed – those secrets for money. Eventually I came to the only logical conclusion: Maximov wanted to be here because he had a secret he wanted to sell. You already said, Mrs Chapman, that he threatened you with vague innuendos about the various tragedies that have befallen the Warren family. He liked to wave his knowledge under people's noses. To let them know he might know something, so that when he hit them with a demand they would have had sleepless nights worrying about just how detailed his knowledge was."

Chapman, begrudgingly, nodded her agreement.

"So who was Maximov hoping to sell this secret to? The Warrens are well off, but not exactly cash rich. Sara Simone? Well, we've seen how precarious her finances are; and someone like Maximov would have known this fact before arriving. Lady Caroline and I," I let the sentence die unfinished.

"Which leaves The Stamfords. A doctor who was about to be ennobled. Nice, but hardly the sort of wealth that would draw someone like Maximov to make a plan like this one. No, to make it worth his while, there had to be vast sums involved.

"The sort of sums a medi-tech company IPO is likely to

generate, when the tech the company has created and patented is set to revolutionise the world of pediatric surgery." I turned back to Karen Stamford. "Mr Smith mentioned billions, I believe."

She nodded grudgingly. "If the IPO's a success, Richard and I would have been set for life."

"Indeed. And so you arrive here, a couple perched on the edge of a glorious future. And within a day, Maximov makes himself known to you with that story about the doctor who sent their patients away to die. He made sure to mix the story in with accusations against Major Henry and suggestions that the Warrens themselves were corrupt, but his modus operandi was always to make his victims aware that he knew something; to torment them. And he tormented you at the dinner table that night. He might have gone further – might have shaken you down that night – if it weren't for the theatrics our American friends arranged.

"But it makes no difference whether he is more explicit or not. You realise that everything you have worked for is about to be destroyed because if he goes public with his story the launch of your company is ruined. And if he can be persuaded to hold his tongue, he will, you know, return to the well again and again and again.

"Because people like Maximov – when there are billions in the well – will never stay away. And so you have a problem that needs to be addressed."

"Not as big as your problem," she stared stonily back at me. "I'm not – and have never been – a doctor. I'm an engineer."

"You met your husband in Serbia," I said. "When he was visiting after the war. You have absolutely no trace of an accent, and almost perfect English. But Mila pointed out to me that – even though her English was excellent too – what she had learned was basically American English. And you, too, learned American English. You've used sidewalk for pavement. And when you referred to your husband's laboratory, you used the American pronunciation – labratree

– rather than the British one, which stresses the first 'O'.

"He was there to help rebuild the country after the war, and you needed an out before people began looking too closely at your past. Because, whilst you're not a medical doctor, you did get a Doctorate in Mechanical Engineering from the University of Ljubljana. And it was while working on your post-doctorate work that you were at a hospital in a small town where a militia arrived and demanded all the Muslim male patients be rounded up and handed over to them."

"Let's say I was," she said quietly, her face softening as her eyes glassed over. "Have you ever been in a war zone Mister Bird? Have you ever had men pointing guns in your face and demanding you do what they want or they will kill you? Terrible things happen at war, but I remind you: When Sergei Maximov was murdered I was standing beside you in the front hall."

"Good point," I answered as the rest of the room came into focus, everyone leaning forward yet again, Caz with a concentrated frown on her face, Nick absent-mindedly stroking Ellie's head as he smiled fondly at me.

"Except, to be more precise, you were standing next to me when we heard the bang that came from the dining room. But by that stage, Sergei Maximov was already dead.

"You must have been in a total panic the night before. You knew what was coming, but you had no idea how to stop it. And then the idea comes to you. There are guns in the house. You've already seen them, already used them that day. But you can't just shoot him. You need an alibi that will make it seem like you are – as you say – standing beside the rest of us when the moment comes.

"And so you decide on your plan: You will go to the shed in the Folly; the one where the fireworks are stored. You will steal some fireworks with which you will create both a diversion and an alibi, and you will break into the gun cupboard and steal a pistol.

"So you break into the fireworks shed by the folly, steal some fireworks and some timers and return to Dukes Halt, setting most of the fireworks up near the front door, as far away from the drawing room as possible, set the timers and return to the house to get yourself a gun.

"Except, on returning from the folly you discover that someone, in your absence, has entered the house and left a pistol on the hall table. This must have felt like divine providence," I added.

Gaia Kennedy had the good grace to blush deeply.

"The next morning, you've agreed to meet Maximov in the dining room – entering by the same door that Arianna Fisher used some time later. He arrives, you arrive shortly after him and, lifting a thick seat cushion from one of the dining chairs to mask the shot, you creep up behind him, press the cushion against the back of his head and before he has a moment to react, you shoot.

"Caz and I were standing sixty feet away by the fountain when we heard a pop. I assumed it was someone in the woods doing target practice," I glanced at Gaia who blushed once again.

"But I now know that would have been impossible."

Karen Stamford's lips were pressed firmly together. I sensed there was so much she wanted to say, but her self-restraint, the very thing that had stood her in good stead all these years, would not allow her to speak.

"Maximov now dead, your next step is to take his mobile phone – the repository of all his evidence against you, and to get rid of the cushion you used to mask the shot. So you overturn furniture, attempting to suggest – as Mrs Geber and Sara Simone had the night before - that some outsider had gained access to the room and killed Maximov.

"You've kept one firework – a banger with a long fuse – which you put in the fireplace, lighting it just as you leave the room and putting the fireguard in place so that the explosive charge sends the banger up the chimney.

"Only the explosion knocked the fire guard over. Nobody noticed it, because the room was already in such disarray, and even if they had, by now your plan is in full flight. You shove the cushion – which now has a large bullet-shaped hole in it – inside your huge coat and head outside to the fountain, intending to dispose of the cushion – the only item that might raise questions about the timeline – only to discover that Lady Caroline and I are in the garden.

"There's no time to adjust your plan. You've already lit the fuse on both the diversion and the alibi. You have to be with us, away from the fireworks and the dining room when it all goes off. Which you are.

"We're crossing the hallway when the diversionary fireworks – the ones designed to draw everyone to the front of the house so that the arrival and departure of your mysterious outsider can be neither noted nor disputed – go off and we're all standing watching them die down when the banger in the dining room goes off.

"Later, you get rid of the cushion by mixing it up with a load of other cushions in the smoking salon. Chapman found it, you know, and assumed the mark was a cigar burn. But the only cigars smoked this weekend were in the Dining Room that first night: Nobody had had time to smoke any since.

"But in the meantime, you're standing with us in the hall listening to the sound of a single shot coming from the drawing room. Of course you couldn't know that Arianna Fisher had entered the dining room just as the first fireworks had gone off."

Again, Karen Stamford said nothing.

"And now we come to Mila."

Over the heads of the crowd I saw Dane on his mobile, clearly calling for backup.

Karen could no longer contain herself. "The cook? Oh do please tell me how – and why – I committed that atrocity."

"I think I explained that last night," I said. "Though I had the wrong Dr Stamford in mind. I won't bore you by repeating the parade of people who went up and down to the kitchen, and who Mila would have seen. But think of this: Mila had worked here some time.

"She knew the Warrens and Mrs Chapman by sight. She

would have seen Sara Simone in magazines, newspapers, films. Mister Smith," I gestured at Digby Smith, "was a regular guest and so would have been known to her. Mrs Gerber, too, went up and down to the kitchen frequently, and Mila met your husband Dr Stamford on the Sunday morning when they were both outside having a cigarette.

"The only person she had not seen was you, Mrs Stamford. Because you never went downstairs, and Mila never came upstairs until she was required to do so when Inspector Dane, following Maximov's death, interviewed everyone in the study.

"She passed you as one of you was entering and the other leaving the room, and she recognised you. And the game began again. Another blackmailer, and another murder."

I glanced across the heads at Dane, saw him replay the order of interviews, saw the light in his eyes that told me my hunch had been correct: Mila and Karen had definitely had the opportunity to pass each other.

"And then – to my eternal shame – I made some incorrect deductions and accused your husband, who – though I was entirely wrong in my accusation – recognised the truth. When you left the room last night with him, you went to his room, and he told you he knew, but I think you managed to persuade him that this could be overcome, that the mess was still salvageable."

I recalled standing out by the fountain with Nick, feeling like my world was falling apart and looking back at the house, the lights blazing in two bedrooms – those allocated to Richard and Karen Stamford. They must have been awake for hours, him slowly piecing the horror together, her desperately trying to persuade him to remain silent, moving back and forth via the connecting bathroom so that nobody else would know of their turmoil.

And suddenly I realised what had been wrong with this morning: Karen Stamford could have entered her husband's room via the connecting bathroom, but she chose not to. And then, having entered his room, she deliberately left the door wide open. Who enters someone's bedroom and leaves the door open?

Someone who wants an audience.

She used me to provide her alibi, to confirm that she was as surprised as I when she found him dead in his bed.

She glared furiously at me as I carried on. "At some point, as an insurance, you took from his bag the syringe and the opioid, and – Dr Stamford still hugely conflicted by the situation – you both went to bed.

"Except he lay awake and finally, in the early hours of the morning, sent you a text that said 'I'm sorry. I can't do this anymore'."

I looked around the room. Realisation – as certainly as it had dawned on me – was dawning on several other faces.

"We thought it was him saying he could no longer live the lie he'd been living, but we knew that couldn't be true, because Sir Phillip had already confirmed that there was no way Dr Stamford could have been the person who sent those men to their deaths. So what was it that Dr Stamford couldn't do any more?"

"Cover for his wife," Pamela said, and I nodded.

"You knew," I turned back to Karen Stamford, "that in the morning he was going to tell the truth. Everything you had worked for – the escape from a war-torn country, the work you had put in to recreate yourself, the lives you had saved with your technology, the money – all that money – that you were on the verge of having. All would be gone.

"And so you went to his room, ostensibly to have one last go at persuading him not to give you up. And you killed him."

"It's a circumstantial case at best," she said quietly.

"There's still enough of it to stick," I answered, as a new trio of uniforms arrived and gathered behind Dane. "And I think once the police start digging back into the atrocity that started the whole thing it will be easy, if not to prove your guilt in these murders, at least to confirm your guilt in that war crime."

Karen Stamford stared at the ceiling for a moment, and her

eyes filled with tears.

Then she passed the back of her hand across them, cleared her throat and stood.

"Well then," she said, ignoring me and turning to Inspector Dane, "I suppose we'd better get started then."

She moved out of the circle and walked towards the policeman, who relegated John Warren to one of the uniforms and stepped towards her.

Karen Stamford paused, turned back to me and smiled sadly. "I really did love him, you know. You talk about my escape from that place as though I latched on to him and used him, but it wasn't like that. We loved each other, and that's why, of all of them, his is the death I will always regret."

And then Dane took her and she, along with John Warren, Sara Simone and Francine Gerber, was taken away.

CHAPTER FORTY-THREE

The first firework exploded above the Folly, the blast of pink painting the ruins below in a cherry wash, and before the flare had faded another starburst – green this time – exploded, then another in white and a shower of smaller explosions – green, pink and white – dancing across the sky and raining down, their lights fading to nothing as our eyes tried to follow their trajectory.

When Karen Stamford, Sara Simone, Francine and John had been taken away, and when the rest of the guests and family were down in the kitchen eating whatever Ali had been able to drag out of the larders, Sir Phillip had asked Caz and I to join him in his study.

He was seated behind his desk when we entered, his tone serious, and he gestured us to the seats opposite him.

"I wanted you to know," he said, "that your friend has been released from custody and will be joining us tonight for the fireworks."

"That was fast," I said, and he shrugged.

"My older brother is the Chief Constable."

"You mentioned," I smiled.

"Yes," he seemed momentarily distracted, then refocussed. "I feel I have to say how impressed I am."

Now it was my turn to shrug. "I'm glad I could help."

"Yes," he said, adding as though it was something playing on his mind: "Chapman has left the premises and will not be returning."

I wasn't sure what response he wanted from me: the woman had killed his youngest son, possibly enabled his wife's suicide, and kept him and his middle son apart for over three decades. A part of me felt that she should have been in prison, but I recalled Sir Phillip's comments, and I heard Nick's voice telling me how impossible perfect justice is.

So I glanced at Caz, and nodded my acknowledgement.

"And I have come to some decisions," he added. "With Chapman gone, there'll be nobody to manage this place, plump the cushions, complain about table settings and manage my correspondence."

"What are you going to do?" Caz asked, and he looked at her in surprise.

"Your friend here," he gestured at me, "would have me employ Mrs Kennedy. But I can't do that."

I opened my mouth to protest, to make one last attempt to get the job I had promised Gaia Kennedy I would get for her mother.

"Because it's no longer my place to do so," he finished. "I've spoken to Henry and Pamela. I'm going to move out of Dukes Halt."

I didn't hide my shock. "Where to?"

"Does it matter? There are lots of suitable places on the estate– the old Estate Manager's cottage for one. It'll need some work; maybe a lick of paint. But I think it's time I let Henry take the reins. Wouldn't be doing it if Pamela hadn't agreed to come on board. Good woman that one. Reminds me of my wife.

"And I know how these things usually go. Well I'm no King Lear, I can tell you. When I'm gone, I shall be gone. I might travel a bit more. Maybe go to Florence. I went as a young man, you know. And I'd like to go to New York. My son George was an artist. But you already know that," he smiled at Caz.

"I'm told that one of their Modern Art museums has a large collection of his work. But you, of course, already knew that too.

"So all I'll need is a place to lay my head when I'm back from time to time. I do hope they'll have me to dinner, but they're not going to need me hanging around or popping out of the woodwork like a phantom."

"And I've strongly recommended to Henry and Pamela that they keep Mrs Kennedy on. She's another good woman. Pragmatic. Strong. Decent. Imaginative. Told Henry they were traits that had been sadly lacking around here and do you know what he said?"

Sir Phillip chuckled. "He said, 'I know,' and went straight off to offer her the job."

He smiled. "And Pamela told me that, as we'd have to cut costs somewhere, she was going to stop wasting money sending Carlotta to those ridiculous schools she so clearly hates and send her, instead, to the village school.

"Insanity, I call it," he blustered, the old Sir Phillip rising briefly from wherever he'd buried him, "but it's their house, their money, what little it is, and their child, and so it's ultimately their choice. And I think – I hope - they'll all make a good go of it. Don't you?"

I smiled and looked at Caz, who nodded, sniffed a tear away and said she thought that they would all make a very good go of it.

"Oh," Sir Phillip added. "Before she left," he dipped down and removed something from his desk drawer, "Chapman returned to me something which she had discovered whilst searching for Maximov's mobile phone."

He rose, the Fortnum's bag in his hand, and placed it, with a heavy metallic thunk, on the desk before he dipped down once more and lifted the urn that I had last seen on the drawing room mantlepiece.

"I have held on to Marion and Edward – together here," he patted the vessel, "for so very long."

Sir Phillip smiled sadly, his gaze going back decades. "Tried to hold on to them even as I pushed George – the boy Marion loved so much – away, because I was angry and lost and because I allowed Chapman to influence me. That ends tonight."

The smile faded, and I saw tears in his eyes as his hand – shaking slightly – opened the Fortnum's bag and extracted the plain urn in which George's ashes were held.

"I assume," he said to Caz "that your plan had been to scatter these somewhere on the premises?"

"It was his final wish," she acknowledged, and Sir Phillip nodded his understanding.

"Then the Folly it is. They loved it there. Painting, sketching, looking down on this place as though it was a magical land and they were gods floating above it. I think it should be there, don't you?"

Caz was silent a moment, and then she nodded.

"I think he'd like that very much," she said.

~

"I'm told congratulations are in order," Arianna sidled up to me, her eyes never leaving the explosions in the sky. "Nick has told me that as soon as we can safely end the marriage he will marry you."

I hadn't expected this to feel so awkward, and yet I did. She sensed my unease and laughed, her gloved hand finding mine and squeezing it.

"I will love Nick forever for what he did. He got me away from a place that was like hell. But you need to understand I do not love Nick in any way that needs to worry you. Do you understand that?"

I nodded.

"I'm sorry," I said. "That I couldn't get from Maximov what you needed."

Above us something shrieked like wind howling through a crack in the ruins, and more blasts of technicolour light flared up, wheeling, whirling, slashing the night sky with colour.

I wondered which of the fireworks had contained the ashes of Lady Marion Warren and her sons.

~

I'd called my parents in Portugal, and the alarm in my mother's voice when she answered her mobile was audible.

"What's up?" She'd asked. "Who's sick? Are the kids alright?" She'd demanded and it took me a while to realise she meant her grandkids and not my siblings and I.

I smiled. "They're fine. We're all fine. Really, we're all great.

How's Portugal?"

"Blissful," she said, relief clear in her voice. "But you really didn't call me to check in on the weather in the Algarve, did you?"

I'd chuckled, asked if she was on speakerphone, and once she'd confirmed that she was and that my dad was with her, I'd told them my news.

There was a silence.

A silence that seemed longer than I was entirely comfortable with.

Then "About bloody time," my father said, his voice thick with emotion. "I was wondering when he'd make an honest man of you. Congratulations, son."

"Mum?" Her silence was really worrying me.

"Does Nick know what he's getting himself into?" She asked, and the wobble in her voice told me that there were probably tears in her eyes too.

"Nick?" I feigned outrage, but the chuckle in my voice gave me away.

"Well he's got you to deal with," she clarified, "but as much as you're going to be marrying into the Fishers, he's going to be a Bird. He's going to be part of this family. Is he sure he's ready for that?"

"Uh, mum, I think you're supposed to be joyful for us and asking me if I'm sure about this, not trying to put my fiancé off the deal."

And then she laughed, the sound so rich and full and happy. A sound I hadn't really heard since she got sick. And she said "I don't think I could put anyone off you, Danny. You're perfect for each other, and you're perfect as you are. And we're perfect as we are with all the messiness of this family.

"And we'll need to go back into town tomorrow," she said, clearly addressing my dad. "There was a hat shop there I want to look at."

And that was that.

~

They'd found Maximov's phone where Karen Stamford had

stashed it: In the priest hole that wasn't a priest hole. And it had immediately vanished into Sir Phillip's safe.

I'd explained how important it might be to Arianna and Sir Phillip had nodded his understanding then sighed deeply and sadly.

"You want me to share the data," he said, and before I could answer, he shook his head. "More than my life's worth. That thing – if we can ever crack the encryption and get in to it – could be a treasure trove of data."

"But I'm fairly sure there was no traitor," I'd explained and he'd looked at me as though I'd just said the most obvious thing in the world.

"But you see," he said, "it makes no difference whether there was or there wasn't. You said it yourself: Maximov was a collector of secrets and – if we can get past his encryption – every secret he knew, every nugget of knowledge – will be ours.

"And the game goes on," I said, resigned to the fact that the phone would be spirited away and that Arianna's sister would never be found.

Sir Phillip's lips curved in a good impersonation of a smile. "Well some games simply need to be played to the end."

~

Arianna's eyes were fixed on the sky. "I stopped believing many years ago," she said. "I decided Klara was dead, or that she had decided she didn't want to see me. It was easiest, you see: less painful than knowing she was out there and frightened. Alone. Lost.

"But even though I decided this fact, my heart knew, as it has always known. We are twins, you see. And I know," her voice cracked, "I know in my soul that Klara is still out there."

She sighed, turned to me, tears sparkling silver as they ran down her face. "But the world is cruel. If I had not seen Maximov that day I would never have been shown hope. I wanted you to find him so I could kill him." She nodded. "This much is correct. But an atom of my being, a cell somewhere inside me woke when I saw him and said 'what if she's not dead? What if he knows where she is?'

"And that hope, like a cancer, spread so fast."

I followed her eyes to where Nick, at a respectable distance, was sharing a joke with Caz as Ellie – the only dog on the planet seemingly unphased by fireworks – sat quietly by.

"I think, you know, that hope is worse than despair; or it is when the hope is dashed again and again. I looked for Klara so long, and so far, and now I am alone, and will be forever."

Another explosion of colour illuminated the sky and this time I squeezed her hand, my mind drifting back to the study at Dukes Halt a little earlier this evening.

"You're wrong." I said, releasing her hand, putting my arm around her shoulder and drawing her near. "You're part of our family now, and will never be alone again."

I looked up at the sky and smiled, then caught Sir Phillip's eyes before we both turned back to the skies, and to the light raining down on Dukes Halt.

EPILOGUE

TWO WEEKS LATER, CHARLES DE GAULLE AIRPORT. PARIS

The line is crawling at a snail's pace, and she has to force herself to stay calm, make herself not shout at the people in front that they need to hurry up and get this plane airborn.

So instead, she looks once more at the cutting in her hand.

Delphine hasn't bought a newspaper in years. She doesn't often go out for breakfast. Why would she when she has a perfectly serviceable kitchen in her little apartment in Saint Germain, the spoils of her last divorce?

But yesterday morning she'd been out of coffee and – as she'd had to go to the Monoprix on Boulevard Saint-Michelle, and she'd sold a treatment for a new video game to a Japanese company earlier that week after months of negotiations – she'd decided to hell with it and gone into Les Deux Magots for breakfast.

And it was there, as she was awaiting her Brioche toast (she hated Croissants – all those crumbs) that she'd glanced across at the newspaper the man on the next table had been reading.

And her heart had stopped.

Her sister – back when Delphine had been called Klara – had been murdered by a man named Sergei Maximov. Maximov had told their mother that he would keep the two girls safe, but as soon as they had ceased to be of use to him he had sold Klara, and murdered Arianna in case she told of his secrets.

This story she had been told by the man that Maximov had sold her to.

"Do not look for her, or him; or he will surely murder you too," the man had said.

He'd seemed surprised when, some years later having relocated her to Munich and pimped her out to an army of businessmen, Klara – by then called Irina – had plunged a bread knife into his neck and stood by watching him bleed to death before stepping over him and resuming the video game she'd been playing, achieving a personal best score before stripping naked, spraying the house with gasoline, transferring the contents of the man's safe into her overnight bag, showering, changing clothes and – as she pulled the door of the house shut behind her – throwing a lit match into the hall.

The golden whoof of the flames had echoed in her ears all the way from Munich to Milan.

She'd had to kill him, because she'd looked in the mirror that morning and seen, aligned directly over the centre of her right eye, a single grey hair, and she'd known: as soon as she was of no use to this man, she would be killed as certainly as her beautiful Arianna had been killed.

In Milan she had discovered just how much money the man had in numbered offshore accounts, and had realised that she would not need to work, if she was careful, for the rest of her life, and so – as Nathalie – she had enrolled in a class on coding and games design.

By the time she had met the French man who who asked her to marry him she had been Delphine, and she' d been earning a good income as a designer of computer games.

And so yesterday morning, when she had looked across as the waiter presented her brioche, poured her coffee and smiled as though expecting a round of applause for performing these mundane tasks; when she had seen the photo on the newspaper; when the world had stopped; she had been consumed by, at first, confusion, then emotion.

Grief, loss, relief.

Rage.

The man in Munich had lied to her.

Arianna was alive, and had been alive all this time.

She'd leapt to her feet, tossing a fistful of Euro on the table, and resisted the urge to rip the newspaper from the man's hands, buying one instead from the vendor on the corner and taking it home to pour over the details.

How her sister had been photographed at a fireworks event in an English country house, how she was alive and had been cleared of murdering a man whose name Klara knew only too well.

And an hour of surfing the web had provided her with the address of a pub in South London where the man with his arm around her shoulder could be found.

And she'd purchased a ticket on the next available flight, and so here she is.

Klara-Irina-Nathalie-Delphine looks at the picture torn from the newspaper, at the picture in her passport – her hair is cropped short and dyed auburn while Arianna has kept hers long and blonde – and finally, after almost thirty years, she exhales.

It feels like she's been holding her breath for most of her life. As though, since the moment she was told of Arianna's death, she's been, at best, shallow breathing, afraid to take the air that should have been her sisters.

But now she inhales deeply.

Smiles.

Steps forward and presents her passport to the young man at the gate who smiles back, casts a perfunctory eye over it, returns the document and wishes her a Bon Voyage, and she steps past him, walks down the walkway and on to the plane.

And she cannot stop herself from smiling.

Because life is miserable, and nothing – she has learned – is ever clean.

But maybe.

Just this once, perhaps.

There can be a happy ending.

The End

About the author

Derek Farrell is the author of The Danny Bird Mysteries published by Fahrenheit Press.

The books have been described as "Like The Thin Man meets Will & Grace." "Like M.C. Beaton on MDMA," and – by no less an expert than Eric Idle – as "Quite Fun."

Derek's jobs have included: Burger dresser, Bank teller, David Bowie's paperboy, and Investment Banker, and he has lived and worked in New York, Hong Kong, Istanbul, Tel Aviv, Prague, Dublin, Johannesburg and London.

He's married to the most English man on the planet and lives in West Sussex. They have no goats, chickens, children or pets, but they do have every Kylie Minogue record ever made.

Also by Derek Farrell

- *Death Of A Diva*
- *Death Of A Nobody*
- *Death Of A Devil*
- *Death Of An Angel*
- *Death Of A Sinner*

More books from Fahrenheit Press

The Beloved Children by Tina Jackson

Three young women; Chrysanthemum, Rose & Orage are thrown together on the stage of Fankes' Theatre during the closing days of the Second World War performing as The Three Graces.

It's there they come under the spell of wardrobe mistresses Dolores and Janna – a chance encounter that will guide and change all of their fates forever.

Set in the dying days of vaudeville theatre and laced with mysticism, fortune tellers, ghosts, and evocative descriptions of the closing days of the War - The Beloved Children will literally make you laugh out loud and perhaps even shed the odd tear.

The Beloved Children is wise, funny, heart-breaking, joyous, poignant, and entirely entirely enthralling.

"There is some really atmospheric storytelling and joyful language at play here, with Jackson as an entertaining mistress of ceremonies." - Ben East, The Observer

The Transit of Lola Jones by Jackie Swift

Debut author Jackie Swift brings some playfulness to the Fahrenheit list with this first book in a series featuring her eponymous hero Lola Jones.

It's fair to say Lola Jones' life is not turning out the way she expected it to.

As the book opens we find Lola recovering from the breast cancer that threatened to prematurely end her life and languishing in a police cell, the main suspect in the murder of businessman Daniel Blain.

As the truth begins to unfold about the events leading up to the untimely demise of the dashing Daniel, we learn more about the journey that brought the normally infectiously vivacious Lola Jones to such an unsatisfactory pass.

But is she guilty, and even if she is guilty, is she to blame?

This is a funny, smart, sexy, modern romp of a book and Lola Jones is a character that you'll instantly want to be your best friend.

Souljourner by Paul Steven Stone

Where to start with Souljourner? Let's start with the author - Paul Steven Stone is either a madman or a genius – probably both – and he's written one of the most gripping and enjoyable books we've ever come across.

It begins with a quote from Pierre Teilhard de Chardin

"We are not human beings on a spiritual journey, we are spiritual beings on a human journey." – and that my friends sets the stage perfectly for all that follows.

The novel, if it is indeed a novel (the narrator insists it is in fact a warning letter from your soul's previous incarnation and aimed directly at you dear reader) - as we will discover though, this narrator is often unreliable - so frankly warning or novel, you pays your money you takes your choice.

One of the central premises of the novel/letter is that our souls make their eternal journey towards enlightenment in the company of a single unchanging 'karmic pod' of companion souls who take on different roles in each of our incarnations.

In one life a soul may appear as your mother, in the next your best friend, in the next your sworn enemy, in the next your lover and so on for eternity. The identities of the souls in your 'karmic pod' are hidden from you in life – this letter/novel seeks to wise you up to who's who in your karmic pod to help you avoid making the same mistakes that landed the narrator, David Rockwood Worthington in prison serving a life sentence for murder.

Know Me From Smoke by Matt Phillips

Stella Radney, long-time lounge singer, still has a bullet lodged in her hip from the night when a rain of gunshots killed her husband.

That was twenty years ago and it's a surprise when the unsolved murder is reopened after the district attorney discovers new evidence. Royal Atkins is a convicted killer who just got out of prison on a legal technicality. At first, he's thinking he'll play it straight. Doesn't take long before that plan turns to smoke—was it ever really an option?

When Stella and Royal meet one night, they're drawn to each other. But Royal has a secret. How long before Stella discovers that the man she's falling for isn't who he seems? A noir of gripping suspense and violence, Know Me from Smoke is a journey into the shadowy terrain of murder, lost love, and the heart's lust for vengeance.

"A beautifully written, brutal & brilliant slice of hardboiled crime fiction. A Knockout."

Printed in Great Britain
by Amazon

71144970R00220